MAY ARMAND BLANC

THE LAST RENDEZVOUS

STORIES AND PROSE POEMS

TRANSLATED AND WITH AN INTRODUCTION BY
BRIAN STABLEFORD

THIS IS A SNUGGLY BOOK

ISBN: 978-1-64525-059-3

THE LAST RENDEZVOUS

MAY ARMAND BLANC (1874-1904), though dying prematurely, was a prolific contributor to many of the journals of her day, most especially the feminist journal *La Fronde*. Her first novel *Bibelot* appeared in 1899, followed in 1900 by her second, *Mila: roman nouveau*, and in 1901, by her last, *La Maison de Roses*. A further novelette, "Ella" was published posthumously in 1909 in the *Mercure de France*. Daughter of the writer who signed herself Madame Mathilde de Saint-Vidal (1849-1911), Blanc was said to have born a striking resemblance to a portrait of Lord Wharton by Van Dyck.

BRIAN STABLEFORD'S scholarly work includes *New Atlantis: A Narrative History of Scientific Romance* (Wildside Press, 2016), *The Plurality of Imaginary Worlds: The Evolution of French roman scientifique* (Black Coat Press, 2017) and *Tales of Enchantment and Disenchantment: A History of Faerie* (Black Coat Press, 2019). In support of the latter projects he has translated more than a hundred volumes of *roman scientifique* and more than twenty volumes of *contes de fées* into English. He has edited *Decadence and Symbolism: A Showcase Anthology* (Snuggly Books, 2018), and is busy translating more Symbolist and Decadent fiction.

His recent fiction, in the genre of metaphysical fantasy, includes a trilogy of novels set in West Wales, consisting of *Spirits of the Vasty Deep* (2018), *The Insubstantial Pageant* (2018) and *The Truths of Darkness* (2019), published by Snuggly Books, and a trilogy set in Paris and the south of France, consisting of *The Painter of Spirits*, *The Quiet Dead* and *Living with the Dead*, all published by Black Coat Press in 2019.

CONTENTS

INTRODUCTION

THE writer who used various versions of the signature "May Armand Blanc," usually with a single hyphen—most frequently, but not invariably, placed between the second and third terms—but occasionally with no hyphen and sometimes with two, remained unidentified for a long time; the catalogue of the Bibliothèque Nationale does not identify her at the time of writing, although it gives her birth date as 1874. Further research employing the current resources of the internet enables the determination than she died prematurely in 1904, having published a handful of books, a number of articles and reviews in various periodicals, and the seventy-six short stories and prose poems collected in the present volume, sixty-five of them in *La Fronde*, a further six in Symbolist periodicals—three in the *Mercure de France*, three in *La Vogue*—and the remaining five in a small collection entitled *Minutes bibliques* (1902) issued by the press associated with the *Mercure de France*, along with the three items previously published in the periodical.

All but four of the fictional contributions to *La Fronde* translated herein were published between October 1898 and April 1900, representing a sustained burst of creativity; the first item had been published in December 1897 and the last three were added in 1903. The items from the *Mercure de France* and *La Vogue* were published in 1899. In the interval between April 1900, and her remaining fictional contributions to *La Fronde*, the press of the *Mercure de France* issued its small collection of prose poems. I cannot be certain that she did not publish other items of a similar sort, because several issues are missing from the set of *La Fronde* reproduced on the Bibliothèque Nationale's *gallica* website, and she might have published others in other periodicals, but if this volume of translations is not complete in representing her work in the format, it is very nearly so.

The first of Blanc's three novels, *Bibelot* (1899), was also published during that short burst of creativity, while *Mila: roman nouveau* (1900, in a volume also containing the novelette "Vers de Paradis") and *La Maison de Roses* (1901) followed not long thereafter. A further novelette, "Ella" (1909) was published posthumously in the *Mercure de France*, but is probably a fragment of an unfinished novel. She appears, therefore, to have switched the principal emphasis of her work from short items to long fiction in 1900—an evolution perhaps forced by marketing difficulties, but not unusual as a career trajectory for writers whose confidence in tackling more time-consuming projects grows with success.

Some additional information regarding the author is given in an obituary by Judith Cladel,[1] a fellow contributor to *La Fronde*, who records that the author's real surname was Saint-Vidal, already "put in relief" by her mother, and that only a handful of intimates were present at her burial at Fontainebleau, where she died in the Autumn of 1904, having left Paris in quest of cleaner air in the interests of her ailing health. Cladel also gives a physical description of the author, saying that she

---

1 Judith Cladel, "May-Armand Blanc" *La Plume*, vol. 17 no. 1 (1905) pp.35-39. Judith Cladel (1873-1958) was the daughter of the prolific writer Léon Cladel (1834-1892), who followed determinedly in his footsteps to become a successful journalist and biographer, most notably of Auguste Rodin. She was one of the first columnists of *La Fronde*, and she and Blanc were at the core of the paper's younger generation of contributors in its early years.

bore a striking resemblance to a portrait of Lord Wharton by Van Dyck (presumably the portrait of 1632), a print of which Blanc possessed, claiming distant descent from the English lord in question, but Cladel gives no further details of her life, not even confirming that "May Armand" were her actual forenames, although she hyphenates them, implying that they were. The reference to her mother's celebrity, however, makes it certain that Blanc was the daughter of the writer who signed herself Madame Mathilde de Saint-Vidal (1849-1911), another contributor to *La Fronde*, who must have been the wife of the sculptor Francis de Saint-Vidal (1840-1900). The claim of descent from Philip, Lord Wharton (1613-1696) is presumably based on the fact that the sculptor's father, Francis Porral de Saint-Vidal, was married to one Elisabeth Warthon [*sic*].

The lack of detail in the obituary is a trifle odd, although it is possible that Cladel simply did not know "May-Armand Blanc" very well, except as a colleague, but it seems more likely that she was respecting the secrecy implicit in the use of the pseudonym, and did not feel entitled to say anything beyond revealing the name behind it. It is, of course, dangerous to infer anything about an author's real life from the contents of her work, but the fact that so many of Blanc's stories feature sick children and delicate adults as protagonists inevitably suggests that the disease that killed her prematurely was an enduring problem from which she had suffered throughout her life— and Cladel does imply that strongly, without being specific. She does not specify the fatal disease either, but it was probably tuberculosis, which features in several of the most horrific stories in Blanc's *oeuvre*.

Cladel states that Blanc struggled heroically against her illness, refusing to allow it to condemn her to inactivity, and during her brief burst of intense creativity she was certainly prolific, but it is very obvious that her entire oeuvre is covered by a dark shadow. The keynote for her work for *La Fronde* is struck plangently by her first story to appear there. "La Dernière rendezvous" (tr. as "The Last Rendezvous"), a harrowing snapshot of heartbreak, and that note echoes continually in her fiction, which is exceedingly sentimental and relentlessly downbeat, ranging in emphasis from exercises in sadly wistful nostalgia to subtly brutal *contes cruel*. Although she never removes the velvet glove from her iron fist, even in her most savage narratives, that does not prevent them from hitting hard, sometimes with uncontained fury. Doubtless her ill health had much to do with that, but it was not the only factor that needs to be taken into consideration; as a feminist symbolist trying to make a living as a professional writer, Blanc was thrice damned in the eyes of many contemporary critics, even had she been in the best of health, and the tone and themes of her work are markedly akin to those of half a dozen other authors in the same position, whose work was fugitive at the time and virtually eclipsed thereafter; it is only now being rediscovered and properly appreciated by a new generation of feminist academics, writers and literary historians.

The work translated in the present volume was produced in a rather narrow interval of opportunity for Parisian writers, when a boom in the productions of daily newspapers that began in the mid-1880s, as a consequence of technological improvements in automated printing presses and papermaking, made them much cheaper to produce. For fifty years French newspapers had been using "feuilleton" serials—novels published in daily episodes contained in a separate ruled-off section at the bottom of a page. From 1880 onwards, however, many of the leading dailies also began featuring short fiction, the word-length of which the restriction of four-page newspapers printed on a single sheet of paper limited drastically. Some papers restricted such work to weekly "supplements," but several began making an important almost-daily feature of them, routinely running them as the leading item on page one.

By the end of the 1890s the most pretentious of all the *fin-de-siècle* dailies, *Le Journal*, had a stable of writers contracted to produce a short story or a combative essay either every week or once a fortnight, although that practice faded away in the early years of the twentieth century as its value as a circulation-builder was tested and found wanting.

While that boom lasted, however, it provided a golden opportunity for a whole generation of Parisian writers, some of whom rapidly cultivated a remarkable skill in the mass production of short stories ranging in length from a few hundred words to two thousand. The principal contemporary exemplar was Catulle Mendès, followed by Octave Mirbeau, Jean Lorrain, Jean Richepin, Marcel Schwob, Edmond Haraucourt, Léon Bloy and others. Only a handful proved capable of maintaining a fortnightly schedule, let alone a weekly one, for any length of time before running out of inspiration, and several of those who lasted longest began to cheat, clumping stories in series or simply cutting up episodic novels into segments, which side-stepped the problem of continually making new beginnings.

The methodology of writing such short stories rapidly acquired a kind of standardization, although the leading writers were able to maintain a measure of distinction, or even uniqueness. They did not, however, have to start from scratch; useful exemplars had been set as long ago as the 1850s in the work of Chares Baudelaire, who had diversified from writing poetry to writing poems in prose, some of which had grown to the dimensions of short stories, taking on more and more narrative elements, and his examples had been followed by other writers interested in that kind of exercise for art's sake, notably Joris-Karl Huysmans and Stéphane Mallarmé, both of whom became key figures in the overlapping Symbolist and Decadent Movements of the *fin-de-siècle*. Many of the writers who mass-produced short fiction in that period were peripherally associated with the Symbolist Movement and found symbolism very useful as a device of encapsulation, permitting short stories to imply far more than they stated.

The *fin-de-siècle* was often represented at the time as a period of literary contest between rival movements of Symbolism and Naturalism, but the opposition between the two was largely illusory, corollary to the fact that Symbolism was primarily a movement in poetry and Naturalism in the novel—but in short fiction, especially the ultra-short fiction designed for newspaper publication, Symbolism and Naturalism collided and fused, necessarily. Although such slots could accommodate *contes* [tales], the compaction of which is contrived by narrative distance and synopsis, the vast majority of newspaper stories were "slice-of-life" stories in which a brief incident is offered as a deft encapsulation of something much larger, an anecdote or a character-sketch implying an entire life by means of a few symbolic details—and not only *a* life, but life in general, *multum in parvo*: a world in a grain of sand.

The world, seen from that perspective, rarely seems good, and can easily seem very depressing indeed, so there is a sense in which the entire genre of ultra-short fiction has an obligatory cynicism, which lends itself very readily to a *conte cruel* brutality. It is not too much of an exaggeration to say that the underlying theme of all fiction in the range accommodated by the Parisian newspapers of the *fin-de-siècle* is the observation of the inhumanity of Providence—the gilded rule that if something can go wrong, it will. It is necessarily the case, however, that the symbolic characterization of that eternal truth differs between men and women, the sexes being very prone to see one another, in general, as the primary instruments of torture employed by Providence to give them a hard time.

In general, the handful of female writers who tried their hand at the mass-production of short stories for newspapers had a very hard time indeed, neglected, if not despised, to a greater extent than their male counterparts, sometimes for no other reason than the fact that they were female. The first woman to try to break into the market in question was Marie Krysinka, the only female member of Emile Goudeau's Hydropathes, who was allowed to play piano and sing in the Chat Noir, like Jean Richepin and Edmond Haraucourt, but was not able to be taken seriously. She managed to collect some of the stories that she contrived to publish in *Gil Blas* and *La Lanterne*, as *L'Amour chemine* (1892; tr. in *The Path of Amour*) but did not attain a regular spot until the founding by Marguerite Durand of *La Fronde*: a feminist newspaper edited and entirely written by women. Jane de La Vaudère managed to maintain near-weekly production over a longer period in *La Presse* and *La Lanterne* between 1897 and 1903, mingling fiction and non-fiction, but her work in the genre was never collected. It was not until Lucie Delarue-Mardrus joined *Le Journal*'s stable in 1903 that any female writer obtained a prime spot, but she worked on a fortnightly schedule, and only contrived to produce thirty-some individual short stories before switching to episodic novelettes and novels; they were never collected in book form, until they were translated into English in *The Last Siren and Other Stories* (2019).

Marguerite Durand's use of fiction in *La Fronde* was always tentative. Initially she only used the occasional short story in addition to the obligatory feuilleton, but when she began to do so regularly, in 1898, in deliberate imitation of *Le Journal*, she swiftly built up a stable of regular contributors, of whom "May Armand-Blanc" was the most prolific. The other leading contributors to the fiction slot at that time were "Myriam Harry" (Maria Shapira, 1869-1968) and "Jacques Fréhel" (Alice Télot, 1861-1918), although the doyenne of the paper, Manoël de Grandfort (1829-1904), and regular columnists "Daniel Lesueur" (Jeanne Loiseau, 1854-1921), and Marcelle Tinayre (1870-1948) mingled items of fiction with their non-fiction to a greater or lesser extent; Séverine (Caroline Rémy Guebhard,

1855-1929), *La Fronde*'s only daily columnist, who also wrote a weekly column for *Le Journal*, did not.

For a brief period at the beginning of 1899 Durand expanded the paper to six pages, using much of the extra space to expand its feuilleton serial, but soon abandoned the experiment. She suspended the use of short fiction during the Dreyfus trial in August 1899, and then dropped it during the election campaign of April 1900, eliminating it from the paper for the next two years, thus obliterating May Armand Blanc's principal market for her fiction. When Durand resumed the regular use of short fiction in the spring of 1903 it was with a new set of irregular contributors, of whom Blanc—who returned to work for the paper but mingled her short fiction with articles and reviews—was no longer the most prolific; and short fiction appears to have faded away entirely from the paper's pages in the autumn, although the near-absence of copies from *gallica* thereafter makes it hard to be sure. That obliteration leaves some cause for regret in the context of French literary history, but is consonant with the general decline of newspaper short fiction, of which Lucie Delarue-Mardrus was arguably the last significant practitioner.

Although Delarue-Mardrus continued publishing occasional items of fiction after her initial sequence came to an end, and Marie Krysinska published numerous items in several newspapers in addition to the twenty-eight stories she published in *La Fronde*, May Armand Blanc remained the most prolific female producer of material for such slots and the one who maintained the consistency of her production most robustly, meeting the pressure of a weekly deadline for some eighteen months. Inevitably, there are signs within the sequence of occasional relaxation into repetition and formularization, and occasional attempts to vary the spectrum of the work simply for the sake of variation, but the difficulty of what she was doing should not be underestimated, and very few writers managed

16

to maintain such production for any longer with a similar fervor and craftsmanship.

As with any writer of the Symbolist school, the ultimate stylistic and thematic roots of May Armand Blanc's work in the formats of prose poetry and short fiction are to be found in Baudelaire, and although her female viewpoint gives her work a markedly different flavor, its fundamental attitude has much in common with the work of the great man. Baudelaire planned to call the definitive collection of his prose poems and short stories—which he did not manage to publish in his lifetime—*Spleen de Paris*, the exaggerated form of ennui that he called "spleen" being the keystone of his attitude to life and the universe. The most blatantly Baudelairean of Blanc's poems in prose is "Neurasthénie" (tr. as "Neurasthenia"), which reflects the march of medical fashionability in the interim between their careers. Many of Blanc's contemporaries, most obviously Octave Mirbeau and Jean Lorrain, made much of the notion in their work in the format, but both treated neurasthenia primarily as a kind of hypochondria, even though their own cases were real enough to kill them. Blanc does not labor her use of the term unduly, generally being content with "ennui" or describing disaffected states of mind without the employment of any specific label, but the symptoms of neurasthenia are nevertheless frequent in her characterizations and their associated narrative prognoses, most of her representations of married women being virtual case-studies.

Because Judith Cladel did not include the detail in her obituary, we can now only guess as to whether May Armand Blanc was married, but one suspects that, like Judith Cladel, she was not. If she was, however, it is difficult to believe that her husband could have read her work without wincing. In the fictional world of her stories, wives are never in love with their husbands, and although they routinely have lovers, that is sometimes a mere matter of meeting social expectations;

whenever real passion comes into play it is almost always one-sided, as well as short-lived, and it is invariably destructive. It is notable that in the keynote story "La Dernière rendezvous," the text does not specify the marital status of either of the two characters, although hints are casually dropped in order to permit, if not to facilitate, inferences. The only story Blanc published in *La Fronde*'s fiction slot that she extended over two episodes, "La Grande fleur" (tr. as "The Great Flower") is a cynical parable about the psychological necessity of passion, but takes it for granted that it is an exceedingly treacherous necessity.

Amour is, of course, the principal mechanism of tragedy throughout the universe of fiction, but is also routinely represented there as the principal mechanism of salvation. In Blanc's personal literary universe, however, there is no salvation, and amour is merely a road to hell, which sometimes goes by the scenic route, but not for long. She was by no means alone in that; there is not one of the female writers cited above as Symbolists whose short fiction would take exception to the judgment—how could it, given that they were living in a society in which *La Fronde* was desperately necessary, and had far more mud slung at it than it ever slung itself?—nor was she the most flamboyant standard-bearer of the small feminist symbolist army, but in her careful and meticulous fashion, she was the most extreme and the most relentless. She was not the only member of the sisterhood to express sympathy for women forced by circumstance into a fatal career of prostitution, but her encapsulated representations of their tragedy are the most deftly heart-rending, in telling juxtaposition with her depictions of terminally ill children.

Along with Marie Krysinska, Alice Télot, Jane de La Vaudère and Lucie Delarue-Mardus, May Armand Blanc formed a curious feminist enclave within the short-lived field of mass-producers of fodder for the short fiction slots of the French newspapers of the Belle Époque. As an episode of the evolution of feminist fiction the work produced within that enclave was neglected at the time and virtually disappeared from view thereafter, until the advent of *gallica*, the newspaper archives of which have made it discoverable again. It was not, however, an insignificant episode—*La Fronde* never matched the circulation figures of *Le Journal*, but at its peak, when it was running short stories as the lead item on page one, it was printing more than a hundred thousand copies a day, and its major contributors were all accomplished writers. May Armand Blanc was one of the most distinctive and eloquent voices of her unfortunately-brief era, and although she was crying in a wilderness, her song warranted being heard and appreciated then, and still does.

All the translations except those taken from *Mimiques bibliques* were taken from copies of periodicals reproduced on *gallica*. The exceptions were made from a virgin copy of the 1902 booklet, the pages of which I had to cut in order to do so, 117 years after it was printed.

—Brian Stableford

THE LAST RENDEZVOUS

THE LAST RENDEZVOUS
(*La Fronde*, 13 December 1897)

A great gust of wind had skimmed the trees overnight; almost naked, they were trembling. Like a light moss, the rust of their leaves covered the avenue that plunged into the mist all the way to the Place Péreire, where the gas jets were already lit.

Catherine walked rapidly, pushed by the chill in the air—and the much greater chill in her heart

As she traversed the square she looked at the station clock: five twenty-five

It's for half past five; he'll be late . . . I'll wait . . .

And already, already, the tears were tightening her throat, for it was the last time she would have to wait for him.

The cruelty of the infinite minutes when she had watched out for him, always having arrived first, appeared to her at that moment as the greatest happiness. She appealed to him very softly by his name: "Georges!" and suddenly desired to flee without ever seeing him again: to flee the determined place to which he was going to come, the city where they might encounter one another, and the land where he lived—to flee herself, and her cowardly heart, which loved him so much.

For the last time—and she was the one who had decided that—they were about to see one another alone, freely.

He no longer loved her. If he was deceiving her, she did not know it; it must be the case, but she did not *know* anything.

He remained affectionate, gentle enough, with returns of the enveloping seductiveness of the great spoiled child who had taken everything from her, his elder. She was dying of it; she was dying of that willful superficial tenderness. Oh, why was he not nasty—she could have been harsh—or infidel: she would be jealous . . . they would have been able to exchange words like bullets, and know the ardent frenzy of making up. But she could not bear the calm indifference of his eyes.

She was carrying the stifling weight of that amour and groaning, feeling it so heavy, knotted in the fibers of her heart, of her flesh, like a profound malady.

She began to go along the Avenue Gourgand, and, almost immediately, heard rapid footsteps. She stopped, without turning round.

"Catherine . . ."

"Georges . . ."

"You see, I'm punctual . . . I'm pressed for time . . ."

"You promised me an hour!"

"An hour is impossible! And in this cold! It's freezing . . ."

"Yes, it's cold . . ." And, taking her hand out of her muff, she slid it under her friend's arm.

He let her do it, slowly disengaging his own hand from his pocket, and repeating: "It's freezing . . ."

They did not know what to say. She feared bursting into tears; he was embarrassed, searching for words.

The great pale sky, green and pink, drank the light of the world, and everything vanished: the mute, gray, closed houses, the uniform line of the fortifications fading away to the right and the left at the corner of the boulevard.

"My love. . ." he commenced.

She turned her face toward that word, toward that mouth, toward that being, abruptly and passionately; and once again,

24

he saw the tenderness and the dolor in her eyes, the pallor of insomnias on her cheeks, all the irremediable bitterness in the crease of the trembling lips.

He smiled, and she: "Oh, Georges, Georges, don't call me that any longer! I'm suffering too much, you can't know! You no longer love me; that isn't your fault, but I see it so clearly . . . forgive me . . . it's better not to see one another any longer . . . as before . . . it hurts me too much, it stifles me . . . I suffer apart from you, but with you I suffer even more. Oh, without comparison! I loved you so much! You'll never know! You were my lover, but you were also my friend; I've given you everything, everything . . . I have nothing left!"

She clenched her hand over her breast, to attest to that terrible verity.

"Oh, I'd like to be cured of you . . . you do me so much harm, so much harm . . . but I can't; I loved you, I love you, so much . . ."

He gazed at her without responding. That face, so familiar, dissolved in the invasive night; in the hollow of the mouth, between parted lips, devoured by shadow, the teeth gleamed; they no longer summoned his desire.

It was necessary to speak; he tried.

"But I love you, my little Cath, you know that. Come on . . ."

And he took her face in his two hands, by force, as one takes the neck of a bird one is going to strangle. She shook her head from right to left to escape the pressure of that hand, that caress, which reminded her too much of other embraces in which she had felt the great flame pass . . . which was now dead.

He kissed her softly. Then she lifted her veil and gave him profound kisses that wanted to devour the flesh and drink the soul of that being, in the desolate fury of the impossible.

Her mouth bruised, her eyes closed, she finally pulled away from him, exhausted, and the tears of a moment before became horrible sobs.

She wept inexhaustibly. A plaint tore her throat: a low, sinister plaint flowing like blood from an open vein.

She repeated: "My God . . . My God . . . !"

He implored: "Catherine, my little Catherine . . ."

He begged her to forgive him, without knowing why or for what; he took her by the shoulders, for she was staggering, shaken by a swell of dolor, drunk, and they walked obliquely in the increasing fog.

He only had one idea: to make her shut up, to stop her tears. To all his pleas she replied: "I can't, I can't . . ."

However, he was sad and emotional, not being bad; but he could only ever find one word to repeat to her, like an invalid who has lost the power of speech.

"My love . . ."

But she expected something else, the things of old, the words that one does not invent, which spring from amour and desire like flame from a fire. She waited . . . but it was dead, his dear amour, and the gauche and compassionate man beside her was no longer the one that she had known.

She sat down on a bench; he remained standing, stunned, enervated and disconcerted by the woman's tears.

A rumble of wheels was heard; he looked, and, still distant, perceived the lanterns of a fiacre.

"Catherine . . ."

"Yes . . . yes . . ."

"It's very late, would you like to take that cab?"

Devoid of strength, she made no reply.

The rumble became louder, and the carriage visible.

He hailed it, with a secret fear that it was not free . . .

It was.

Catherine did not resist. He put her into it, gave the address to the coachman, and leaned through the window for the adieu.

She had believed that he was getting in too, but when she understood, she extended her arms toward him, appealing: "Georges . . . Georges . . . my love . . ." with fear and with despair—with hope, still! So many things to say to him that she had not said! That he would never hear! To part so quickly, so brutally . . . !

He saw those two naked hands agitating piteously, and, moist with tears, shining in the darkness, poor little hands . . .

Already the fiacre was pulling away; he stepped back, and did not see anything more, or hear anything more.

He shook himself, and, his heart rather heavy and his feet icy, he went away rapidly toward Courcelles station.

How she weeps . . . he thought.

HAPPY CHILDREN[1]
(*La Fronde*, 5 October 1898)

POUPÉE

Poupée was three years old—almost.[2]

Her father was an apprentice jeweler and had never seen her; her mother, a supple and insouciant creature, walked with her through the hazards of the life she loved.

Poupée's maman was twenty years old—and very lucky; her limbs were round, her gait suggestive. She had bright skin, the teeth of a young cat, and the nape of her neck had the scent of flowers and pepper. Oh yes, very lucky; the house was small but she would have a bigger one . . . later. She was performing in a Revue—astonishing costumes—and there was talk about her in the newspapers: Mademoiselle Florry . . .

Poupée was three years old. She knew that her mother's role in life was to be very pretty, very cheerful and always to be amusing.

As for her, she had to be good and beautiful in order to "do honor" to her mother.

They went to the Bois together. The victoria was brand new, a little small, light, shiny, not famous though, a gift from the Comte d'Oiselles, and the Comte d'Oiselles loved Poupée.

---

1 The use of this headline implies that the story was intended as the first of a series, but no others followed.
2 Because it is used as a proper name I have left Poupée untranslated; the English equivalent would be Doll.

"It isn't a child, Florry, that you have there! She walks without falling on the sand outside, and remains tranquil in a drawing room, a doll, I tell you . . . but I love her."

Poupée was sometimes forgotten in her bed in the morning; awake in the dark room she sang songs in a tender and soft chirping voice.

Midday . . . one o'clock . . . the chambermaid arrived; the toilette commenced.

In the day, Poupée had one good moment: between four and six, often, her maman had rehearsals and left her in the house. The very long, heavy velvet garments that embarrassed her feet were taken off Poupée; a white apron was put over her short skirt and vest and she was left alone to play in her room.

Poupée asked that her hair should be bound together behind her head, because the curls fell over her eyes as soon as she lowered her head. When she was cold, a red and white shawl was put on her, knotted at the waist, and then, in that odd little accoutrement of an ordinary baby, only bright satin little house-slippers with pompoms striking a discordant note in the ensemble, Poupée devoted herself to her favorite amusements, and she was always very good—habitually—even with the temptations of fire and light around her.

Poupée's bedroom was bizarre; her maman relegated unimportant gifts there. Poupée venerated those objects because they belonged to her maman—her beautiful little maman, joyful and flowing, who carried her away in the turbulence of her skirts and her crazy life like a light feather. She made it the subject of amorous and touching meditations. There were statuettes there—gifts of a poor devil who had talent but no fortune and could only give his works to the woman he loved.

She would have liked to be his, because he was a handsome fellow, but did not care for his modelings, although they were often made in her image, the ingrate. In giving her daughter one of those statuettes one day, Florry had said: "It's your maman, my love, see what a pretty maman you have!"

That form without a dress, was it possible? She thought that her maman had deceived her, and was greatly chagrined. She did not mention that chagrin to anyone, because she had a little reserved and proud soul—her papa's soul.

There were also peignoirs in need of repair, to which the chambermaid incessantly devoted hasty needlework: a split seam where the sleeve was attached, a neckline prolonged by a rip in the cloth. Poupée thought: *Maman would rather have her dresses here than me*, but with respectful adoration.

What Poupée found most fatiguing was going out in the evening.

Quickly, after her solitary dinner, she was taken, manhandled, turned around, and when she was ready she was sat on a chair, her curls lined up over her forehead, very regularly, her dress spread out; she was instructed not to move and maman was helped to dress diabolically with a host of people around her who drank a last glass of champagne while slamming the doors. Then, in a gust of wind, Poupée was borne away in someone's arms, engulfed in a carriage, and *en route*.

Oh, the theater, the dressing-room, the wings! What a bore . . . it was so hot!

Poor Poupée, overwhelmed by her Empire mantle, which no one thought of taking off, a publicity baby planted like an advertising flag, she made great and heroic efforts to stay awake, but always, before the final act, she was laid down on two chairs and a man's overcoat folded in four, and she went to sleep, her mouth open, very round, like a flower, her hat yawning above her head.

Poupée traveled. In addition to Paris, already well-known to her, she had seen the sea, the mountains and the Midi. But all of that had seemed to her like a stage-set put up by invisible scene-shifters, which she distinguished poorly, made of painted canvas and theatrical supports.

Of the sea she knew the ends of the blonde beach, covered with the variegations of women and children like herself and her maman, summer beaches, restricted and encumbered with the preoccupations of five costumes per day, plus the bath. Of the mountains she knew the corners transformed into subsidiary branches of Paris for six weeks of strong heat, full hotels in which, more than ever, she was overworked and neglected, with orders only to go for walks in fashionable places at fashionable times, better behaved, more correct and more Poupée than ever.

She knew the Midi in a similar fashion, and always, everywhere, the exhibition of her little person, followed by ostentatious playthings that did not amuse her much.

People talked to her during walks; they stopped her. She played her role so well, unconsciously, and lent it an unexpected charm by means of her serious little face and her sad and attractive gravity.

＊

But here it is: there is a big dinner at Florry's house. Poupée's maman is very naked and very well-dressed, her hair somewhat loose and admirably curled.

Poupée is alone in her room. She will appear shortly in a beautiful dress ordered expressly, which is there, on the bed, the sleeves displayed in a cross. Poupée is very hungry—it is half past nine—perhaps she has been forgotten? She is sad.

But the door opens and a chambermaid throws a tablecloth over a corner of the table, pushing before Poupée a slice of salmon, cut up for form's sake . . . the soup has been omitted today . . . Poupée utters a sigh of regret—she is so hungry! She is so hungry! But she does not say anything and picks up, in order to console herself, a rubber cat of which she is fond, and then timidly, gazing at her incomplete meal, asks for something to drink.

"Soon!" And the chambermaid goes out, running. Through the lifted door-curtain the sound of voices and laughter arrives.

Poupée's maman is having a good time. The door-curtain falls back and the room becomes silent again. Poupée picks up her fork with a hasty and awkward gesture. She has been given a big fork today, which is inconvenient. She spears a large piece of pretty pink fish, without her other hand letting go of the favorite cat . . . she opens her hungry mouth . . .

Oh! how tight her collar is all of a sudden. She lifts her hand to it . . . drops the fork . . . and it is stinging inside now . . .

Oh, that hurts a lot . . . Poupée tips back in her chair in order to breathe more easily, the cat falls in the sauce, she agitates her arms desperately . . . and the room spins before Poupées' eyes, the statuettes shift; the one that is Poupée's maman is still smiling, her arms extended in a harmonious movement toward something that is not Poupée . . .

Poupée tries to cry out, but only utters a scarcely-perceptible, frightful sigh, and, her mouth twisted, her eyes dilated, green and convulsed, Poupée, stiff on her high chair, her two little awkward hands clenched and clutching her collar, remains mute, choked.

What is happening? Is it a new toy, a big toy sent by someone she does not know?

It is a box. So many boxes arrive, of all forms, when Poupée moves, in her long dresses or her white aprons, with her little pony-tail of bright wisps knotted in a ribbon, or sometimes a piece of string.

Now Poupée is no longer moving. She has become pale and pretty, without any sign in her thin face of her last horrible solitary suffering.

A fishbone . . . oh, that hurt a lot! And in such a little throat . . . imagine a flower that has a throat, it's almost like that, such a little child . . . and when one is all alone there is a very hard moment—that isn't explained, of course, but one is very unhappy—in sum, it's quickly done, quickly over . . .

Oh, Poupée's maman has wept a lot. She almost went mad. Besides which, it had a very bad effect on everyone. They were so gay, and they suddenly hear a terrible scream; the chambermaid is questioned, she is frightened—everyone comes running and sees this: Poupée, her eyes open, in a nightmare pose—dead.

But in sum, that box?

The box is long, but not very long. It is brought into Poupée's room and opened. Oh, the pretty box, lined with white satin, with lace and knots . . .

It's a sachet, it's a jewel-case . . .

Poupée's maman has received many sachets, many jewel-cases; this one makes her shiver and turn away.

It has been made pretty very pretty, you see, but it is still what it is, and when it is for lying a little child within it, your little child, one can be cheerful, have gaiety in the blood and insouciance in the spirit—and not much tenderness in the heart—but that always has a particular effect.

Poupée is very dainty in her jewel-case. A little girl who is there is deceived by her and extends her arms with desire, crying: "I want the lovely doll!" For she has not changed at all, except that she is asleep.

She is asleep . . .

Florry throws handfuls of rose petals over her daughter, detached expressly that morning, and then it is finished. The jewel-case is closed, and taken away.

It is taken to a garden that is not the Bois de Boulogne in a carriage that is not the new and light victoria.

Florry weeps like a child, repeating: "Oh, how pretty she was, how funny . . ."

And the Comte d'Oiselles says, indulgently: "I'll give you another, darling . . ."

DAY'S END
(*La Fronde*, 19 October 1898)

FOUR O'CLOCK; in November.

Between the violet-tinted marshes in which the naked russet rushes were mirrored and the mown verdigris-colored meadows the road extended like a long and interminable ribbon, in a broad curve, with the neutral gray of dried mud. A petty north wind, low and harsh, stung that mud, crumbling it into fine, acrid dust. The advent of a frost could be sensed—one of the first—merely by seeing the earth cracked, split and pale here, brown and dewy in the fields, in closed soft shells in which seeds were dormant.

The sky was immense and empty, a uniform pallor of water and ash, which melted over the fluid blue line of a circle of pines beyond the fields. That distant horizon was interrupted by large gaps of sandy dunes, livid scars carved in the forests incessantly devoured by fires.

The dry branches of the trees cried softly under the breeze: a thin, halting note . . . more profound, a broad, continuous clamor seemed to come from the very heart of those trees; that was the pinada, which sent forth its incessant, anguishing lamentation: the wind in the dense, high branches of the overlapping crowns, which stirred the forest with a long swell, with an appeal of waves.

The low tide, the water retired in an uncertain line confounded with the pallor of the sky, left the marshes uncovered,
exhaling their savage odor. And in its nudity, that ancient
port—with its light glaze of stagnant water, pink and strange
beneath a faded reflection, come from who knows where, wandering in that uniform sky, its sharp excrescences as regular as a
drawing—resembled a relief map placed there, very delicately,
like a plaything.

The silhouettes of two or three pinnaces, antique boats,
black and long, almost devoid of a keel, flat-bottomed, loomed
over it. Very old, useless henceforth, they were finishing rotting
far from great breezes and powerful salts, amid that stagnant
water and those flat dead plants.

On the road: a woman and a donkey. The donkey was old,
the woman had no age. Their métier: she a merchant and he a
bearer of woodchips.

"Who wants . . . wood . . . chips? Who wants . . . wood . . .
chips?"

From dawn to dusk, all her life, she had moaned that phrase,
dragging out each word, each syllable, almost every letter.
Always the same phrase, spoken slowly, tearful and penetrating, twice over, and over . . .

That took five minutes; then a brief halt, and it began again.

Thus, every day . . . thus, every day, she paraded that chant
through the town orientated toward the sunset, elegant, new
and rich, situated on the large blue bay opening into the ocean
beyond the sandy points edged by pines that enclosed it. Then
she returned to the forest by the same long, pale route unfurling between the mown meadows and the violet-tinted marshes,
and that for long years, with the same donkey.

Living in that forest and on that forest, she seemed to have
become one of its roots: dry and brown, bent over the earth,
picking up the woodchips, collecting the pine cones, her gnarled
ankles seemingly attached to the earth and coming away from
it effortfully: dark things and a mute life.

Her feet were naked in her clogs, her skirt, short and color-less, made of all fabrics, floated as if hung from a stick, and around her waist, thick and square in spite of the thinness of her limbs, her *caraco* was tightened by a rope belt.

She wore the black hat of sewn straw, as large as a plat-ter with edges drooping uniformly all around her head, of the women of the region, with a strip of black velvet tightening the low skullcap.

Her figure was sculpted like a knife-blade, with long, sharp, stiff features, immutably arrested, it seemed, the yellow of old—very old—ivory. Her mouth could not be seen; age had eaten it away, anticipating death.

Her eyes: two black holes, devoid of gleam, devoid of lashes, devoid of eyebrows, like two little painted round dots.

That woman, for all those who knew her, was eternal. She was earth, wood, that which is brown, solid and seemingly in-sensible. The years had fixed upon her like a patina that forms and that expression . . . that lack of expression.

Under the rod, ballasted by two sacks that remained unsold, the donkey went, as russet as his burden, dull, frightful, very scabby and very thin; his even pace, so slow that at first glance one might think him motionless, was a protest, and his head low—very low—his ears dangling, said: *I expect blows* . . . for he knew them. He did not know anything else, anything except his quotidian, unchangeable trajectory, but he knew that he was beaten.

This evening, the old woman with the woodchips was not beating him. She was not talking to him either.

Her gait, her head bowed like that of the beast, similarly profiled on the horizon oppressed by the dusk, was dejected and pensive. But she was not thinking. She did not compare the lassitude that attached to every step her legs took on the pale and solitary road with that of the day before, in order to find it heavier.

The forest drew away as she went toward it; that was the impression caused by the heavy line of pines, so high and black, so uniform that one always thought that one was close to it, but which fled before you, disconcertingly.

And the fading day took the light away toward the distant and invisible water.

When she passed the edge and went into the great shadow, shadow itself, she sighed: "How tired I am . . ."

That was all.

With a habitual gesture, her hands unloaded the donkey, and he went toward the hut of his own accord. She sat down.

Pinadas are magicians; the obscure and monotonous rampart of their exterior lines is deceptive.

From the road down below it was redoubtable, so black. And under the forest, Nature, like a tall red-haired and blonde woman, extended her finishing beauty.

The low, thickset oaks, mingled and united by bushes with a thousand rusty branches, dressed the ground inextricably.

A giant and symbolic downcast form, prolonged beyond the visible confines, lying down to die, died gloriously, an adorable tawny autumnal flora devoid of flowers.

The gold, the flame and the copper streamed and overflowed like a wave of a unique and infimal color, as violent as a conflagration, drowned like delicate flesh; and in that splendor, that madness of yellow, nothing contrasted . . . The humidity emerging from the soil misted that brightness with its glistening shroud. The eye was caught as if by a gaze: a long, bewitching gaze of topaz, amber and sunlight. Something of the light remained under those branches, marvelous and inexplicable.

The old woman gazed stupidly through a gap in front of her.

In the light of the setting sun a thin golden line also appeared, a long narrow stripe along the distant sea; it was a day that was dying out there on the horizon.

A long and tender frisson passed. In the silence, so great and so sad, the intermittent fall of leaves was frightening. Little black tree-trunks, rude and gnarled stumps, enveloped the old woman with their projected shadow, invasive and tenacious.

She got up; it was necessary to shelter the two intact sacks, have supper and go to bed. She repeated: "How tired I am . . ." even though no one was there to hear her. The donkey, very hungry, was licking the bare ground.

Then the great forest, the mysterious forest—invisible from the roads—all golden, started spinning . . . the old woman fell, and her form was confounded with the relief of the stumps and the clods of earth. She moaned a little, plaintively.

The cold of the night, of the winter, suddenly seemed to her to increase, and to enter into her body like a blade.

In the silence, the frisson of dusk, she died without suffering.

The blonde fête of the forest paled, recoiled, captured by the large prompt shadows of autumn.

The gold of the western sky melted.

The black, avid hour settled upon its prey.

WHITE FURNITURE
(*La Fronde*, 22 November 1898)

VIVIANE BRUNE looked at Mimi Badaud, and Mimi Badaud looked at the white furniture.

They knew one another well. Viviane, nicknamed "the snake," had a face of pale shadow into which profound eyes and a voluptuous mouth put their flame and their grace; Mimi Badaud, fifteen years old, her bright hair windblown under the four-sou straw hat secured by green ribbons, had the body of a child, a doll, a statuette, so frail—frail enough almost to disappear behind the large boxes covered with waxed cloth that she carried every day in Paris.

They knew one another . . . and this evening, in November, at five o'clock, the hour when the clouds fall, as heavy and prompt as misfortune, Mimi Badaud arrived at Viviane Brune's new apartment, and entered the disorder of the recent removal.

The door to the landing was still open, the electric light was blazing on the straw, and in the slightly lugubrious silence of half-empty and sonorous rooms, Mimi had reached the threshold of the room with the white furniture: the fragile, ornamental furniture, shiny in its new prettiness. Leaning on the mantelpiece of that room, Viviane Brune, her eyes directed at the mirror, was weeping and watching the tears roll down her cheeks, so pale beneath the shadow of her hair.

That had surprised Mimi greatly; she did not understand why Viviane Brune was weeping . . .

"It's me Madame!" she announced.

Viviane turned round.

"Ah! It's you, the kid! How did you find me here?"

"I've come from the Rue Fortuny; I came to show you the spangled bodice. They said: Madame is in the Avenue de Messine. I came . . . it's very chic here," she added, with conviction.

"You think so?"

"Madame is hard to please?"

"Yes, a little, so they say, but I don't believe it. Sit down; put the box down . . . I'm bored, I'm alone . . ."

She fell into an armchair, and Mimi Badaud sat down in the armchair facing her, delighted, her eyes laughing, going from the very low bed, immense, sculpted like a jewel, to the wardrobe with three panels, those to the side ornamented with lattices, like windows—and she sighed a little, seeing herself there entirely: her mud-spattered skirt, her sorry cat-fur collar, her hands thickened by woolen gloves, displayed wretchedly under the bright light. . . But her gaze stopped at her muzzle in the mirror, and she smiled: that bloody mouth, those eyes of lively water—she was pretty, yes, quite pretty . . .

Curled up like a large artful she-cat in her green and mauve silks, coiffed with violets like a priestess of pleasure, Viviane made an adorable patch among the old-fashioned fabrics thrown at hazard over the furniture . . . and then, there was a great silence . . .

Life was suspended around them, only sensible by virtue of the heavy, incessant movement that rose in regular and muted waves from the street; arrested in the great struggle, the hunt for money, bread and desire, they were pensive . . .

A chime of folly, desire and enjoyment rang, overflowing, beneath the bright hair and small forehead of Mimi Badaud: her unknown destiny, before her, intoxicated her.

Viviane Brune, having become Anne de Nordelles again, saw the past, twelve years old, the arrival in Paris of a young provincial girl, the installation amid the family furniture, the heavy furniture, brown, square and honest, which encumbered the narrow rooms disgracefully. The miserable past between the rancor of the household and the disappointment of researches, the fatal race to the abyss . . . her, finally, on evenings like this one, climbing the stinking stairs of the lodgings in Batignolles, feet heavy with fatigue and mud, heart sunk in a frightful bitterness.

On the sixth floor she found her infirm father and her sister, her eyes worn out by the reproduction of miniatures.

The omnipotent disgust for that existence grabbed her by the throat, with the acrid smoke of the match struck on the kitchen wall. She swallowed both, and her tears too. One such evening she looked at herself before going to bed, desperately— as Mimi had surprised her a little while ago—and the gulf of her eyes, the beauty of her lips, and the divine softness of her skin calmed her down, and she slept deeply for a long time: those eyes, that mouth and that skin would save her.

With the father dead and the sister returned to the province, blind, Viviane emerged from the shadow, was advertised on posters, adored, and very well dressed.

And this evening, in the bustle of the change of evidence, something distant, sad and pure came to trouble her . . .

Mimi Badaud sighed deeply . . .

Viviane got up with one of those long abrupt movements she had, as if ready to break something, or to beat someone, and which threw her, supple and melting under caresses, into someone's arms, an item of furniture, or to the floor. She came to kneel against the fresh silk armchair dishonored by the skirts of the poor errand-girl Mimi. The latter made a small gesture of surprise, without understanding, bewildered and slightly mocking.

"You like this, the pretty furniture?" said Viviane. "You like pretty dresses, like these? You're cold in the street, where you live? Show your feet . . . they're small . . . the fatigue of walking a great deal, but it's good for the calves; you're thin—that's because you're young . . . you laughed when you looked at yourself just now; do you think you're pretty? I pleased myself once too. Am I still pretty . . . ?"

She was so exquisite saying that, that Mimi kissed her.

"You see my teeth, you see my eyes . . . it's those, etc., that gave me all this. There—you can have as much, my dear!"

She laughed like an amour as she got up again. Mimi Badaud laughed, got up too, and very simply, said: "That's what Maman tells me every day."

Immobile, Viviane Brune saw in a light mist her dead father and her blind sister, their innocent hearts and their simple thoughts.

"Adieu, Mimi, go and walk. I like you a lot; if you say that you saw me weeping, no one will believe you . . . adieu, little Badaud, choose your furniture; when you have a beautiful bed like this one, come back and tell me how you paid for it . . . For myself, it's eight years that I've been working for it—eight years is a long time, but I'm a bungler, you'll get there quicker—and now, it doesn't give me any pleasure . . . bad luck, eh?"

She stopped, slightly breathless, and went on: "Do you know why? But no, you wouldn't understand . . . go away . . ."

She watched her depart; then, returning to the large mirrors, so pretty, like a tall green and mauve flower, she smiled with her amorous eyes and her mouth full of promises, murmuring: "I don't have the soul of my body—could I tell her that? Damned white furniture! It reminds me of the old buffet where I searched for a crust at night, on the road . . . !

"When one is alone in the evening, how stupid one becomes . . . !"

REGARDING PIGEONS
(*La Fronde*, 1 December 1898)

WHILE passing along the Rue de Prony this morning, I remembered Florence. Why? The uniformity of the houses, only broken by the mosaics of silks and embroideries lining their windows; the pale and glacial lapis blue of the sky, the cleanliness of the sidewalks, nothing recalled the Loggia della Orcagna such as I saw it again in one of those violences of memory that suppress the present. I saw again those lines of an oppressive splendor in the profound light, and, on the threshold of their shadow, the old lions of ancient Firenze, which seem to be guarding the ardent life of the marbles.

Image of beauty, of purity, of eternity, and beneath, in the vibrancy of the sunlight, the whiteness of the dust; the people in bright rags, the fresh and perfumed profusion of fruits, an orgy of color, a *furia* of yapping more vertiginous for a Parisian than the eddies of the boulevards at six o'clock in the evening.

I remembered Florence because, over the neat asphalt, the cabs arranged at the station and the coachmen in cloaks, a bright flock of pigeons went past with a silken noise: about twenty, perhaps more; a great living fan, nacreous, mauve and luminous, descending on to the causeway amid the gilded filth; a scatter of snow, of feathers . . . and a few memories also rose up . . .

Florence: a heavy summer, too blue, too beautiful, which seized my heart, head and limbs—my entire being—like a gigantic hand.

I had gone to Italy in order to distract a sting of the soul, the slight pain of a banal deceived amour, and my little scratch slyly became a large wound. My body flaccid and my mind slack, I slid from nostalgias to regrets far above the real level of my trouble.

The moment was dangerous. It was then that I met outside the loggia, got to know and loved Giuseppe—and Giuseppe cured me. This is how: Giuseppe was twelve years old, he sold lemons and resembled a pretty bronze. He loved the pigeons that enveloped him from sunrise to sunset with their wings and their tenderness, and he loved a little girl.

He told me, in his amorous singing language, all sorts of very touching little things—immense for his heart—and I had no desire to laugh before the slender creature who pronounced very gravely the grave words of amour.

I inspired confidence in Giuseppe, and he introduced me to Catarina.

When I saw her I felt sorry for my little friend. She bore in her face and her movements all the certain signs of domination.

She was taller than Giuseppe and in a more elevated social situation; she was the only child of a wine merchant in the Via Calzaioli. "*Ecco il signor de Parigi* . . ." said Giuseppe, pointing him out to me.

She cooed like a dove, and her curls, her eyelids and her little flat plump breast palpitated with a malicious breath of curiosity, desire and ambition.

I tried to make her talk, but she laughed without responding, with all caresses already possible in her somber golden eyes and her lips like fruit.

The thin little face of Giuseppe, of a dullness almost green with fever, and the bitter crease of his mouth, struck me more forcefully at that moment.

I saw him every day; he talked to me about "her" without reserve, but with sadness.

"She doesn't love you?" I asked.

"Oh, yes, a lot, she told me so . . ."

"She isn't nice?"

I thought he was about to bite me. Then, hesitantly: "I'll tell you . . . she doesn't like pigeons."

Again, I saw my little living bronze with the excessively sensitive heart; again. I heard his naïve lament that morning and his childish and profound story appeared to me with a new meaning.

He loved them, Giuseppe, "his" pigeons, for, in the number, the anonymous, the unknown, the strangers that spread out over the stones, casting light there in great wing-beats, warm and amorous life, he had his own. He nourished them in his mouth, his hair mingled with their feathers, and he was so tender and so twittering with them, poor boy—a little bird himself, a bird of the street, seeking his grain in the sun and in the gutter . . .

In the evening, when the old palaces extended their great tragic shadow over the square like a mantle, he watched his companions flee that shadow, rising in the sky like white and rapid smoke, and disappearing, returning to their unknown nests—and he watched that desirously.

"If you don't want to, I'm going to pluck a pigeon alive . . . yes, entirely alive . . ."

What was that about? A mystery . . .

But if Giuseppe "didn't want to," it was surely because he couldn't. And I saw his heartbroken face, and the ravishing anger of his mistress—for she was that, in the old and veritable sense of the word, the queen of his heart. Perceiving me, she fled, and I calmed Giuseppe down.

But the next day I found Giuseppe in tears.

"*Ha fatto, signor, ha fatto . . .*"

She's done it, Monsieur, she's done it.

And he told me the whole story, in detail.

Before his eyes, with her little robust and sinewy hand, she had plucked one of his birds.

The victim was there, quivering, pink, with frissons in the flesh, anxiety fixed in its little eye, as round and black as a nail. On the ground, around Giuseppe, like frail snow, the little feathers were spread, fluttering, as if each of them still had its own independent life.

The poor child was sobbing, repeating: "*È crudele, è crudele.*" She's cruel, she's cruel. The true word, the bitter word, the bloody word, he seized, savoring it, turning it over in his mouth and in his heart with a sensuality of chagrin.

✻

Years have passed since that little humble intimacy, that little story, that little minute in which I had seen a heart entirely open, wounded, laid bare like the little creature he was mourning—and by the same work, the same hands.

Years . . . I was wondering how a few abrupt, white, fugitive wing-beats had been able to bring back, from so far away, such a clear memory, when my thought deviated—or, rather, by reconnecting fragments united by the mysterious underside of things, I recalled a more recent caprice of a little girl. She had sent two turtle-doves in a perforated hatbox to a milliner in the Rue de Paix, at about five o'clock on a certain day, with an order to attach them, alive to her toque; and that evening, in a forestage box, at a sensational premiere, she had appeared thus coiffed—which had enchanted her lovers.

There are pigeons and pigeons, and various fashions of plucking both kinds.

THE DAY AFTER CHRISTMAS, THE DAY AFTER AMOUR
(*La Fronde*, 20 December 1898)

HE woke up . . . at what time? His body weary, his soul flaccid, his head heavy, not yet out of slumber, with fragments of memories deformed into dreams; and, in the utmost depths of his consciousness, recapturing an ennui, an oppression, he woke up . . . at what time?

The bedroom was mute and gray, with the reflections of the night-light and the pallors of daylight making the familiar things silky.

And suddenly, abruptly, in an infinite yawn, and stretching his limbs:

"Oh yes! Christmas . . . yesterday . . . midnight supper . . . Bouquette . . . Charmer . . . attempt at orgiastic joy . . . lots of flowers, flesh, light, wine, in order to be cheerful . . . then, the departure, in the middle of the night, when being awake seems an abnormal sin amid the enormous repose of beings, the immense silence of things . . . Very short, that moment, on such a Parisian night of December twenty-fourth . . ."

Finally, the memory becoming more precise, he suddenly saw again the face, drowned in sensuality, of Marceline d'Ambre. Then, his eyes still closed, it seemed to him that behind those recent memories, hours scarcely gone my, distantly—like a landscape trembling in the hectic clarity of a summer morning, poorly visible to eyes blinded by the mirage of the undulating light at the level of the fields—he seemed to glimpse, almost to perceive, indistinctly, the line of another image, another décor, the face of another woman—and the malaise of a bad awakening oppressed him more . . .

Perhaps the broad daylight and a cup of tea would chase all that away . . . and, stretching out his arm, he rang.

"What time is it?"

"Three o'clock, Monsieur."

And the valet de chambre placed newspapers, letters and a parcel on the table.

That parcel was very light. He could not recognize the handwriting of the address, for the gray daylight outside scarcely made the room less gloomy. He weighed it and undid it, his soft fingers struggling with the knotted string. Separated, a sheet of silk paper, and a slightly broken cardboard box appeared, and, suddenly opened, spread a strong sweet perfume . . .

A little scattered bouquet, partly shredded: carnations, roses, resedas—delicate, odorous flowers—fell on to the bed and on to the young man's breast, under his dry lips and his nostrils, covered his hands like a light amorous harvest, a gentle weight of an immaterial phantom—and the memory of a little while ago returned, tugging at his heart, as a physical pain twists a muscle.

Quickly, he searched among the letters, had the curtains drawn completely, and, leaning on his elbow on the edge of the bed, having found the expected pages, he read:

> *My love, it's me, as before, who will be there when you awake, with these flowers that you once loved . . . I picked them myself in the garden full of the sunlight that I need to "drink" in order to be cured quickly, quickly . . . (I'm much better, I'm still coughing, but that doesn't prove anything.) What would cure me*

would be news of you . . . but you scarcely write, oh, no . . . And for myself, you see, discouraged, I don't pester you any more as before . . . Before! That sad word comes back to me incessantly. And in spite of so much dolor, and so many tears, it is the time when you loved me, when there were Christmas Eves of amour when, by virtue of a superstitious weakness, I searched for you and I wanted you more than ever, which always fills my life, my heart . . . But forgive me, I don't want to be sad; I know that you too have troubles, cares, I know—in spite of what you have made me suffer—that you're not wicked and that you'll keep—I want to believe it—the promise you made to me, as a sacred promise . . . the oath that I couldn't help asking of you in the horrible wrench of the last hour we spent together: Do what you wish, always, love others—I know you, you can't do otherwise—but once, once alone in the year, on Christmas Eve, I'd like to be sure that you're mine, mine alone . . .

I'd like, for one night, not to be subject to doubts, jealousies, frightful imaginations, in the certainty that you haven't entirely forgotten our dear divine tenderness . . . Oh, yes, that little sacrifice you'll be able to make for me; you won't deceive me to that extent, especially this year, the first of our separation, the first distant Christmas, my love, my dear, dear love, I love you . . .

He dropped the letter, picked up the flowers that long hours of traveling had stained: a slight fading of the petals, weary stems, leaves slightly rusted by frost, and the hearts crumpled, closed, half-dead . . .

And as such, slightly wretched, they were able to revive, in such a recent past, the great exquisite past of their riveted hearts, once, and those three ardent years into which she had been able to put enough sensuality and enough soul to be *the one who remains* . . .

The oppression of the awakening weighed more heavily upon his soul, upon his entire being; he had a bitter taste in his mouth as if he had chewed his existence, and without knowing why, a phrase that she had pronounced one day when, cowardly and brutal, he had put her in distress, returned to him incessantly: *The happiness that one has, you see, is like a poison that one has in the blood, which never, ever goes away* . . .

Then, in a low voice, in response to obscure thoughts, he murmured: "There! It's the day after, the day after!"

FORGOTTEN . . .
(*La Fronde*, 5 January 1899)

(Fragment of the journal of an unemployed man)

A sky of the end of winter, impossible in painting, . . . made of a transparency of the atmosphere and a gray of twilight—a special gray that rose from the earth, from the shadow of gorse and heather, invading the pale, washed, final mauve like a dust, which went, thickening, toward the sunset, accumulating very low, touching the water, in the form of somnolent monsters . . . and vapors like long pink tongues, licked those heavy chimeras crouching on the horizon, awakening them with a caress, dissolving them over the crests of the waves that were coming, slow and fleecy, to stretch over the sand—tranquil under the darkening sky, almost mute in the motionless calm air.

The heath behind us, and before us, the sea . . .

Sitting with her hands crossed over her knees and her eyes distant—in a dream before her, very pale under the delicate plumage of her toque and the foam of her bright hair—she spoke to me.

"It was last winter; I was coming home after the ball; it was four o'clock in the morning.

"My room, my beautiful bedroom of a spoiled only child, was being redecorated. The fire had caught a silk curtain, quickly extinguished, but everything was in the air . . . I was lodged for a few days, camping in an uninhabited place, with cupboards all around, on the second floor of the house, near the linen cupboard and the bathroom. A room with which one isn't familiar, you know, by night—especially a woman's—that did something to me . . . not fear, no, but in sum, in looking round, one is curious . . .

"At first, I wasn't thinking about anything; I had a beautiful dress, I was very pretty that evening—and I had been having fun: me, a dreamer, as you say, by habit. Then, in spite of all the comfort established temporarily, the sentiment of curiosity I mentioned just now came to me . . . to open a cupboard: dresses; another: old linen and books; a third . . . it resists; I force it, the batten yields with a sigh . . . something white, doubtless caught in the groove, crumbles and falls on a raised floorboard . . . a little frail debris of porcelain, foliage, the shiny fragment of a fake pearl, which runs over the parquet with a little crick-crack, all the way to my feet . . . my satin shoe stops it involuntarily.

"I take a chair, I climb on to it, a candle in hand, and I see a little mortuary wreath, a humble little floral crown, brittle and shiny, attached by disjointed strings of pearls . . . a very old and dusty little crown . . . and alongside it, two minuscule shoes in white leather, with satin bows, worn away by time, but which had never been subjected to the continual friction of a child's feet, impatient and bold, which act in the void . . .

"Where did those objects come from? That crown and those shoes were so wretched, dolorous and forgotten in that deliberately relegation, that obstinate abandonment in a corner of rubbish . . .

"Maman, that evening, again, had been very beautiful—as always, adored and surrounded. She had been so regally worldly, for such a long time! I had always seen her animated, occupied, overworked, caught in the gears of so many duties—chores,

52

she said. Papa needed her so much! And I had always seen both of them breathless, busy, their hands encumbered all day long with papers, notes, lists—and in the evening, those hands were charming and captivating, gestures extended, on papa's part, to influential and respectable men, and on maman's part, coquettish and ravishing, handling a scepter under the soft and facile grace of an unfolded fan. An outdoor life of movement and noise, brilliant and vibrant . . . I was born inside myself, very thoughtful, I had been obliged to make do . . . But suddenly, in that existence flowing free and clear, without any apparent underside, a shadow was revealed, by chance . . . I felt it . . . something unknown took hold of me, tormented me . . .

"Maman, confronted with it by me, cried: 'What, it's still there!'

"And, to my question: 'Oh, little girl . . . in this life, one doesn't have time . . . we never told you . . . you had a brother; he died before you were born . . . he had . . . let's see . . . ah, I remember . . . those shoes I bought him the day before the day when . . . he had the croup . . . that lasted one night—he was so small! It's his nounou who must have put them there . . . she had given him the crown . . . there were so many flowers! She was kept here . . . At that moment your father needed me for . . . how far away it is already! Oh, little girl, that's life! Oh, I had a great chagrin . . . but you came . . .'

"The brief and interrupted phrases, those phrases of society, the society in which time is necessary for everything, and in which time for troubles can't be taken, she had them by habitude, before that wreckage of a past more than twenty years old . . .

"Life, as she said . . .

"Life: forgetfulness, indifference, in the heart of a woman, a mother, the memory of a dead child, the first child, sunk, disappeared! Life made by society—that's it!"

And with something savage in her large eyes, delivering the secret of a proud and sad reserve, in a detached voice with the harmonious modulations of a simple conversation, she added:

"That, life? No . . . I'm not a sentimentalist, a soft heart, no, you know that full well, but I'm disgusted, weary . . . Life is something short and eternal, and although that brief interval is populated by fleeting and changing events, the soul that lives it is made to be subject to the great living and eternal force— and that force is profound; it's love, memory, dolor . . . *that* is life, and not the feverish agitation of an empty and sonorous bustle—sonorous, yes, like the echo of stone at the bottom of a well."

With a broad gesture, standing up now, her skirts lifted up around her, and then stuck to her body by the wind that had risen a minute ago, she pointed at the sea, more mysterious in the night and bloodier, the sky, higher and more immense, swept clean and bright, with the nascent clarity of a new moon, and the heath, extending darkly, perfumed by a harsh odor, unfurling in the distance . . .

"That is profound, beautiful and immortal; that is life as I want it, as I understand it—dolorous, yes, but tomorrow there will be sunshine!"

And as I sighed, thinking of the chimerical vision of existence of that young soul, she wept, saying:

"How sad it all is!"

ONE OF THEM
(*La Fronde*, 12 January 1899)

THE city groaned in the gold of the setting sun and the ash of the evening: the dust of a June evening—six o'clock, when vehicles and people circulate—which made the trees gray and faded, and veiled the Madeleine lightly.

In front of the omnibus bureau, the crowd was shuffling feet, weary and enervated.

Sitting at a table of the nearby café, he was thinking. The women passing by fastened their eyes to the tender eyes of the handsome fellow, but he did not look at them, and did not hear the rumor of the intersection of the street and the boulevard. He was looking beyond, far beyond, into the mirror of his memory, at a calm and cool evening descending upon tranquil meadows rosy with flowers; a bell was tolling, and in that profound peace, it was the very air that seemed vibrant under the leaves.

That was the frame around a narrow house and a woman in black: his mother, his house.

And he took two letters from his pocket, one already crumpled, slightly tarnished, bearing on its stamp a date more than fifteen years ago, the other received the previous evening. He reread both of them, in order, amid the eddies of breathless life:

The first:

My child,

Time goes by, however, and that has ended up astonishing me, for I believed it in advance to be eternal, and to have stopped at your departure, in order to take you even further away from me, and for a long time!

But no, you will soon return! How will I find you, my René? What will it have made of you, the big city, your Paris, which you love so much? I want to tell you right away myself that you will find me somewhat changed . . . I prefer to warn you—but don't be afraid.

She's no longer very young, your maman, you know—but seeing you will put me right . . .

A year, a whole year, you've been away from me . . .

Would you like to know? That's what made me ill . . . I didn't have the strength. I didn't say anything to you then; you wanted to leave, and that was quite natural! I couldn't go with you, for several reasons that you know. You know what difficulty I've had installing us in our home here, since I've had a little work: those infinite embroideries that you've seen in my hands day after day, evening after evening, for so many years . . . You said to me, at fifteen: "How can you do that all the time?" It was necessary, my child. When I took you back from your father, René, when I took you away with me, it was necessary to keep you and it was necessary to work. Our means didn't permit both of us to live in Paris . . . from here I can still help you a little. And then, I didn't feel very strong . . .

I've always been fortunate with you, especially when we've been able to be entirely at home. I knew that you wouldn't stay forever in the country with me, but I thought that you'd easily find an occupation in Dijon; you'd be able to come home in the evening, and then, you'd get married. Anyway, let's not talk about all that. That wasn't your idea, and when I saw you dragging your feet so languidly and talking to me distractedly, and above all—above all!—when I saw something troubled and obscure in the depths of my child's bright eyes, I said to myself: "René has a chagrin!" What you had was ennui. One evening, weeping you said to me: "I'm stifling here!"

Well, it was necessary, then, for you to leave, and that's what happened . . . and I stayed.

Why am I talking about all that this morning? I always think about it without saying anything, for you know all these things like midday . . . is it because everything seems today so similar to the morning of your departure . . .

At that point, René stopped and looked ahead of him again. With the eyes of his soul this time, and through the mist of tenderness that was shown to his pupils, he saw again the April morning that she was evoking.

The last meal in the dining room where the great golden light of midday was flamboyant: the linen, the furniture, the shiny carafes; a buzzing bee circulating; beyond the gaping windows there were blond fields, green trees, roses—a beautiful new spring in the radiant youth of the countryside.

The memory of all those humble things and those great tranquil lines attached and wrung his heart . . . And the last words:

"Don't weep . . ."

"No,"

"Write to me . . ."

"Yes."

And he had written; she had seen the fever of tenderness that he had for the city, and that, like a shrewd and cruel mistress, because it was so seductive, the city had been hard on him.

She had suffered more than him from all that suffering, and had not been hopeful of all his hopes . . .

The objective attained thus far was very far from his dreams, as an action is different from a phrase. She sensed him weakening, sickened; she also sensed him infected by an ardent ambition ignited by the maleficent friction of adventures and ambient glories . . .

But in sum, she waited for him to come back to her for a few days, and that wait was not only that of her immense tenderness but also the excessive impatience of a being who knows that she only has a short time to live and wants to possess everything beloved with a frenzy of the soul that will make such a short time eternal in depth . . . For she knew her illness, and that it would take her slyly, like an assassin, at some imminent and unexpected hour. She only wanted to see her child again and to live a few calm days with him, before the end.

Oh, but let him come, let him come quickly!

All that anguish and all that desire were contained under the tranquil phrases of her letter. She had said almost nothing, because she loved him too much to worry him; he had understood almost nothing.

Thus, in response, he told her all about a new affair that had surged forth for him. It was a matter of a post in Madagascar, important enough to fix his future with a rapidity that he could not hope to achieve in any situation retaining him in France. Everything was in question, he was overloaded; if the matter were decided, if the proposition were made and he accepted it, it would be necessary for him to depart straight away, if not it would be an opportunity missed, lost; it was only designated to him on that condition, of *departing straight away* . . .

Oh, that phrase, underlined in the letter as if to demonstrate fully to his mother that, from then on, the brief journey to see her had become impossible, had entered into his mother's eyes and into her heart like a dagger . . .

Afterwards, among many words, he had mentioned the chagrin he had in going away without embracing her, but it was the future, *their* future! In any case, in three years he would have a leave, a long leave, and afterwards . . . afterwards . . . !

She saw that he was happy, intoxicated by expectation, made for the unknown. She knew that all that was serious, that it was indeed his future, and, not revealing anything about her health in order that he would not have any remorse, and no regrets, she wrote: *Accept; I can wait a little longer.*

And that very morning, in response to those words, which he reread now, he had sent a telegram saying that the affair was concluded and his departure fixed. It added: *Letter follows.*

Yes, that was it; a calm and fresh evening descended over the meadows pink with flowers, a bell was tolling, and in that profound peace it was the very air that vibrated under the leaves.

The cemetery was like a garden, not very large, enclosed by a low wall and a tall grille, always open. There were a few cypresses, many young fir-trees with shoots of tender golden green, and blond willows as abundant as tresses. A very distant, very high bird was singing: a monotonous, melancholy and soft cry . . . so distant, so high! One searched for it but could not see it; it was like the voice of the cloud that was passing on high, a slow beast, over the pale extent of a crepuscular sky . . . What anguish . . . ! What peace . . .

Along the grass of the path in the part of the "garden" that was still desert she went, at an unsteady pace, and it was there that she stopped to read the blue paper the dispatch received a little while ago. Her eyes remained attached for an infinite time to those few words, but when she raised her head she was not weeping, she was smiling, and, looking around her as if she were searching for something, she said in a low voice: "Yes, my child, I'll wait . . . here."

And, still standing in the long and beautiful grass, she was suddenly afraid of dying too quickly, and that that might stop her child, who was going away unconsciously, so strong and so joyful in life.

THE WIND BLOWS . . .
(*La Fronde*, 19 January 1899)

TOUSLING the forests, covering the plain and lifting up the sea, the wind shrieked its enormous cry of eternity; but on entering the houses it took on a human voice; behind the doors it moaned like a pauper, wept like a child between the shutters, and then, in some empty, poorly closed room it led a sabbat in which howls of madness, gasps of debauchery and the plaints of murder victims were confused.

From the sea, magnificent and terrifying as it was in the open sky, in the middle of the ocean and skimming the ground, the gallop of the wind collided with the stone of walls, ripped and fragmented in cracks in the woodwork, strangled in chimney flues, became sinister and low in the houses, and could not be heard without a frisson, on rediscovering therein all the misery of familiar appeals.

Thérèse, lying down, listened avidly, shaken by that frisson, almost voluptuous because it was combined with a profound sentiment of security; then, at a longer and more violent gust, she plunged her delicate face into the lace of her pillow and drew the fine sheet, perfumed with vervain, all the way up to her ears.

No more could then be seen but the top of her juvenile cheek, the soft wave of her brown hair above her eyebrows, as neat as the stroke of a paint-brush, and her half-closed eyes, mysterious and tender beneath her eyelids.

She could feel her entire body, slightly worn out by a long excursion made in the afternoon, when the tempest was not yet aggravated by turbulent downpours. She and Jean had gone a long way, along the solid and shiny beach, the admirable ocean beach that unrolls, all golden, from Biarritz to Saint-Jean-de-Luz. On departing, along the foot of the Basque coast, when the tide was at its lowest, she had taken pleasure in imagining, in one of those crises of perverse joy that grip people in the midst of happiness and repose, how frightened they would be if, suddenly seeing unleashed waves advancing beyond the anticipated limit and ahead of the normal time, they found themselves trapped between the sheer cliff and the sea: the implacable, monstrous, marvelous sea . . .

And that supposition had been the pretext for both of them to press against one another more tightly, while holding their breath, cut off by the wind, the kisses and the delightful fear of the impossible, and to recount the legend of the "Chamber of Amour."

The Chamber of Amour was a grotto hollowed out in the basalt cliff overlooking the sea, where two lovers had taken refuge and, having forgotten the time in their happiness, the sea had surprised them and enabled them to pass, mercifully, from that happiness into death.

At a detour of the beach, the wind being cut off by an accumulation of rocks, they had run like two children.

She had picked up seashells as frail and fresh as mouths; he searched little rock pools, discovering dark violet or pale pink sea-urchins, profoundly anchored in fissures, which would not allow themselves to be detached easily.

They exchanged their treasures with smiles, and then, after a short time, were saddened by seeing them tarnished, dried on contact with their hands and, deprived of the powerful juice of the sea, losing their light colors.

On recognizing the puerility of those childish activities they made fun of one another, very gently and without conviction, for that puerility was something exquisite and infinite, and so many small gestures and banal words were affirmed and rejuvenated by their great amour.

The return had been more silent, rendered difficult by the increasing strength of the tempest, and they had been obliged to struggle, really struggle, with a continuous, tenacious, breathless effort, and, arm in arm and shoulder to shoulder, they had been rolled so forcefully by the storm wind that they had almost been wrenched apart and disunited, and had only been able to come together again with difficulty, emotional, stumbling and slightly pale . . .

So this evening, feeling very weary, Thérèse had gone to bed very quickly, and now, as eleven o'clock chimed, she was waiting for Jean, who had stayed to smoke a cigar and read the last editions of the newspapers, to come up to join her.

She sank into a semi-slumber, a refrain going round in her head, as heavy as a bee buzzing in a closed room. It was the song of Gastibelza, the man with the carbine:[1]

The wind that blows through the mountains
Has driven me mad . . .

Meanwhile, she perceived vaguely from below an unaccustomed noise, of voices . . . then doors closed, locks grated, shutters were sealed; they were definitively and perfectly defended against the blind and ferocious forces of water and wind . . .

Here, one is at home; the tempest cannot enter . . .

And Jean opened the bedroom door quietly.

She raised herself up slightly, her delightful face and charming body emerging from the curtains of the bed, into the soft glow of a night-light in a bracket fixed to the wall.

"Oh, it's you, finally. I thought you'd never come up . . . but what's the matter?"

1 "Gastibelza, l'homme à la carabine" is the first line of "Guitare," a poem by Victor Hugo set to music more than once, nowadays best known in a modern version by Georges Brassens.

He said: "Listen!"

And, punctuating the gusts of the wind, she heard dull, prolonged, repeated detonations.

"What is it?"

"The alarm cannon. There's a ship in distress. The semaphore is signaling the fear that the tide might bring it on to the coast . . . near here, on those rocks . . ."

He did not finish. Her eyes wide open in the shadow, she saw again the maternal beach of their childish games, indulgent to their amour, the blond and firm beach of that day's end, into which a February twilight put some softness even amid the hurricane . . .

She shivered.

"Oh! That's horrible . . ."

He made an evasive, approving gesture . . .

Having lit a lamp, he arranged a few small objects on the mantelpiece, pushing aside the frail seashells and the poor sea-urchins, which were dying, exhaling a raw odor of brine and another odor, slightly insipid, strange and unnamable, an almost imperceptible odor of corruption.

Thérèse, sitting on the bed, listened to the regular beat of the cannon, almost stifled by the mad clamor of the wind, and her heart responded with beats of anguish. She said: "What time is the high tide?"

"Forty minutes after midnight."

Midnight chimed.

She said: "Ah . . . !" and as Jean approached the bed she seized him frenetically, as if finding him again after a separation, and they kissed with a sort of desperate ardor in which was mingled, in order to make their passion more vivid, a kind of shame for that happy passion and their protected life, a pity—infinite for being impotent—and, prey to that sacred terror and terrible sweetness, they hardly heard the wind any longer, which was blowing so forcefully . . .

64

THE LITTLE QUEEN OF THE MEADOWS AND PRINCESS MIRETTE

(*La Fronde*, 26 January 1899)

"I believe," said Princess Mirette, "that I'm going to die."

"Die! My darling child, oh, what a foolish idea in your foolish little head!" And Princes Mirette's nurse, who was keeping vigil at the foot of the bed, stopped winding the flax around her distaff, and let her hands fall back along her skirts, as if prey to a great amazement.

Princess Mirette was very small—oh, truly a very little girl, not yet fifteen years old. She had a thin, delicate face. Her cheeks were like two white flower petals, and under her dark hair, cut straight, a smooth and heavy fringe over her narrow forehead, her eyes resembled two weary violets, sad and ravishing: eyes of dream and anguish. She did not say much, and over the silence of her soul, her sinuous lips—scarcely pink lines—were obstinately sealed, grim, haughty and scornful. Her entire frail body disappeared, hieratically, in a long sheath of precious fabrics embroidered with gold and trimmed with silver, in which a fulgurant design of precious stones traced flocks of birds and ignited fiery constellations of stars. So the breath of her little child's bosom was insensible beneath the gorgerin woven with pearls and heavy with royal turquoises; her hands and feet were immobilized under the weight of the gems with which they were laden, and Princess Mirette truly resembled a corpse already in her heavy, icy, discolored flesh—but a corpse that had retained a hallucinatory gaze, a terrible and invincible gaze. And thus, under that sumptuous and inanimate appearance, she spoke, the little girl, and said in a low voice:

"I believe that I'm going to die."

Her golden ball, playing with which sometimes occupied her pale and fragile fingers momentarily, had escaped her, and it lay, round and shiny, on the floor, very close to the silvery coats of long silky hair of her favorite greyhounds, lying on the carpet, their narrow muzzles posed on their delicate paws.

The large open missal allowed to escape, like a reflection, the bright colors of its illumination, and from a casket whose complicated sculptures were decorated with ivory inlays, on which mythological scenes were engraved, a stream of precious stones emerged. Violet fires and light fires rose up, irradiated, from those jewels, those clouds, a changing and charming soul of things that, evaporated, seemed to fill the room: the vast chamber that the shadow penetrated, coming from the gaping window, full of the immense and mild dusk of the countryside, and from the very depths of the room, its walls hung with yellow and green tapestries in which hinds fled before naïve Dianas with bare legs.

And the shadow invaded and bathed that room like a wave, a profound wave of water, a dark, almost violet blue . . .

"I'm going to light the lamps," said the nurse.

But the child said: "Oh, no, Syna, let me watch the night that is coming . . . see, it's emerging from the wood out there at the end of the park . . . oh, it's very slow, and I can still distinguish the colors of the flowers in the grass, but soon, very soon, without one knowing how it happens, I shall no longer see those flowers, nor the grass . . . the roses will be black, the grass will be black, everything, everything, will be black . . . oh . . . !"

And Princess Mirette had a frisson so profound and so long that the frightened Syna leaned over and took the two small pale hands in her robust brown hands, as if to retain the child and prevent a terrible, mortal fall . . .

Meanwhile, gazing outside, she too was gripped by the charm of the death of the day, and, the entire landscape still being golden green and golden pink, dazzling with the glorious light of the sun, broken into arrows and united in beams—a magnificent adornment—both of them, the royal child and the humble nurse, oppressed and overwhelmed by the divine beauty of the evening, heard the fluted appeal of the arboreal toads moaning in the distance, and the uniform and untiring croaking of the population of frogs amusing themselves under the nenuphars in the dormant pond at the far end of the meadow.

The meadow . . . bordered by pink rose-bushes and black cedars, it was velvety and mysterious, appearing thus to be a magical place, chosen for the round-dances of elves in the moonlight or the intrigues of sylphs and fays playing ball with fireflies . . . And then, very softly, very softly, not knowing for sure whether the cherished child was asleep or awake, the nurse Syna began to tell the story of the little queen of the meadows, in order to lull that wakefulness, if it was sad, or to mingle one dream more with the dreams of that slumber.

"The little queen of the meadows is all blonde, all white and pure silver, she is the moon and the rose . . . she was born one morning with the first crocuses and before the hour when the flowers of the apple tree turn pink. Immediately, very grave, she sat down, as if on a stool, in the golden heart of a daisy, and the passing butterflies mistook her for another flower, a new flower.

"But the little queen of the meadows was vivacious and coquettish; she made a girdle and a skirt of fresh leaves, she was shod in primroses and coiffed with dragonflies; she was joyful and so light that with one bound she rose all the way to the branches of the trees, and it's there that she hides when human beings pass through her domains—that is why no one ever sees her. She is good, and she weeps when a storm breaks the poppies and lays them down in the grass, but with the tip of her little finger she stands them up again, and then she laughs and talks to them, and kisses them delicately with her little lips, and the flower of the poppy can no longer be distinguished from her mouth. It's the little queen of the meadows who drinks all the morning dew, which one sees in the fields like a river of pearls, and which disappears as soon as the sun rises . . .

"She is always cheerful and strong . . ."

"She's very fortunate," murmured Princess Mirette, who was not asleep.

Syna continued: "She is free, she is never unoccupied, she doesn't have time to think about herself; she is the queen of all the meadows in the world, but there are meadows she prefers and I believe that the one that extends before us, from the terrace to the pond, is one of that number . . ."

"I'd like very much to see her," said the little princess languidly. And she raised herself up on her elbow, in an excess of ennui and anxious curiosity, as if to go toward the impossible apparition, which would disrupt that ennui and slake that curiosity . . . but what . . . ?

Suddenly, close by, so close that Mirette and her nurse shivered in surprise, a minuscule form emerged: a little girl, very blonde, very white, with so many leaves and flowers over her hair, her shoulders and her back that she seemed entirely enveloped by a supple green stem blooming in corollas.

Believing in everything—because she did not believe in anything—Mirette said: "It's her, the little queen of the meadows.

But the vivid eyes of a wild cat encountered and exchanged glances with her weary violet pupils, and the intruder would already have been far away if the nurse had not retained her by the floating flap of her herbal tunic.

"Who are you?"

"I'm all alone and I'm lost . . ."

"What is your name?"

"I don't know . . . I'm all alone I play in the woods . . . this evening I lost my way and I arrived here . . . let me go, I want to go away. . ."

But Princess Mirette shifted and took off the network of fabrics and precious stones, seized the child in her turn, and interrogated her. She wanted to know everything. Where did she live? How? What did she do?

And the child responded: "My father cuts wood in the forest; he lets me run around on my own; I eat fruits and I drink the water of streams; when the streams are frozen my father lights big fires with the wood he has cut in summer, and I stay by the fire. The fire tells me beautiful stories, like those the green branches tell in spring . . ."

"Are you never bored?" asked Mirette.

"Bored? I don't understand what you mean."

"You don't find the time long sometimes?"

"The time long! With the morning and evenings, and the plants and the animals! Oh!" She started to laugh.

Mirette fell back on the cushions very pale.

"Is she ill," the child asked Syna, fearfully.

The latter wept, but the little princess said: "No . . . speak, talk to me, tell me everything, everything . . ."

And the child spoke; she talked about the free life, the strong life, the life of movement and dream in the midst of vivacious nature; and, through the filter of her ingenuous and simple words, all of the rude and healthy poetry of things passed, an overflowing river carrying the tenacious and obscure power of seeds and fecund shoots of the earth under the sun, and an admirable sky changing the color of that infinite landscape, for Mirette's closed eyes . . .

Of not having known all that, she became anguished and died . . . and, the hour having come when roses are black, invisible in the black grass, poor little Princess Mirette died, in fact, rocked in the eternal passage by the words of the little queen of the meadows . . .

A FEVERISH HOUR IN AN ITALIAN PARK
(*La Fronde*, 2 February 1899)

PASSING along the pathway of roses at the end of the paved terrace, she entered the park. It was a very old, immense park, and in that late afternoon in summer, entirely voluptuous and mild, it was like a chapel of amour.

The crowns of the trees were mingled: secular cedars with gray-green plumes of foliage, giant magnolias bearing their heavy flowers, swollen by perfume, like censers, as bright and motionless as flowers of wax, and prodigious acacias, svelte and blonde, and poplars in sheaths rustling like silken robes; and other trees too—enormous trees with split trunks, the black wounds of storms, which, lifting the earth with the knots of their powerful roots, like the arms of wrestlers, were crowned victoriously by a victorious sap, renewed by fresh, green and shiny foliage . . . and also frail trees, frail and disappearing entirely beneath their florescence, as abundant and light as hair.

And everywhere, under that moving cool vault lining the blue and burning vault of the sky, marble figures slept and laughed: antiquated figures, which the usury of centuries, the rust of rain and the hazards of storms or human carelessness had marked and disfigured . . . It was thus that a faun with a broken ear resembled a bewildered rabbit with a little green moss corroding its lip; and again, lying down at the edge of a stagnant pond invaded by yellow lilies, a feminine form, half-disappeared, the legs and hips veiled by long grass, with the smiling and mysterious face of a sleeping siren—for some implement of a stupid gardener had broken her charming eyelids.

On the tall pedestals at the entrances of avenues, the busts of young goddesses stared arrogantly.

But that was still the edge of the park, and the fields of roses and the wood of orange-trees that linked the park to the villa still filled those avenues, always obscure even in the most ardent midday, with their violent and sweet breath . . . a breath of vertigo. On respiring it, sensing it mingle with each aspiration of her short breath to enter her mouth, her throat and her breast, Adrienne felt oppressed, with a stifling malaise that increased to anguish and fear as she advanced further, as if she were penetrated to the soul and that soul were filled by a maleficent atmosphere of mortal intoxication.

In order to escape that empire she walked more rapidly, dragging around her delicate little feet, naked in sandals of white embroidered silk—the bizarre and pretty little sandals of a fay—the flounces and lace of her pink lawn skirt, where, scarcely rosier, painted in pastel shades, large roses flourished, barely open and devoid of petals. And there were more roses over the cloud of her blonde hair, which dusted her pink face with gold, and over her bosom, where satin and lace paler than her flesh were wound: roses in a diadem over her tulle capeline, fresh roses, an enormous bunch picked in handfuls, planted diabolically, which blossomed there, between her dimpled chin and her narrow belt, crushing her shoulders with their nacreous and bloody corollas.

She murmured: "What a detestable perfume . . . I only like roses . . ." And she suddenly respired deeply, bathed by a slightly acrid freshness, a freshness of water, shade, repose . . .

The pond! It was the pond, very deep: motionless water, black under the dense branches, and always icy.

Countless animalcules on its surface made shiny frissons there, which died away at the high, sheer banks of greasy, slippery earth, where admirable black irises grew and a hedge of rose-bushes. On one side, the pond was closed by a grille over a substructure of stone. It was there that Adrienne often came to sit down, and it was there that she stopped once again, and the dream of her eyes went toward the islet as flowery as a bouquet, which rose in the center of the miniature lake, and where, among the thick tangle of plants, mutilated statues were crumbling.

It was a temple erected long ago, a pagan temple devoid of walls, a roof and a steeple, with Venus for a saint and Amour for a god . . .

And that god could still be divined by a quiver that remained intact between two broken wings; the head, severed neatly, had doubtless rolled into the black lake. A little extended arm still indicated a grotto hollowed in the rock, veiled today by a supple curtain of verdure. Doubtless once a tabernacle of pagan masses, of which perverse princes and mad princesses made use . . . for surely a voluptuous, ingenious and frivolous soul had animated this park in past centuries, and that soul still respired here, and also there, in that hemicycle, where one divined a court of amour with its marble benches, which had seen and heard the languorous follies of noble ladies and their chevaliers, in sumptuous costumes.

Having arrived with Pierre in that celebrated villa on the marvelous gulf coast near Genoa, hired by the caprice of their young amour, Adrienne had loved everything in the first days in that park where a population of ruined statues testified to the amorous concerns of those who had once lived here.

In one of the flat boats, like splayed bats, he and she had crossed the pond and landed on the pagan isle; in the moonlight, in a satin dress with bare shoulders, with him alone for a gallant crowd, she had held her court in the enchanted hemicycle . . .

Today, she could no longer see again without dolor these places where the soul of her amour had died, as so many other souls and so many other amours had died, before her and before him . . .

Today, as almost every day, he was in Genoa, departing in the morning and often not returning until dinner time, exhausting—she saw that clearly—the excessively long lease—O, the imprudence of always being passionate!—that retained them there. She was enervated by solitude, but repelled by the idea of following her lover, escaping the slavery of caresses, of her ardent soul, foolish and miserable on her plaything body, her body of a beautiful pink doll, a child of pleasure who flew into rages that abolished the will, of desperate desires for death and crime; and she had divined the truth—the amour not only extinct here but reignited elsewhere—the fire that corrodes and blinds, bloody dreams and awakenings to horror . . .

Thus, like some magic living flower born of all the rich juices and saps of the immense park with the heavy, greasy, humid, waterlogged park, like an exquisite corolla fallen from the high branches into a cradle, where flocks of white pigeons passed over, filling the woods with the long and tender sigh of their cooing throats, Adrienne went forth; she marched, avoiding the places where she and he had made love, fleeing the waves of perfume and the calling of doves; but everywhere, she recognized and rediscovered amour . . . Yes, the lax, sensual and bitter amour that she had for him and the drunken, delectable and torturing amour that he had had for her . . . Amour, in that broad velvety and starry meadow, from which one could see the whole of the bay of Genoa, dazzling and motionless, beneath the sky resembling an immense blue cup, overturned . . .

And now, in the narrow, stony path, steeply sloping, which she was climbing breathlessly, she recalled the memory of that climb made à deux; and, the earth becoming red, clayey, with a strange reflection of brick, she recognized the zone of the parasol pines: a furnace zone where she commenced to pant, burned by the vapors of the resin, the exhalations of the crimson soil, the color of conflagration, and, skidding at every step on the pine-needles, she took off her capeline, threw it behind her insouciantly into the thorn-bushes, where diadems of roses were withering and fading, forgotten there, never seen again by her or by him.

Adrienne went up, still climbing, and suddenly stopped; the torn curtain of the trees, cut by skill or marvelous hazard, opened an infinite window over the sea, the open sea all the way to Genoa, an entire splendor of a gilded horizon. And leaning slightly over the edge of that "window" cut sheer above a prodigious gulf of trees—another sea, green and undulating, unfurling all the way to the shore—by leaning over one could see the little towns on the shore with the names of birds, perched pink and green on the edge of the blue sea: Arenzano, Voltri, Pra, Sestri-Ponente—not to mention Pegli, which was directly below and which remained invisible.

She stopped . . . and she remembered . . .

A marble bench buried all the way to the seat in moss, said: *One rests here* . . . and on that bench, on that moss, in one another's arms, above the abyss of the forest rolling the swell of the branches at their feet, they had spent an entire night, a blue night, a clear night, a warm night, a night of amour, a treacherous night also, where, in the open air of the dangerous midnights of Italy, she had caught a bad fever . . .

A fever that she still felt on certain days, and with which, at this very moment, she was shivering; and, abhorring that excessively cherished place, she started running, madly, descending the steep path at the gallop of a wounded, pursued animal . . .

She tore her delicate feet, her little bare feet, on the roots; her sandals remained in shreds stuck to the stones like dead flesh, her dress was caught on bushes, and all the roses of the dress were soiled with dust, and all the fresh roses spread over her bosom were shredded by the wind of her course, and soon she no longer had anything of her corsage but broken stems and thorns, which pricked her in her disorderly movements; drops of blood pearled under the lace and made little round rosy patches, like other roses . . .

When she stopped running, she was near the villa. She was afraid; she was in pain. Someone said: "Monsieur has just returned," and almost immediately, she encountered Pierre, who exclaimed:

"What are you doing? Where have you come from? Are you mad? Decidedly, the air here isn't good for you; I knew you were crazy, but not to this point . . ."

She smiled, without responding, and that smile was so soft on her pink mouth, and the fever put such a violent languor into her eyes, that her lover forgot that he thought that she was crazy and that he was deceiving her, *forgot that he no longer loved her*, and because she was so pretty and had such charming weakness, consented in the hour following the hour in the park to one of their walks, *as before* . . .

And, as every evening, they went out into the park, and that evening, he was not distracted, and she did not make a jealous scene. She was child-like, all coaxing grace. She drew him to the pond.

"Let's take the boat," she said, "and go to the isle of amour . . ."

And as he did not appear to care, and tried to kiss her, she repeated: "No, no . . . on the island . . . only on the island."

He gave in, and, by turns, whistled lightly and smoked his cigarette. Between the black bank and the isle bathed in moonlight, the boat like a splayed bat glided soundlessly . . .

And suddenly, she started to laugh, laugh and laugh . . . the laughter rose up and filled the night, the woods, the park, awakening the wood-pigeons, and from all the amorous places the echoes came back, softer and more muted . . .

"What's the matter with you?"

"Oh, nothing; I'm just laughing at something I thought this morning."

"What did you think?"

And she leaned toward him. "That I'd like to die here, with you."

She was no longer laughing and he saw her eyes glittering in the darkness. He tried to say: "What a crackpot!" but, prompter than speech, she was standing on the edge of the boat and, taking her lover by the shoulders, she weighed with all her strength—she, so pink, so fragile, who only liked pink roses!—toward the black water, the icy water . . .

The boat went: *glllouu . . . u . . . u . . . u . . . u . . . flac!*

And an anxious toad cried . . .

A minute later they were on the bank—for Pierre was a very good swimmer—her unconscious, him furious.

Their amour lived for a few more days and nights on the memory of that troubled and savage hour—after which they quit the old Italian park for separate destinies. She retained therefrom intermittent fevers, and he a more masculine memory of satisfied self-esteem. He said, in confidence:

"I was once loved by an adorable woman who tried to kill me . . ."

THE SOUL OF LACE
(*La Fronde*, 9 February 1899)

A ND the princesses and the courtesans, and the lace-
... A makers and the artistes and the *mignons* and all the
Froufrous—all of them, a sumptuous, silky, multicolored, noisy,
dazzling host—crowded into the hall.

What hall? In what place? It doesn't matter. In an unknown
country, and the hall was beautiful, truly beautiful, with the
only oppressive and intangible beauty—because it was not
real.

The walls were aerial, transparent, all in superb appliqué,
of an intricate, scrupulous design, and they vacillated lightly
to the feeble wing-beats of butterflies of living gold and blue
dragonflies, which fixed them in the fire of precious stones in
the inferior part of the vault—a vault of tulle . . . yes, bright,
soft, nacreous and fluid tulle, similar to a summer night, one of
those nights that seem to glide over the sky like a caress, their
kiss flowing all the way to the ground, which they envelop and
embrace . . .

The parquet was embroideries; there were marvelous and
very delicate ones, and over the perforated arabesques, over the
birds in motionless flight, and over the flowers blooming in
white with black holes for hearts, the joyful people, the charming people, the madly amorous population of gallants and
art-workers, passed with a light step—and that step, so light,

amid so much frail grace and magical celebration, would have frightened a living person, for it was the immaterial tread of Death . . .

There were dead men and dead women there, not livid, not fleshless, with smiles still on their puerile lips similar to blown kisses, but which buried in the open air the great silence of Death, and which, beneath the sumptuousness of their adornments, hid a strange flesh as imponderable as dust . . . But the mild phantoms of both sexes retained the attributes of their former roles of animate days.

The princesses were wearing their jewels, the artists their dreams, the courtesans their beauty; and while the *mignons* kept the large greyhounds given by the king attached to their languid footsteps, the lace-makers with the worn-out eyes and supple hands held the embroidered pin-cushions against their breasts, in which the thread and the needles were wrapped.

And it came, and kept coming, from distant lands where unobtainable fabrics were women, and cities with royal or tender names: Alençon, Bruges, Valenciennes and others; it came from the depths of slow and somnolent provinces, and green and blonde countrysides where, on the secular thresholds of her dwelling the solitary worker had once tried her hand, weaving until dusk, as she had the previous day and would the next, and always, weaving her dream with the agile play of needles and bobbins. And when a great deal of that dream had formed an admirable fragile point, it had gone to cities and courts, galas and weddings, to extend over royal beds and to veil virgins, and then, after many hours, many days, the soul and the life of the lace-maker—a worn weave, the last lace—was exhaled in a final dream . . . which might form, out there, on high, the beautiful robe of an angel . . .

So, the crowd jostled, and the hall grew, was enlarged, became immense, prodigious, as high as a church, as vast as a palace, filled by a singular murmur like that of a forest in the middle of the night, so soft, so beautiful, so clear that it seemed to hold that miraculous hall with all the charm of a woman, all sensuality and amour.

Meanwhile, along the walls, without speaking, all of them, all the elegant dead, arrested gazes full of a singular trouble, like those one arrests on the portrait of a beloved disappeared individual discovered on the wall of a house abandoned long ago . . .

And, strangely, on those walls, the hangings and the lace broke their uniformity and were divided into large creases of scarves, or were cut into dresses, and had small motifs: frills, friezes, collarets, coiffures and chemises, then children's bonnets, and then veils, veils and more veils, and, as if under a gust of wind or an excessively brutal hand, those charming treasures showed hitches and tears—and many had a mat ivory tint, as if they had been shut away for a long time in cupboards between sachets of iris and dried rose leaves . . .

Doubtless thus, whether glorious and intact, or miserable and worn, the crowd recognized those relics, and its memory wept—but the dead have no visible tears, the dead are no longer able to weep, since their inanimate eyes become estranged from their immortal hearts . . .

However, that population of the disappeared have not assembled in vain. What common desire, what common anguish has united them, the disquieting ephebes and the great artists with infantile souls, the prostitutes and humble seamstresses side by side with sovereigns? What could it be, except a similar amour?

O little frail soul, precious soul of chiffon, lace, you were their work, their task, their passion, their joy, their folly!

They loved you, those more womanly in that amour and those effeminate, having that amour, you were their adornment—more mystery—their veil, more immodesty; such complicated and marvelous patience; and always, everywhere, in the divine tabernacle as in the couches of amour, on the heads of wives and the bosoms of courtesans, you were the symbol of the dream and—so fragile!—of annihilation. But now that the secret of your luxury is grossly debased, and factories and tradesmen and all of barbaric mechanism has been substituted for the slow human hand, the creative brain, the great prince of fantasy who forgot a unique model in order to seek and find a new one—those urgent, devouring, vulgar forces are mocking you, little soul, and threatening to kill you . . .

But no, little soul, you shall not die, you will retain your enchanted poetry, your occult power and your quivering grace, for you have, in your favor, the women and the artists who adore you, soul of lace . . .

THE UNKNOWN HOUR
(*La Fronde*, 16 February 1899)

NARROW mirrors, green and somnolent like pools of marshy water, were illuminated by a light reflection in their white frames, wrought in stonework shells and garlands, when she went into the bedroom, candle in hand—a little high, as if to penetrate more fully the darkness in which the entire high and immense room reposed, buried.

"It isn't warm here," she declared, tightening the pleats of her violet mantle with a chilly hand.

And an analogous interior movement had to envelop her soul with an energetic determination of courage—the courage that had brought her here tonight, alone, into an atmosphere of memory icier than that outside, which caused her poor heart to tremble with cold.

Memory . . . At first she scarcely seemed to recognize that bedroom, so strange had it become to the memory enchanted by past days lived among present things.

She had only slept and loved in this room in clement seasons when the high windows, always open, had let in the tender enchantment of blue days with burning middays, the silent magic of a horizon of stars, of delectable nights. Then, on the delicately sculpted white marble mantelpiece, on the chest of drawers with brilliant copper handles, an ever-renewed crop of roses always rained, one by one, the thin perfumed drizzle of weary petals, and the gilded side-tables in the corners bore the pretty small trinkets of her toilette, those petty feminine labors, puerile chiffons.

In those days, strangely, the two portraits hanging from the wall—a young woman coiffed in powder, with her cleavage bare, rosy and rounded, emerging from a flower-patterned dress; and a young man with a catogan wig and a lace ruff—had smiled with an indulgent and voluptuous smile, a complicit, amicable smile, as if the ancestor and the ancestress had foreseen from the depth of their young years the sweet sin of amour of their great granddaughter, and that seeing her offer her hereditary blonde beauty to her infatuated lover was such a beautiful and natural thing that they were touched by it in an occult manner beyond the years and the tomb . . .

This evening, the portraits were grave, and Valentine felt even more alone in the familiar room.

However, as the fire was beginning to exhale its warm and resinous breath, the young woman wanted to rid herself of the respectfully mute but avid curiosity, prowling and searching around her, of the guardian maidservant of the château—that name had been retained for the historic pavilion, which royal amours unraveled in an obscure drama had rendered famous . . .

"Give me my bag and go away; go back to bed . . ."

"Will Madame not be afraid? It's just that Victor and I lodge some distance away, and Madame hasn't brought Lise . . . Madame doesn't want me . . . ?"

"No, no . . . you can go . . ."

And as Valentine sometimes had the voice of her imperious soul there were no more objections. She remained definitively alone.

She heard the noise of footsteps fading away along the corridors, and the heavy sound of a door closing . . . a few more faint echoes of human presence, and that was all.

Very calm, without fever, but without slowness, Valentine prepared for sleep with the habitual rites of careful coquetry.

That was a mechanical operation for her, which she accomplished with an absent soul.

When her bare feet were in her mules, however, and her bare shoulders in the lawn peignoir, she opened the recently prepared bed, and the disturbed linen exhaled a perfume of hay, lavender and fresh grass, as if the entire countryside were contained in the alcove, between the wood-paneled walls veiled with muslin; she let the pillow fall back as if it were something redoubtable and disquieting, let go of the pleat of the parted sheet, and came back to the fire, the living and murmuring flame.

As she was about to sit down by the fireside, her eyes encountered her face in the mirror, and, as the large gilded bronze candelabras, illuminated, inundated that mirror fully with a raw light very different from the veiled and rosy light that bathed the mirrors of her dressing room in Paris, Valentine remained immobile and attentive, leaning toward herself, toward that faithful, revelatory and cruel image. After a long time, she said, aloud: "Oh! yes . . . I understand . . . !"

She could now understand that her lover had deceived her and deceived her again, and that she was abandoned and scorned by him, and that he had gone toward other mouths and other eyes, taking from both new caresses and dreams, and that by virtue of that, and for that reason, she was defeated and miserable. She *had* to understand, to admit those horrible things, for she was *growing old*. Growing old! Was it credible? For a long time, never—with the aid of savant lighting, the resources of scrupulous artistry and skillful make-up—a woman cannot believe that terror: growing old.

And suddenly one day, one evening, it is necessary to submit to it, as one submits to death . . . and one suffers from it . . . one suffers . . .

That was the word she murmured: "I'm suffering! I'm suffering!"

She no longer had courage; her soul was drowned in chagrin, flaccid, drunk and lamentable . . .

She cursed her impulse, the decision she had made a few hours before to quit Paris, to flee the city complicit with easy treasons, and the man whose letter she had just discovered, the new proof of one of his renewed treasons. Oh, this time she had not wanted to subject herself to the sickening of the lie that he would have told and she would have accepted, nor the debasement of a scene, and she had departed in a moment of haughty revolt, of courageous repossession of herself . . .

He would come home at the usual hour.

"Madame?"

"Madame has departed on a voyage."

"A voyage? Where?"

"We don't know. Madame departed without saying anything."

She had a desire to laugh at the idea of the face he must have pulled momentarily. She did not hope for a torment or a regret on his part; no, but had she not shown, for eight years, the most admirable—the most foolish—confident expansion? And she knew that, in spite of everything, he still had a tenacious tenderness for her—an egotistical tenderness made above all of the amour she had for him, but all the same his fine casual nonchalance of a beloved infidel must have received a shock. What was he doing now? Where was he?

Valentine looked at her watch, but it had stopped. Mechanically, she directed her eyes at the Saxe clock on the mantelpiece, but the secret little life of its pendulum had been suspended since last summer. A reminiscence of reading came to her: *The little Saxe clock that is slow and chimes thirteen . . .* Her memory was not sure of being exact and she wondered where she had read that. *Mallarmé, I think . . .* and something analogous immediately haunted her, a very sharp memory:

The clock had just struck thirteen
In the silence of the accursed room.

That, she was certain, was Rollinat.[1]

Had they read them together, he and she, the verse and the prose? Were they sitting, in repose between embraces, in infinite days, exalted by the contact of nervous, sensitive art, and, mingling their living and strong passion with so many passionate dreams they could often have believed their love eternal, in finding it universal . . .

Suddenly, she felt terribly weary. She had not eaten since the morning, and she had wept so much . . . Fearfully, her eyes went to their reflection in the mirror . . . but the violent movement of her soul brushed them, and over her fatigued face passionate emotion put a magical mask: the supreme revenge of amour, which, having used up young freshness, seems to extract from all the voluptuous fatigue of late nights and all the ardent misery of dolor, a superior immortal youth, an imperishable beauty that comes from further away than the flesh submissive to time . . .

Yes, her eyelids were bruised and her pale lips weary over her dazzling teeth, but if the man she loved had only been there she would have been victorious and strong because the gaze of her eyes and the kisses of her mouth would have been those that one does not forget . . . but she was alone . . . And, suddenly seized by impotent rage, anger against herself, she detested herself for having been able, for an hour, to be more proud than amorous. Without that accursed pride, that cowardly energy, she would doubtless be seeing him at this very moment; she would have scorned him, hated him, covered him with her fury and her tears, exasperated him with her jealous plaints, but in sum, she would have had him there before her, would have seen him,

---

1 Maurice Rollinat in *Les névroses* (1883).

would have heard his voice, his lying voice; she would have slaked herself on his eyes, his seductive, cheating eyes . . . And now that she was here, alone, far away from him, she had left him to the caprice of his desires, the liberty of the hazards he loved. Oh, fool, fool!

Exhausted by tears and regrets, she ended up falling on to the bed and curling up there, huddling like a fearful child . . .'

✳

The candles having burned to the level of the holders, the sockets flared up, the logs in the ashes crumbled, hissing faintly—and behind the partition, a mysterious appeal exhaled through the wall from a neighboring room, from who knew where, a clock chimed. In the shadow and the terrible silence of the middle of the night the chimes were clear, definitive and imperious—and their number, to the enervated hearing of the young woman, surpassed the usual number.

Thirteen strokes? Perhaps . . .

But an unknown hour was sounding. What hour? Was it the heavy one that closes evenings of pleasure, or the light one that indicates the imminent morning, the awakening, the tomorrow?

She did not know . . .

An unknown hour, ironic and full of mystery, which found her alone, the amorous woman, alone and distant from her amour.

Her entire body was chilled by an unnamable terror, her heart agonized by anguish. She had the frightful memory of bloody legends of the past populating the dwelling, and the more frightful memory—a hundred times more—of mild seasons, a passionate rosary told in that same dwelling . . .

An unknown hour . . . which dos not exist and sounds in a dream, is that not everyone's secret desire? Is that not what changing hearts seek when they have exhausted, without living them, the twenty-four hours of a day and a night? An unknown hour—which one avoids and fears, which hammers time at some unexpected moment . . . the hour palpitating now in the white room—and Valentine thought that perhaps she was already dead and laid down to sleep without awakening in the great bed of amour . . .

And she sensed the heart of a dead woman—an immense heart that the flesh no longer oppressed—an indulgent, blissful heart, outside the world.

She saw again her imminent miseries, and her dolor and her pride, and her regret and her trouble—everything that agitates and fills human hours, making them eternal and brief—with a sentiment of deliverance. She would be able, therefore, to see him again, to master her emotion, without being torn apart and ravaged by jealousies and desires, and to be gentle to him without cowardice, and finally to love him, love him without hatred.

Oh, the peace of the unknown hour in which such a dream seems possible . . . the fugitive, ironic, mysterious hour.

Awakened in brilliant and icy mid-morning, when the entire countryside is shiny and shivering, she rang . . . In the mirrors, she saw herself so blonde, her face remade, reposed, pink with cold, her eyes resolved, her mouth imperious.

"Breakfast, quickly! My bag! The carriage! What time is the next train to Paris?"

"Ten twenty-five . . . Madame is leaving again?"

Before the ever-respectful bewilderment and the sharp curiosity, Valentine conceded: "Yes. I thought I'd stay here for a few days but it's too cold. I'd definitely be too cold here. Let's go! Quickly!"

And, having climbed into the train at ten twenty-five—a real hour!—she thought, smiling, that they could still have lunch together . . . She would forget everything, would put on a semblance of knowing nothing, would be malicious, calm, furious and tender by turns, would suffer and cause suffering, would be forgiven and would forgive, amid the worst troubles—and the most foolish . . .

A real hour . . .

COLORED TALES
(*Mercure de France*, March 1899)

THE SINCERE CLOCK
(An Orange Tale)

SHE had the name of a fruit: Mandarine; and I had picked her one winter evening as one picks a "beautiful Valencia" from a street-vendor's cart, in order to bite her soft golden flesh, in order to respire her bitter and fresh odor of young Spring, which rises from mosses and runs from trees in blonde sap . . .

But she rolled me in her hair, her words and her kisses with a sort of anger, and beyond her I was caught by an invisible and intangible being, the future being that doubles a creature and lives a terrible and unconscious life of future "things."

Oh, the strange little friend . . .

She was delightfully young. And, savant in gentle guises, still awkward in ruses, she had visibly passed from unpolluted infancy to amorous science with an absent soul—a gracious, absurd, moving, tenderizing soul.

Everything in her was obscure and luminous, like twilight over the sea. She loved the sun like a plant and had it in her skin, in her blood; it shone in coppery floods in her dark hair and in her eyes, which were extraordinarily bright, but above all, she bore it on her body like a glory.

The color of amber concentrated on her face, all her being irritated her brightly—the color of celebration and joy that makes a body blonde, marvelously blonde.

She had the custom of sleeping naked, and I surrounded her with soft silks, which were brightened by the sumptuousness of her flesh. Delicate and energetic, she passed through the flame of caresses like a well-tempered blade, always supple and always strong. She huddled in the brutal nest of my desire, and it was a pity to see that the gestures of amour—bold because they were sincere—made an impression of peace and protection on her.

※

The chamber of bright silks still appeared obscure to me around my little friend, and I took her away to lands of sunlight and left.

And it was in Urrugne, in the heart of the Basque country, that I found her natural and harmonic frame: that land of a violent and solid saffron color, where such a rude and soft language is spoken, like every language of a sensual and savage race: a guttural, hoarse speech in which inhuman—or superhuman—troubled accents are found and mingled, wrenched from the throat and teeth of a creature by unexpected or extreme sensations.

Passing through there in a carriage one Sunday, an anguish and inexpressible charm seized us and we stopped. We spent a sweet hour of amour, and commenced to feel the delectable torpor of happiness descending on our limbs and our hearts.

We loved one another. We had crossed the ardent frontier of caresses, and we stopped in order to live there in autumn, when, every night, rain covered the trees and the roads with rust, where, every morning, broad sunlight made all the countryside golden, radiant and shiny.

We lived together there, and outside Life. The high road was before us; we ignored the road.

Yes, it was happiness, and yet I felt, at certain times, gripped by fear: an irrational and strong fear.

I seemed to see something new appearing in Mandarine . . .
But what . . . ?

An unexpected grace in movement, a supernatural seduction thrown like a net over her beauty, the survival of an excessive passion, making her almost frightening in amour . . . but although I had observed her, I could not discover anything that motivated my anxieties *rationally*.

Mandarine did not like the church of Urrugne. It is high and ancient; its clock bears the words: *Vulneant omnes ultima necat*. For that she did not like it. She was superstitious about delights, and the motto: "All wound, the last kills," cast a shadow over her joy.

Something else moved her: an ancient local custom—a funerary custom—dictated that in the church, at services every family in recent mourning had a lighted candle before it, placed on the ground and protected by a wooden screen.

Those short vacillating flames were to recall the souls of the dead to the prayers. Mandarine feared exteriorizations that made Death precise, and words that brought it to mind.

One night, she spoke in her sleep:

"It lies . . . it lies . . ." She agitated. "The clock . . . the clock . . . it isn't true . . ." And, waking up, she seized me with the ravishing fury that was like a force of nature in her, and amid the happy tears and the anguish of joy: "It isn't true; the hours are beautiful, all beautiful!"

Ah! I didn't hear her real voice, the imperious voice pronouncing Fate, nor the eternal lies she cried out in the profound instinct of that Fate, the terror that she had of it . . .

The russet, enchanted season was about to end; the sadness that emerged from the woods was between us, and the shadow of the ancient church extended further every day toward our house; as the sun paled the arrested hands of the clock indicated the cruel words.

✳

I brought Mandarine back to Paris. Oh, the strange little friend! How did she come to me through the hazards of life without her past occupying me, as if she had only commenced to live on the day when I took her mouth? How did she go away without me understanding anything of the near future that would take her, because she enchanted the present days?

But she went away . . .

She passed through the suffering and the languors of the end like a vivid ray of light: it burns, it exists, but one cannot seize it.

One evening, one ruddy evening when, in the direction of the Bois, the splendors of the invisible sunset rose, my friend's eyes, her great staring eyes, became anguished.

I took her on my knees like a sick child, a weak, pitiful child—and she was all of that.

She smiled at me and, oppressed, spoke about happy things—they passed the beauty of her lips, and I forgot them, on seeing them on that mouth . . .

Thus the entirely gilded hour shines of her memory and my desire; then, she settled herself "for sleep." and as the shadow came and the hour chimed, she said, twice:

"Oh, the clock . . . the sincere clock . . ."

And died.

LITTLE APPLES
(A Green Tale)

TWO little green apples; yes, truly, two little green apples, slightly acidic, hard to the tooth—so young!—and an aftertaste bitter enough to bring tears to the eyes.

When one goes, in midday in August, along the edge of a field bordered by thickset trees, in the low, broad shade, one looks at the round fruits, the color of leaves, with a violent, rapid, insatiable desire . . .

"Not ripe, not ripe, my handsome passer-by, come back later . . ."

Well, their eyes, their lips, their downy faces, the sketch of their mouths, said the same:

"Later! Later!"

And among the flowery blue vases of oleanders, between the creamy walls covered in smooth mats, they lived a petty closed life, the life of a seed—tenacious, patient, seemingly slightly confused: Fou-ti and Mou-ni.

Mou-ni's father being dead, his wife drowned in opium the joy of being liberated from him.

The mother of Fou-ti being dead, her husband ran by night to the grilles behind which the ivory smiled, with a little ironic and disquieting smile . . .

Thin streaks of kohl and carmine indicated on those faces the eyes and mouths of dolls.

Thus abandoned, the two friends formed a household—a playful, genteel and ridiculous household.

They did not wear knotted tunics as yet, nor their hair in terrible coiffures.

Fou-ti had a very round face, the eyes of a cunning mouse and the voice of a parakeet, and her mouth was like a tiny doll's kiss that one might have drawn awkwardly.

Mou-ni, a little taller—by three centimeters—a shadow of a dream under her very Japanese eyebrows, kept her lips taut, and the feminine mystery was already upon her asexual body, like an adorable paradox.

Before their door often passed—more often than one could believe—a Chinaman . . . and what a nasty Chinaman!

The two little green apples, unable to bear the sight of him, acquired the malicious habit of scourging everything that displeased them with the term: *it's Chinese* . . . for the natural hereditary antipathy of their race for the race of the sons of Heaven was combined with the pretty repulsion of little creatures as delicate as cats with regard to what is pot-bellied, hairy, too yellow and stinking. The Chinaman united these various qualities.

He went by . . . it was him who, from the edge of a field, sees the fruits the color of leaves and advances his hand to pick them, in order to refresh a heavy and burning tongue with them . . .

By night they slept together, Mou-ni and Fou-ti, while their parents were far, far away from them, one delivered to grotesque contortions and the other plunged into bewildering torpors.

In their slumber, populated by minuscule dreams made to their measure—like a puppet or a cart—they sometimes laughed . . . and sometimes woke up, frightened . . .

Something deformed had traversed their brains: the little black room where the atoms of thoughts stirred.

They spoke to one another then in low voices, embracing one another candidly, confidently and tenderly, and then falling into pure and delectable forgetfulness . . .

Then—their kiss having calmed them, saying to them: "You're not alone; I love you . . ." before their closed eyes there were flocks of birds with enormous feet and long beaks, traversing the rice-fields under a beautiful sky . . . and even the gods with horrible faces became paternal and jolly in the mirror of their dreams . . .

Thus, the two little green apples were happy. Childhood and purity had recreated for them a little blank hearth. They forgot the mother and father somewhat, and already, they were moved on seeing the elders, in complicated tunics with pins in their hair, rocking yellow and howling parcels.

One night, a very nasty dream entered beneath Mou-ni's forehead. It made a large black mass in the bedroom between their couch and the lamp, still lit.

She murmured: "It's Chinese," without believing it, and woke up, about to burst into laughter, finding it funny—that and herself, and everything, very funny—in a surge of gaiety, unconscious and innocent life; but the laughter died on the edge of her lips, her soul and her thought . . .

He was there . . . *Him* . . . the horrible creases striping his face, and his eyes shining like glass pearls. He was walking slowly . . . he leaned over . . . Then Mou-ni opened her eyes fully, mute with fear. Seeing those eyes open, *It's Chinese* started to laugh . . .

He laughed lugubriously, hideously. Knowing that appeals passed in vain through the bright walls, he did not hurry.

His hands were trembling, though—but that was not from fear.

He took pleasure in the abominable, while laments died away between the blue vases . . .

When, in a very long, very sad scream, Fou-ti woke up, tortured, she saw her friend tied up, rolling on the ground in the disorder of stained silks.

And over her, the gentle shadow of feminine mystery was no more—aborted in its flower . . .

Two little green apples, yes, truly, two little apples, slightly acidic, hard to the tooth—so young!—and an aftertaste bitter enough to bring tears to the eyes.

THE WEDDING OF TIME AND DEATH
(A Black Tale)

IT was beyond the leaves and the clouds, further away than the white horizons trembling in the light and the tender enchantments of the sky, on blue days.

It was *out there*.

Out there?

Up above? Under the ground?

Nowhere . . . perhaps . . .

But the sad eyes of the living and the calm eyes of the dead gaze at that ardent and unknown place—and wait.

Out there, Time and Death spoke: "O You! You go so quickly . . . so quickly, so quickly, do you know that your name on the lips of the sage cannot by 'present' but only 'past' or 'future' . . . stop . . ."

"O You, multiple and multiform, who run with a silent dread by the side of every living being, grimacing at his laughter, drinking his tears, and who finally tips him, on a whim, into the grave where you will have his spasm and his breath . . . listen to me . . ."

They stopped—a frightful thing! The motionless hours convulsed hearts, the infinity of agonies howled with terror.

Death neglected the living, Time neglected the open tombs of souls that only had hope in him.

It was the *duration* of the *moment*. Their imprecise form was affirmed. Who can tell the line of their appearance? Human folly has made a crude image of it: ugliness and old age.

Ugly? Death? The supreme administer of justice, the great dispenser carrying away, with a gesture invisible to the sighted, the nameless and priceless burden that makes the entire creature in a miserable body?

Old? Time? Time that had no commencement and will have no end . . .

They are not born. the eternal ephebes of primordial dawns, having been neither the seed not the embryo: *they were out there, once*—and remain, bearing in their features the grace and the color of an age unknown to humans.

Weary of their labor, then, the great laborers, they spoke.

"Are you not sated, O my Sister?"

"Are you not exhausted, my Brother?"

"All those who have gone to bed are afraid of you—for the attitude of slumber inclines to thoughts of you . . ."

"Yes, they are afraid—and I save them. They give me a strange name that I do not understand: *Death?* Thus they understand 'that,' non-existence. I know what 'atoms' are, for, being everywhere, I see everything . . . I know that pure delightful faces and all flowers are similar, that shivering bones and great trees bent under the tempest have the same cry; I know that, but *I don't exist.*"

"Yes, they're mad; they say incredible things; I pass before their eyes and their hearts, always the same, but I never find the same eyes, the same hearts . . . other mirages shine there . . . and they say: Time . . . I am the immutable, the absolute, *I am not . . .*"

Then, silent, eyes riveted to eyes, they forgot the earth, human beings and human concerns.

They ignored the clamor that wanted them, wanted their caress, their cold and insatiable caress, which makes the heart

light, the flesh heavy and icy: the accursed and redoubted caress—the unforgettable . . . They discovered one another—and
loved one another. They loved one another, the Brother and the
Sister, nameless, formless and ageless.

The human habit, they broke. He, having passed through
so many amours, and She, having mingled her rattle with so
many spasms, were subject to the avid contagion of desire and
annihilation, and, on the far side of the clouds, they embraced
in the light.

Then the leaves and the clouds, the trembling horizons and the
great sky, so tender, sank into the primal Darkness, for, without
Death and without Time, there could no longer be Life.

Is it a dream beneath the eyelids—or a shadow in the room . . . ?

Voluptuous and naked, she sleeps.

At the breath of her heart, her breast undulates, and under
a pale light, her flesh is as silky as very clear water.

It is the terrible silence of the middle of the night—that
unfathomable silence in which awakening seems an abnormal
sin . . . Not a dream—and not a shadow either.

Time is upon us and Death before—unique certainty. What
does it matter?

Thrown upon the beautiful and the fragile—the creature of
an hour—I defy Time and Death . . .

It is necessary to drink, to drink, to drink . . .

POLICHINELLE HAD A HEART . . .
(*La Fronde*, 2 March 1899)

IT was a miserable puppet show:[1] a sort of formless stall, all its walls cracking, the canvas agitating in the slightest gust of wind, a pitiful, colorless, patched rag like the sail of a boat in distress—one of those boats of the Mediterranean coast with red sails, the color of blood and the color of glory, washed repeatedly by the sea, their weave becoming threadbare before losing that color . . .

But such as it was, so poor and pitiful as truly to wring the heart, that grotesque miniature theater was the whole of the fair, the whole of the fête, in the little square of the little town. That square had eight secular plane trees and four stone benches crumbling at the base and engraved with more inscriptions—dates and names—than an Egyptian stele, which had seen uniform successive generations pass, with habits so identical that the individual disappeared therein, confounded, too similar to neighboring individuals before, in parallel and afterwards, to the extent that those dates of dead springs and those names, which one would have found written on other stones, behind the church in the garden where an entire race

---

1 The traditional English equivalent of the French *guignol* [puppet show] was the "Punch-and-Judy" show, in which Punch, the equivalent of the French Polichinelle, similarly invited laughter by employing a stick to beat others, including a policeman.

slept, those varied figures and words, seemed futile, mysterious, troubling and amusing, like the Japanese characters of our trinkets of modern exoticism.

But the summer poured its golden rain between the large palpitating leaves of the old trees, and on those beeches, which the sunlight and the shadow of the branches covered with a light and fluid watery shimmering in the pink mornings and the blue afternoons, there was a crazy waltz of blonde fays, a vertiginous ballet of ephemerae spiraling vertically in every sunbeam. And in that calm and splendid décor, the puppet show seemed less sad, less ugly, stealing from the tall trees a shade propitious to its misery, it was draped by a sheet of sunlight and took from the dancing rays what was necessary to put a star on its inglorious fronton.

Then, as it was the artificial, the unknown, fantasy and laughter, a population of children soon began prowling around it in the manner of inquisitive cats, with the slyness of malign little animals. They all came, the bourgeois children dragging their nursemaids by the corners of their white aprons, and the children of the streets, the shops and elsewhere, the very chic and the very dirty all rubbing shoulders, the preparations sharpening their curiosity, their desire and their dream: a dozen wooden benches in an area enclosed by a rope wound around poles stuck in the ground—well, it wasn't the Opéra . . . !

But, the mind of a child, being sage—almost magical—does not stop at visible appearances; it creates them all, and thus transforms and dominates them; it is a beautiful soul, a brand new soul, instinctive and powerful, which casts the charming, immaterial veil of the imagination over unpleasant exteriors—a veil that will be so quickly torn and soiled by reason . . .

Now, as soon as the curtain—the frightful curtain—rose, on a stage vaster than ordinary puppet-show scenery, and extravagant, magnificent and miraculous Polichinelle appeared!

It was not that he was newly painted, and his costume was threadbare in twenty places, but his construction was superior.

Like a good Polichinelle, his humps had a human amplitude, his arms were as ridiculously thin as one could wish, and on his marvelously articulate neck, his head had contortions so admirable that all the members of the audience stamped their feet with admiration; the spontaneous soul of the claque animated the public, and the worthy public gave Polichinelle an unforgettable welcome.

Polichinelle's face was a masterpiece: what marionette artist had been able to knead and fashion a cardboard-paste malleable enough to give such verity to that physiognomy? The eyelids and the temples were clad like make-up in an intense shadow of dolorous fury, and a hilarious rictus was designed around the mouth. The hilarity was contagious; before the mouth had simulated words, people were writhing, rolling under the benches, laughing until it hurt, dying of it, simply from looking at Polichinelle's silent, prodigious and absurd laugh.

But he spoke, and his song responded to his plumage; and, something not yet seen, he did indeed *appear* to speak, and one had the inappreciable illusion of believing in the reality of that being, of believing that the voice was not heard emerging from the depths of the puppet-show box, in order to lend itself to the marionette's gestures, but was wrenched from the deformed throat and breast of the doll. One could believe that the doll was alive, that the monstrous packet was a creature of flesh and blood. That was believable, and the worthy public was joyful.

And that joy increased, that joy endured; it was renewed every evening, and every evening there was a thunder of laughter, the breath of which agitated the smoky flame of the Argand lamps; there was a clinking river of coins rolling from the pockets of the population—the emptiest were there, for that laughter—into the pockets of the exhibitor of marionettes. They knew him, and his family: a wife and three children. They could be seen by day taking the golden air of summer afternoons and reposing on the centenarian benches under the old trees. The tranquil square was stirred by their presence and filled with a murmur of delirious bees by the crowd of children, who returned even in the hours of closure, tenacious and fascinated, to the enchanted place where the frisson of a benevolent error and the delirium of the farce retained them there every evening. Thus, the days and the evenings were cheerful. Then, there was the obscure, profound and inviolate reign of the night.

It seemed to descend, as soon the lights were extinct and the footsteps died away in the surrounding area, retired to the dormant dwellings, as blue and mild as a fay from the realm of the moon, and over the deserted square, under the immobile branches, its beauty was suddenly deployed, like a woman lying down to sleep, all white, all brown and delectable, with only the soft veil of her hair between the tender light of the stars and the splendid light of her body . . .

Thus, the narrow square, liberated from human noise, was returned to the great eternal peace . . . but every night, in that light, that shadow and that magic, a form glided, intrusively . . . and it was a crawling, filthy and horrible being . . . perhaps a phenomenal animal from a secret menagerie?

That deformed shape emerged from beneath the gray canvas that enclosed the puppet theater and went as far as a bench, climbed on to it, lay down with a groaning sigh, and extraordinary paint, and stayed there, looking up at the sky, its simian hands crossed over the hump on its chest . . . stayed there until morning, its eyes wide open: an apparition that would have been frightful to a sensible heart . . .

It was a man—and it was dreaming . . .

Dreams? Perhaps not even that . . .

A monstrous appearance, animated by a sort of genius; and because Chance—a very reliable god—enabled that genius and that appearance to serve the fortune of a poor director of a puppet-theater and the joys of populations, the thought of that nightmarish embryo was alimented by one and the other.

What he saw repeatedly in his nocturnal awakenings was always the variegated crowd whose emotions he agitated like a gambler shaking dice in his cup. Before his eyes, in pathways all the way to the stars, there were pink faces, youthful, smiling faces, faces tranquil with happy health, the ignorant, calm and simple faces of children and adolescents, impulsive amour, the future and force of imminent embraces, all of nature, all of life that germinates, continues and renews itself . . . and before that bright horizon, that immeasurable and unlimited horizon, he sensed himself, as stagnant and derisory as a marsh rotting one step away from the vast and fecund sea . . . and his sighs groaned, monotonously, in the adorable night . . .

So, after many days in which the spectacle he took was the miserable inverse of the one he gave, after many nights spent under the gentle stars, when the last evening came and Polichinelle had seen the eruption of the naïve and full satisfaction of his director, gorged with money, Polichinelle felt weary . . . oh, weary of so much laughter crackling in bursts, weary to the point of disgust, horror, hatred and death . . . and the misery of his soul broke through his role, overflowing in his gestures and his words. He was sublime—and the enthusiasm of the crowd was ferocious . . .

Then, suddenly, before the abruptly fixed gaze of that crowd, he drew a blade from the wooden stick with which he beat the authority: a solid, humble little kitchen-knife, and he plunged it to the hilt in his truly exaggerated hump, and that hump gushed blood—blood, yes, truly!—which one could have believed to be human blood.

Then, in the public, the worthy public, and in the town, the calm little town, people said over and over again that evening, and for many evenings to come:

"Oh, what a strange thing! Polichinelle had a heart . . ."

THE BELOVED LITTLE FOOL
(*La Fronde*, 9 March 1899)

"THE water is much too blue today," she said. "We can't go sailing in a boat."

"Really? Why not?"

"You know very well that it's because the sirens had their beautiful bright eyes put out last night by some frightened mariner, and all their sisters are dissolving their intact eyes in tears, weeping for that disaster . . ."

He responded very humbly that it was the first news he had had of any such adventure. She seemed more shocked and saddened by that than one might believe, and they remained silent, gazing at the sea.

It really was a surprising blue, bluer than the sky, corn-flowers and the purest blue eyes, dazzling with an intense and magnificent color that circled it toward the horizon with an orb as neat as a design. It was not velvety or silky, as on charming days when light clouds covering it make it similar to a gaze, and it was not troubled by a swell; it was scarcely stirred by a slight frisson, which raised the splash of slow and lazy little wavelets on its shore., and it seemed that nothing was calmer, more reliable, more divinely cradling and appeasing than that immense blue sea.

"Well," Mireline repeated, "we won't go on the water today."

But he protested; he was madly fond of the sea, boats and the daily excursion, in which the adventurous and divine reverie dreamed better to the gentle rocking of the great seductress, and he did not renounce it easily. What! For a caprice, a whim of a stubborn little fool . . . no! He had had enough of tolerating such burlesque flights of fantasy of an infantile and unhinged mind, and the continual cries of "Do this!" and "Don't do that!" for veritably absurd reasons—which were not reasons— with which she made his own mind swerve back and forth, not knowing which way to turn, entirely tamed and submissive to the humor of the woman, were becoming intolerable.

He looked at her and he felt a hatred for the delicate and pale creature. He detested that charming woman, he despised the delectable details of her beauty: her black hair and her blue eyes, her little hands—frivolous jewels—and that whole air of melancholy mischief, that allure of fascinating tenderness.

He went as far as denying within himself that he had ever loved the gracious and stupid little soul, who was astonished by the simplest and most familiar things, and easily imagined chimeras good for putting little children to sleep in the laps of their nurses.

From such violent sentiments came a banal gesture; he shrugged his shoulders.

She saw that, and started to weep.

She was very pretty when she wept, because they were tears without conviction. Then he became troubled. He said, harshly: "Speak, then! What's the matter?"

Naturally, she murmured in a broken voice: "Nothing . . ."

That would have appeared to be quite exact to superficial eyes, but she had, on the contrary, a thousand reasons for dolor. Confusedly, because her soul was indeed little and fluttering, she recalled the time when her mobile fantasy was precisely what he adored in her, and at such an extravagantly inebriated and seductive imagination he would immediately have seized her, embracing and kissing her, and calling her, passionately, his *beloved little fool* . . .

Now, by virtue of an inconceivable change, he was particularly irritated today by identical things! Of course, she did not believe in the least in that story of sirens with their eyes put out—how such a tale had come to mind she would have had great difficulty explaining—but she thought she recalled that when she left the house she had had the sly thought of preventing that day's excursion in a boat. Was she not free not to have a desire to go out on the water?

Certainly, she could have said that she was tired, that she had a headache, that she had a visit to make or an errand to run— reasonable reasons—and, by showing herself very amorous, retained him with her. But no. A ludicrous idea had striped her little mind with its flight, and here they were! She was sulking and he was furious . . .

And very rapidly, utterly envenomed, he said: "That's all right; I'll go on my own . . ."

She judged herself neglected, afflicted in her dignity, and sought by means of all ruses to prevent him from accomplishing such a black design. He proved to be intractable; and as, without paying any more heed to her angry and promising words, having given his orders, he was supervising the maneuvering of the boat, suddenly, she could not stand it any longer and she leapt aboard. Embarrassed by the high heels of her white ankle-boots, the flounces and lace of her dress, her umbrella, and the crossed chains and tulle bow of her veil, which the wind caught and stuck to her face, she nearly lost her balance, but she finally found herself settled at the back of the cabin, and she stayed there, as motionless as a little modern idol.

The boat was detached and moved off. As he kept away from her, silent, she only had her own resources to distract and console her. She gazed at the blue water, so blue . . . and as they brushed the long, undulating seaweed, she thought about the sirens . . . the poor sirens who were weeping for their mutilated sisters . . .

My God! That stupid story, he had been right to laugh at it . . . what if she were to try again, now that she had given in, now that she was there and he was content . . . ?

Content? He scarcely gave that impression, his eyebrows in a bar over his ferocious eyes and his lips clenched over his cigarette . . .

Awkwardly, she made the attempt. And, with a movement toward him, an adorable movement of her whole body, of which it would have been sufficient for him to take hold . . . if only she had had the wisdom not to say anything! . . . she said, in a whisper: "So you don't believe in the sirens?"

He desired sincerely, ardently, to kill her, to annihilate her there and then, like and importunate little animal. He realized that he was savage, brutal, and was horrified by himself.

"Leave me alone, will you, please . . ."

Tuning away from one another, they contemplated, he sinister and she frightened and full of rancor, the marvelous sea, bluer than the sky, cornflowers and the purest eyes . . . and all around them, the water and the atmosphere enveloped them with that same color of happiness, of festivity, building them an imponderable aerial palace of amour, where it would have been delightful to live an hour without shadows, an hour of dream and light grace, and through which they passed, he with his soul poisoned by the desire to be rid of her, and she the beloved little fool, saying to herself:

I don't understand anything.

BETWEEN THE BOX-TREES
AND THE MYRTLES
(*La Fronde*, 30 March 1899)

The perfume of myrtles vibrates like a crystalline tinkle . . .
Gabriele D'Annunzio

THE box-trees, on the edge of the bowling green, where the grass was short and velvety, like watered silk in the moonlight, and the myrtles, in clumps, which were exhaling the voluptuous breath of their perfume in the gentle evening breeze, ornamented the narrow French garden with the charming, slightly dry grace—so puerile and so neat!—of ancient things that seem eternal.

A toy-garden, like those that come from Nuremberg in a box at Christmas, bursting with vivid colors, with fresh florid fir-trees and wet varnish; in this one, there were almost no blooms in the flower-beds, where only the corollas of violet and old gold pansies opened large sad eyes, and where, between the yews trimmed into cones and arranged and interlaced in precise curves, the little paths strewn with fine sand were reminiscent, in the moonlight, of minuscule painted streams in some minutely-finished painting, with a silvery and nacreous glaze.

Dormant and melancholy, that garden seemed to resemble very closely a stage-set chosen in order for ballads to be sung there by lovers in antiquated costumes: a mysterious and precious place, a divine, undiscoverable place, in which a vagabond dream might encounter gentle phantoms.

One evening in spring, the poet came into it to take the cherished follies of his dream for a stroll; and, his feet taking care not to collide with and bruise the dense and obscure box-hedge—a black margin designing the light pathways—and his hands caressing the frail branches of myrtles filled with tenacious and sweet odor without plucking them, he thus possessed, without spoiling or depriving it, the entire charming garden. Then he sat down on a stone bench adjacent to the pedestal of a statue: a Pomona who was laughing, clutching fruits and flowers to her beautiful breasts, which flowed in clusters and garlands over her loins and her plump legs, veiling the fruit and the flower of her radiant young flesh.

And the poet, immobile and charmed, gazed ahead of him, watching the cherished follies of his dream, which he had brought to stroll, in order to delight them and set them free, wandering amid the neatly-trimmed boscage, naked and sumptuous, leading their magical saraband. They are bold and supple, like proud lovers, the daughters of dream; their allure and caprice, and their light souls, make them reliable consolers and incomparable lovers. There is no human pain that they do not appease, and no joy that they do not render pensive when they dance, with doll-like steps, their round of benevolent fays.

That night, better than anywhere else, between the box-trees and the myrtles, they were evocative and triumphant; and then, from all directions, surging from the heart of the yews trimmed into cones and surmounted by balls like absurd minarets, and appearing on the near horizon of pathways as pale as water, a population of shadows rose up . . . shadows lighter than the lightest daughters of the dream. They were gentle phantoms, marching with slow steps, with a strange gleam on their charming foreheads, oppressed by an invisible weight, and they were beings with an appearance paler than ash, but who wore their immortal names sparkling in terrible light around their dead faces . . . And more and more of them came . . . the tender faces of women, which a smile or a tear would have made eternal; faces prostrate in a kneeling position and faces tipped back in a kiss . . . for they had retained the appearance of their terrestrial lives . . .

There were also bloody effigies and visions of the dawn, for there were heroes there and virgins, lovers and martyrs, saints and kings, and the air in the silent garden, where an enormous crowd was not gathered, vibrated with the triumphant resonance of the cortege, with the thunder of clarions over battlefields and profound church music—all that human harmony has desired of pomp and plaints around mourning and celebration . . .

And the poet recognized the creatures of that crowd, named them with their names of fear or grace, those whom one fears and those whom one adores, the very pure and the very terrible, some bearing all their soul in their eyes like a divine liquor in a sacred chalice, and others whose feet were weighed down by bloodstains, who had made the earth, in the four corners of the world, red and greasy with the life of generations.

But of those beings, so various, Death had made almost similar shadows, and between the box-trees and the myrtles, for crowns or for offerings, they rushed to the harvest of glory and amour, they wanted from those embalmed boughs and those sacred branches, which were still emblematic for them, a little of the life of old . . .

But as the moon, all golden, slid over the pink horizon, and the sky became pale and dazzling for a new day, those shadows vanished, dying a second death with the enchanted dream of the poet, and all the cherished follies, daughters of the dream, went to sleep, invisibly, in the enclosed garden, melancholy and charming, which the box-hedge and the clumps of myrtle ornamented with the grace of ancient things that seem eternal . . .

THE LIFE, DREAM AND DEATH OF ARLIE
(*La Fronde*, 13 April 1899)

ARLIE was a poor little orphan girl. Her aunt, a domestic servant of a rich family, brought her up. From the house of her foster-parents in the country Arlie had passed to a little room on the sixth floor where she slept alone, after days at the communal school.

Arlie loved the appearances of life passionately and, instinctively, her soul stripped them of their scoria, in order to make them hers in all beauty.

Thus, at eleven years of age, having had a childhood without kindness, she recalled with the most tender joy the beautiful rosy mornings and the long warm evenings in the heart of the fields. The blonde ears of wheat, the birds in the branches and the heavy tawny cows lying in the lush grass had been her friends.

She loved the city for its colored streets, shop displays, carriages, florid rattletraps, the rumor and movement of the crowd. Submissive to such uncomprehended charms, she was able to forget the miserable ugliness of her little individual life, so humble and so dull.

Having caught a chill one rainy day, however, and, coughing very badly, Arlie had to stay in bed. Alone for long hours, with her eyes raised toward the skylight that perforated the ceiling like a pale, fixed, dead eye, the misery and ugliness of that life oppressed her for the first time: a profound oppression that mingled with the painful exhalation of the cough squeezing her frail throat and her poor narrow breast like a huge evil hand.

One evening, Arlie tried in vain to recall the rosy mornings and the long warm evenings. The oil lamp was giving off an acrid smoke, and its light, vacillating in the wind that slid through the cracks in the skylight, cast hideous shadows on the walls.

Then, "in order not to weep," Arlie extended her hand, like a pauper asking for alms, toward a heap of old books, and among those books she found a volume of Andersen's tales—oh, a wretched volume, tattered and dirty, with missing pages—but scarcely is it open than it effaces the hideous shadows . . . it becomes forgetfulness and joy . . . Arlie is outside life, outside the world, in the lands of sirens, enchanted swans and lead soldiers smitten with dancers cut out in paper . . . and now, wearied by attention, dazzled, she slides into that magic in slumber. She sleeps . . . she dreams . . .

The lamp crackles, is no more than a red dot, and goes out. The full moon high in the sky strikes the little skylight and designs a white square in the center of the room, but on that bright place, as neat as a beautiful piece of paper, a singular black silhouette is profiled . . . the silhouette moves, stretching like a Chinese shadow: a large back, two ears, and a feathery tail—it is a cat, a black cat; it miaows.

Arlie hears that miaow, opens her eyes in the darkness, sees the white patch, the black patch, raises her eyes toward the skylight, and encounters the phosphorescent gaze of the cat.

Childishly, playfully, "for a laugh," she miaows a little herself, very softly: "*Mia-a-a-ow*" . . . but—what a surprise!—the cat responds immediately, and it does not respond "*Mia-a-a-ow*," as one might expect, it responds in words, human words that Arlie understands, having miaowed without understanding what her "*Mia-a-a-ow*" signified.

116

The black cat says: "I'm cold, you know, on this roof; it's freezing tonight, everything is white, and I'm also hungry, and I can see milk in your room . . . you know that we cats can see in the dark . . ."

Arlie is good; she is moved to pity; she gets up, opens the skylight and, briskly and unceremoniously, the supple and silent black cat leaps into the room. But what? Now Arlie feels very odd all of a sudden; by means of an involuntary movement she has hoisted herself up on to the roof and is sitting there, melancholy and astonished . . .

Her chemise has been transformed into a black pelt, she has claws at the end of her little hands, and famished entrails. Through the window, closed again, her astonishingly clear-sighted eyes see a strange little Arlie in the room, lying asleep, and she sees Arlie's dreams: she sees a charming population of swans of surprising intelligence and entire armies of lead soldiers, and the entire roof, sparkling with frost, seems to her to have become a moving sea in which sirens are floating . . . she hears their songs and sees their long, flowing hair . . . She pursues them; they flee; and in the strangest vision she sees herself, metamorphosed into a black cat, running over the roofs after the sirens . . .

A choking sensation, of dolorous efforts . . . and Arlie wakes up; she is lying in her bed, her whole body trembling, her head aching terribly and her tongue dry with thirst. Around her people are agitating, talking; he understands a few words through the sonorous buzz that fills her ears: "Found unconscious on the floor . . . the skylight open . . . it's doubtless the delirium . . . must have got up, stifling, wanted air . . . very ill . . . oh, very!"

Meanwhile, someone has picked up the old volume of tales; Arlie sees it; imminent memories of so many marvels—which seem to her to be so distant!—accumulate in her head, on her lips . . . she speaks quickly . . . quickly . . . quickly . . . and she sees all the extravagant images again, and speaks them again, smiling at them . . . the sorcerer cat, the sirens on the rooftops . . .

On hearing her, a grave person frowns, leafs through the book and cries: "How can one put such things in the head of a child? It's a stupid fantasy!"—phrases that can be found exactly on page 105 of the said book . . .

Arlie can no longer hear . . . she suffers, and then consciousness returns: the hospital; fluid days, bleak and slow, and finally, life again—still . . . Arlie is cured; she is alive . . .

She is alive; and there is misery and ugliness, the suffocating odor of excessively narrow rooms where her sad youth goes by, and, in the evenings, on the walls, the hideous shadows of insufficient lamps . . .

With lightning rapidity a vision sometimes passes: enchantments of princesses and fantastic round-dances of animals, with the prettiest magical story unfolding in those charming décors . . . but those visions fade . . . and Arlie always has greater difficulty stripping reality of scoria . . .

She is alive; she has a lover, difficulty, children, hunger and tears . . . she becomes ugly long before becoming old, and she becomes old a long time before dying . . .

Finally, having lived a long time, she dies, almost idiotic, and as she dies she whispers, with an imbecilic smile:

"What . . . can one put . . . so many things . . . into the head . . . the head . . . of a child . . . it's . . . it's . . . a stupid . . . fantasy!"

That is all that she recalls of such a beautiful dream . . .

THE ROMANCE OF A DELFT PORCELAIN VASE
(*La Fronde*, 20 April 1899)

BETWEEN the wall perforated by bright windows, which formed a singularly real canvas backcloth, the wings, and the true backcloth, which undulated with an almost imperceptible ripple in the air currents, there was an extraordinary ornamentation: all the potteries and porcelains of the world, magnified to human proportions, were accumulated there, reproduced in colored cardboard paste. Next to blood-red and solar-gold Satsumas bearing dragons on their bellies, Sèvres the color of the Mediterranean and the sky were aligned, and close by, smiling and simpering, rosy, fragile, garlanded Saxes in an adorable pretty group mingled with Spanish flames of the Belle Époque. Behind, all white and all blue, were the Delfts: a population of vases, tall ones with narrow necks and bizarre stoppers and short, plump ones, heavy and amusing; then there were bottles coiffed with pewter, with beautiful figure-eight handles, inkwells, and salt-cellars.

And next to all that, motionless, arranged on parade, was a population of children: kids of all ages from five to sixteen, perhaps a little more, perhaps a little less. The smallest, so slender, emaciated and dull, with pale faces and snuff-colored baby clothes, almost disappeared, overwhelmed by the sumptuous colored simili-porcelains.

In groups, in heaps, two by two or sitting on the ground for a moment's rest, they were the little souls of that décor, which, thanks to them, sheathed in those cardboards, their little arms passed into interior handles, were about to come to life, to move and form a comical, delightful hallucinatory procession . . .

Leaning on one of those containers, a young woman—fifteen years old or eighteen? one cannot tell, she so thin and dainty, but with such a passionate and meditative face—is listening . . . If one looks closely one can see the fine reciter of foolish songs half-simulated behind that same container. Handsome? Perhaps not excessively, and surely of modest employment; in his métier as a figurant he is an inkwell—a magnificent inkwell, of course, square and important.

So, the "inkwell" is talking, and the vase . . . oh my God, the vase is weeping! She is weeping silently, with the little sobs of an abandoned child who would be afraid of being beaten if she were found . . . and there is a little of all that in the story of the little vase. She is going to be, she is, abandoned, and, being very familiar with slaps, she fears them, and her despair has become indiscreet. She had foreseen it, clearly, several days ago; the delicate Saxe shepherdess over there had been preferred to her, and with what a surge of hatred, rage, punches and kicks she had tried to knock over, roll and kill that little brunette creature, all round, so absurdly different from the painted image that she will be in a little while! But there will be no scandal here, or death, for here comes the chief of the figuration, and he does not tolerate any nonsense. The moment to don the costumes has come, and "every man to his jug," as they say in Brussels. Still not entirely self-controlled, and not resigned, she attempts a delay, a supplication, and toward the boy who is lifting the vast inkwell, slipping into it as if into a barrel, she implores: "Then . . . you won't wait for me afterwards?"

"No." The voice from the depths of the box is distant.

"Oh! Say! This evening . . . again . . . I . . ." A sob—but she is called.

"Hey, you over there, the vase. Get a move on, and quicker than that!"

She goes, the little vase, but, shaken by tears, in a dolorous swell, she totters with a grotesque gait, with the ridiculous hops of a drunken vase . . .

An abrupt hand knocks on the side. "Stand up straight, damn it! Do you want to be shown the door?"

And in the triumphant fanfare of the procession, the little vase, galvanized by the idea of losing her twenty sous per evening, marches straight ahead, without even being able, her two hands being caught in the handles, to contain her breaking heart . . .

THE CROSSING
(*La Fronde*, 27 April 1899)

UNDER great starry skies, like inverted cups dotted with gems, covering the oceans with immense names, and out of a port of rust and sulfur reeking of tar, garlic and salt, in some blue and gold bay, its soil red with flowers and crushed fruits—a bay full of bitter and sweet odors, unknown odors, nausea and languor—is it an infinite crossing and, poetically, a nostalgic crossing?

Yes, nostalgic, charged with dream, but not distant, and without a paltry concern of detail, it is, on a gray spring day, a miraculous crossing, the one that passes over a simple iron bridge shaking with the movement of vehicles, leading from the Quai Malaquais to the Louvre.

The most adorable sky, made of pearl dust and blonde ash, mobile silky smoke like tresses undone by invisible lovers, and so gray, as white, of a blue so pale and a gold so dull, like an immense, changing and soft eye, that sky ignites and catches fire in the occident. A strange fire of blood and flame, and that fire sizzles, splashes in sparks, is torn apart in magnificent shreds by the sieve of the Tower, which resembles a fantastic perforated factory chimney—the factory of the world, the fire of the vast forge that is Paris, and which, symbolically, burns and sets ablaze the sky in capricious and seductive April dusks.

To the left, like a silken knot, the Seine deploys the double ribbon of its waters, a ravishing cord: soft, invincible and full of frissons, which moors the city . . . and at the tip of Saint-Louis-en-Î'le a clump of trees shakes over the river, from all its branches more blonde than green, the light pollen of buds. And in that narrow stone horizon, in that atmosphere made of fluid light and mist rising from the water and falling from the clouds, there is the strangest appearance of phantasmal architecture, blurred and cut out of an aerial design of an impalpable model. All of that backcloth to the heart of Paris is indescribably soft; invaded by shadow, sadness and melancholy and miraculous peace, it slips into slumber at night, and almost, it seems, into death and eternity . . .

In that drowned landscape the soul is clutched with tenderness and regret, but, rapid and bounding—very human—it turns away, and its eyes go to the blazing façade of the palace: red windows and golden balconies, *The Triumph of Apollo* drawn in violent strokes above the delicate line of trees with tremulous crowns. And that thin green line, like a fresh, murmuring stream, runs in a curve of inexpressible grace all the way to the bushy foliage of the Champs-Élysées, where it dissolves and is lost in a gulf uplifted in light waves—it is like a hump-backed port—cupolas and scaffolding—constructions invisible at their bases in a gentle flow of leaves; and, cords of knotty wood, the scintillating slates, the gleam of new stone with the whiteness of sails, make one think of a squadron, a fantastic, aerial squadron run aground there, far from ocean breezes and powerful salts—face to face with the realm of gold that opens over the sea when the sun goes away . . . frightful splendors of the evening, fortresses crumbling into royal ruins in the jasper, the ruby and the amber—the glorious death of Sahil . . .

NOTHING
(*La Fronde*, 4 May 1899)

HE said to her: "What are you thinking about?"

Naturally, she replied: "Nothing," because she no longer loved him.

At that little word, which had become frequent between them, he was invaded by a murderous desire: to put his hand, his strong hand, which would not tremble, on that delicate nape curved under the mat golden knot of her heavy, warm hair, and, holding that pale and tender neck in his ten fingers, see that charming head tip back in death, as in amour.

A violent appetite for murder poisoned his heart.

Meanwhile, before the staring eyes of her lover, she interrogated in her turn: "What's the matter?"

And he said: "Nothing."

Then he gave her rapid, passionate kisses, in order that the lie would be more firmly established between them—mute, and with eyes closed.

Nothing . . . oh, truly nothing—silence . . . infinite mortal silences in which the future that was about to separate them was woven. Nothing, doubtless, the new thought fluttering, a profligate little bird, behind that forehead, which seemed charged with dream and light speech and folly; the minuscule word that speaks the unspeakable, expresses the voice, really was the only exactitude to define the delicious wave that he saw in her heart, the changing cloud in her changing eyes, the hesitation, which does not refuse the habitual kiss—it costs so little!—of the mouth become slow at the frisson, and on that unconscious mouth he chewed the word like an insult, like an appeal: *nothing!*

"What did you say?"

"Nothing."

He saw her smile . . . not a smile of tenderness, nor of languor, but a fugitive, ironic smile of a stranger, of a creature departed, definitively gone away, and yet conserving an omniscient and occult power of a torturer . . .

He was about to say: "Why are you laughing?" but he foresaw the response and, in order not to hear it, in order never to hear that woman's light and foolish little word again, he strangled her . . .

There was an effort of ignoble struggle . . . she didn't want to die . . . her eyes dilated and her mouth open—her pink mouth and her blue eyes—she was certainly still hoping, against all hope, to live! But almost immediately, the head fell back; as they had a little while ago, with the same heavy and graceful movement, the eyelids fluttered two or three times, like the little wings of a toy bird, the lips remaining parted and a redness rose like a flame to the cheeks; she had a second death, a marvelous appearance of voluptuous life, asleep in a dream that wakefulness would not know . . .

Then he let her fall on to the cushions and gazed at her with a sentiment of deliverance, a great benevolent calm.

How he loved her thus!

He wanted to tell her so, to shout it to her, to embrace her soul, her thought and her hearing in a prodigious music of amour. But he thought that she would make no response . . . and he shivered slightly.

However, he could not succeed in judging himself worthy of the name of murderer, and when, later, he was asked with interest: "For what reason did you kill that woman?" he responded truthfully.

"For nothing."

And they thought he was mad.

THE GREAT FLOWER
(*La Fronde*, 11 & 18 May 1899)

"SOMETHING strange is certainly happening in that little pot!" cried Dominique Privat one morning, while making the daily inspection of his "garden."

That garden, a wooden box solidly fixed to the external sill of the window, contained a dwarf rose-bush, two primrose plants, three dumpy crocuses, a hyacinth bulb in an old bottle of fruits-in-brandy and a second, minuscule, box forming a margin in the first, which was to be a lawn, and where Mahon grass was already pointing its fine green needles. Finally, in a corner, there were two or three pots without tenants, half full of earth, to which the "tools" were fixed—an old pewter fork, a wooden spoon with a broken handle, and a rusty pair of scissors—heaped up humbly. It was one of those pots that had attracted Dominique Privat's vigilant attention.

"Something strange is certainly happening in that little pot!"

And he drew it into the center of the garden, and leaned toward it with an anxious and happy solicitude.

In order to understand that sentiment on Dominque Privat's part, it is necessary to know that he had a soul fond of the unexpected.

At first glance, the person and existence of the worthy fellow did not allow any suspicion of that taste for adventure. A modest employment, feebly recompensed, delicate health and an uncomplicated mind certainly made him an undistinguished exemplar of humankind. He had always been sufficiently ignorant of passions to be scornful of them, and yet he believed he loved, and truly loved, the unknown.

Of that weakness, which he had to recognize, he accused himself, but that was the principle of his liking for horticulture. To hear him pronounce that slightly bristly and climbing word, armored with a thorny *r*, one might have thought that one saw in him a master gardener versed in the science of grafts and the culture of cuttings, or a fervent amateur of audacious collections: orchids, tulips or ferns. However, his universe, Nature, his entire floral folly was contained in those half-dozen vulgar plants, and at the slightest manifestation of germination raising a bump in those four centimeters of earth deprived of juices, he shivered as if in expectation of the impossible, of a magnificent mystery.

O triumph of amour and imagination!

So, that little pot presented a singular appearance, at least in the prejudiced eyes of Dominique Privat.

The gray and dry earth that half-filled it, deprived of water—because it had not rained for days and Dominque did not include it in his irrigation—was slight swollen in places, seemingly inflated by new life . . .

But I haven't sown any seed in there, the worthy fellow meditated. *Perhaps it's a worm.*

But the supposition that it might be a miserable animalcule that was causing such a singular convulsion scarcely pleased him. Thus, he did not disturb the earth in the little pot, and resolved to wait. Oh, but this time it was no longer a matter of the usual wait for a germination—charming certainly, but foreseen.

All the heroic hours of life having as the inverse of their weave quotidian banality, Dominique Privat was extracted from his ecstasy by the shrill voice of his concierge's little daughter, who was bringing him a bowl of hot milk, as she did habitually every morning.

"Will M'sieur Dominique perhaps give me a flower this morning?"

And, feline, seductive, womanly, caressant and endearing, the child—eleven years old, with an amusing muzzle—added: "They're so very pretty, your flowers, and they grow so well in your garden!"

Flattered, the fellow could not contain himself, and said in a low voice: "What you can see is nothing much, but I believe I'm going to have an extraordinary flower—yes, truly extraordinary!"

"Ah! And what will your flower be?"

Monsieur Dominique did not want to compromise himself. "You'll see," he said. "You'll see!"

"Right away! I want to see it!"

With the superb faith of amour he leaned toward the little pot with the mysterious womb, half full of slightly inflated dry and gray earth, and said: "Look."

The child thought he was joking, and, being naturally cheerful, started to laugh; but Monsieur Dominique's gravity impressed her, and before nightfall, the entire quarter knew that Monsieur Dominique was going to have a magnificent flower.

That same evening, Monsieur Dominique believed that he might die of fright. With his lamp extinct and the moonlight paling the window, he saw a strange form behind the glass, half flower and half woman, with a beautiful smiling face, who tapped on the window pane with her five fingers splayed like petals.

Not naturally brave but impelled by an unknown force, Monsieur Dominique ran to the ensorcelled window, opened it—and saw nothing, except for his flowers sagely asleep under the moon's rays, and the little brown and gray pot, which kept quiet. However, he repeated, as in the morning:

"Something strange is certainly happening in that little pot!"

Having gone to sleep full of joy, emotion and uncertainty, Dominique Privat woke up prey to a vague sadness. His soul supported the weight of passions poorly, and doubts, expectations and hopes fatigued him rapidly.

In fact, the soul of Dominique Privat, somewhat weary, would have welcomed a salutary repose.

Living very quietly, from one trivial habitude to another—spending his time in the grave, futile occupations of a clerk at the ministry, and in the preoccupations devoid of dolor of biweekly nourishment—suited Dominique Privat's faithful nature admirably. But it is necessary to believe that he had a demon in his spirit, whose perverse pleasure consisted of knocking over like a house of cards the beautiful equilibrium of negative virtues, and Dominique Privat's first concern was to run to the window in his nightshirt, open it, at the risk of catching a cold, and examine the mysterious little pot ardently.

The cool morning breeze, the weak sunlight and the soft breath of the modest little neighboring flowers, open and respiring with full corollas: none of those charming realities touched the fellow's senses. The crocuses, like golden stars, the primroses, as fresh and round a children's mouths, were shining and smiling with all their frail petals, but he ignored them. The white filaments of the hyacinth, considerably elongated since the previous day, quivered in vain in the bottle in order to attract his benevolent attention, and similarly wasting their time, if they expected any affection in return, were the needlelike tips of the Mahon grass.

In his folly, Dominique Privat even forgot the dwarf rosebush, his former pride, and did not see that the frail shrub had produced two buds, very delicate and pink, like miniature shells of floral nacre.

He was blind . . .

The swallows under the gutter mocked him—but he was deaf.

In truth, there was reason to be. Utterly absorbed, he compared mentally the secret condition of the little pot with that of a volcano before an imminent eruption. That image born of his excited brain enchanted him.

A volcano on a sixth-floor window-sill is already not banal. To anyone who had made the observation to Dominique Privat, full of the most deferential tact, that the present aspect of the pot did not differ sensibly from the aspect it had presented the day before, Dominique would have replied with the most profound scorn.

Now, scorn for reality, if it is not the commencement of wisdom, perhaps being that of happiness, Dominique Privat knew for a week all amorous deliria. He pretended to ignore nourishment, gave short measure to slumber and neglected every concern foreign to the object of his amour, and did it so much and so well that by the end of the said week he was pale and thin—and his garden, by analogy, was in full decline. But what did it matter? The mysterious seed in the little pot was prospering magnificently.

It was not that its fruit had become visible to the naked eye. No, the earth was no longer gray or swollen, because Dominique Privat watered it with a jealous intoxication with the air of a florist's vaporizer. It had become a blackish-brown, even, unified earth similar to the soil in any pot in which nothing has ever been sown; but Dominique Privat knew now what was happening: before appearing in the light, the unknown plant was establishing profound roots.

However, by reaction, after a fortnight of fever, Dominique Privat felt very fatigued. He no longer knew the calm joy of eating well and sleeping well. His uneven and nervous humor surprised his colleagues, his concierge and his concierge's little daughter disagreeably. He became unbearable. He took society in hatred, and yet could not suffer the solitude that his unadmitted disappointment exacerbated further.

He was unable to renounce by free and forceful will the happiness that he had promised himself, but was no more able to give evidence of the patent and superb mildness of true faith, of veritable amour.

By virtue of an excess of misery and disgrace, he was subject to the vulgar allusions of envy and malice. His friends and neighbors, without modesty and without pity, heaped him with questions about "the great rare flower." Divining that he was unfortunate in that regard, they were ingenious in irritating his doubts and soiling his dead enthusiasm . . .

Anxious, maddened, hunted and desperate, Dominique Privat, in those bad hours, was unable to keep intact his still-vibrant but utterly unslaked passion for the cherished mystery, the unknown dream.

He floundered in hesitations and suspicions, he saw himself abandoned by the entire world; his "garden" was like a cemetery—and a single month had sufficed for such great disasters!

So, one evening, one mild moonlit evening, the soul of Dominique Privat, fond of the unexpected but utterly out of tune, became criminal, and, the prompt gesture following the fatal thought, he smashed the poor little pot and, angrily taking handfuls of the soil, scattered them to the four winds of the sky—but as there was not the slightest breeze that evening, the earth fell vertically, in little moist lumps, on to the neck of the concierge, who was sitting on the threshold of her lodge taking the fresh air. She flew into a terrible anger; there was an animated scene on the staircase, and Dominique Privat went to bed very agitated.

✳

Scarcely was he in bed than his room filled with a strange light, as if the moonlight had established itself there as in open country. A subtle and exquisite odor floated, the window opened, and, trembling all over, wonderstruck and fearful, Dominique Privat saw, surging from the gaping frame, an admirable, tall flower, with a profound double calyx, similar to the twin gaze of two large velvet eyes, with petals of a dazzling whiteness, as bulbous and satiny as a woman's breasts, and the leaves and the stem tapered like supple arms, and that entire long, sinuous, undulating stem had an inexpressibly voluptuous allure . . . Dominique was greatly oppressed. He recognized *her*, the promise of his dream!

He spoke to her and appealed to her, but she remained distant and made a sign . . . immediately, a thousand flowers appeared, which invaded the room and the bed in hectic round dances, and began, the mad things, a frenetic and bewildering sabbat, emitting mortal perfumes.

The poor fellow thought: *I'm dead!* and he resigned himself to it stoically, by virtue of an excess of physical weakness.

Then the torture ceased momentarily, and the great flower spoke—yes, truly, she spoke. She said:

"Your soul is cowardly, miserable creature, since, after having had the promise of my beauty, such as you saw me on the first evening, you have not had either the courage to wait or the strength to hope even so; you have been infidel by virtue of weakness, unworthy fellow, not equal to the proof; thus, you have lost me forever, and I am more than a flower, I am passion itself; you have withered it forever, but you will be punished, for you ought not to be unaware that, as the sage says, *it is necessary not to resist one's passions* . . . for they are women, and will avenge themselves . . ."

THE EXPERIMENT
(*La Fronde*, 25 May 1899)

O N the evening of Saturday the nineteenth of January 189*, Marquise Simone d'Ailesvives disappeared.

Having left home in her carriage at five o'clock, she got out at the Louvre shops, and had not been seen since.

Her family, her husband, her lover—an intimate friend of her husband and the family—and the police expended all the time, money and efforts of research appropriate to such an occurrence.

Had there been a murder? A suicide?

The latter hypothesis, to those who knew Simone d'Ailesvives, with her pretty mask of a modern fauness, in which a cheerful mouth laughed, appeared utterly implausible. She loved life, and the charming or violet events of life. She had an appetite for amour, luxury and the arts. It is true that she brought to everything, in her lively and gracious manner, the singular and seductive paradox of her gaze, which seemed foreign to her behavior. She had sad eyes. To anyone who remarked on that, she replied: "It's not my fault!" And immediately, one observed the rare animated beauty of her smile.

In fact, it was not her fault; and her long, heavy eyelids, cut in the Egyptian style, veiled the blue and obscure irises of her eyes, the indefinably melancholy smile that gave them such a hazardous line was belied by all the exterior manifestations of her soul, so mild, so supple and so vibrant.

Because of that character of amiable grace, and because of her alert intelligence, Simone was able to be odd without being criticized; she was well liked.

Her father, who divided his time between hunting and gambling, had always found time between those passions to pamper his daughter. He was proud of her; she was pretty and amusing.

Madame de Fonville, her mother, was grateful to Simone for having a beauty very different from the one whose remains she flattered herself with having conserved.

Married at eighteen, after seven years of union, Simone found in her husband, whose correct nullity she appreciated, a sufficiently fortunate mixture of tenderness and indifference to make conjugal life with him tolerable.

Having found herself sufficiently moved by the elegant passion for her testified by a young man, André de Rovières, she had taken him for a lover with the vague sentiment of obeying a necessity that, by chance, presented itself to her in an agreeable form.

Sixteen months had passed without him dropping her, and he even assured her that he loved and desired her "even more than on the first day"—which did honor to the ingenious and varied grace that she was able to bring to amour.

Thus provided with everything that constituted a well-comprised and perfectly organized social and sentimental existence, Simone d'Ailesvives existed without collisions in pleasant surroundings. In solitary hours the sadness of her eyes seemed to flow like a shadow and invade her entire pretty face from her eyelids to her lips, but such an inexplicable appearance of lassitude of the soul was doubtless, once again, *not her fault*.

Perhaps it was the fault of an intimate Simone—a Simone so intimate that no one knew her, and she even considered her to be a stranger herself, that inconceivable Simone who permitted herself not to be completely satisfied, and who, astonishingly, sometimes breathed insistent questions with her beautiful cheerful mouth such as, addressed to André:

"Do you love me?"

A kiss for a response.

"Then you'd be chagrined if you didn't have me any longer? If I suddenly died, for example?"

"Shut up! Are you mad? I forbid you to say such things."

"Truly—as chagrined as that! She would be missed as much as that in the world, little Simone, eh?"

And he said the eternal things; that the world was for him, precisely that little Simone—so crazy!—and words of happiness, passion, a fine fire of desire and delirium that collapsed into ardent and silent caresses, as a flame evaporates in light and burning smoke.

On other days, before her invincibly coquettish mother, preoccupied with sumptuous chores, and her father returning from the club or riding, she judged the movement of their lives infinitely unnecessary. She sensed that such ideas were out of place, but that *wasn't her fault*; she had them.

Her husband alone did not suggest any of those strange sentiments to her. She considered him as an associate with whom one maintained courteous relations, and no more. She could imagine exactly what Max's exterior concerns and measured dolor would be if she were to die.

If she were to die . . .

And she was, in fact, considered to be dead when, after several weeks, nothing came to clarify the mystery of her disappearance, and especially when a certain mantle of dark cloth found in the Seine and bearing the label of the Louvre shops was recognized in those shops as having been purchased on the nineteenth of January, between five and six o'clock in the evening, paid for and taken away immediately. A model even

135

remembered the young woman to whom the mantle had been delivered. But that clue, which accentuated the drama, did not explain it.

It was equally recognized that on the fatal day, Simone had not been wearing any but her most meager habitual jewelry, and if very little money was found in her private cash-box, there was nothing astonishing about that, for she dispensed quickly and abundantly on whims and in alms.

She was therefore considered to be dead, no more and no less than if she had been seen ill, and then asleep, immobile and icy, on the large bed in the red room.

There were notes of condolence in the newspapers, and the Fonville and Ailesvives families put on mourning. The saddened memory of Simone, aggravated by the tragic mystery of her premature end, weighed upon those who had loved her.

However, when summer arrived, as they were making arrangement for the holidays, they tried—perhaps unconsciously—to conciliate with the reserve imposed by that mourning with the perfectly natural concern of not succumbing to ennui, and with regard to André de Rovières, the strictest honor forbade him to testify an exaggerated sentiment of remorse for the death of the wife of his friend Max d'Ailesvives.

The following year, one evening in February, a short while after a service had been held a year after Simone's disappearance, on a bright and keen evening, as the Marquis d'Ailesvives was returning home at a brisk pace in the company of André de Rovières, scarcely had he crossed the threshold of the house when he saw an alarmed domestic running toward him.

"Monsieur! Monsieur! Madame is here!"

"Madame . . . ?"

Truly, he did not understand, and if, in the short space of time that it took him to reach the drawing room, his incredulous but bewildered mind was able to believe that some troublesome hallucination had afflicted his domestic, he had to agree, on penetrating into the drawing room and seeing Simone there unchanged—perhaps slightly rejuvenated—sitting by the foreside under the lamp and extending her delicate little feet toward the fire, that it was not a matter of a mirage.

"You!"

"You!"

"Yes me!"

And suddenly, an extraordinary embarrassment overtook them.

"But how? But after all . . . ? But why . . . ?"

She remained silent momentarily, looking at the two men, feeling sorry for their alarm, devoid of real emotion, and then looked at the fire and relived the folly for a second time: that irresistible, extraordinary desire to know whether she was *really* loved by anyone to the point of a regret, if not eternal—the worst follies ought not to become too foolish!—at least durable, profound enough to change a person's habits; and that desire impelling her to the singular comedy, that dramatic game, that cunning plan of the mantle bought and thrown in the water—a false trail—and then, with savings hidden for a semester, money that no one suspected, the flight, the departure for a destination in Bretagne, soberly but surely disguised in her costume of matching blue cloth, a white apron—taken from the linen cupboard before leaving the house—and her blonde hair hidden under a black woolen shawl taken from the poor box.

And it was out there in Bretagne that she had lived, very simply, on a little remote and sheltered beach, representing herself as a delicate young woman of modest condition . . .

All of that she related tranquilly, but they looked at her anxiously.

The motive that had pushed her to such an action she skimped, speaking about a caprice and pronouncing the word "experiment." They did not appear to comprehend—and, in fact, they did not understand such an extraordinary impulse of an unsatisfied soul.

In sum, they held it against her that she had wanted to create such an absurd situation, so equivocal, for two honorable families whose rank and habitudes designated them to too many observations . . .

The sadness of the sad eyes was accentuated, and the amusing tone of the words of the cheerful mouth became a little more ironic than in the past—but that was all. Time and various events enabled such a strange adventure to be forgotten around her, and Simone only obtained from it the instruction—which one ought to possess instinctively—that subtle experiments are discordant with reasonable life.

THREE POEMS IN PROSE

(*La Vogue*, June 1899)

HAMLET

HAMLET—you who were asleep in the divine shroud of immortal pages, now liberated, before us, you live, animating our soul with your soul—terrible in being so various . . .

. . . Oh, but what a strange shade yours is—more real than our dream of the real? Your shade, mysterious sister, seems to have obtained, from long slumber, the secret of fear and a voluptuous tender grace . . . your shade, as delicate as youth—and ardent among its puerile songs—totters on the edge of dolor, but it is upright, and a hundred cubits magnified in hatred . . .

You roll your childlike body in wild gestures at the feet of the child you love, and, because you love her and horror embitters your heart, you reject her, and wound her, and kill her . . . were you ever more beautiful, shade of Hamlet, mysterious sister, than in the beautiful rage of no longer being able to love?

. . . Or again, the movement of your arms in a cross above crimes and maternal terrors, immeasurable movement in the shadow, was that—revealing all vengeful glory in a gesture of forgiveness—more beautiful?

But when, ceasing your frightful pursuit, your pursuit of damnation, in which you mingled the appearances of the most sublime unreason, you stop suddenly, and for an instant, on the edge of the tomb that yawns in the slippery earth—the well-rotted earth!—here you are more admirable, O Shade, sister of Hamlet, superior to him. You who recreate him in the magnificent form of a living genius . . . stop, with that skull of one you knew and loved between your delicate hands: that skull in which everything that was animate and sensible is no longer revealed except by one thing—a frightful thing—odor . . . something that still persists after everything . . .

. . . Halted, vacillating between the life that is crumbling around you, within you, and—repose? death?—*words . . . words . . . words* . . . for what name names the unknown?

Is it then that we adore you more for being so beautiful? so human in your terror—and eternal in your thought? Where do you come from, if not from having fathomed the unfathomable that dominates genius—august mystery—the unfathomable—whence comes that level, slow voice, that voice which already seems no longer to be sounding in the free air? and that sadness, so calm—even sadder perhaps than the clamor of your approaching despair?

But, after so many agitations, and such a prodigious movement in which your prodigious soul—in combat with the one who was almost your brother—your soul trembles and writhes, as if, unchained from the chains of the flesh, it is about to spring forth from your pure body, your supernatural eyes, like a great bird of prey . . .

. . . Here you are standing in death, as if in a last and immortal victory . . . finally, your body, Hamlet, lying in the hollows of walls, is borne away—and it seems that everything is finished of your tragic history . . .

But no, from the crowd, and above the crowd, your head appears and is visible again, so young, so blond, so beautiful, tilted back, facing the sky, O Hamlet! And thus, magnificent, you finally live, You who were asleep in the divine shroud of immortal pages . . .

MEDEA

IMPERIOUS and terrifying, she draws her robe woven of moonlight and shadow . . . a dazzling veil, an obscure veil, which, on her body, seems the magnificent shroud of joys that cannot die . . .

And, all embroidered with emblems, wrapped around her svelte legs, lifted around her narrow feet, it loosens and tightens like coiling serpents submissive to enchantments.

And from her neck to her cleavage, and sliding from her cleavage to her loins, and flowing from her loins to the ground, there is the bright and rattling splendor of gemstones the color of water and the color of the sky—a blue river, a softly noisy river that sobs and sings to the movement of her—Medea's—howling march amid the rocks.

But in her face haloed by metal in frozen flames, her eyes are murderous and her mouth voluptuous.

O hatred, so supple, insinuated between the amorous teeth that grip the Kiss . . . O tender folly gasping the breath of caresses until drawing blood . . . her eyes and her mouth desire all crime and all amour.

And now, here is all the blood of Hecate upon her, Medea, and now, again, here is also all the gold of Helios . . . here she is bathed and burned by light on the threshold of the temple, which she bars with her arms in a cross . . . her arms imaging terror . . . charm . . . and, the flowers of gold in your golden hair, witch, are not so much flowers as your frail hands, your blonde hands, borne by the marvelous stems of your arms . . . your arms from which spring forth—horrible dew!—the pink blood of your murdered sons . . .

LORENZACCIO

A DOLESCENT, feminine soul . . . almost no soul . . . frail and devouring soul in which the universe is held: and the monster and the apostle in the body of an ephebe . . . an asexual silhouette: visage so pale, figure so somber, sensuality ignites in his abyssal gaze, anxiety clings—a very human rag—to your androgynous feline allure . . . Here you are alone . . .

Here you are also, at the lunar hour, before dormant Florence, between yesterday, which was all debauchery in royal company, and tomorrow, which will be the dawn . . .

Death.

You lean over the window-sill toward the sumptuous City, obscure at the base of its palaces, brightened by its steeples, where the pale sea of stars, as it flows—so slowly—unfurls in a surf of light . . . the city sated—for the hour is nearer to morning than dusk—on the bloody ferment of embraces and murders.

Your hands, Lorenzaccio—ardent, sinuous name, full of languor and strength, like you!—lean on the broad stone where a few handfuls of gilded barley have been thrown for domesticated pigeons . . .

. . . But, because you are also leaning on your soul, your soul, which is approaching its moment of spasm and horrible joy— because all that unslaked soul, Lorenzaccio is not asleep—for that, and because its horizon is vaster, darker and purer than the horizon of the sky and Florence, for that, your hands now clench mortally on the light seeds, the golden seeds spread here for the doves; and, those hands so pale, those caressant hands, after the gesture that enfevers, exasperates, claws, strangles and murders—in dream!—rise up, appealing to the gods, to the clouds . . . to everything that is not, floating and disappearing . . . and as in a similar interior movement your crushed heart opens, intoxicated by energy, now, around you, all the seeds of golden barley escape from your gaping arms, stream and scatter with a sound of hail . . .

Gesture of your flesh, admirable, triumphant . . . exact gesture of your soul—almost no soul . . . frail and devouring soul in which the universe is held: and the monster and the apostle . . . destructive gesture . . . and liberating . . .

THE SONG AND THE ROSE
(*La Fronde*, 1 June 1899)

THE music that was audible through the wall came from an unknown hearth, and, sung by a foreign mouth, it took on something mysterious, almost not human with its pauses, its reprises, the sudden extinction of its excessively soft sound, no longer crossing the distance, and then, abruptly, like a screech, a high note bursting forth violent and victorious . . .

Lying on her bed, pale and weak, the invalid was not even listening to that music any longer; she heard it as one hears the wind, the waves and the rolling of carriages. It became a familiar sound to her, and without thinking, without suffering, she gazed at a large rose in a cup, which was shedding, petal by petal, the blood of its crimson heart, weary of too much sunlight and too much stormy heat.

She did not take her eyes off the flower, no longer daring to look at the clock, which was ticking, and filling the room with the regular and sonorous pulsation.

She preferred not to know the time, since the hour no longer gave her joy, and she would have liked already to be where the hours are dead.

Through the wall, the song recommenced, to a familiar rhythm, relentlessly, a tedious study.

Someone coming into the room said in a low voice: "God! How wearying those people are with their eternal music!" Then, after a circular glance: "These flowers are faded; it's necessary to throw them away . . ."

Suzanne was anguished, agitated her hands, made a sign that she did not want that—no, no, she did not want that!

Naturally, they yielded to her caprice; she had so few nowadays, not even the petty infantile desires of invalids. And certainly, all her malaise stemmed from that: not desiring anything. She was sliding into death, without shocks, very gently, with a frightening facility and security.

She gazed at the rose, therefore, with a desolate and calm happiness.

That unique flower showed her hedges, fields and forests of flowers. There were distant meadows trodden by her insouciant infantile feet, and a thousand harvests of more recent spring that her feverish hands had reaped.

That poor rose, the color of blood, reminded her of dazzling sheaves that she had shredded with full voluptuous hands in order to make the mild leaves, perfumed like flesh, flow over her own flesh, in order better to sense the kisses that had covered it.

It seemed to be still living a little, and so well, to remember the delightful life . . .

And then the music, my God, that music, behind the wall, a trailing and sorrowful song, had she not heard it before, a hundred times over?

However, fatigued, she had difficulty following the indecisive harmony. Seized by vertigo, truly too weary, she closed her eyes, no longer saw anything but the rose, no longer heard anything but the song.

. . . She saw an admirable landscape full of shadow and light. A cooling fan of branches shook over fine grass, with a dust of flowers.

In narrow basins with marble rims, nympheas opened their pink hearts. A hedge of rose-bushes circled that charming square, and beyond, above and below it, there was the blue realm of the sky and the sea, the one so pure and the other so brilliant, and she found herself there on one of those marvelous mornings that seem the youth of the world, a primordial, infinite aurora . . .

Someone she could not see said to her: "You too are all rosy, as rosy as the roses and blonder than the sun!" She felt the vivid heat of that sun on her hair—but perhaps it was a kiss? And at the same time, behind the hedge, in the road, a hurdy-gurdy intoned a trailing and tedious song . . .

Then, seized by vertigo, she no longer saw or heard anything, neither the roses nor the song . . .

When she opened her eyes again and awoke, a little less weary, she looked at the rose—but the rose was no longer there. She wanted to protest, becoming annoyed, but almost immediately, more attentive, she understood: the stem of the rose was still there, intact, and four green tapering leaves sustained the young, dead heart, but all the petals had fallen and had become invisible, strewn on the floor.

Then, as it was late, the wall was silent; the song was no longer being sung, Suzanne was frightened . . . could she live without that flower and that music? And with the desire for life, life increased within her.

She found her strength. She sat up, seized a mirror and said, in a low voice: "That's me! Is that me?" and she sensed that she would not die, since she was already dead, in truth, and yet still active, and in pain.

People hastened around her. They admired her energy; she accepted their cares, smiling and reasonable.

They brought her other roses, and behind the wall, other songs were sung, but always, before the end of the day, she had the flowers in her room changed, and against the wall of the room she had a magnificent fabric hung, very thick, all silk, embroidered and re-embroidered with flowers and gold and silver birds. Truly, when that work was finished, the sound of the music was so faint that it could scarcely be distinguished from the most distant and indistinct rumor. No one would ever have recognized a song in it! Then Suzanne was cured.

When she felt entirely well, she went out—alone. She wanted it thus. She had a visit to make; she had only thought about that of the day of her dream in the admirable landscape.

She made that visit.

She heard, as if in a dream, the same voice saying to her: "You're as pale as your dress, oh, and your hair! Your hair is almost like snow!"

And that was almost true, for she had powdered it a little, out of coquetry.

Then she and he looked at one another tearfully, and she wept—a great deal—thinking about hard hours, and he wept—a little—thinking about beautiful hours . . .

NOSTALGIA
(*La Fronde*, 8 June 1899)

To Madame Tola Dorian[1]

PALER than the pale lace whose light weight covered her frail shoulders, but with a brighter pallor than the white velvet woven with flowers in silver thread that enveloped her feet and legs with its heavy folds, little Princess Mérévah yawned infinitely her infinite ennui . . . A prisoner, a prisoner in this city of crimson dust and ash, a prisoner of malady, of the slow and tenacious malady that left her stretched out, curled up and weak, like a poor little faded flower—or, rather, a broken flower that a great storm wind had laid there in all its fresh beauty, and which was destined by that blow for imminent death, the stem no longer supporting its heart, open in a pink and perfumed corolla.

Her sixteen years, in order to play, had nothing but memories and books—such a fine repose is a game wearying for youth, but if she scarcely liked the one she adored the other. No, Mérévah's almost imperial blood could not support without fear and dolor the excessively tragic memory of her early

1 The poet, dramatist and novelist born Kapitolina Serguéïevna Maltsov (1841-1918), who became Princess Metscherskaia by her first marriage and Madame Dorian by her second. She was the author of *Âmes slaves* (1890).

years. And in any case, she could not yet fathom and explain that memory entirely, which caused her thought to recoil, like something crawling and choking in a subterrain full of black mystery, where the terrifying contact of horrible nocturnal beasts can be divined.

When she remembered, she always heard screams and she always saw blood; it was a distant night, with calls for help and gasps, and the murderer was her father and the victim was . . . surely a fay, the delightful creature seen on nights more distant still, next to her cradle of ivory and gold; the creature she would have liked to call *Maman* . . . but that name had never been given by her to any woman, for neither her father nor anyone else had ever said to her, designated any woman or portrait: "This is your mother."

And another shadow prowled between those two beings, its face invisible, with an appearance of flight, cunning and mystery . . . and there had been such sinister screaming and so much blood on the furniture, and even on the walls, that for a long time afterwards, and even now, Mérévah suddenly woke up at night in an agony of fear, and saw, *saw* that blood everywhere around her—heard those screams of beasts having their throats cut—heard the silence that had followed after the throat-cutting . . .

Then the strangers, the strange dwellings, the awakenings at night, the confused, low, rapid words . . . unknown lands— then, again, her father . . . at least, he said to her: "I am your father," and she believed him, without recognizing him; and the royal existence recommenced. She had palaces, furniture, fabrics, horses; she lived in a frenzy of luxury and solitude.

She lived everywhere, especially in Paris, but never in the land of the drama, the land of the first happy unconscious hours in the land of the fay whom she would have liked to call Maman.

That land, she discovered much later, was Russia, and it seemed to her that if she could return there and breathe the pure and savage air again that she had breathed in the dwelling and in the countryside that remained in her brain—embryonic and unconscious then, almost automatic in its indecision—then she would revive, would be strong, would be cured.

But to that desire, expressed one day, she had received a response from her father frightening in its harshness, in which it was impossible to tell whether rage or dolor was dominant. Questions asked of her father by his secretary—more friend and counselor, faithful and meek—received a partial explanation; the prince was in exile, prohibited from living in his homeland—but the reasons remained veiled, secret and terrible. Then the little, nervous, violent soul of Mérévah was impassioned, and she wanted, wanted that impossibility—impossible because she knew full well what a strange, profoundly jealous and exclusive tenderness her father had for her, and that she would never, never travel without him . . .

That day, like so many days, in her dazzling pallor, beauty and languor, little princess Mérévah was weak with sadness amid the perfumes of narcissi and lilies, which she loved, her eyes, her long eyes, rays of obscure light beneath long silky eyelids, went toward the books piled up next to her and suddenly shone as if a mute prayer had been granted. She read the words: *Âmes slaves*. Her soul, her anxious soul, her desire, her folly, her obscure memory, she would doubtless find therein . . .

. . . When, toward evening, the glorious crimson and gold evening that lit up the sky, little princess Mérévah let the volume fall again from her exhausted hands, she saw passing, in tragic and magical procession, the ardent and tender people who animated those enchanted pages.

There was the Souka who told her story of vertiginous horror and amid the décor of the sumptuous orgy, brutal visions that made Mérévah pale; there was the calm and noble face of Raïsa, divine in simple grandeur; and Domna, gliding over the silvery waters of the Dnieper, a sublime little girl who only knew amour and death; and the Lesghienne, who only knew amour and death—a marvelous female, to the point of the murder that avenged her desperate entrails . . .

Then, here, adorable and mild, is Pana Geneviève passing, "carrying on her regular features the expression of saintly girls who, on a golden background, paint old masters for missals with the patience of profound faith." But because she is so beautiful, the drama of amour will bloody her child's feet . . .

And here too is Marina, the centenarian, who displays to the eyes and weary heart of a sister of Mérevah, a nostalgic little child princess, as vast, profound, regular, bitter and infinite as the ocean, the memory of her life—of universal, tumultuous life, avid and without restraint . . .

And among those figures, looming up in eternal landscapes of light and shadow, there are other vivid images of legend, delicate images of tender sensuality, of cruel verity.

Little Princess Mérévah, dazzled, is mortally anguished in their contemplation. She summons them and loves them, those creatures of misery or dream, she senses that she is of their race, she would like to be as brutal, as dull of savage strength in the free and glacial atmosphere of the steppes, and would like to swoon with blissful sensuality, full of amorous force, in those landscapes of nacre and emerald, those marvelous springs of the North, exploding in foliage, in flowers, fireworks of sap, and where all the ice melted in a single morning, streams everywhere in silver and gold tears under the new sun . . .

Little Princess Mérévah suffers, sobbing, agonized; but in the delirium and her nostalgia, paler than the pale lace whose light weight covers her frail shoulders, but with a brighter pallor than the white velvet woven with flowers in silver thread that envelops her feet and legs with its heavy folds, little Princess Mérévah seizes the book again and applies her mouth to it in a fervent kiss, kissing the souls that respond to her soul, an homage of grace to the magical grace that divinizes, in exalting, the nostalgic desire of that prisoner soul . . .

THE JOYFUL CITY
(*La Fronde*, 15 June 1899)

THE crowd swelled the streets of the City as a fever fills the arteries of the body and causes them to beat. Ebbing and flowing, the black tide dappled by the beautiful pink, violet and green patches of women's hats seemed, in filling them, to enlarge the avenues and boulevards immeasurably. Cleaving through the eddies where the causeways and the sidewalks were confounded, the carriages traced difficult furrows with the slowness of larvae: narrow, uncertain holes from which cries of fright and insults immediately leaked, like drool. Meanwhile, the people, their heads raised and hands high, applauded and acclaimed a cortege, of which nothing could be distinguished except vague ornamentations, a great deal of dust, and, amid smiles constrained by dint of fatigue, the double flash of teeth and eyes marking each face.

Traversing that clamor and delirium at the cadenced and trampling gait of his carriage, which seemed, at such a pace, to be following a hearse, André felt himself gripped by rage and mad impatience. He was furious with his coachman, who, maladroitly, had allowed himself to be caught in the current, which he was no longer thinking of opposing.

Finally, deafened by the howling of the crowd, his eyes tired by the flamboyance of the flags, he respired, for the carriage now disengaged, was hastening toward the Place de la Concorde, which seemed as broad and fresh as a lake.

"Go up toward the Étoile," he ordered, and he was finally about to pass from imbecilic material miseries to the complete misery, almost voluptuous in its acuity, of his chagrin. Scarcely had he seen again and grasped again the terrible recent image than his eyes were filled with the present image: all the way to the Étoile, the slope before him rose into light and ink like the most marvelous road of glory and joy.

His entire soul, seized by vertigo, skimmed with dazzled glances in order to more intoxicated seeing from below, up above, the Arc de Triomphe, still invisible at its base, seemed to be suspended—a magnificent and paradoxical obscure rainbow—on seeing the round Sun in the midst of a sky ablaze with golden flames, red and enormous, a giant eye fixed on the City.

And the city, yellow at that hour, rolled and cried with pleasure, like a madly amorous creature, sublime in that spring evening, that evening of celebration . . .

Returning from the Bois, victorias as profound as baths, filed past at the supple and gentle trot of horses, in a rattle of creaking leather and shaken bits. The hats of the women, as large as umbrellas, and their flowery umbrellas embroidered like hats, shone and agitated like flowers in the magical light, the bright and golden apotheosis of the setting sun.

Suddenly, André's gaze was caught by a coiffure of blue tulle, heightened by mauve hortensias, twisted like a turban around blonde hair, which he thought he recognized. That small face of a pink doll, with the large eyes of a pure child; that delicate body, mounted like an absurd jewel in the dark blue satin cushions of the vehicle, that whole little creature dressed in the most skillful disorder of muslins and guipures, could only be Fifiane, the amusing and fragile crazy Fifi. He saw immediately, by her little smile and a little hand gesture toward him, that he had been recognized too. With the same movement they both had their carriages stop. Already Fifi was crying: "Well? Is the lunch still on, next week?"

But André retorted, brusquely: "You don't know? Louise is dead . . ." And the word that he pronounced brought the young woman back before his eyes, Louise Silvère, Loulette with the pale cheeks amid her black hair, her slow eyes and her beautiful creole mouth; Loulette, whom he had loved well enough three years ago, since after having quit one another, after travels and avatars, they had rediscovered one another decently, good friends, nothing more. She, a tender and delicate creature, of whom it was said: *Her soul doesn't know what it's doing . . .* he a capriciously sad individual: on both sides a little amour and a great deal of appetite, some esteem, enough to re-form a charming liaison.

But now, she was dead. Fifiane, her face of a pink doll less pink, and her large eyes of a pure child even larger, did not believe it and said: "But that's impossible! I saw her the day before yesterday, and on Saturday we arranged that party together. It's impossible!"

Stubborn and pale, André, seeing again the agony full of horror, then the great definitive calm that had followed and was now upon her, affirmed it with brief words.

Fifiane interrogated: "But how did she die?"

"The consequences of an operation . . ."

Fifiane repeated, without understanding: "An operation? Just like that, suddenly? What operation?"

He kept silent. He heard again, in the dolorous delirium, the confession of poor Loulette, saying: "I was pregnant. I didn't want . . . so I went to a midwife . . . I'd done it once before, when I was very young, and it had succeeded completely . . . but this time, see, I'm going to die . . ."

Then other strange words, mad, tender and desolate, which she had spoken on the brink of death, telling him, him, the friend—among many others, from before—the visitor arrived today unexpectedly, that he was the only one she had ever loved, addressing to him the multiple and unconscious tenderness of her poor little tender soul, and, in the course of those crazy, touching, phrases, passing like a flood overflowing from a large river, desires, regrets, appeals, miseries—the wreckage of her heart, sincere at the last minute . . .

To Fifiane's reiterated question, "What operation?" André replied: "I don't know. I arrived there at the last minute, without knowing. The doctors didn't explain anything . . ."

She shivered.

"Oh, to die so quickly! It's frightful!"

And in her lace, her silks and her flowers, all of the delicate little body seemed to be trying to escape some brutal and harmful assault.

André recalled vividly one of Loulette's last remarks: "To die so young, that's nothing—but not to be loved, mourned, regretted . . . !"

He had said: "Don't say that! I love you, me, you know that very well!"

She had almost smiled a little, and in a whisper she had said a terrible: "Thank you!"

Now André felt his heart empty and his eyes dry. That pink rose of the beautiful evening, that pretty woman with the odors of fresh flowers, made him desire bitterly to live, to forget . . ."

After a second of reverie, Fifiane said, mechanically: "And what are you doing, this evening?"

He made a vague, indecisive gesture.

At first he had thought of going to the Bois at the obscure hour and savoring profoundly the bitterness of destiny, but now he was hesitating.

Fifiane, also hesitating, with desire and the simultaneous fear of death and emotion said, in a low voice:

"I'd like . . . to see her . . . if you're going back there, I'll go with you, if you like . . . ?"

He nodded his head, and after a few words to agree the rendezvous and the hour, they separated.

André, having changed his plans, turned his back on the Arc de Triomphe. In the sky, the giant eye was dead. The Place de la Concorde was covered by and full of a dust as fine as a cloud of ash; the streets, which André regained at the rapid velocity of his vehicle, displayed the saddening ugliness of their eddies and the grotesque, sometimes sublime, terrifying anonymity of the crowd.

Because a feeble little creature had risked a dangerous little action and had died of it, André saw all that with momentarily open eyes, full of irony and emotion. He no longer knew very well to whom—Fifiane or Loulette—to distribute that irony and that emotion.

He gave them both, in thought, an equal share, and while he traversed the joyful City, after having ordered admirable flowers—for both of them—he sensed his empty heart filling up and taking form—like the heavy earth over a very small light corpse . . . light . . .

LIRE, LIRE, LIRE, LON . . .
LIRE, LIRE, LA . . .
(*La Fronde*, 22 June 1899)

BECAUSE, that Sunday in spring, the chorus of a roundelay rose from the street to the open window, the old woman sitting at the window wept . . . Slow, calm, rare tears, as old people weep who no longer have hatred or prodigality for anything.

A ray of sunlight on the pale, wrinkled and meager hands seemed a frail jewel of gold filigree mounted on ivory. Those poor hands were trembling slightly, and from the equally jaundiced face, creased by a thousand wrinkles, where the framework of the nose, chin and cheekbones indicated the mask of death, the gaze of the watery eyes went around the room, toward the familiar objects, the secular objects stained by time and usage, but which seemed eternal.

The color of water, those gray eyes: troubled water, tarnished by too many reflections, which, after having passed a rapid and light image, had once left them the color of bright water, blue and green water—silky water, spangled with gold—but were dormant there today and stagnant, charging them to the edges with heavy memories.

Facing the armchair in which the old woman was slumped, curled up shapelessly, a little heap of disgraceful black fabrics: cashmere hemmed obliquely with silk, a mohair shawl—another empty armchair seemed to be waiting. That armchair, like all the furniture in the drawing room, was bastard Empire style. Economical and uncomfortable, that mahogany furniture, upholstered with rep that had once been garnet, and retained in places the hue of crushed raspberries, was all decorated, in a puerile fashion, with crocheted veils in white cotton with fringes. On the seats, the backs and the arms of the armchairs those veils were spread in squares and diamond-shapes, neat and dazzling.

To either side of the englobed clock, two Chinese vases bearing gilded copper candelabra reposed on circles of chenille wool embroidered in relief with large flowers.

In front of the window, between the two twin armchairs, a round occasional table bore a golden basket overflowing with black knitting-wool, a prayer-book and a blonde horn candy-box.

In the street, the roundelay dragged out its refrain:

Lire, lire, lire, lon,
Lire, lire, la.

On that beautiful Sunday, free and gay, the little girls of the neighboring shops, in short skirts and neat aprons, were leading the ancient dance . . .

On the wall, hung with gray wallpaper with red lintels on which gilded staffs were leaning, a few painted portraits were gazing before them with grave eyes. The troubled eyes of the old woman went to an oval frame in a corner: a five-year-old girl in a white muslin dress with flounces, with embroidered pantaloons projecting from her skirt by several centimeters, was represented there standing, placing her right hand on the head of an enormous black dog, and, very blonde, with blue bows in her curly fleece and amid the frills of her dress, she resembled a pretty little white sheep. That little girl had sung the light roundelays . . .

Leaning over, with a painful movement, toward the window full of the warm and fluid gold of the sunlight, and the blue of happiness of the sky, the old woman tried to catch the words of the song, but she could only make out the refrain:

> *Lire, lire, lire, lon,*
> *Lire, lire, la.*

But a louder music suddenly drowned out the shrill high-pitched voices. The tune was not unknown to the old woman; she recognized it as a ballad by Mendelssohn.

And, still gray and dull, her eyes turned to a piano that stood in the corner of the room in its tall case, in the antique fashion; for a long time the lid had been closed over the keyboard with its old yellow keys . . .

Doubtless a young woman was playing, a trifle inelegantly, that wordless ballad, the title of which the old woman could not remember. She closed her eyelids, and imagined that she could see her: her figure a trifle flat and perhaps gauche, but the skin, the eyes and the hair dazzling, and if those hands were trembling, it was with impatient youth . . .

Now, with an effort, the old woman has sat down again by the window sill. Slightly intoxicated by the sunlight, she watches the carriages that are rolling almost soundlessly along the road, gliding like boats on a river, for the avenue has recently been paved with wood. Those carriages seem to be full of flowers, for all the women have bright dresses and rosy hats.

For the old eyes that no longer see very well, all bright colors are the colors of roses . . .

And thus, in couples, the amorous are doubtless going toward the roads to the country.

With slow steps, tottering, the old woman crosses the room and goes to take a daguerrotype from a dresser, which resembles a minuscule fixed pool in which shadows and light mingle, only settling momentarily the strangest appearances.

What is it, then, that thing, so vague, so faded, scarcely an image, which has been under water for a long time? Is it the only thing that the old woman's poor old dull and troubled eyes, which are on the point of permanent extinction, can distinguish clearly, bright and magnificent?

Looking hard, strange, distracted eyes can distinguish the image of a blond young man dressed in a cornflower blue jacket.

The eyes must be keen, the mouth beautiful, and he is holding a cane with a golden pommel with a spirited gesture. He must be a very elegant cavalier . . .

But now the door of the drawing room opens in a gust of wind; a young woman comes in with two little children. The young woman exclaims: "Well, grandmother, you aren't expecting us any longer!"

Surprised, almost ashamed, trembling, with her eyes misted by tears, the old woman hides the daguerreotype, with an awkward gesture, under the knitting wool in the basket. The piano having fallen silent, the roundelay rings out more loudly and the refrain itself:

Lire, lire, lire, lon,
Lire, lire, la,

seems to be mocking the poor old sentimentalist gently . . .

She pulls herself together, she smiles, she gives her great-grandchildren kisses and balls of gum that have the same insipid flavor. She hardly has the strength to hug them in her arms. Her animated and cheerful granddaughter says: "How you make yourself beautiful! You've become a coquette!" and chats, recounting things of yesterday, today and tomorrow, which seem singularly distant and foreign to the old woman.

"We went to the theater yesterday evening, where we saw Aréah, ever more beautiful, more incredible . . ."

The old woman, slightly astonished interrogates hesitantly: "But . . . I saw her once! How old is she?"

"Oh, she's a grandmother, but her age . . . does she have an age? She's always younger, a marvelous figure, the legs of a twenty-year-old, and the grace! And golden hair . . . she lights up the stage!" And, pensively, the young woman adds: "When I think about you, grandmama, I've always known you almost similar to now, even when I was very small—and in this same drawing room! It makes one think that the vertiginous, changing life conserves and remakes youth!"

In a wave of silence, the refrain goes up yet again:

> *Lire, lire, lire, lon,*
> *Lire, lire, la,*

and the old woman murmurs, joining her chilly hands where the sunlight, a changing jewel, has slid:

"Yes, perhaps . . . while memory doesn't rejuvenate . . ."

CONSOLATION
(*La Fronde*, 29 June 1899)

TWO women were leaning on the parapet of the Pont Saint-Michel at eight o'clock on a winter evening. Paris, as terrifying as a marvelous etching, and the river, in a festival of light, extended to the right and the left, in front and behind, a horizon prolonged in an architecture of enormous shadows, punctuated and cut up in a capricious and brilliant design, like one of those pieces of paper pricked with holes, which, when held up in front of a lamp, display a silhouette traced in points of light . . .

Two women: Céleste, known as la Vadrouille,[1] and Tonton Mitaine. The latter, coiffed in an inglorious hat, her head slumped between her shoulders, was weeping untiringly, and the poor formless packet—any old garments and a humiliated back—agitated by hiccupping sobs, leaning over the silent, silky water, seemed sinister and lamentable, as if the enormous red and obscure reflection of the enormous city had driven that human rag into a corner and crushed her, forbidding her to go any further, only giving her the choice between that windswept spot, the rim of that parapet sticky with the noxious damp of the fog, the smoke and the sweat of poor hands, or the mov-

---

1 i.e., the idler, or the slut. "Mitaine" is usually an abbreviation of Croque-Mitaine, a kind of bogey-man, and Tonton is usually a familiar term for "uncle."

ing, icy bed, the undulating, fleeting and ever-ready bed of the river, propitious to long, black dreams . . .

Meanwhile, Céleste, a good girl, fully dolled-up, was making every effort to combat that despair, like someone shaking a stopped watch.

"Well, so what!" she said. "He's gone . . . but isn't it necessary to live? Didn't he leave you anything? No heritage?"

A moist, broken voice eked out in humble speech: "The poor friend! You know very well that he didn't have anything . . . and he shared everything with me . . . when he was there . . . Jean! Jean . . . my Jean . . ."

The voice dissolved in tears as soon as it collided with that name, the name of the beloved individual, which acquired in the ear and the heart a particular, animate, mysterious meaning.

Jean, the blond student who, pursuing his studies with very little money, had always said to his little, timid and tender mistress: "Tonton, I'll be leaving once the examinations are over; I'll be going home, because my father won't send me any more; he's already sacrificed a great deal, and Maman too; I promised them to go back, to make a career out there, with them . . ."

Those words, so often heard, haunted Tonton, and she found enough breath to say aloud, but very quietly: "He told me: don't stay with me, think about your future. He told me that!"

"That's because he didn't love you," Céleste declared, imperatively.

The voice found the strength to affirm: "It's because he loved me better . . ."

Then her companion, shrugging her shoulders under her beautiful sheepskin, burst out: "Get away! What a story! If he loved you so much he'd have stayed. But all that's not important! It's necessary to eat, to live. Me, you know, I'd like to, but I can't continue to lend you . . ."

166

"I know . . . I know . . ." The narrow shoulders slumped further, inclining toward he tempting water, and in a whisper, again: "It's all right under there . . . one no longer has any pain, no need for bread . . . for . . ."

But she was rudely shaken. "Come in! Stop it! You give me chills in my spine! And you're weeping, you're always weeping . . ."

A pause—then, resolutely, like someone risking the supreme remedy: "Monsieur Chaton would find you much to his taste, you know . . ."

"Monsieur Chaton! Shut up!"

Stubbornly, the other continued: "No, but you need to be healthy. What can you do like this, all thin and pale."

Very humbly, Tonton acquiesced: "Oh, yes, I know, I'm ugly . . ."

"Anyway, even as you are, you please him . . . and he'll be at the brasserie near Cluny at nine o'clock . . . then you'll see . . . the time to be there . . ."

Tonton clenched her little hands on the cold stone. That cold penetrated her palms, where the fever was beating, rose to her breast and entered her heart like a good little knife, very sharp, very clement . . .

For a moment, that cold was so great and so profound that she was intoxicated and hallucinated by it; she was almost no longer suffering. She only said: "Tomorrow . . . if you like?"

"Tomorrow! Tomorrow! But you're mad; will it keep until tomorrow? I've arranged everything so well for this evening! Tomorrow! Do you even have enough to eat tomorrow?"

Very quickly, Tonton said: "Oh, yes, I have thirteen sous."

Then Céleste, even more quickly, pressing the words: "That's lucky! I know a boutique before arriving at Cluny where they have superb bunches of violets for five centimes; we'll buy one and stick it to your hat with a double pin, and do it up . . . but hurry, the shop will be closed; it's eight twenty-five! I'm catching a cold myself here. Let's go—you've dirtied the Seine enough with your tears! It's stupid to be here! What's the point, I ask you! He wasn't your first man, why should he be your last? And then . . ."

"I don't know what to say to you," Tonton tried to explain, vanquished in advance. "You're right . . . but all the same, he was the only one . . . the only one . . ."

"I know that! We've all gone through it . . . but you, you're beginning to annoy me with your whining! And then, it has to be said, you have too much pride! You ought to think a little about what you owe to me, to others . . . to weep to your heart's content, my girl, you need time and money—the great luxury, what! It costs dear, chagrin . . ."

While speaking she rummaged in her pocket, drew Tonton under a street-lamp like a mannequin, wiped her face with a violently perfumed handkerchief and powdered it with little dabs.

"And your mouth! How pale it is! Let's go!" And rapidly, rouge was applied with a brush-stroke. Tonton Mitaine extended her muzzle, meekly, her eyelids lowered, like a wax mask being painted.

Finally, Céleste having given her a little slap in the lower back in order to restore her aplomb—poor broken marionette!—they went away, toward the thirteen violets, the Boul'Mich—and Monsieur Chaton . . .

A few hours later, at the exit from the brasserie, Tonton, a little drunk, was laughing on the arm of Monsieur Chaton. He was red-faced, obese, with eyes sunk in the yellow fat of his eyelids, and a prominent snout like a pig's.

And Céleste, delighted and her soul serene, whispered in Tonton's ear: "You see, eh? What did I tell you! Here you are, consoled . . ."

PASSAGE
(*La Fronde*, 6 July 1899)

THE great forest, immobile and obscure, was tender in the silence that followed their kisses. Patches of sky no larger than hand-mirrors shone between the high branches, and in places, the green, lush and beautiful moss around them became blonde when the sunbeams rained down beneath the lightly-agitated foliage. By those signs alone they recognized the blue and magnificent afternoon that was burning the entire countryside outside the enchanted circle of the forest.

Suddenly, he said: "Look!"

She followed his gaze over the ground, docile and attentive, but sincere, and had to admit: "I can't see anything. What is it?"

"Shh! Wait . . . there . . . see . . ."

Ten paces away, a little snake was passing over that gilded moss. It was thin and black; its pale head was starred with a yellow patch . . . it looked nasty.

She said: "Oh!" very quietly, alarmed, and threw herself further back against Pierre although he was already holding her very close. Meanwhile, Pierre slowly advanced his hand toward his cane, at his feet, saying: "Don't move . . . you'll see . . ."

But at that moment the shrewd reptile turned its flat head toward them, and immediately disappeared.

"But where is it?" Suzanne cried, getting to her feet with an abrupt, nervous movement.

"Oh, doubtless far away . . . have no fear then, my beloved!"

She looked everywhere, advancing her head, lifting up her skirt with both hands, shivering all over. She murmured: "It passed just there, where I was lying a little while ago. Oh, Pierre! Let's go—quickly, quickly!"

And it seemed to her that she could never quit promptly enough that clearing bathed in shadow and gold, where their amour, a divine jewel, had found such a sweet refuge on that summer day . . .

She tore her light dress, her blue dress, on the bushes, and scraps of cloth remained hooked there, as if patches of the blue sky sustained on the poles of the high branches like a veil had fallen to the ground. She ran like a child, dragging Pierre along, who repeated:

"What folly! How nervous you are!"

"Well, yes, there, I'm nervous! What do you want? It's necessary to take me as I am."

He could have responded to that with charming—and true—things, for he really loved her; but, being nervous himself, he only found an awkward phrase: "Your friend young Yzell wouldn't be frightened like that. There's a very modern young woman! I'll wager that she would have seized my cane and killed the beast herself before I had time to think about it."

Then Suzanne stopped dead. "Since you find her so agreeable, Germaine Yzell, what prevents you, my dear friend, from consecrating your promenades to her? Don't put yourself out for me, I beg you . . ."

In her anger she appeared prettier than ever; he thought he would be truly stupid if he did not kiss her immediately—which he did, saying: "But Suze! My little Suze! When I tell you that you're foolish . . . !"

With that, a little intoxicated by sunlight, kisses, fear and irritation, Suze went on; he became tender and alarmed, and the return was worthy of the trip.

When they were on the road, however, the highway pink with the evening dust, they turned with a single movement toward the immobile and obscure forest so gentle to their kisses—and then to their silence . . . and at the same instant, they both saw again, with a slight anguish, the rapid passage of the little black snake over the golden moss . . .

GARDENER AND GRAVEDIGGER
(*La Fronde*, 13 July 1899)

*GARDENER AND GRAVEDIG*GER. Painted in black letters on a wooden board, these two words served as a sign for the little house invaded by climbing plants, amid the foliage of which pale marigolds opened like large sad eyes.

Gardener and gravedigger . . . the soil occupied his life from the bright dawn until dusk. He turned it over, excavated it, filled it in. From that soil sprang beautiful rose-bushes, which he contemplated with an amorous gaze; then those fresh roses shed their petals, returning in a light rain to the soil; and in mingling with the bitter odor of that shifted soil, it seemed the breath of the petals, like a thousand minuscule mouths, had never been so sweet.

In rosy mornings and tranquil evenings, before and after the double and uniform quotidian labor, the old man always sat down for a few moments on the bench at the threshold of his house.

The façade of the house, situated at an angle to the road and the cemetery—a road that was almost always deserted and a cemetery that had become too narrow—overlooked the countryside, the vast countryside extending in broad meadows and blonde fields all the way to the sea; and from one edge of the horizon to the other there was, on summer days, the magnificent coloration of the grass and the water that seemed to fill the world. The lush, thick grass covered the gentle slopes of the hills, invading the paths, confounded with the flowery hedges, and rising from the beach all the way to the house of the "gardener and gravedigger" like another ocean, a green ocean with enormous waves, but of a mild tranquility, an ocean, the limit of which, made of the rude plants of the coast, gray and pale yellow, with a savage and delicious odor, dissolved on the shore—a singularly delicate line—in the white foam of true waves, waves the color of nacre and pearl, waves that, further away, became a somber blue, or shiny in the sunlight; and at certain hours, all the sky over all the sea was covered by that same marvelous color like an inverted cup.

In winter, there was a mosaic of gray, washed-out tones, a frail design of dust and ash, which traced in delectably fine streaks the form of the fields and meadows, blurred the edges of the woods that accentuated the landscape with russet and mauve hues; and, prolonged as far as the beach, that architecture of dream seemed entirely duplicated and reproduced by the ripple and swell of the ocean, with the same broad calm and gray planes, and the same reflections of golden violet . . .

But of all that, the man rooted for thirty years in the little house halfway between the road and the cemetery, at an angle, saw nothing. The soil alone interested him, the heavy earth populated by a thousand ugly little beasts, blind and sly. He liked it thus, and only liked it thus. He spoke to it like a child, like a mistress. He apologized with a surly and tender familiarity for the trusts of the spade that he gave it; he announced to it the travelers that it was about to receive for an eternal sojourn, and thanked it for its flowers and its plants, for the robust verdure that it produced generously, being well-nourished. In order to live bent over it, he had adopted, and now always conserved, a broken curbed appearance, in an eternal gesture of welcoming appeal toward the soil, as if he were incessantly saying to it: "Yes, yes, I'm coming . . . here I am . . . !"

So he never looked into the distance, toward the blonde and bright horizons. He never even looked as far as the bend in the road! He knew well in advance what might be coming that way, and his curiosity knew all the corteges. As for the isolated individuals who penetrated into the enclosure, they were rare. They usually entrusted to him the care of the occupied places in the calm garden, for the road from the little town on the edge of the sea to that garden had a rather steep slope.

One autumn day, however, a young man and a young woman came along that road. They did not look very far in front of them either, so they found themselves in front of the house of the "gardener and gravedigger" without knowing exactly where they were or how they had arrived there. Seeing the roses over the hedge, the young woman exclaimed: "Oh, the beautiful roses! I'd like some!"

"That will be easy; there must be a horticulturalist here." And, perceiving the old man coming to his door by virtue of the sound of his footsteps: "We'd like some flowers, my worthy man . . ."

"Flowers? For a grave?"

The two young people started.

"What! What grave? For what grave?"

But immediately, the young woman, more attentive, exclaimed: "Oh, but we didn't see . . . it's a cemetery . . ."

"Ah! You're strangers," said the old man.

She continued: "Oh, how quiet and pretty it seems . . . let's go in, shall we?"

They went in, and suddenly, in the enclosure, the warm sunlight, the light air, all the delightful charm of that afternoon in October, seemed to become more delightful and more golden, and with the same frisson, the lovers, more smitten, agreed in the same voice, broken by amour, with similar gazes of tender languor: "Oh, how I love you!"

They affirmed amid the great silence and the perfect peace that intoxicated tumult of their being; they judged it immortal and more beautiful in contact with death and all its hideousness.

A little tree, very blonde, was weeping the gold of its branches leaf by leaf. They sat down on a flat, slightly inclined stone, slightly oppressed.

Around them, on similar stones, names and dates related the existence of a disappeared population.

They read those words mechanically, as if they were the words of a strange language. Meanwhile, the old man appeared, jealous of the order of his garden, a brown and disarticulated silhouette, like a marionette, at the corners of the pathways; and suddenly, in those two young people full of life and amour, pity was born, an immense compassion toward that other individual, whom they judged to be miserable.

"Poor man! So old and always alone here—how sad that must be!" said the woman. And, as the fellow approached, without appearing to look at them, his eyes on his rose bushes, where the last roses were growing and shining, she interrogated him in a soft voice—so soft that her lover suddenly had a sharp, absurd, insurmountable jealousy of such a seduction going toward someone other than him, even though that other was only an infimal and grotesque old man.

"Are you the only guardian of the cemetery?"

The old man, doubtless for lack of habitude, did not like talking much; obliged by politeness to reply, his little "Yes," was so curt and icy that she dared not say any more. She added, however, in a banal fashion: "That can't be very cheerful . . ."

But the old man immediately growled: "I wouldn't want a companion," and turned his hostile heels toward those people who were two, and who had arrived smiling, having stupidly asked him for his flowers . . .

His flowers! As if they were for sale, the flowers of the dead . . . his flowers! And he cast an evil glance at them through the branches . . . but *the two*, already forgetting him, were exalted by the ensorcelled and marvelous charm of the place, the hour, and themselves; and because they possessed all the grace and all the plenitude of life, the imperious and dangerous ardor of annihilation came to them quite naturally.

"Oh, to die together here . . . !" she murmured, hallucinated by the obscure vision of hours to come, less beautiful, less full, and the mad desire to escape them, to complete her happiness by death. But he escaped, and saved her from her haunting with kisses . . .

Furious at such unconsciousness, the old man returned, and with a cry like a thunderclap full of bright lightning, he said: "Leave! We're closing!"

It was a flagrant lie, for the cemetery had no gate.

Mute, they went out.

On the road, returning toward the town, the young man said: "Brrr! He isn't accommodating, the animal!"

But she, indulgent and mild, said: "Poor old man! What do you expect? *He doesn't know.*"

THE RED UMBRELLA
(*La Fronde*, 20 July 1899)

EVERY day, at three o'clock, Zizi pushed the green shutter gently and looked out . . .

From the kitchen, her mother, who saw a golden stripe on the window pane, shouted: "Zélie! What are you doing? Don't open it! The sun isn't far enough away yet."

And Zizi—ten years old, a little face with an expression of misery and suffering—closed the shutter to a crack with a sigh, keeping her eyes fixed on the section of road, bright with dust, visible from her window, from the window at which, eternally—the eternity of her short, sad and dolorous little life—she sat on an uncomfortable little chair. Zélie, almost infirm, her atrophied legs impotent to make the beautiful free movements of the children, had no knowledge of running madly along the road, adventures, climbs on the steep slopes of the mountain from which one brought back flowers and fruits with a savage and sweet taste. Zélie did not know anything, almost nothing, except the monotony of hours, which overflowed in that inert body, in the most vagabond little soul, nothing but desire, that prestigious and desolating desire!

Imprisoned in a paltry dwelling between the plaintive shrillness of her mother, overloaded with children, chores and cares, and the enervated chirping of her brothers and sisters, Zizi knew the mild folly that pushes toward impossible happiness; apart from that, a few books in which the dullest protestant morality was treated in a style devoid of brightness, and a charming artistry that she had, quite naturally, for weaving little baskets from stems of rushes or straw, Zizi did not know anything.

Every day, however, from three o'clock onwards, she was agitated by all the delicious misery of expectation, and she gazed and gazed at the dazzling bend in the road, until her eyes were burning and almost blind . . . Then, suddenly, there was the rumble of a carriage, and her heart ceased to beat, her poor little heart, with such an irregular, feeble movement. In the back of that carriage there was a woman in a white dress, with a face like a flower under a large red umbrella, with a great soft pink light over her face, a light of tranquil caress, of serene beauty . . .

Because the turning was a little steep on one side, the vehicle went slowly, and the young woman like a great red and white flower, with the double petal of a lace hat tapering into a big bow, had in that slow and quiet movement a relaxed, happy, mild expression, under the umbrella that illuminated her pale face with a reflection . . .

And always, at that vision of luxurious and peaceful loveliness, the same words came to Zizi's tremulous lips:

"Oh, how lucky *she* is!"

She: the unknown woman, the rich stranger passing through the little summer station, who paraded her lassitude or her leisure indolently in the daily excursion, which the hazard of the route had given the sick and poor child more than a friend—a dream!

Like a fabulous sun by night, that red umbrella shone in Zélie's dreams; her meager little hands reached out toward it as if toward a light and a benevolent warmth. She thought them ugly, those poor hands, and also ugly, her little jaundiced face, comparing them to the beautiful floral pink face and the delicate, nacreous hands of the young woman with the red umbrella. She did not know that without the reflection of that umbrella—carefully chosen—that face was also very pale and those hands truly too bloodless. Ignorant of that reality, Zizi could delight in the adorable charm of the appearance, intoxicated by the chimerical ambition that she too might be an enviable creature who possessed, as in a fairy tale, a carriage and a red umbrella . . .

On some days, by chance, the distracted gaze of the young woman went as far as the crack in the shutter where Zizi was spying; then Zizi's emotion was enfevered . . . and in the evening, amid all the vulgarities, she remained silent, she felt like a stranger, distant, delivered from the frightful and incessant weight of her suffering and misery, she escaped to a glorious land of dream, a little vagabond soul.

Sometimes, a charitable neighbor took Zélie and carried her down on to the doorstep in order for her to breathe a little and to be distracted by the movement of the street—but that was only ever toward evening, after the hours of work, and not at the hour when the great living flower, the lucky individual, passed by.

One afternoon, on the road a little before the bend where she was awaited, without being aware of it, with such a fervent admiration, the young woman awakened in her passage the enthusiasm of a little boy about five years old, who, returning from school, put down his basket at the side of the road and cried: "Oh, the beautiful lady!" He was very pretty, it was hot, and the basket seemed heavy—at which a caprice or whim moved the young woman to compassion; she smiled and said: "Would you like me to take you home in the carriage?"

Seized by fear and stupid with astonishment, the little boy said nothing; but in two movements, with the sort of seductive coquetry that recognizes all homages and does not disdain any, even—especially—those coming from the smallest, the young woman sat the child down facing her and gave him sous, and bonbons from a golden candy-box, amusing herself with that toy for a moment with the unconscious hidden agenda of being in that minuscule life a sort of miracle, an extraordinary event . . .

And it was in that state that they both appeared, *she* and the intruder, to Zizi's eyes . . . She thought she was dreaming . . . she believed she might die . . . What! Under the same pink reflection of the umbrella, which illuminated his paltry existence, a child almost similar to herself! Not an ornamental, foreign child—no, the child of a neighbor whom she knew! But why? How? Questions that she could not resolve—and with a strange word, a new word, which rose obscurely from her obscure little desolate soul, violent, bitter and untranslatable sentiments came to her lips:

"And I love her so much!"

She, so weary, so deprived of everything, since such a chance of happiness could exist, why had she not had her turn? And for such a long time in her memory: *the lucky woman?* Why? That too she did not know . . .

She simply suffered. And the next day, poor little soul open to dreams, she kept the window closed through which, for so many days, the light joy of a dream had come to her . . .

THE GRASS
(*La Fronde*, 27 July 1899)

FROM close to the ground, level with the vigorous thick grass—not the velvety, lustrous and almost artificial grass of the lawns of civilized gardens, no, an uneven, solid grass starred with mauve, blue, pink and gold flowers—from such a place the entire world seems singularly small and the human movement that animates it strangely futile . . .

An ant scaling a flower-head impassions a soul easily moved by symbols, and in a column of light, the ephemerae that are born and die with the hour seem an admirable image. They are floating and free pleasures of life; links more delicate than those that retain the weary body of the hectic, tall supple grass to the maternal earth, and attach the light distracted thought of the exposed fresh and beautiful grass to the interests of insects that populate a life of vertigo: a noisy, humming, turbulent and crawling life. A green frisson undulates over the plain; the branches under the blue sky, seen from so low down, and backwards, seem to be animated with a particular life . . . the soul of leaves and the heart of flowers are slowly and quietly revealed, seeming to say: "Well, yes, it's us, and this is how we are and how we feel; you've taken the time to comprehend us."

And that is a reproach, a regret and a tenderness—something human . . . without bitterness . . . speech without a voice . . . an immaterial caress—and, from such a calm vegetal mildness the

181

animal creature obtains a slight hallucination; it is then that the universe disappears . . .

And now the population of trefoils—with three or four leaves—speaks . . .

The latter, naturally, are a little scornful of the others, for having recognized on fine days delicate wrists circled with gold nonchalantly reposing on the grass. Their brother "four-leaves," envy the glory of transparent prisons of glass and, similarly wanting—the fools!—the almost-flowers that they are to become not-quite-jewels. In the hope of a searching eye they stand up straight, hoisting their frail stems above their companions, the very ordinary billions of three-leaves—in truth, the only true trefoils.

In certain places, the meadow being covered by that tenacious little vegetation, speckling it, green on green, with so many humble stars, palpitates on bright golden evenings—pale gold, the dazzling evenings of summer—with a prodigious life.

Those who stand up, marching and treading, do not see or hear anything, of course—but the others, the sage, the women, the very small, the height of grains, the asleep and the unconscious, those who abandon themselves without a struggle to the slow softness of the hours, to facile attitudes, to placid nature: all those are initiated to the tumult—how comical to want to be enormous!—that shakes the population of trefoils like a furious wind.

A recent event had plunged the four-leaves into stupor. Disdaining one of them, little pink, capricious hand had plucked a nearby three-leaf with a mischievous gesture, and with an even more mischievous voice had cried:

"A four-leafed clover? Oh, no, we don't need any more of them, it's become so banal. Me, I want a simple one, one like all the rest, a little three-leaf, and I'll answer for the good luck it will bring me."

Kisses, naturally, had responded to that deliberate choice and that bold profession of amour . . . but the population of trefoils had remained blue—if it is permissible to express it thus—and after several hours, in their language, a quivering of crumpled petals, they expressed the most degraded passions: rage, hatred, jealousy and revolt against the four-leaves; as for the others, the always-disdained, those who had pullulated, resigned and miserable, after their recent triumph they acquired the basest vanities, the souls of parvenus inflated their pretty little stems and the twin demons of pride and desire dilated the exquisite filaments of their little green foreheads to breaking point. Some of them burst! Latent rivalries burst forth and they were sensed to be furious all the way to the root—the solid little root that attached them to the soil and prevented them from throwing themselves on one another in a terrible melee!

But there is a god for the most infimal vengeances, for suddenly, a malign little breeze undulated a kind of frisson over the meadow and its invincible pressure curbed the revolutionaries in a thousand directions, and that became brutal. Then the sage—those who remained at the level of the beautiful and gentle grass—discovered with horror that a quasi-human soul, a soul of combat and hatred, lifted up those thousand little vegetal lives, so frail, so gentle and hospitable in repose . . .

"What's the matter? Did you cry out?"

"Me? yes, perhaps . . . I went to sleep and I had a bad dream . . ."

"What dream?"

"Oh, almost nothing . . . I saw a reality . . ."

"Rascal! I'm the reality, me alone, whom you love and am here beside you . . . I wasn't asleep . . . and yet I was dreaming . . . but it wasn't a bad dream . . ."

✳

"My dream, you say? Oh, it was idiotic . . ." And he recounted the struggle of the three- and four-leaves.

"You're silly," she said, simply, very tenderly. And she added: "That's what you get for having a nasty agitated soul! Personally, when I'm like this, lying in the grass"—she lay down—"with my hands knotted behind my head"—she matched her gesture to her words—"and my eyes in the blue sky like this"—she raised her eyelids—"well, I'm happy, happy! It seems to me that I'm stripped of all anxiety, that I can only see mildness, peace and happiness everywhere. And yet, you say that I'm nervous! Poor little calumniated trefoils . . ."

She separated her hands and passed them lightly over the ground, seeming to filter the grass like fresh water between her white fingers . . . and the soul of the heart and leaves of flowers enveloped them with a thousand tremulous bonds—and the whole universe appeared to them to be singularly small, and the human life that imitates it strangely futile . . .

SILHOUETTES
(*La Fronde*, 3 & 10 August and 19 September 1899)

1

MABEL LOVELY is eleven years old, with wavy hair— half by nature, half by art—eyes that are already very feminine, sold calves and the complexion of an English baby— which she was yesterday . . .

Mabel Lovely, staying in a hotel in the mountains with her father, her mother, her two sisters, her five brothers, two governesses and three "nurses," has a very accurate sentiment of life, the benefits of this world, and understands what she owes to herself and to the English nation, being very fond of football and tennis, and sufficiently anti-nervous to resist the most subtle intoxication by tea . . .

Mabel Lovely has a boy-friend.

Her boy-friend is fourteen, with red hair, broad shoulders, indefatigable feet and a heart that is certainly brand new, still poorly accustomed to nuances, and sometimes Mabel is heard to cry in a shrill little voice: "How rude you are!" Which could be translated, if one does not stick to the literal meaning, as: "You're full of asperities, my poor boy!"—for it is necessary to take account of the soul and the impulse that pushes Mabel to such an exclamation.

However, three weeks of intimacy—they spend twelve hours out of fourteen together, on average—have acted considerably upon Harry. Harry is becoming increasingly tender and less a comrade. By dint of picking magnificent violet thistles, gentians and campanulas in the mountains, they have discovered the little blue flower . . .

It is certainly very small . . . it is a nascent and fragile floret almost devoid of perfume; as such, they respire it with a charming and comical gaucherie. In the morning, Mabel, straight and flat in her costume of freshly-starched white piqué, with her boater on her bouffant hair, or, in the evening , in her muslin and tulle greenaway dress, bare-headed, her narrow feet, like swallows, in vanished shoes, smiling or grave, leads Harry by the hand in excursions or improvised dances; she leads him like a blind man, a blind athlete with wide eyes, the large eyes of a good calf or an excellent dog; and she has unexpected finesses, delightful coquetries, the mannerisms of an innocent cat, and very gently, draws him into her game . . .

And this is what happens on the day of departure. It is Mabel, in the bosom of her family, who is to go away first. Harry's heart is disagreeably constricted.

He gets up at dawn; Mabel, the day before, has given him one last rendezvous on the bench under the fir tree near the little stream that always sings. They arrive together, not having reached the age at which one or other of them will count on the fever of waiting to extract more ardor from the other.

Facing one another, they cannot find anything to say. Suddenly, abruptly and decisively (how rude), Harry takes a pen-knife out of his pocket . . .

Is he going to kill her, perhaps?

No, with great care, he engraves their two initials on the back of the bench, observing with satisfaction that they are initials of a regular design, easy to interlace correctly, then the date, and finally, very red, proffers the opinion that each of them, by way of a signature, ought to write a word—only one—containing, if possible, all the words that cannot succeed in emerging from their throats.

188

With a sign, Mabel approves, and begs him to commence.

Immediately, boldly, he finds a banal word—*Remember*—and engraves it, still with application.

Pretty, like the prettiest of English images, Mabel gazes with increasingly feminine eyes, and as soon as he has finished his little task, writes the word *Lovely*—her name—which contains everything.

And it is over. Four tears roll down the bright cheeks and the old brown wood. They go back hand in hand until the imminent hour that will separate their destinies—petty, gracious and romantic existences of a minute—which will become very English existences, regular, full of an accurate sentiment of life and the benefits of this world . . .

2

WHEN she came in, so thin, so white and bent over, like a beautiful tall pale flower with a heart rendered heavy by the water and wind of a storm, around the huge table the same mute and pitying thought seized the seventy or eighty people gathered there

Poor woman, how ill she is!

A robust young man with a brown and anxious face drawn painfully by a perpetual effort to smile followed her. Three times they changed places because the inevitable air currents necessary to maintain a reasonable temperature in the vast hall. Finally, they found a sheltered corner and sat down.

She coughed, with a charming smile that seemed to say: "Excuse me . . . I'm embarrassing you and troubling you, but I'm suffering and can't do otherwise."

She was full of grace, and docile to the cares of her companion—her husband. Around them, and because, so young, so pretty and similar to an unreal fay, that woman differed so much from the whole population of Anglo-Saxon idlers and invalids that a common accord gathered in that climacteric station, curiosity made enquiries, and soon knew that they were Parisians: a young family; and with a redoubled interest, the most adorable baby was soon seen to appear in the garden, fifteen months old, a little face to delight or make one weep, so much did he resemble the maternal face already marked by destiny for an imminent hour, with even more thin delicacy, with the same weary violet eyes that already opened to life with the same astonished and dolorous expression. And the little mouth, the little hands and the little fragile voice had all the hereditary charm in their touching appeals for tenderness, protection, toward the robust universal living force of placid nature, and that, more immediate, of humans: amour and science . . . the husband, the father, and the doctor, to whom they wanted to listen and believe when they said: "It will get better . . . hope . . . patience . . . courage . . ." Admirable words, but only words.

Days went by. From her bedroom to the drawing rooms and from the drawing rooms to the gardens, on chaises longues, among the cushions of flower-patterned silk, Madame d'Allevreuse dragged her languishing supple grace, with ever more grace and ever more languor. Next to her, incessantly, she asked imploringly for the presence of her child. "Jacques, my little Jacques, where is he? Go and fetch him. Bring him to me," she said to her husband; and when, obeying her, he went away to look for the child, the father had an expression of mortal distress and fear before the irreparable.

Afterwards, before her and the child, he insisted: "Don't take him on your knees, you'll tire yourself out . . . ! Don't kiss him so much, you'll give him a fever . . . ! Jacqueline, Linc, Linette, my beloved, listen to me, be reasonable, you know that the doctor orders repose, calm, not playing so much with our little treasure . . . I beg you . . . !"

Oh, the irresistible eyes she had then, the poor invalid, who begged in her turn, with a caressant reproach in her hoarse voice: "Oh, Georges, don't be so wicked. Let me have him; you can see that he's not tiring me out. It seems to me that all the life I've given him is returning to me through him, my jewel, my angel, my adored! It's him who will enable me to live!"

One day, to one of the chance friends that one makes in such places, where identical torments and a similar horror of solitude create abrupt, astonishing intimacies, with an untranslatable intonation of dolor, impotent rage and brutal sincerity, Monsieur d'Allévreuse confessed:

"She says that he's enabling her to live, the poor child, and she, she's killing him! She's killing him for me," he repeated, with a force of inexpressible and obscure rancor, a frightful anger against the future. After a moment, and in a low voice, he went on:

"Understand! That child born of her, of that woman I adored"—already, cruelly, he was speaking in the past tense—"whom I've watched agonizing for three years, knowing that the disease is so profound that no human aid can reach it in order to combat it, that child of my flesh and her flesh, our soul, all that she can leave me, all that will remain to me of her, I sense, I know, that she's going to take him with her when she goes!

"And how, my God! By means of her caresses, her kisses, which are poisoning the poor little innocent already poisoned at birth! Every gesture of her fever-moistened hand and every breath of her mouth over him takes him from me in the future. With him, when she's no longer here, I'll relive her agony! By isolating him right away, and with incessant care, I could protect him, keep him, save him, my child, my son. The doctor has told me that, for mingled with that blood charged with death he also carries my blood, and I'm strong, healthy. But he also told me that this love in caresses, in animal possession, this proudly exclusive love of the mother is murderous! Do you understand now why I torment the unhappy woman with my refusals, with my dreads? I can't tell her the truth, that would assassinate her, for, naturally, among her miseries, she doesn't believe in the danger! And I adore her!

"I adore both of them! Both of them! Oh, I'm suffering, I'm suffering!"

He gasped and moaned his suffering with wild movements, as if to rid himself of that evil beast attached to him—and suddenly, from the depths of the garden, the laughter of a happy little girl was heard; to which replied, like an echo, softer and weaker but similar, the delightful laughter of a cheerful, playful baby . . .

Monsieur d'Alévreuse stopped, leaned over, parted the branches, and we saw them: the mother and the child, in a ray of sunlight: beauty, innocent grace, happiness, caught in the grip of an embrace full of kisses, and he was crying: "Maman!" and she was saying: "My son!" All the purest human joy was there.

"You see, you see!" sobbed the father.

And his interlocutor, oppressed, could find nothing, not a word, for there was nothing to say.

MONA

ARE her eyes ten years old or twenty? She does not have the gaze of the little brunette girl, thin and lively, that she is, with her capricious allure of a little wild goat, but rather that of the woman she will be when her little thin face has acquired the downy and velvety softness of a beautiful bright amber fruit.

Mona is, therefore, only a little girl. She is English. However, one might believe that she is Italian; she seems to have the charming ardor, and also the nonchalance of that race. Her forename also fixes her image, like a portrait: Mona.

Mona is simultaneously slothful and ambitious; it is necessary that she learn that those are rival forces and that, if a beautiful thoughtful idleness can be fertile for artists, who prefer to action the solitary grace of their dream, it does not suit ambition.

Mona drew and wrote, she loved fixing on paper lines that seemed pretty to her and scenery that her eyes loved, and the sentiments that caused all of her strange, amusing little soul to flourish in her eyes . . .

And Mona was already thinking of the future: she wanted to be a professor in a great women's college in England. She would like that . . . she does like that . . . projects . . . dreams . . . the unconscious happiness of the being who does not know herself, but divines herself . . . a future in seed: a touching and august thing in a frail creature full of promises.

194

Here she is, camped in the direct sunlight in the meadow; she is wearing a bright red short skirt, a white blouse; she is holding her large hat in one hand and a bunch of wild flowers in the other; her brown hair, in a gust of wind, casts a great shadow over her laughing eyes. She is so fresh, so small and so gay that one smiles and one's heart softens merely by looking at her. She is called and she comes in her genteel and savage manner—she truly has something about her of the kitten and the squirrel—and with all the natural grace that she has she gives us her flowers. She is interrogated—not too much!—with a certain circumspection, for she has a slightly mutinous little soul, to the point of frankness in her expansions, and none of the naïve and gauche confidence of ordinary children.

She declares to you that she finds the years too rapid, for among all her desires, she does not desire to grow up . . . her independence would accommodate poorly to long skirts, and duties become more numerous; and as she is very shrewd, she senses that; and she also senses that her appearance, even more mischievous than her age is mischievous, serves her fantasy admirably.

Sometimes she stops in her hectic movement, and her eyes— are they ten years old, or twenty?—fix upon a passing cloud, a beautiful color posed like a tranquil caress on the mountain or the soft reflection of the waters of the lake . . . she loves those immaterial and fugitive beauties for all that she senses in them of eternity—how it would please her, with a little gesture of the hand and a little word of her thought to force those things to take on a durable and evocative life by virtue of the image and the story . . .

Will she succeed one day, little slothful and ambitious Mona?

Is there a secret that delivers those magnificent gifts to who-ever dreams of them?

Perhaps . . . but it is a secret almost as soft as amour, which blooms in the same mystery. You bear it within you, strange, amusing and moving, little Mona; it comes to you in the cloud that passes and the mild reflection of air and water, because you love that cloud and that reflection, and because, those fugitive things, you see them eternal in your eyes, which are—what age? ten or twenty?—the age of your destiny . . . of your future . . .

THE WAX STATUE
(*La Fronde*, 7 September 1899)

A great sculptor, weary of rude combats delivered over twenty years against bronze and marble, resolved to make a statue of wax.

Not finding any human model sufficiently beautiful, he modeled it on the image of his dream, so it was perfect. He finished it one winter evening, a roseate and pale dusk in February, as prompt as a flash of lightning, which filled the studio with a nacreous light, and then an ashen shadow, and everything was thus veiled and marvelous.

However, the atmosphere outside being glacial, a great fire of wood in the vast room soon made that light ardent and bloody.

Long and pale, the wax statue loomed up, distant from the fire, and from a distance, amorously, the blaze illuminated it.

The light glided, as fresh as life, over the delicate hip and the small resplendent breasts. The face of the statue, turned toward the fire, seemed to drink it avidly, through her hollow eyes, in which burned the profound beauty of the heart—which she did not have.

No drapery fettered her svelte legs; her loins were pure—and still virginal . . .

The sculptor knelt down between the flame and the statue; both were anguished by an inexpressible and divine anguish.

Sensing the animal splendor of the former and contemplating the motionless grace of the latter, he could not imagine one without the other, and it suddenly seemed to him that, separated, they would not be able to exist.

Far from the fire the statue would lose her beauty, and without the statue, the fire would go out.

It appeared to him that they loved one another: he the devouring force and she the tangible dream, and, in the folly of such an imagination, he brought the statue closer to the fire. The fire became hotter, the statue smaller; and soon, the empty eyes wept.

The limbs lost their supple grace . . .

The elegance of the skeleton appeared, admirably! But it was the skeleton, and suddenly the heart of the sculptor broke, on seeing the languor of the body.

He touched her shoulder with his finger and cried out; that shoulder of wax was hot, like flesh in a fever, and, under the pressure of his hand, the statue yielded and swooned like a woman.

He wanted to hug her, to lift her up, to adore her, but his eyes could have gone blind searching for her—she was no more . . .

Like a poor child, the great sculptor was about to weep, but a knock on his door obliged him to a beneficent calm. He opened the door and found himself facing one of his dearest friends, who, penetrating into the obscurity of the studio, exclaimed: "Of what are you dreaming, then, like this, all alone in the dark?"

Softly, with an invisible smile, the sculptor replied: "I was thinking that the flames of life consume dreams!"

The friend thought the response banal—and he was right, for there are light and profound things that the best friends cannot comprehend.

THE DESTROYED LETTER
(*La Fronde*, 24 September 1899)

AND thus, my dear amour, all alone, that night, in the country, I thought of all these pleasant things . . . oppressing in their sweetness . . .

The afternoon spent in the depths of the garden, the hour preceding your departure, slipped by so quickly into the past, into memory, I revived with an unexpected violence, and it seemed to me that it contained our entire life, our entire amour—like one of those narrow mirrors that receive the image of a whole room in its smallest details.

Charged with sadness and tenderness, gilded by the magnificent light of summer, and heavy with the storm that was already rising with coppery and blazing clouds on the horizon, it was good—was it not, my friend?—the reflection of our dear happiness full of anguish. I was entirely enveloped by those thoughts; they took me by the soul like grand passionate caresses . . . I had no fear of thunder and lightning . . . they accorded well, tearing the sky and the air, to the beating of my heart, which followed you on your route during that night, which was taking you away from me. A strange thing! I did not feel very clearly the sharp pain of the separation . . . I loved you so much—understand me well—at that moment that I did not sense your absence. Can you comprehend all this, my love? Does it not cause you pain?

The house was shaken by the wind like a vessel at sea. I had left my shutters open and at every instant the room was filled with the vivid glare of lightning flashes . . . Yes . . . I loved that torment, that almost-danger, when I suddenly found myself awakened from that sort of voluptuous torpor . . . and, standing up, trembling and desperate, I had only one desolating obsession . . . You remember that yesterday I had taken several of your letters into the garden in order to reread some of them with you . . . you know in what deliciously intoxicated memory that reading had plunged us . . . then I had gathered them all together preciously . . . but suddenly we perceived that you were late, and departed quickly. As we went away I turned my head and looked back at the place we were quitting, and I saw on the ground a little piece of white paper: it was one of the letters, fallen there . . .

We were in a hurry, and I didn't want to lose a single minute of your presence; that is why I didn't return immediately to pick it up, to fetch it. Oh, how I regret it and bemoan it now, that moment of delay, negligence at first, and then forgetfulness, for, having returned from the station, utterly absorbed and absent—had you not extracted me from myself and taken me with you?—I shut myself in my room, where the night surprised me immobile . . . still having my hat on!

Almost immediately, the storm burst. I went to bed, too weary and too enervated to have dinner, and it was only in the middle of the night that I suddenly saw my poor letter again in thought—*your* letter—lost there in the garden under that frightful rain, and, who knows, perhaps carried far away by the wind. Then I burst into sobs, into tears . . . Alas, the full consciousness of my solitude, of your departure—that terrible reality!—finally came to me, and I suffered, oh, I suffered in an intolerable fashion!

It seemed impossible to me that it could be true, that so many dolors could afflict me at the same time: your absence and the loss of one of your letters, of those first ancient letters. But I wanted to know which one might be missing . . . surely one of the most tender, of the most beautiful, of the most adored, since they all were, for me . . .

Trembling, I picked up the packet again, leafed through them, rereading again, always, and as their dates and what they contained of trivial facts are living and burning things for me, I very quickly realized—with what constriction of the heart!—the identity of the one that had disappeared . . . immediately, I sensed that it was really the one, in fact, that I treasured most profoundly, the favorite, the most cherished of all.

Then—don't scold me!—no longer able to stand it, I wrapped myself up as best I could and I went out to go and search for it immediately . . . in the dread of not being able to find it. I did not feel either the wind or the rain.

Finally, I arrived at the place, so calm and so pleasant only a few hours before . . . who would have recognized it?

A broken tree branch blocked the pathway; the ground was covered with leaves riddled by hail! By the light of lightning-flashes I searched, painfully, feverishly, desperately—for how could I find the exact place? Everything was ravaged and turned upside-down by the hurricane. But there are miracles in amour—we know that well!—and beneath my rain-soaked hand I encountered my letter! Oh, my poor, poor letter! In what state it appeared to me when I had looked at it—as I would have looked at you, I believe!—by the light of my lamp in my bedroom. Undoubtedly, it was really the one—that rag of paper was really the one that you had employed to write to me, but where were the words traced by your hand? Illegible! Dissolved by the rain, annihilated . . .

Oh, how chagrined I am, my love; if you knew! But you cannot know, cannot understand what I have experienced before that destroyed letter . . . the sentiment that pursues me, haunts me, maddens me before that shred! I'm afraid . . . yes, afraid, as if I have clearly seen our amour, our dear great amour, afflicted in that . . . wounded, irreparably depleted. Oh, I know full well, you're smiling in reading this, you're saying that I'm mad, and you're right . . . but what do you expect? I am thus . . . I think thus—in sum, I'm suffering. You can't change that . . .

✳

And she added a thousand more things, crazier and crazier and more and more amorous.

That letter, not destroyed, reached the lover. In reading it, he murmured:

"Oh, yes, she's crazy! It will be necessary, however, that I make her understand one day how much she bores me with these exaltations and exaggerations!"

THE AUTUMNAL HOUR
(*La Fronde*, 5 October 1899)

FROM the golden sky, the great sky of pale silk crumpled into a thousand pleats by threads of pink cloud, slate-blue shadows and nacreous white; from velvet clouds extended over the infinite horizon; and from the blonde branches of trees, where autumn leaves rained down, frail and light, like butterflies, like improbable flowers cut out from rich, worn fabrics; from all that changing splendor and that slow vanishing of nature, a bleak sadness was exhaled: a sadness charged with languor like an amorous fatigue, a sadness similar to a desire, a frenetic nostalgia to savor in such a décor some superhuman happiness, an immortal forgetfulness of the fleeting brief hour . . .

That mild autumn dusk in which a little warm wind blew, which seemed to murmur incomprehensible words among the trees, gave an incredible ardor to life, to devour that short and infinite life, to fill it as one fills in a profound and obscure grave. With what flowers? with what mud? No matter!—but to escape the maleficent enchantment of the void, of nothingness and the irreparable that seizes us in that season and the agonizing hour that dies with such charm under the golden sky and the blonde branches . . .

It was in such a sentiment of extreme violence and heartbroken tenderness that Simone suddenly stopped walking in order to press her heart with both hands, with a sigh similar to a sob.

"Oh . . . ! Oh . . . !" she murmured, with a sort of nameless, causeless, goalless despair.

Where was she going? And what was she doing here, in this deserted place in the country, having escaped from the enveloping movement of her animated house, where twenty people around her pampered her, loved her and amused her—sometimes. The terraces and the park had not sufficed for her abrupt and imperious desire for air and for space, and so, before her, straight ahead and all alone, into the distance, she had gone . . .

At first she had hoped to calm in that rapid march, in that appeasing solitude, the strange enervation and melancholy that had been breaking her dully with stabbing impulses, like a physical pain, for several days. But instead, on the contrary, her ill-feeling had increased, increased continually, until the moment that she stopped in order to groan aloud in a high-pitched voice, with a gesture of extinguishing her soul in her breast, in order to make it shut up, the disordered and impatient soul that was weeping like a feeble and sickly child . . .

Simone: thirty-two years old, a fine slender and youthful face, tender eyes and a beautiful mouth, amid dark hair, relaxed in fluid waves of light alongside the little pink ears and the delicate neck.

Supple and neat, with a svelte and bold figure, enveloped by a long ash-gray mantle and coiffed with a pink silk hat as pretty as a flower, in delightful harmony with the sky and the hour, Simone appeared to be going thus, mysterious and charming, to some amorous rendezvous where she knew that invincible amour would make her suffer.

She seemed to know in advance, the young woman with sad eyes, that her lover was no longer amorous, and for that reason he would be, even in his affectionate pity, his silences and his slightest banal words, infinitely cruel . . .

To the right and left of the fields, red and mauve trees enveloped by glory and softness undulated, drawing the softest and gentlest lines all the way to the horizon. In the pale sky, little pale spirals of smoke in the distance revealed human presences and humble dwellings. Those gray fumes, frail and warm in the fresh and fine air like blue spun crystal, were in Simone's eyes a complete symbol of life: labor, ardor, the hearth . . .

A crow rose up nearby from the ditch on the edge of the road with a cry; she shivered, and her memory suddenly quivered, tore and opened:

A distant evening, at this same hour, in the same season, in an analogous place—an isolated and crepuscular countryside—she had walked with a similar passionate languor . . . a melancholy as vivid . . .

How many seasons had passed since that season? She counted: seven years.

She was not alone then. All of her soul and all of her flesh were supported and sustained by a proximal heart and body.

She murmured a name.

What name?

What did it matter? The name of the person one loves is always the same, various syllables taking on the value of a unique word, of an almost supernatural meaning.

And yet she had forgotten that name a long time ago; in her memory it had been a name that had become similar to a thousand other names—had not the very memory been covered slowly and unconsciously by so many new cares? Had she not been, after the separation—a separation without rupture, which external, omniscient events had decided, without her or him having the necessary passionate energy to vanquish the events and make the separation impossible—had she not been simply, and, oh my God, *almost* purely, a very pretty woman, loving amour as one loves an art, without splendor, without exclusivity, without sentimental or sensual violence; had she not, with delicate gestures and subtle words, woven the most exquisite existence?

Alongside secret sweetness, had she not had estimable affections, and the strongest chains of her heart, she firmly believed she had riveted to the two fragile little lives issued from her: her children, whom she loved with adoration. Was that not happiness? And how such frail things coalesced: the color of a cloud that floats and disappears, the fugitive breath of October under the gold of leaves already dead and the hazard of a horizon seen before; had they such a magnetic power over her soul and her senses that, attracted here, she was suddenly able to feel so irreparably alone and desperate, sunk in such a nostalgia that she sobbed and fell into the grass and the dust of the road as if her heart was about to break?

Now she recalled the whole of the distant hour: how she had loved, her amour—and then, how she had ceased to love him; and, from that, what bitter, infinite regret! Oh, how, one autumnal evening, while nature, the day and the hour were agonizing, they had both sensed so ardently, one in the other and one for the other, that the entire universe seemed concentrated in them alone—forever. She had wept with happiness; full of tender sweetness, he had understood her tears.

More profoundly and perfectly than in the embraces, their hearts had embraced, and they had exhausted their mouths in kisses . . .

Other tendernesses, other kisses and other décors had been able to pass and sink into the perfect oblivion into which only that which never really existed falls; but that minute, reawakened and tenacious, really was the great wound of amour, which does not heal.

Among many joys and pleasures, how to recover that hour and live it, to drink it again as one drinks a strong wine?

Something troubled floats before Simone's veiled eyes; on the deserted road, she imagines the ancient image, and feels herself becoming cold, disenchanted, unsatisfied . . .

She evokes other companions of a similar dream. But to play that role they are incomplete, and she is not serious.

In the distance, a bell chimes: an appeal devoid of melody. Simone murmurs: "Dinner! I'll be late . . ."

She goes back, she runs . . . the golden sky is black. She senses her face, pale, ardent and distraught. She wonders whether she can go in without being seen . . .

She no longer had time to stop to calm her disordered and impatient soul, which was weeping like a feeble and sickly child . . . and she even had a singular kind of fear, as if she knew full well that that soul was going to fall silent again, quickly, soon leaving her, for long hours, days and years, devoid of memory, devoid of dolor, devoid of that brief and infinite life that one would like to fill in as one fills in a profound and obscure grave—with what flowers? with what mud . . . ?

FORTUNE
(*La Fronde*, 12 October 1899)

"DO you believe in chiromancy?"

"I don't know, but I believe in chiromancers."

"How's that?"

"Listen . . . Three friends, young and strong, were walking one day in the country. One of them, a charming fellow, a painter full of talent—one can say that since he's dead—sees something red and brown in a field. He asks one of his companions: 'What's that, a flower or a monkey?'

"'Perhaps both,' replies the second, 'it's a woman . . .'

"'And it's even a gipsy,' says the third.

"'That's good,' says the first, 'we'll have some fun.' And he calls to the woman and asks her to tell their fortunes.

"She's a beautiful, lively creature who smells good. The charming fellow—we'll cal him André to simplify things, if you wish—willingly recognizes her qualities, but treats her with a certain scorn, or, rather, with a scornful certainty. He argues and jokes, and treats all the gipsy's predictions regarding his two companions ironically, and when she asks him in his turn for his hand, in order to read it, he puts it in his pocket, clowning, and swearing that he won't let it be taken for such an absurd and grotesque game, and that he'll save it for a better occasion.

"Then the woman throws herself upon him, seizes his other hand, which is holding a cigarette, tears away that burning cigarette with her teeth, remains leaning for two seconds over the open palm while he continues laughing and declares: 'In a year, to the day, at one o'clock in the morning, you will die a violent death.'

"Then she disappeared . . ."

Having spoken thus, Gustave Mardochée stopped

"And then? And then?" demanded a dozen women, with interest.

They had dined well, felt pretty, and desired to experience a little fear.

"Then, it was the twentieth of October. André immediately invited his comrades to supper for the twentieth of October of the following year, in order that at one o'clock in the morning they could all drink together to their reciprocal good health

"And that was agreed.

"The year was very clement to André. He had a charming mistress who was only unfaithful to the extent necessary to animate his amour, rapid success, almost as much money as he spent, and his health was perfect.

"He therefore felt that his muscles were supple and solid, his soul serene and light. The friends of the previous year and others were invited on the appointed day to his studio, converted into a banqueting hall.

"By virtue of a hazard that no one could explain subsequently, or a malice whose author was never revealed, the big clock was set forward an hour that evening. Thus, it was in reality at midnight that, deceived by the chime and drunk on words, cheerful youth and blonde wine for an hour, the young folk drank a joyful toast to their comrade in defiance of the sinister prediction.

"Then, some time afterwards, they all departed together with the last *au revoirs* to their host, who, from the threshold of the small pavilion he occupied at the end of a garden in the Rue Lepic, illuminated their way, holding a lighted lamp high. When they reached the gate to the passage, André went back.

"But before they had passed through the gate and closed it again, and a single stroke rang out in the night from a church bell, they were stopped by a frightful scream—the cry of a beast with its throat cut—and then nothing more: silence.

"When they returned to the pavilion they saw their friend lying dead in the studio full of light, flowers and the disorder of the supper . . ."

"My God! Dead!"

"But of what?"

"But how?"

"Had he killed himself?"

"Had he been murdered?"

"But by whom?"

"But why?"

"But how?"

They were all talking at the same time, shivering, shocked, ravishing and pale . . .

"A dagger-thrust in the heart," said Mardochée.

The interrogations resumed.

"I don't know—and no one ever knew any more—but as I said, I believe in chiromancers . . ."

And he was content, his story having pleased.

They heard in one corner: "Oh my dear, what horror!"

And further away: "No, no, it's very feminine!"

And, some wit in the gathering, having declared that he knew something about the lines of the hand, instantly received an offering of a host of hands, like a rain of flowers . . .

THE IMMATERIAL RIVER
(*La Fronde*, 19 October 1899)

THE night, as soft and sad as a woman who senses the light of her beauty agonizing within her, descended over the closed windows. Only the bright or pale things in the bedroom still held faint reflections of the dying daylight, and in such a strange fashion that one could not tell whether the radiance came from those things or the daylight.

Among the bright things: eyes; among the pale things: hands.

And the aged great artist, sprawling, warmly wrapped in a fur blanket, where he had been immobilized for weeks, nailed there by a dislocation of the ankle, complicated by rheumatic pains, the celebrated painter lowered his eyes, still vivid in his ravaged face to his hands, still singularly alive, which stood out sharply and palely and the thick dark fur.

Having been so handsome in a prolonged youth, he had had beautiful young hands, long supple hands with nervous fingers, hands sculpted like works of art, from which the delightful art of his oeuvre had flowed.

He gazed at those hands—his own—with a sort of anxious curiosity, like the hands of a stranger. It seemed to him that he had not seen them for a long time: those swollen veins, designed like a frail skeleton, doubling the bone structure, had become apparent since he had become thin; those knotty articulations deforming the fingers that had become numb, as if shrunk . . .

He moved those fingers, lifted that hand—how slow they were! how heavy it was!—and he let it fall back . . .

His eyes went to the window: an adorable sky, as delicate as a large unfolded veil, a sky in which invisible flowers were shredded in flakes of blue and mauve petals, a great sky of light ash and blonde smoke, undulated like a sheet of cloth fastened to the corners of black roofs and the edges of gray walls . . . It was the sky of Paris in that October twilight, a marvelous and lamentable thing, an exquisite thing, which one sensed so fleeting, so frail and so beautiful that one was seized, before such fragile grace, by a desire and a violent despair: to retain the image, and then to see it again, to sense forever the unexpected charm of the nevermore!

But that smoke, that ash-gray, that drowned gold, that mist of a blue washed and washed again seemed not to be descending from the great sky on to the poor earth, but rather to be rising from the stones of the city, from the fever of the streets, from souls, from the hair and the eyes of the women of the city and the street, toward the inaccessible sky, in order to bring it closer, make it more human, more changeable and more miraculous . . .

The living soul, infatuated with the ambient and pretty life, and the sharpened senses of the great artist, quivered . . . By means of an effort of will he leaned over, and through the closed windows he looked toward the road as wide as a square, the road dappled with light, multicolored by decomposing shadows, which the rapid crowd activated with a prodigious fire of movement, which sprang in invisible flames from mortal eyes, from down below to up above, in order to make that adorable sky of pale flowers, that ragged sky like a gauze, the sky of Paris with which the city enveloped itself in order to sleep with the voluptuousness of a prostitute and a queen accumulating the stream of her sovereign ornamentation . . .

The artist's eyelids fluttered, his hands trembled . . . he had loved all those fugitive and profound things so much, which are the soul of the world and make the soul of a work of art. His own work was entirely infatuated, impregnated and saturated with the dissolved frisson of that life, as a being dissolves and is saturated by amour.

So many images had passed through his eyes thus, and when those images had pleased him, like the color and the impalpable and floating heart of the present moment, the joy of his eyes had always been animated by a palpable existence . . .

The adorable river of lines and shades had filled and overflowed his nervous hands and had gone to enchant eyes without number, forming the gentle shores of art where peoples repose and slake their thirst.

This evening, an agitation lifted those two hands, which became so pale and so alive in the shadow. Like idols, supernatural and sacred individuals . . . They went toward the dying and tender light, toward the fleeting moment, toward the immense swell of life, which they wanted to seize as one would like to seize a beautiful wild bird that passes over the ocean with a cry of anguish . . . oh, to materialize with a gesture that wants and creates, the divine fever of the dream . . .

The great artist sighs for the first time, with violence, he senses the energy of the omnipotent and immediate will stealing away before his desire; he sighs and suffers bitterly, for now the moment is dead, and the room is black, and his hands have remained inert and nothing will remain of the delectable vision . . .

Suddenly, a door opens, the light of lamps and the sound of human voices break the maleficent melancholy, and there are charming visitors around the master, an entire petty court of female admirers, who bow and smile, and evaporate and exhale a youthful perfume of incense and grace within the room, in which the thought of the great artist, momentarily alighted in sadness like a bird on the edge of an obscure wood, can revive and respire; he is animated, he is happy, his hands, in prompt harmonious movements, design his rapidly and colored ideas in impalpable lines.

Observing such gestures admiringly, someone remarks on the inexpressible beauty of those hands, which become singularly young and active again; in a few words, it is suggested that the initial point of the master's melancholy was a little while ago; then the latter opens his hands wide in the light; the light seems to filter through his fingers like a golden veil; gold marvelous in beauty, gold filling his life as the sun fills a beautiful day from dawn to sunset, gold of a royal fortune glistening in the sparkling shimmer of his changing and sumptuous fantasy—and before that multiple symbol there is a silence, a great silence similar to that of a forest at midday, made of all the breaths of life and the swell of all saps.

And suddenly, the master, with a tender and triumphant mockery: "Ah! Christi, my children—and they will work again!—you can see that!"

THE OLD KNIFE
(*La Fronde*, 26 October 1899)

"WHERE did you find it?"

"In the garden, among the debris of the summer-house that was demolished yesterday."

They held the old knife between them in a ray of sunlight under the fan-like caress of a Bengal rose-bush. It was shiny . . . it was not pretty, but it was curious.

"What might it have cut?" René interrogated, in a low voice, with a mild and dreamy expression. "Game or throats?"

"Oh, what horror! How disgusting you are, my love! What a perverse imagination you have!" she cried, with a charming expression of fear. "And I wanted to have it cleaned, and was already thinking of putting it in the vestibule in a panoply, with your weapons!"

"Have it cleaned! Never in my life! Leave it with those beautiful rust patches, which make the intact places stand out more clearly—and then, perhaps it's blood, you see . . . that's sacred . . . You see, dear, that rusty brown stuff on the metal, rough to the touch. That was blood, fine young blood, fresh and warm, odorous and strong . . . No, no, let's keep it as it is, this old knife. I'm going to put it on the table in our bedroom, and one night it will tell us its story—a terrible story, surely! Think about it: a knife found on the Spanish frontier, buried amid the foliage and the rotten wood of a summer-house ornamented

215

with amorous arabesques at the bottom of the old garden of that old property! Yes, yes, a terrible story with many kisses and a great deal of violence! You'll see, you'll see!"

"Oh, René, how can you? You're wicked, you're scaring me. I'll always see that frightful knife between our kisses now!"

"No, no, Madame!" And changing his tone: "But you're mad, my dear."

"It's you who are mad, with your ideas!"

"Do you think so?"

Yes, the same double phrase . . .

Now he applied his finger to her forehead between the two eyebrows, crying: "Ah! Ah! Who can tell me, who can know, what there is in there? There!" Then, immediately, with an insouciant whistle, he turned away, picked up the weapon, and with a single stroke, he scythed a sheaf of roses, which he held out to his mistress with an air of humble adoration.

She took them, smiled, reassured, and looked at the old knife with a shrewd and victorious gaze. The old knife looked back at her with its bright, invincible reflection.

Indulgently she said: "Go on, go and find its place, your trinket!"

And in fact, they were installed in that house in the middle of the Basque country with a thousand sumptuous and useless things, as if to live there for long years before dying there in an infinite union. It was, however, nothing but a lover's caprice, the sojourn in that rude, savage and charming land.

His desire as an artist and her amorous grace made an eternity of that caprice in dream. That is the entire secret of human happiness: to believe it to be long when it is inevitably short.

In their bedroom, when the evening of amber and roses came in through windows open over the sea, to the west, like a victorious young prince charged with all the harvests of glory and spring, a few hours later, when they got up from embraces full of languor and ardor, he had not yet chosen the place where he would exhibit the old knife . . .

And other similar evenings went by, broad rivers of light; and other morning palpitated in frissons of foliage and wings around the house—a seasonal retreat—which they made heavy with an amour as impetuous as a hurricane. And between those evenings and mornings, the nights lived, insomniac and stormy.

She, totally tender and totally supple, was the queen of caresses—and the slave of her master's fits of anger . . .

He did not spare her one or the other, exalting himself to the worst follies of laughter and despair, while she, an incomparable lover, showed herself more malign and more seductive, in the fashion of a she-cat with an unexpected humor.

That was because, even in that isolated land, she had been able to create her realm of bewitchment, and he held everything against her. He wrote willingly, on such subjects, cruel and defective verses. She approved—impenetrably.

But his manners outside testified to an independence and an increasing impatience with the already-ancient yoke.

One morning, René said to her: "Last night, while you were asleep, the old knife told me its story . . ."

"Oh!" she said turning her brunette head on her naked shoulders. "Tell me, will you?"

"It's just that it's a frightful story . . . you won't be afraid?"

"No, no, I've become very brave; haven't you perceived that?"

"Listen, then: a long time ago, there was a young and pretty girl who lived in the village nearby. She brought fruits and vegetables to the owner of the house in which we're presently living. That man was old, rich, debauched and generous.

"Now, a young Spanish smuggler being smitten with Haleja—the young and pretty girl—she responded with kisses to his amorous words. Our lover was happy.

"He dreamed of marrying Haleja in order to possess her more fully, he said . . . but one evening, as he was passing behind the hedge at the bottom of the garden that you can see through those windows, as he was going along without thinking about anything but her beauty and his smuggling business, a voice nailed him to the ground; he listened. It was Haleja who was speaking . . . and she was speaking to the rich and debauched old man, and she was talking about him, her young lover, and what she said made him turn the point of his knife on himself, the man she was betraying, instantly, full in the heart.

"That instant, as rapid as lightning, having passed, Haleja and the old man saw a terrible and somber figure appear on the threshold of the voluptuously-illuminated summer-house with the amorous arabesques, whom Haleja scarcely recognized . . .

"She recognized him as she died, when the blood from her young breast inundated the body, already stiff, of her old lover, at her feet . . ."

René stopped. Calm, loosening and tightening her dark hair over her dazzling throat, the young woman said: "And that's all?"

"You're not content?"

"Oh, yes; it's a very, very pretty story—albeit a little banal; but well-arranged, as you know how to do—in a short story, it would be nice . . ."

"Wouldn't it?"

When the sun rose the following morning, the lover had finally found the right, the unique place for the old knife. He had planted it like a jewel in the breast of his mistress, and young fresh blood covered the dark patches of rust . . .

THE WOMAN RELUCTANT
TO LEAVE PARIS
(*La Fronde*, 2 November 1899)

FIVE O'CLOCK. The hour when Paris is prey to its quotidian fit of fever; when, after the great frisson of dusk, which, on beautiful evenings lights up in fireworks, all green and pink, a sky of enchantment; when, after the palpitation of anxiety, of the *petit mort* that comes to us with the death of the sun, an ardor hotter than the warmth of life invades the people and the streets.

And the latter, symbolic with their lights and their mud, attach the former, having become less conscious, submissive to the atmosphere.

This evening, one of those streets at a corner of the boulevard, and one of those people, stationed there and stamping her feet, seemed so similar in essence that Lise Dorée, on the threshold of the shop where she was waiting for her carriage, forgot herself, in one of those rapid and eccentric imaginations that were habitual to her, to the extent of expressing a profound and dolorous sympathy for the life of the person in question: a woman.

A woman who, doubtless having found herself too pale—her skin drained of blood, as old age, hunger and amour do—was too heavily made up. Her cheeks shone like false gems; her eyes, which desired to be vivid, welcoming and inviting, seemed absent, going toward something invisible, an unknown, far from the enormous décor of the quotidian labor, too heavy for that pitiful little body, almost that of a child. And the mouth—oh, the mouth, looked as if it had been made and remade carefully in order not to appear—which it was—desolate. The corners of the lips, heightened and sculpted in vermilion, designed on that poor, delicate, young and faded face, so expressive in spite of so much real life, terribly human and tragic, the mouth of a doll, the artificial, bloody mouth of a mask. Around that face, a tired Mongolian fur and the large brim of a velvet hat put a halo of pitiful luxury.

"Madame's carriage is here . . ."

Lise Dorée shivered. In a little dazzle of her beautiful large passionate eyes, which always retained such a voluptuous sadness even in joy; between her—all in sable, supple fabric and pink flowers—and the creature waking ten paces away from her, she had just seen another woman pass: herself, much younger, when, poor, vibrant and delectable, she had known, in all their misery and magic, the follies of evenings like this one.

"That's good . . ." And before his surprised eyes, she advanced toward the young woman who was too heavily made-up because she was too pale, and said, abruptly: "You seem to be fatigued and suffering? Are you going far? Would you like me to take you in my carriage?"

She is conscious herself of the apparent ludicrousness of the step, and, in fact, almost immediately after an initial stupor, sees an ambiguous supposition rise into her eyes.

But those thoughts are so prompt and the movement around her so rapid that they act first; they can be explained later.

Anyway, what does she want? What is she doing? What does Lise Dorée want, above all, from this woman who is now beside her in the victoria—Lise, huddled in her furs, likes the rudeness of these icy evenings—observing her covertly, understanding poorly, not understanding at all . . .

But Lise understands everything, and, half laughing and half serious:

"I'll tell you . . . someone that I loved very much . . . often suffered during the winter, in Paris, without my being able to do anything about it . . . you resemble that person . . ." Lise was lying; she had never resembled that poor, slightly bewildered, humble, effaced and maladroit creature.

She interrogated: "What's the matter with you? What do you do?"

Then the other, with a touching naivety: "What do I do? What am I? Oh, Madame can see very well . . ."

"You're not from Paris?"

"No, Madame.

"Undoubtedly . . . that's obvious too . . ."

The other becomes embroiled in explanations, in confused words. Lise Dorée glimpses a calm and narrow province, monotonous days, and beyond, all around, the great horizon of the countryside, pure, green and blonde. She has similar mirages in her own memory.

"Why don't you go back there?" she says,

"Oh, I don't want to leave Paris!"

At that exclamation Lise Dorée shivers. She leans forward, with more curiosity and even more pity. Around them, the swell of Paris seems to rise, rocking and bearing the carriage softly and vertiginously at the same time, gliding along the boulevard like a boat along a river. The ocean of human faces and lights, at the level of the two women engulfed in the profound vehicle, overflows and immerses them all the way to the shoulders—all the way to the soul.

"Ah? You don't want to leave Paris? You love someone here?"

"No . . . no . . ." The voice is low, the expression weary and sincere.

"You want to go into the theater, perhaps?"

The other did not perceive the involuntary tone of bitter irony.

"No . . . no . . . at least, I don't think so . . . I don't know . . ."

Lise Dorée suggested a few more possible, probable mirages. And to all of them, there was the same definitive syllable in response: "No . . . no . . ." followed by the timid, irritating, stupid: "I don't think so . . . I don't know . . ."

At that dialogue, Lise's bold and impatient mind became enervated and scornful . . . and then her heart took on a pity even more profound; her heart was ashamed of her mind. And it was against herself that she turned her scorn.

What was that if not egotism, of the most secret and the strongest kind—the one that transposes us with another, supposedly in order to make us feel sorry for and love her, but in reality to be better able to love and feel sorry for oneself? What was it, if not that narrow and paltry sentiment, under its multiple forms, that had made her seize this creature in passing, in order to confess her and take an interest in her, in one of those unexpected, apparently disruptive, impulses that were familiar to her?

She gazed more intently at the stubborn little face of the woman, her square chin, her stupid mouth, her vague eyes, and repeated without conviction:

"You ought to leave Paris . . ."

"No . . . no . . ."

"But why? What is it that retains you here so strongly?"

"I don't know . . . Everything . . . all this . . ."

She made a circular gesture.

Lise Dorée did not insist. She was still mocking herself a little internally for her rage for salvation. She also thought: *I can't do anything* . . . No, nothing except insignificant, temporary material aid; only the gift of a momentary respite. And when, with a practical good sense and tact, she had made arrangements with her companion of an hour—the sister of old, the stranger of tomorrow—to act thus, when she found herself alone again, traveling toward her own tasks, her own pains, Lise Dorée grasped again the phrase dated in exclamation:

"I don't want to leave Paris!"

That cry had been her own, that speech was the one carried their hearts, clenched and exalted, by how many other individuals in the enormous crowd!

She had justified that desire, not only by her beauty, which had woven the amorous and luxurious story of her life, but also by her soul of an artist, which had embellished that story with details of glory, independence and fantasy . . .

Many others had followed that same arid and enchanting route, and, telling in her memory the rosary of celebrated names, she found in almost all of them a savor of the soil: the country, the province, the frontier territory, the incessant and forceful alluvion of Paris . . .

But how many had been assassinated by the same burning fever that enabled the energetic beauties to live?

And they were the ones similar to the little girl drawn momentarily from anonymity just now—too many narrow chests adapting poorly to the dust, tottering wills yielding lamentable to all impacts, the latent sloth of flaccid souls: mortal maladies!

And all of them—all of them, both the conquerors and the vanquished—had one day, one evening, prey to the great frisson of the *petit mort*, the devouring ardor that exalts Paris in the crepuscular hour, shouted: "I don't want to leave Paris . . ." because they had the city in their blood and skin, like a creature; and they were prepared to die, even wretched, mad or degraded, but they no longer wanted to live elsewhere . . .

ALMOST INVISIBLE
(*La Fronde*, 9 November 1899)

WITH a silky sound the sea stirred, slow and invisible under the great pale sky, the dying color of the new moon. On the horizon, in a frail and violet line, the mountains seemed to be dreaming, and amid so much profound shadow and light clarity, a single bright light burned and shone: that of the lighthouse to the right, which illuminated in rays as rhythmic as the swing of a pendulum the sea and the sky.

From the beach, behind the breakwater, came the refrain of a waltz; the echo of an orchestra whose full sound was carried from another coast by the breath, very contained and warm that night, of the wind blowing from the south-west.

They remained silent, leaning on the broad stone parapet, alone at the tip of the breakwater. The chime of a bell counted eleven strokes, which quivered and died in the extreme immobility of the night; the hour seemed to pass overhead thus, with a flap of wings, like a great bird, and then disappeared, flown toward other oceans, other shores . . .

A group of people paused momentarily at the entrance to the jetty. They were talking loudly and laughing; the pure and sonorous atmosphere carried the echo of their words as far as the two friends; they were insignificant, puerile words—large pebbles thrown into the calm splendor of the admirable night, and then disappearing also, falling into oblivion . . .

Thus those faint echoes of life made it seem as if that life itself had never existed . . .

Jacques and Pierre summarized their sensation in a few words:

"It's beautiful."

"Yes . . . and what brutes, those people . . ."

Then, all that could not be said was expressed in a double sigh.

However, they were fortunate.

Their life was good; they were not subject to present chagrin. They were young enough, and in robust health.

"All the same, old man, eh?" said Pierre.

"Well, yes," replied Jacques, in a melancholy tone.

And they knew one another sufficiently for such banal words to be intimate and entire confidences.

As the sky became darker—the moon was dying on the horizon—the stars became brighter.

With reflections of red, pink, white and green gems, they dotted the water like a swarm of fireflies.

Footsteps resounded on the paving stones. The two men turned round.

From the obscurity accumulated behind them like heavy creases of black cloth, a small bright and delicate form emerged: a woman.

But she could not see them, for, in dark garments they were confounded with the night.

The woman was walking slowly, with pauses and returns, sometimes leaning on the iron rail of the bridge that led to the sculpted rocks of a breakwater. She too was gazing at the magic of the night: the almost invisible sea was visible to her, and the great pale sky dazzling . . . or perhaps she had arrived first at some rendezvous?

Jacques and Pierre had that same thought at the same time, and a scruple: they were in excess, they found themselves indiscreet, awkward, ashamed. They suddenly desired to be able to slip away without their presence even being suspected, for they imagined sharply the disappointment of the lovers at not finding this delightful location for their amour deserted. In the absolute and complicit beauty of the great ambient charm, they represented a human gaffe . . .

But it was impossible to withdraw without being seen, since it would be necessary to go past the woman . . .

They waited, without budging, reserving the option of making their presence known on the arrival of the probable partner, and they gazed with eyes that, adapted to the darkness, were sharpened by attentive curiosity. But the partner did not come—and perhaps was not expected . . . Perhaps it was simply a nostalgia for solitude, an anxious caprice, a secret dolor or an avid desire for the immensity that had brought the woman there that night. She had drawn gradually closer, and they could see her more clearly.

Young? Pretty?

Without a doubt! At least, they wanted to believe it, for love of harmony, and nothing apparent forbade such suppositions.

Her stride was light and supple, the movement of her arms and head full of grace. She wore a dress of bright fabric and an elegant mantle, the ribbons and flounces of which enfolded the evidently slim body well. Around the invisible face, a patch scarcely paler than the pallors of her clothing, one divined beneath the raised borders of the hat a cloud of soft dark hair. In the shadow, the unknown woman seemed a silhouette so frail and bright as to be almost unreal.

Pierre said in a whisper: "No, she isn't waiting for anyone . . ."

"How do you know?"

"She hasn't turned once toward the beach . . ."

"That's true; she's only looking toward us . . ."

"Whom she can't see."

"No matter . . . it's a fortunate augury . . ."

"I . . ."

But what he was about to say was cut off abruptly.

A voice rose up: a song, a lament, an appeal? Who could tell?

The unknown woman sang; and with the same frisson, Pierre and Jacques understood that they possessed, there in the inviolable and supreme beauty of the night, something even more supreme and even more inviolable: the soul of a woman exhaled in complete liberty in the unusual enchantment of a marvelous voice.

She sang tears of sensuality . . . the light laughter of delirium, infinite unconscious desires, oppressed happiness—everything passed in notes and words through those parted lips, which cried to the sea and the night more kisses and more dreams than a human breast and mouth could contain without dying of them.

She sang . . . and what repose awaited her, then? What soul and what face did she have, the woman who had a beautiful voice?

She fell silent.

Pierre said: "Ah! But I want to see her!"

"Oh, to be able to love her!" murmured Jacques.

Hasty footsteps resounded again on the paving stones . . .

The two men, who were already advancing, stopped. They saw a masculine form join their unknown woman.

"Rosa! What folly! You're exposing yourself thus to the humidity of the night, of the sea! To sing here! Tomorrow, you'll have a sore throat, you'll no longer have a voice! And I've been searching for you everywhere for an hour . . ."

He continued talking, but as he had taken the woman rapidly by the arm, his words became vague and indecisive in the ears of the two friends . . .

They made suppositions:

"A husband-impresario?"

"A lover-director?"

"Oh, but it's necessary to find her again, to hear her again," said Pierre.

And Jacques: "Oh, that, no, never! To see her face made up, and to divine all the threads of the métier in the voice! Such as she was there, I would have put myself on my knees before her and adored her—for an hour! That hour she has stolen from her life—God knows for what reason! Almost invisible to our eyes, she has given it to us, without being aware of it. If it is true that it is unconsciousness that creates infinity, let us try to be worthy of such a fine gift . . ."

THE JADE FROG
(*La Fronde*, 16 November 1899)

IT was a frog of bright green jade striped with yellow like a cat's eyes: a pretty trinket that Strymans placed with an equal indifference on invoices, love-letters, circulars, tickets for general rehearsals and telegrams: in sum, everything that constitutes in written or printed form the daily life of a man—or woman—who does not respect his tranquility.

Strymans held on to that frog as one holds on to a habit; he did so with an affected negligence that dissimulated a real affection.

One evening, as Ceramea was putting up her hair again with long pins with baroque pearl heads, amid the roses of her toque and her undone hair, she spotted the frog, which she had seen a hundred times before—a hundred times is perhaps an exaggeration—and recognized a furious desire to take the little beast away, in order to have it in her own home, on her own table, among her own overly familiar knick-knacks . . .

She expressed that desire. Immediately, Strymans looked at his property with more complaisance, and tried to resist.

"What an idea! You have a thousand things much more artistic, more precious . . ."

He was flattering her, for only the day before he had confessed to a friend that Ceramea's apartment was "like a veritable bazaar."

"No, no! And then, if I find it pretty? If it gives me pleasure? What more is necessary?"

Elementary politeness dictated to Strymans these simple words: "Well, then darling, nothing at all! Take my frog away, quickly; it has become *your* frog."

Unfortunately, Strymans remained deaf to the voice of politeness; he recalled immediately charming memories attached to that animal. It was his friend Marande who had given it to him in the course of a delightful little voyage of comrades to the north of Italy.

And suddenly he imagined that, in a vivid and permanent fashion, his frog, his dear jade frog, reminded him of the intelligent hours of that voyage, the walks full of good humor and the unexpected, with the goal of pure beauty.

Meanwhile, Ceramea, with the calm of a conscience to whom nothing is refused, put the frog into her muff, and already, outside the simulated bag of silk and flowers, where Ceramea sincerely believed that her hands were protected from the cold, nothing could any longer be seen but the golden yellow eyes, scarcely more yellow than the blonde stripes of the frog's body, the color of grass . . .

When Ceramea had departed with it, the draught from the door and the fireplace lifted up all the thin papers previously maintained on the table by the weight of the little beast.

Strymans grumbled, shrugged his shoulders, and took a small bronze at random from a sideboard, which became a useful paperweight.

But Strymans could not console himself for the loss of his frog.

A few days went by; his friend Marande came to see him.

"Don't you find anything changed here?" Strymans asked him.

After an inspection, Marande said: "No, nothing. What is it, then?"

Strymans told him about the theft.

"It's a beast like any other," he concluded, "but you can't imagine how I miss it. It's reached the point that I can't write tranquilly. I always look toward the place where it sat, so green and so yellow, with its broad back and its little feet."

Marande considered him, bewildered, and then started laughing.

"No! But you're going soft!"

"Don't laugh. Yes, I know, it's doubtless a mania, even a malady; they even have a name, these maladies . . ."

"Undoubtedly!" And Marande tapped his forehead with his index finger between his eyebrows. "But can't you ask Ceramea to bring it back to you when she comes?"

"That's idiotic, old man, what you're saying. When Mea is here I have no need of the frog."

"One of them is sufficient for you?"

"I don't like these jokes. No, you don't understand; it's when I'm working that my eyes need to discover the habitual décor around them . . . and then, it's very strange . . . but you're going to mock again."

"No! Go on, then, go on! I'm sure that it will be a pity if you don't finish!"

"Certainly! That frog . . . your frog . . . my frog . . ."

"*Her* frog! Conjugate, my friend!"

". . . Has often breathed me the word that wouldn't come . . . you know, those vocables that remain in the air, suspended from the thread of thought . . . one only knows them, one has them on the edge of the brain, but damned if they'll fall on the edge of the phrase, which remains incomplete, displayed, flat, in the middle of the page. Well, in those annoying situations, I had only to look attentively at my frog, which gleamed like a little sun under the light, and *bang!* my little vocable, the fine, the true, the only vocable, quickly trotted out under my pen!"

"Damn! I understand—it's a collaboration you're losing."

"You've said it. For now, you know, it's aphasia, amnesia, all along the line."

"That's serious!"

"I believe so."

A silence, and then Marande jumped.

"I've got it!"

"What?"

"Is she nervous, Ceramea?"

"I'll lend her to you one stormy evening—you can judge for yourself."

"Perfect . . . but I don't ask as much—have us to dinner together on evening soon, and I won't give you a week before the frog is back here—like a good dog!"

Ceramea, Strymans and Marande dined together.

Marande was exceedingly seductive, and, above all, prodigiously interesting.

He told scientifico-terrifying stories, and when he saw that the young woman was moved he said: "And besides, have you not noticed, dear Madame, what a singular power of suggestion animates certain objects? Principally ancient works of art; one could believe them truly imprinted with black magic, with spells. I, who am talking to you, had in my possession a little onyx camel of very curious workmanship—well, you wouldn't believe what strange things happened in my home during the time I was obstinate in keeping that trinket—for you must be aware that of all objects, those that are sculpted images of animals, especially in certain precious materials, are particularly endowed with that mysterious power. Oh, the ancient religions had a profound meaning," he added, in a fatal tone.

With a slight shiver in her voice, Cereama turned to Strymans and said:

"You don't know? At home, last week . . ." (a pause) ". . . two days after you made me that gift . . . you know . . . of the nice little frog?"

"I know," Strymans affirmed.

Marande listened with an expression of innocent interest.

Cereamea continued: "Well, I've had horrible nightmares, I've dreamed about enormous snakes . . . I couldn't wake up . . . it was terrible! I had eaten lobster that evening . . . but that often happens, and I always sleep well . . . and then, the morning after that frightful night I found one of my parakeets dead, and . . ."

"A frog, did you say, Madame? And of what is that frog made?" Marande interrogated, mildly.

"Jade."

Marande shook his head.

"Jade . . . hmm . . . very bad, jades . . ."

Then Ceramea got carried away:

"That's an idea! You've given me that frog too! You must have known that! It's very lucky that nothing worse has happened to us!"

"Than snakes, lobsters and parakeets!" murmured Strymans—but Ceramea was too angry to hear him. .

The next day, full of hope, Marande went to visit Strymans, to obtain news of the frog.

"Well? Your fetish?"

"Alas, my dear, don't talk about it!"

"What, she's keeping it?"

"Oh yes! Keeping it! She threw it out of the window when she went home. Before I had time to jump I heard it shatter on the pavement, while she said: 'There you go! Filthy beast!'"

"Oh!"

"Yes, Oh!—and do you know what she replied to me when, containing myself, I asked her why she hadn't simply returned it to me?"

"No, what?

"In order that no misfortune should befall me. 'Do you, think, then, that I don't love you?' she said to me.

"That's perfect."

"Isn't it?"

PETER GANEUS' IDEA
(*La Fronde*, 23 November 1899)

PETER GANEUS often had, in addition to talent and enemies, ideas.

He had had generous ones and eccentric ones—pretty and crazy girls—bad ones, like little black beasts, and beautiful ideas similar to pure statues, and others as funny as little inquisitive and comical kittens—but in that number, very few were practical.

One gray, foggy morning, before the insinuating article of a colleague, with the stinging memory of the recent defection of the "dear friend" and the prospect of imminent beatings and struggles that would hamper his progress on the work of which he was dreaming, a ravishing idea occurred to him, and as he was in an impetuous and expansive mood, he immediately leapt out of bed, nightshirt flying, and cried:

"I'll make people believe that I've suddenly gone gaga!"

And he did.

His young domestic was the first to be admitted to the sad spectacle, offered to him by way of a trial by Peter Ganeus, who, in memory of ancient clowneries that had seemed delightful to him in his early youth, simulated marvelously a senility in its early stages but already severe. Seized by fear and commiseration, the man, after having run to inform the doctor, an intimate friend of "Monsieur" took care to warn everyone within a rather extensive radius of the poor Monsieur's condition.

Apart from Doctor Sautoir, journalists and "maids" sick with curiosity came to the concierge's lodge and all the way to the entresol occupied by the celebrated Peter Ganeas. Former mistresses and future creditors, the eternally hostile and the temporarily friendly, came; it was a select crowd.

Peter Ganeus, collapsed in a soft armchair, glowering and drooling slightly—a trifle fatiguing to obtain that continuous jet—from the corner of his slack mouth, his limbs agitated by continual, slight and varied twitches, uttering inarticulate grunts, gazed at those people without laughing, for the first symptom of senility ought to be a great seriousness before humanity. It was with the same spasmodic impassivity that he allowed himself to be put to bed and cared for; toward midday he gave certain signs of a general amelioration in his sad state. He pronounced a few words, vague in their ensemble but precise in their meaning. He obtained broth and jelly by that means, and thus gave his doctor and friend a great satisfaction in seeing the fortunate result of his care after the devastating and terrifying diagnosis that he had furnished. Then he appeared to take a well-earned rest, only suffering from a slight impatience in his legs—for it was the hour of his habitual walk.

The day was calm and rather bleak. He sensed that he was watched by avid eyes; the evening was infinitely more cheerful.

Between five and eight the news spread in the newspapers. People came to sniff the truth at close range, with a pitying sympathy that was, alas, futile; Peter Ganeus evidently received no comfort from it.

With his eyes veiled by perfect idiocy, in which his sight remained piercing, he scrutinized the faces of many in which the heart rose like lees; on some, too old, the wrinkles hid thought to well—it was necessary to wait for other experiments—while on others, too young, there was a certain sincere beauty. Those, Peter Ganeus marked in his memory.

He heard himself called master, poor old friend, eternal friend (by those with whom he had quarreled after too many disappointments), a misunderstood genius (by those who had cried in their articles that real genius is always manifest and that, in consequence, if someone remains modest and obscure, it is because . . . etc.) So many words slid over him like water off a duck's back. Then the bedroom, on the order and the plea of the doctors, became empty again, full of propitious shadow and reverie. Then, in his brain, lucid from repose and a light but substantial diet, and sharpened by an observation impossible for recognized good sense, Peter Ganeus composed a page as solid as a rock and as bitter as sea-water . . .

And the days went by; Peter Ganeus sustained his role with an infinite patience and art. He was the sublime actor who has no comrade and does not even know his dresser.

Before an entire week had gone by he led a charming life and no longer had a single enemy. The faculty considering him to be doomed, the homages were rendered to him of the dead who can no longer write. He was adored, and people said so in choice terms; since he could no longer understand, one could be gracious and generous, and the "copy" on the case of Peter Ganeus was placed without delay.

Now, Peter Ganeus having witnessed his "case" with an even, facile humor, which had taken a chronic and definitive allure, medical consultations had regulated for him like a musical score a most hygienic petty existence, capable of curing the most inveterate neurasthenics. As his income was sufficient, he did not have to move out of his entresol. He had a domestic—a busy, careful and vigilant nurse—with whom he no longer had to struggle, as with his previous servant. He was taken into the country by carriage on sunny days. He avoided the general rehearsals in which he had been due to praise the authors in the corridors, authors who would have hated him if he had avoided their plays. Unknowns no longer requested that he read their dedicated works. His mistress of whom he was weary—being in the animal and anemic state in which a change of air and body is necessary to recover an appetite for amour—was replaced by a doctor's prescription. Finally, after a fortnight of observation, when it was recognized that his nights were more serene, he was liberated from nocturnal surveillance.

Then, on those nights and their liberty after and between days of complete repose—sleep, regular nourishment and excursions—he set to work: beautiful, good, magnificent work, freed from cares and preoccupation; the delight of work nourished his marrow and his blood, and his thought, as firm and sculpted as a jewel, was incrusted in sequences of phrases that were fluid and supple, with a harmony of pearls rolled in water.

And thus he did his work, the cherished work of which he had dreamed with a poignant desire and a dull bitterness at not attaining it amid the paltriness and the chores of old.

While he was working thus he was so completely forgotten that he had been forgiven everything, including his talent. He no longer had around him either hostility or rancor, and he had been able, in full knowledge, to choose his friends, those whose solicitude did not weary him—and even a sweet woman to love, one who, previously unknown, dared in his decadence to approach the man whose glory had frightened her somewhat. She was delicate and tender, with a timid and charming grace. She was a stranger to his entourage and all alone. She spoke before him to the doctor, with whom she had solicited an interview, she had all the divine little words; before her, Peter Ganeus almost forgot his role for the first time, but she went away quickly because she was visibly fearful of tiring the invalid, of appearing curious and indiscreet—but not so quickly that Peter Ganeus did not have time to see that she was weeping.

Then he resolved to be cured. And slowly, he commenced to reconquer his intelligence and his faculties. The doctors were perplexed at first, having declared him incurable, and then marveled. However, one day, one of them said: "You know Peter Ganeus; they said he was f***ed? Well, not at all; he's getting better."

As no one wanted to believe it, they were not risking anything in welcoming that good news with ardent demonstrations of joy. The comedy of the procession was repeated successfully in Peter Ganeus' entresol.

As they went out, many of them said: "It's unexpected, what extraordinary nervous things one sees today; he appears never to have been sicker than you or me!" It was often confirmed ataxics who spoke thus.

A month had not gone by since the official convalescence of when two notes in the newspapers—the seeds of innumerable chronicles—informed the public of the engagement of Pater Ganeus with a young woman previously unknown in Paris, and the appearance of his latest volume, entitled *Verily, I say unto you . . .*

And there was for everyone an abysm of uncertainty.

NEURASTHENIA
(*La Fronde*, 2 December 1899)

IN a sky like the face of a cadaver, the sky of a winter night in a lunar epoch—without a moon—a leaden sky dusted with rice powder and verdigris, in which the drool of the clouds spat flakes of ash and smoke, the lightning flashes at the zenith, tinting enormous roundels with sulfur and blue, seemed immaterial gemstones incrusted with reflections of nacre, snow and amber: vertiginous adornments that crowned the narrow wan brow of Neurasthenia. In that sky, after midnight, she surged forth, tall stretched and magnificent, queen and she-cat, ferocious and light, over the City, yawning her breath of pleasure through the stinking and perfumed mouths of theaters, splashing the sidewalk with a human foam. Wild beast and ballerina, with the backbone of a tiger and the sharp eyes, wearing little golden bells attached to her thin ankles, with all the frills of follies that dance and swoon and pant and commit suicide, Neurasthenia pirouetted and leapt in a somersault that stirred the city and the sky with a convulsion of atrocious joy . . .

In eyes, she fixed her eyes, carved in metal and sculpted in flame, burning and brilliant; and nostrils sniffed the warm, humid air, the ambiguous air of the night, recognizing her passage by the strange reek of hatred and sweetness that she trailed after her, while she lifted her veil woven of rotten flowers, in order to freshen the streets—rivers of mud—and in tearing away the clouds she had carried away the stars, which fell into the gutter . . .

Select brains that passed that way under human appearances, picked up those stars in order to make works of them—art, poetry, beauty, happiness . . . and many, at that strong odor of putrescence and roses, at the delicate odor of decomposed flowers that marked her trail, panted in following her . . .

It was the abomination and the adoration of a people: prostitutes and princesses, perverse and vanquished in the soul, who sought her at the crossroads and in the ditches by the roadside for an embrace or a union.

They suffered in that imperious hour when she held them, Neurasthenia, but they knew that in the next hour she would sting them with a needle charged with a liquor surer than ether or morphine . . . a sweet poison that would slide into their flaccid soul a surge of energy, and into their empty veins the great flood of desire, the illusion of blood!

And for her court and her valets Neurasthenia shakes her little, short, thick mane the color of rust and hemp over her neck, of a delicacy to tempt the guillotine, and at moments that head tilts back with an abrupt shock like a broken corolla at the end of a stem devoid of sap—and then the entire body, the long, pale and sinuous body, agitates: a snake that does not want to die. That is because Neurasthenia, in her course, receives blows along with the kisses that attain her, snatching her like the bites of a rabid animal: a flagellation in the manner of the filthy and sublime parvenu who has climbed from the footlights all the way to pure thresholds . . .

Neurasthenia laughs like a child; she has a delightful and victorious laugh; dead chrysanthemums, lilies and irises exhale death and lust over her, in a shower of petals, while in her appearance as a fay who will play with a simple human creature, she extends her arms, which seem weak—so thin!—and stops . . .

One can approach her, touch her—take her, in sum, for what violations, or what triumphs, or what murders?—but her skin is so soft, so very soft . . . too soft, too fresh a flower, a flower splendid with divine pallor; it is silk the color of the moon, prestigious flesh of a fluid suppleness, flesh morbid with languor, flesh of caress and dream, to the point of not knowing what it imports from here or there . . . both doubtless, which pour out the same weakness—and thus escapes and flees again.

Neurasthenia . . .

Then, with a thrust of her crimson-tinted claw, she has departed to kiss the sky with the face of a cadaver . . . each of the nails of her narrow feet and her open hands—but filed like hallucinatory weapons—seems a jewel: pink rubies and red rubies . . . There she is, above the shiny roofs and the soot-colored reflection of blazing hearths, prodigious: a wild beast with a taut back, a ballerina scaling the clouds with an entrechat, Neurasthenia traverses the sky and reflects her disquieting and marvelous image in the moving mirror of the river; the river receives it with the silent and fugitive kiss of its bed . . .

And Neurasthenia finally snags her robe of putrid flowers, of beautiful deflowered blooms, on the new stones, the stones in domes, minarets, balusters, capitals, gables, pylons, stones that want to be of all ages, all epochs and all races—bastard styles coupled in deception and sham, in plaster and slapdash, in order to express to the crowds the immense adultery of time with hideousness and the lie: and that through the most magnificent effort of labor, Effort toward Beauty—who refuses herself.

Neurasthenia contemplates it, in the Field where the plowshare and the gesture of an invisible sower cause a new city to sprout from the bosom of the old city; and she sees that young city—which one might believe to be in ruins, given its disorder, so similarly chaotic are formation and destruction—already made up and ornamented like a whore for tomorrow: the spring of a young century . . .

A formidable hole—in which what remains of the palace of yesteryear will sink, and which seems the skeleton of a phantom vessel run aground, with its framework of scaffolding and ropes—will enlarge the horizon of the Élysée, where sumptuous life flows, above the bridge that will be made the color of gold and ash—what gold and for what conflagrations?—all the way to the Esplanade guarded by narrow mouths of bronze . . . They will be seen, from one bank to the other, those little round black mouths mounted like lorgnettes, which will have for targets . . . fêtes?

In the sky, Neurasthenia blinks, and seems to go to sleep—a repose . . .

The monstrous silence of the night, in which wakefulness seems an abnormal sin, is over the city . . . Neurasthenia sleeps . . . Whence comes that strange slumber, which does not put to sleep the smile of her teeth? Out there, toward the west, where a faint radiance indicates the undulation of little hills under frail winter woods carved in slate and drawn in blue ink under a timid moon, a delicate and white young woman places her fresh finger on her closed lips, takes refuge and disappears . . . That is the Beauty of the word, who has a savage and solitary caprice; she has escaped the new prisons in which some believed they had imprisoned her, so the lines remain graceless and the contours do not retain the prism of light and shadow . . .

However, because the exhausted crowd has fallen into the repose of drunkenness or agonizing pleasures, Neurasthenia raises her eyelids ringed with blue and mauve like crumpled petals . . .

It is the hour of mortal dawn, in which she throws to her own the fodder of bile and honey, the sickening nourishment that assassinates the appetite without satisfying the marrow . . . and Neurasthenia laughs again, because she knows full well that hunger will drive humans to carnage, and that, queen and she-cat, wild beast and ballerina, with the backbone and sharp eyes of a tiger, wearing little golden bells on her ankles and all the frills of follies that dance and swoon and commit suicide, she will be the mistress of the Universe, in the same Field where one believes that strong and virginal life is being grown, in which she sows the execrable seed, reeking of hatred and sweetness, while trailing her veil of corrupted flowers . . .

LITTLE MILA
(*La Fronde*, 7 December 1899)

W HEN MILA opened her eyes she was considerably astonished, for the space of a minute, not to be able to
take account of the place where she was: a hotel room, which
eight o'clock on a November morning and the dying smoke of
the night-light illuminated hideously. The velvet-upholstered
furniture the color of wine-lees, had positions both banal and
complicated throughout the room.

On the walls, four paintings—fortunately indiscernible as
yet—could be divined by the bright surrounds of their frames
of gilded sticks. The carpet resembled an old meadow over
which too much livestock had passed, grazing all its grass.

An open door in the partition wall cut out in a white square
a narrow dressing-room, with deplorable porcelains.

My God, why and how am I here? thought Mila. And she
curled up, with a little frisson, thinking that she was still
dreaming and that in a little while, in a second, on opening
her eyes, she would see around her the delicate harmony of her
bedroom, all ash-gray silks and silks the color of snow, with
the beautiful motionless efflorescence of violet irises and moss-
roses, cut out in metal and glass on the panel mirrors and the
bay windows, which filled that bedroom with light and a pure
and profound reflection of clear water . . . the bedroom, so
mild, fresh and soft, where Mila slept and lived in a tender

light unconsciousness of the whole world, with the security of the great regular movement—muffled by discreetly leather-clad doors and felted carpets—which enveloped her, rose in waves toward her from the offices of the ground floor and the entresol, served by a double staircase, where her husband and her brothers activated the movement of their labor and their energy precisely in order to ensure her that cushioned and delicate life, the life of a little bird in full down, which only knows the warmth of plumage and the ripple of chirps and trills of little throats like its own . . .

And in that bedroom—*her* gray and white bedroom—where lace, her folly, snowed incessantly in flakes of adornment, Mila also heard, coming from above, from the highest and most fragile, and closest to the sky, little shrill cries and minuscule laughter, spun in crystal and silver, an entire puerile and infinite song: her children, murmuring their frail and pampered little existence on the floor above, where Mila had installed them in the most ingenious luxury of refined maternal tenderness . . .

Abruptly, Mila opened her eyes again—her poor, large, beautiful eyes, full of alarm.

I know . . . I'm here waiting for my lover . . . my lover, whom I love, whom I love, whom I love . . .

She repeated that word mutely, in her heart, with an expression of dolorous and passionate intensity on her face, of which one would not have thought that face capable, all infantile grace sculpted in the blondest flesh with the ravishing details of rosy lips, the pink of eglantines, and eyes the blue of happiness . . .

And yet, the mysterious and ironic awakening had not immediately given her the thought and image of that lover, the returned memory of whom now made that visage tragic, in which the face became almost black, charged with all the shadows of desire . . .

Definitively returned to the reality of life, having opened the curtains and stood up in the middle of the room, Mila looked at its desolating ugliness, and with that sight and that of her case of toilette necessities, in which the profusion of her habitual trinkets of feminine coquetry shone and overflowed, Mila remembers everything quite clearly.

Nine o'clock. He will arrive at eleven o'clock. Mila has time for all impatiences and all fevers; she sits down next to the reanimated fire in order to study her memories more carefully . . . And Mila fixes all her will-power and all her attention—but, strangely, although they are all there, pressed and faithful, a variegated crowd, she cannot succeed in distinguishing them clearly. She is astonished and anxious, and interrogates them:

"Is that really you?"

Yes, of course! It's us, us, who . . .

And they talk—but Mila cannot hear them. Her ears are full of a loud confused noise, violent and imperious, like that of the ocean, and her heart leaps and dances like a mad thing in her breast, repeating in the hostile silence of the room and the unusual silence of her soul:

I love him . . . I love him . . . I love him . . .

And it is a terrible cry in all her being, that nascent lament, a cry that drinks her blood, her life, her reason and her consciousness with an insatiable hunger and thirst.

And Mila remains sitting, motionless, with eyes that do not see and ears that no longer hear, in that hotel room to which she has come to wait for and meet her lover . . .

After an adroit escape from her hearth, accomplished with clever ruses and schemes with regard to her brothers, while her husband is away, she arrived here the evening before in their little provincial town, cold and closed, like a disagreeable face, chosen not very far from the city—the great city where they have rolled their amour for a year in the swell of the enormous complicit anonymity.

Not very far . . . for a possible prompt return; for the definitive departure toward the great distance, the very great distance, where the lover whom she loves is going, does not yet seem admissible to Mila—little Mila, who, all her life, has gone to sleep and then been animated, by turns, in the tenderest slight unconsciousness . . .

And now Mila's heart has ceased to dance and leap; it has fallen back upon itself, exhausted; the immense void that it senses to be close at hand, is an infinite weight for it . . . It is dragging the murderous millstone of or a mortal dolor in a reiteration, a stupefied repetition of the same phrase.

What will become of me? What will become of me?

Yes, what will become of her when *he* has gone? When he is out there, having rejoined his post in those gilded and dangerous lands? When the letters, from him and from her, the feeble letters, will only arrive, and the colorless responses will only return, after weeks and weeks? When she will not know anything, when he will be ignorant of everything . . . when one and the other can imagine everything, suppose and suffer . . .

He's deceiving me . . . She's forgotten me . . .

And one or the other might die and that death might only be, to him or to her, a sudden, significant silence, an eternal silence fallen like the blow of an ax . . .

With the cold of that winter morning and that strange room, Mila feels the chill of that blow attain her heart.

How far away she is from the security, the calm happiness of her house, her children—a puerile song in a soft feathery nest, effaced and annihilated. And yet, scarcely an hour's travel and she could find them, identical: peace, ignorance, innocence . . .

Mila closes her eyes and sinks into anguish . . .

Something like a bright light in front of her causes her to raise her eyelids abruptly . . .

It's him! He's here! How rapid those long hours, those two hours, have been. She wanted to get dressed, to do her hair with amour, in order to be delectable one last time, so that he would carry her away in his eyes as one carries away a torch . . . ! But she is no longer thinking about all that . . . She looks at him; he is so pale and his eyes are so sad . . . Crushed against his breast, drowned in her hair, her tears and her vertigo, she says:

"Oh, my love, my love! How you're suffering!"

He says: "Yes, I'm suffering . . ."

She moans: "Oh . . . ! Oh . . . ! Oh . . . !" as if she were giving birth in agony. He cradles her, without words. They say adieu thus, with a fear of words—imperfect, impotent, maladroit words . . . and the time flies by around them relentlessly, a great bird of prey that will henceforth devour so slowly and so cruelly their empty life, from which their hearts have been torn out . . .

And when, finally, it is necessary to say things, to settle details, to fix dates, their dolor becomes more acute, full of rancor and bitterness, with a sensation of stupid, imbecilic disaster . . .

In the depths of her instinct, closer to the truth, Mila penetrates that sensation first, and immediately stops in her tears and misery, with a strangely resolute expression that says: "No, I won't go any further in suffering . . . *I don't want to suffer . . .*"

She does not want to suffer, and repels the softening anticipation of regrets to come, simply in order to avoid the atrocious present dolor.

She had never loved, she will never love again, *like this* . . . she wants to preserve and keep amour—and when the evening comes and the moment that would have been the disenlacement and tearing apart, she goes away, little Mila, through all the mortal perils to her amour and her life, she goes away from them, scarcely pale, toward the golden and dangerous lands, with that amour, to which she has given that life . . .

THE GOOD WORKER
(*La Fronde*, 16 December 1899)

SHE was a worker in glass, but in the very special industry of *eyes for dolls*.

As she was very skillful—a little Parisienne hand prompt in labor and adornment—she succeeded in earning four francs fifty a day when times were good.

She worked from morning until evening in a studio that was completely dark.

Only the pale and tremulous flames of the burners illuminated the room and the population of women who leaned over attentively, rotating the milky white globe on the end of the vitreous stem that, in a little while, when they had added the pupil, would be an eye, a beautiful blue, brown or golden eye . . .

Then, thus completed, before being placed, those eyes, in hundreds and thousands, filled baskets and glistened there, caressant and motionless, catching reflections of the little pale flames, and giving birth to dreams of perverse ferocity . . .

But the good worker has no time for the dream. She gazes with satisfaction at that appearance of massacre, which is her livelihood.

Earn your daily bread, good worker, thinking about your life.

This morning in December is a moment of feverish haste, because an entire avid people is awaiting joy with the toy.

Margot has arrived a little late. All her comrades are already there, vague shadows with slow, precise gestures, and it is by an exceptional favor that Margot is able to take her place after the hour and escape a fine.

For that she has had, before observations, such eyes and such a voice, and has also demonstrated her constant zeal and the fervor found therein, that her excuses and her pleas are admitted.

To say everything, the supervisor is not insensible to Margot's eyes and voice. That is because, young as she is, she does not yet wear the faded appearance that is the mask of the enormous flock of workers. Her pallor is as fresh as that of a flower born without color but more dazzling than the roses. A delectable sad smile accompanies her child-like voice.

Her eyes are an indescribable color, and their form always gives the impression of weeping and loving. Caresses and tears: she seems to be made thus. Almost a little girl, Margot is pitiable, and yet, behind her, when she is installed at work or departed toward her life, which remains hidden and mysterious, the others say, astonished: "How can such a woman be leading such a life?"

Undoubtedly, a life that is entirely obscure, like the hours of her work: no light and no air, a mediocre existence in a heavy atmosphere.

Marghot is proud and never complains, but it can clearly be seen that her neat garments are worn and thin. But in the shadow, this morning, no one can see her shivering.

She is, however, trembling very forcefully, the good worker, and the more she tries to steady the frail implement in her little hand, the more the terrible frisson that envelops her from the nape of her neck to her heels increases, increases to the point of chilling her heart . . .

Oh, the heart, when it becomes so heavy and so cold, ought it not to cease beating?

However, the little hand, by dint of energy, has assured the quotidian labor. The good worker works, and the irises as brilliant as cornflowers blossom, fragile pure gazes that, set in the round and rosy faces of beautiful dolls, will give maternal hearts to all little girls . . .

And in the meantime, all those unseeing eyes are only fixed on Margot; their number increases and they are very bright and very soft; they are eyes that do not know tears, eyes full of light, invisible to light.

Oh, how cruel their softness is, to be unalterable like that!

In the shadow where Margot creates artificial gazes in that fashion, what Margot sees are two poor living eyes, two suffering eyes, two large child-like eyes, two eyes that are slowly extinguishing . . . slowly . . .

And as, her shoulders bent, broken by dolor, Margot seems to collapse toward the work-bench, her neighbor, who divines something, asks: "What's the matter?"

Drunk on chagrin, Margot sobs: "It's my child . . . my little boy, who is going blind!"

There is a little rumor of curiosity in the studio; they are astonished.

How can the good worker, so thin, who seems so fearful and was thought to be sage, have a child?

The labor—the hasty and urgent task—stops, takes a breath on the edge of that news, and immediately, Margot takes refuge in the silent reserve for which she has been reproached so much. She is afraid; she regrets her exclamation. She is not habituated and never will be habituated, to prompt confidence. Passionate and savage, the story of her passion and her savagery she keeps secret. One can imagine that it is a sad and proud story, but nothing is known.

Today, however, her silence is pardonable, because of her pain, even if they do not understand it very well. And in the penumbra, young women with unkempt hair and thin mouths, with profiles as if sculpted in green wax, the closed and gray faces of women who seem old but are perhaps not, can be seen turning toward her place.

All companions in labor, comrades in misery, have the unconscious but profound sensation of a monstrous irony of destiny that wants to double with its needle the pain of the good worker . . .

And all the artificial eyes radiate and wink on the work-benches, in the baskets, having taken, with a little flame and great deal of cleverness, the breath from all those emaciated torsos, and their frail beauty . . .

Margot looks at the past—oh, a very small past, scarcely yesterday: six months; the nascent gaze, a double flower, of two blue eyes: two eyes like those she had loved, which had deceived her.

And in that fragile clarity, she had had all dreams, and had lived happily . . .

Her entire life was arranged modestly with the work, which pleased her simple and worthy soul; in that obscure workshop, she had known abundant happiness.

What would that madly beloved child not become? He would be intelligent and strong, and for the joy of those two blue eyes, of what would she not have been capable?

But one morning, she was astonished by the vacillation of those adored eyes . . . then she panicked, finding her child unwell . . .

The first consultations had only left her with an impression of indefinite anguish; it was only this morning that she had received the crushing truth like a frightful blow.

"Mysterious causes . . . doubtless congenital weakness—perhaps distant heredity—and then, congestion, anemia . . ." But to save the sight of the child, it would require a miracle. He would be blind . . .

Blind . . . blind . . . blind . . .

A disaster and a terror, that black word—all of her joy and pride sank within it.

She pulls herself together; she is hallucinated by the thousand vitreous and disquieting gazes that seem to be around her, enveloping her and filling her with bitterness . . .

The hours of the day pass over that pain, which does not pass . . . but to fathom misfortune, few hearts are fortified.

The heart of the good worker strives to accomplish the quotidian task as perfectly and as promptly, because, for two eyes that will no longer be able to see, for more charges, for more difficulties, more labor will be required; and among all those caressant and motionless artificial gazes that so many soft living eyes will contemplate, the good worker thinks without weeping—for tears alter the breath and tarnish the glass—about the poor dead eyes of her child, who will live in the infinite shadow without ever knowing the joys of colors and lines . . .

A DEBUT
(*La Fronde*, 21 December 1899)

"YOU aren't afraid, at least?"
     "No, Monsieur . . ."

She was lying brazenly.

She was in a blue funk, which made her face green and her gestures stiff.

It seemed to her to be no more than a poor little wooden doll, poorly articulated and incapable of an accurate movement—and its throat was cardboard; the voice passed through it without timbre. And yet it was necessary to have a supple body and a lively voice to enter into that role, which had fallen to her unexpectedly the day before . . .

Fleurange, the beautiful Fleurange, was ill, and she had several important numbers in the Revue. It was her who represented the florid automobile, the latest scandal of the press, "An exchange of views" had resulted, ministerial, etc., etc., etc.

In sum, neither the play nor the public could do without her in her creations—her, so blonde, so white, such *fresh flesh* . . .

The stage-manager and the director had been in despair, therefore, when someone suddenly said: "What about Aurélie? Aurélie could replace her."

The director had pulled a face at first. What was being proposed to him? Aurélie—Timid Lily, they called her—that little girl who had wept the first evenings over the obligation of the leotard? Get away! Would she ever be able to pull it off? Even though she knew the lines—better than Fleurange, perhaps, for she was a true musicienne, the kid, who knew all the parts entirely by heart—she wouldn't have the laughs, the tics of the burner of the boards who tickled the crowd.

In great embarrassment, however, he consented.

"Call her!"

She only had derisory roles in both plays. Four lines, stupid, naturally, replies that made no use of her pretty voice. However, she was always punctual, full of zeal, often replacing the accompanist on the piano after the regulation hours, helping the inexperienced with modest but precious advice, indefatigably making her comrades rehearse, but always effaced and almost unperceived: Timid Lily.

She arrived in her poor woolen skirt with a thin collar over her ribbed velvet blouse. Having already taken off her hat, and a trifle tremulous, thinking that she was late.

In the bright light of the two reflector lams she seemed very blonde and very pink, having run downstairs—the dressing room she shared with two comrades was on the third floor—her immense blue eyes delightfully fearful on seeing herself observed by everyone without knowing why . . .

The director said: "My word, its true, she resembles Fleurange!" And he thought: *That's because she's very pretty, that kid, much better than Fleurange!*

He examined her. He knew full well—only having engaged her for that reason—that she was nicely put together, but that face without make-up on the cheeks, without rouge in the lips, without black under the eyes, in which the color of triumphant youth was entirely dazzling, once made up under the curly floral wigs, as tall and upright, slender and supple as she was, would be able to wear Fleurange's sumptuous costumes admirably.

And it was decided: twenty-four hours to learn the role, immediate costume fittings for any useful alterations and not a second for anxiety!

254

"Oh, Monsieur . . . ! But Monsieur . . . !" Timid Lily risked, seized by terror at the thought of that abrupt shove forward of her poor person, so savage, already so unhappy, for months, in the most effaced of employments.

She had had fear and rancor, bitterness and rebuff, mockery and cares! She detested her beauty and her pretty voice, which had decided her fate one ironic day.

Eighteen years old, the oldest of five children, her mother ill, since the death of her father two years before, after the near-luxury of life while that father was alive, having made serious studies in music with a great deal of taste, this was where she had arrived, with the sole aim of helping her family more rapidly, and with the fallacious, ignorant, preliminary assurance that the life in question "wasn't incompatible with virtue."

But she kept her disappointments to herself, along with the virtue that was still her own, and having escaped many snags and vengeances thanks to hazards and miracles, Timid Lily was able to laugh like the child she was at home when she brought back her monthly wages—the figure will remain unspecified, for fear of not being believed . . .

However, having thus affirmed that she was not afraid, Lily works bravely on her face, which has until now hardly frequented the pots of red and white liquid, having never been called upon to honor the foreground. As that work advances she can no longer recognize herself, but cannot help finding herself beautiful. Yes, undoubtedly, beautiful like a marvelous wax doll, for on that firm and smooth skin, not a single scratch of fatigue breaks the mask that she executes patiently under the advice of her dresser and hairdresser.

When it is finished and she is expertly undressed, those individuals full of experience congratulate her.

It seems to her that she is dreaming, and truly, she no longer feels anything—all this is not real and why, at this precise moment, in looking at her painted, brilliant image in the mirror, in satin, flowers and skin, should she see a little girl in a black dress, very well-behaved, her heart inflated with emotion and joy, playing on the piano for her mother and father a melody learned with tenderness and care? And over her frail little shoulders her blonde tresses quiver, without a single hair surpassing another on her pure forehead, above her calm blue eyes. Yes, that image of the past, at the moment when her director exhorts: "And above all, be vulgar, very vulgar! Everything depends on that!"

She inclines her head without speaking. She has understood; she will obey. And then a kind comrade comes to whisper in her ear: "You know, the boss is furious with Fleurange! Stories to make you writhe! If you can carry off the role, he's capable of taking it away from her. That would settle your affair."

Then Timid Lily . . . and it is necessary to believe that she "carries it off" because here she is, stunned and prettier than ever in her dressing room, invaded by numerous strangers— and, as the evening progresses, bouquets, cards covered with scribbles, as comprehensible as they are illegible . . .

Then the little friend of a little while ago, in the confides of admiration and jealousy: "No, but you're lucky. X*** (an obscene word—no, sorry, an obscene name) hasn't quit you with his opera-glasses; I'll wager that . . ."

But there is a stir, a silence . . . it is X*** in person who advances. He smiles, he speaks. Lily listens, more timid than ever . . . and more exquisite . . .

She does not know, she does not know any longer . . . she would like to weep; she laughs . . . and confusedly, as if in a dream, she hears the voice of her director.

"Eh? For a debut, that's a fine debut."

And how! Superb . . .

IN HER WHITE DRESS . . .
(*La Fronde*, 4 January 1900)

"IN her white dress, a little girl was laughing . . .

"A fiancée was dreaming.

"A crazy woman was dancing.

"And a year died . . ."

It was an old song that commenced thus, no one had ever known the end, but—this is a very long time ago—a painter who was a poet painted four panels based on those four lines, and then mounted them in a screen and offered them to a young woman.

She found them pretty and made them a frame for her coquetry. They were both taken with that game, and found it very good to begin with . . . and then very bad. Eventually, when she found that she had grown older, the young woman looked at the screen, repeated: "And a year died . . ." and so many distant hours, often bad, made a charming chaplet: a profane rosary of winter evenings.

When many years had died thus "in their white dress" the amorous woman died in her turn and was buried one snowy day.

Her heirs, who were rich, thought the screen with the tarnished moldings and the misted paintings wretched, and they relegated it to an attic.

And many little girls, many fiancées and joyful crazy women laughed, dreamed and danced in the large drawing room where the screen had been the frame of out-of-date coquetries.

Then, one day, a little girl more malicious than the others, ferreting in the attic, found the image of someone very similar to her amusing: the one that was laughing in a white embroidered dress with the sun in her eyes and on her hair. She cut out the "pretty picture" covertly and stuck it to the wall of her playroom. No one worried about it, or even exclaimed with indifference: "Oh, that child has unearthed that horror!" And one day, as the caprice had passed and they were "tidying up," the "horror" was burned. Nothing remained of it but slightly sticky ash, which appeared not to want to allow itself to be completely annihilated . . .

Now, not long afterwards, in the wake of romantic and dramatic adventures, a young woman in whom the soul of some amorous ancestor seemed to be reincarnate became dreamy before the "fiancée who was dreaming." The other figures being of no interest to her, she cut out that oval carefully and had it fitted into a gray and gold frame of a melancholy brilliance.

That charming painting followed her everywhere—and she had a great many dwellings and made great voyages—and one day, someone said to her:

"You have an exquisite work there that might be signed ****(a celebrated name of a celebrated epoch of art) where did you buy it?"

She remembered the attic and the old screen; research was carried out but nothing was found. The old house had been demolished along with a block of old cottages that hindered the construction of a rental property; as for what it had contained—"a heap of old rubbish"—that had been sold at auction to a swarm of second-hand dealers.

Toward the end of her life, the owner of the portrait of the dreaming fiancée, finding herself embarrassed in her affairs, sold the painting and obtained a tidy sum for it, but much less than its new owner, who sold it on for sixty thousand to a keen collector.

Meanwhile, experts having been sent on campaign, after many errors, the veritable fourth panel, "And the year died . . ." was finally found. The defunct year was represented as an old woman with almost blonde or almost white hair—one could not be entirely sure—and a face of a pallor, a melancholy and a divine finesse that fade and evaporated and dissolved in veils of lace that were clouds, and of ash that were snowflakes, and fumes that were flowers. The canvas was cleaned and the magic of the whites reappeared. "And the year died," a work of genius, on the word of the forgotten poet, entered a great museum and into glory . . .

Meanwhile, the wood of the screen had been eaten away by woodworm for a long time; what remained of it had been burned; the smoke of such a fire was perfumed like the breath of a cassolette . . .

And the third panel? The crazy woman who was dancing . . . ?

In her white robe, still dancing, the beautiful, joyful crazy woman had been devoured by rats. She had disappeared completely, and no one any longer knew anything about her.

The people who had chanced to have her in their possession, who had thrown her into their cellar with an ignorant scorn, truly had no luck . . . but they never knew it . . .

ONE FROM THE OLD DAYS
(*La Fronde*, 11 January 1900)

"WHEN you open the drawer of the decorative table in the corner by the window, pay careful attention; there's an old piece of paper in there, which might get caught in the groove; I wouldn't want you to let it fall and lose it . . ."

Those were her last words; then she died, the old spinster, and her immobile ashen face amid her gray hair appeared even softer and more peaceful than when she was alive.

Her niece, her only relative and heir, wept silently.

It was an exquisite soul that had just cast off all mortal human appearance, so humble and so gentle: Aunt Luce.

Over the entire life of Claire, an orphan, that calm and pale face had inclined; around all the collisions of her existence, which had not been happy and had not been fortunate, there had been that enveloping consolation, the cradling arms of the old spinster. Without saying much, she had been able to testify the most delicate comprehension—and now she was no more, and Claire, infinitely alone, wept.

But the hours carried away the dead woman, and the days brought the implacable action. The heritage was composed of a meager income, some old furniture, and a few poor objects devoid of art and beauty, having only the value of distant sentiments that had gathered them around Aunt Luce when Aunt Luce, still young, had relatives and friends . . .

Those objects had been naively admired by Claire as a child, and then respected by the profound affection that she had for Aunt Luce; now, finally, she venerated them. She would have liked it if present custom had wanted, in the tombs of the dead, as of old, a touching entourage of small familiar trinkets, as if a little of the floating soul and the body in dust could still take pleasure in those fragile witnesses of their life . . .

But Claire lacked the material means to edify for the memory and her relative's remains a mausoleum in which such things could be gathered. She therefore kept them around her, and, having already surpassed the age of great hopes and having once, as an ardent soul, realized, lived and then seen those hopes agonize, Claire resolved to remain for some time in a narrow intimacy with those humble and pure memories, perhaps hoping that the soul, so pure and so humble, that had made them such might narcotize her heart, still burning with the blood of an amour that did not want to die—and that the poor amour in question might finally expire, passing from the slumber of pardon to that of forgetfulness.

She commenced piously to make an inventory, in accordance with an old wish of Aunt Luce, of everything that had belonged to her.

The order that reigned in the cupboards and drawers was so perfect that the occupation in question was easy and untroubled. A dusk like an autumnal wind rolled the dead leaves outside. Claire, sitting by the window, gazed at the little ornamental table left in the lace that it had occupied for thirty years. She noticed the narrow drawer and remembered Aunt Luce's last words.

The drawer was locked with a key.

She immediately searched for that key among others, and opened the drawer. There was a grating sound—almost a sigh—as it was drawn with difficulty. It was filled with letters, and, indeed, because it was overflowing and that piece of paper was on top of all the others, a little piece of yellow paper caught in the groove was lifted up, fluttered and fell, as Aunt Luce had foreseen.

Claire picked up the piece of paper and read it.

Today, Thursday the twenty-eighth of November 1844, Michel left at two o'clock in the afternoon for Jamaica. He told me that he would always love me and that he would come back. I want to believe him and wait for him; I'm shutting this piece of paper in this drawer that he alone will open when he returns.

I want to believe him and wait for him!

Claire's beautiful fatigued face quivered, and was covered by a smile of heart-broken irony.

Then, sensing the consent of the dead woman, she plunged her hands, her eyes and her soul into the little flood of pages, in which two handwritings alternated: a frail little flood, an ocean in which two hearts had once bathed their fever.

Claire recognized there all the passion of eternal cries and immortal puerilities, but she also recognized that the passion in question had stopped on the edge of its desire, and she remembered more clearly the ardent intoxication with which she had wanted to fuse her own desire with her own passion . . .

She had the obscure instinct of feeling sorry for the dead woman . . . and she continued reading. As she turned the leaves she went back over the course of life, and when several hours had gone by and, raising her tear-bathed eyes again, she saw all the surrounding things—a décor identical to the ancient pain, illuminated by the glare of the old lamp—she was subjected to the hallucinating vertigo of a transmutation of her being. Was she the ancient amorous woman, full of a dolorous patience—but without bitterness—or had the soul of Aunt Luce entered into her with those vibrant words of a life renewed, to contact with a young heart and another amour?

And now, gradually, in Claire's mind, a memory became precise: that Michel! But she had known him! He had come back from the colonies; he had married a pretty and delicate little creole there. Claire could now remember that young woman very clearly, with the excessively pale face, the excessively black hair, the excessively bright eyes and the excessively red lips. He adored her.

And now, that whole story, vaguely known, became very clear: the little creole had died of a malady of the lungs and the consequences of unfortunate childbirths. Claire remembered very well the great chagrin of Aunt Luce during those events and before the husband's dolor.

Then Michel had left again, and nothing more had been heard of him, nor had anyone ever talked about him.

It was definitely him.

Weary of her overloaded soul, weary of remembering and weeping, Claire suddenly had an irresistible ardent desire to flee the melancholy of that room and its sterile nostalgia. She appealed violently for forgetfulness in order to live again, in order always to live fully—desperately, perhaps, but, finally, to live, to act even in tears rather than let those tears fall back on the hearts like this . . .

She detested her suffering and the solitude that maintained it; she did not feel either the appetite to exhaust it or the strength to accept it. And then, in imagining vividly an entire existence reflected in a unique sentiment like an image in a mirror, she was frightened and admiring . . .

Were they absurd or sublime, such hearts, which, for want of exterior efforts that might conquer and tame life, have the energy to live for a long time and even die with a patient and secret strength?

In the morning, Claire burned the little piece of yellow paper: *Today, Thursday the twenty-eight of November1844, etc.,* and also all the ancient correspondence; then she closed everything with a tender care, and left . . .

She left for a new city, new faces and a new destiny. She fled the atmosphere that immobilized her soul and her being, full of a sentiment of the brevity of the longest life and the fullest days . . .

SYLVAINE'S NEW YEAR'S EVE
(*La Fronde*, 18 January 1900)

WHEN SYLVAINE came out of her house, which was the last one in the village—the lodge of the guardians of the Château de Cirlac—she had a great shudder before the dazzling whiteness of the country and the sky: a land of brilliant snow and ice under the satin of frost, a nacreous and fluid lunar sky like an enormous opal set from one end of the horizon to the other between large clouds similar to heavy prowling polar bears . . .

All the village to traverse in its length to reach the forest in that clarity of broad daylight! And on that festival eve, one or other of the inhabitants might be up late . . . a shutter or a door might open . . . she would be seen, and people knew that her husband, a gamekeeper, was on watch in the thickets, where poachers had been seen. . .

With infinite precautions, Sylvaine reclosed the latch of the door and remained still for a moment on the threshold, holding her breath, listening to see whether any suspect noise was coming from the first floor, where her parents-in-law slept.

No . . . nothing . . .

She set forth. Her woolen slippers left no imprints on the frozen ground. She traversed the orchards.

The trees charged with icicles cut out exquisite architectures against the pallor of the sky. Sylvaine did not see them; she went on . . .

Sylvaine had been a little girl from the city placed in the country by the cares of the Public Assistance. When she grew up, one might have been able to imagine a magnificent past for her by the light of her enigmatic eyes, so clear and so dark, the grace of her figure and the obscure and small paradoxes of her manner and speech, which gave her an extraordinary living harmony among the vulgarities of her surroundings and her condition. The condition in question, when she reached her sixteenth year, was that of a farm girl, but a certain innate disgust protected her from the promiscuities to which she was exposed. Women found her proud and did not like her. Men found her beautiful and desired her. Children feared her, and yet she attracted them by virtue of the enveloping gentleness of her gestures and her smile, and the pretty stories she was able to tell. At that moment, Bernard, the son of the guardians of the Château de Cirlac, came back to his parents' house after studies made with the brothers of the nearby town.

Ardent in spirit and delicate in health, he became passionately infatuated with Sylvaine, He adored her savagery, which he confounded with purity, and her indifference, which he mistook for timid reserve. He vanquished the resistance of his parents, who had dreamed of another alliance than that for their only child, and married Sylvaine after a year. That change of existence refined her further.

She lived placidly in an ease of security with the old couple who had spent their thirty-five years of united and laborious marriage in the same place, and her husband, who now replaced the father in the hardest parts of the métier of gamekeeper, and who was ingenious in delicate and touching tenderness with regard to his pretty wife.

After eighteen months of marriage, as she approached her twentieth year, she wore that strange beauty as a stem bears its flowers and its fruits. Her movements were both lively and indolent, full of eurhythmia.

Her natural grace had seduced her parents-in-law, rebellious at first, and her good fortune had made her enemies shut up.

Perhaps they watched her but they did not attack her any longer.

Bernard's mother had only one grievance against her.

"Isn't she going to give us a grandson, your wife?"

Bernard smiled. "A little patience, Mother. We're young; you know how you waited for me!"

"That's true, that's true." And she was mollified, remembering that she had, in fact, despaired for five years before Bernard came.

And one spring, after an Easter sojourn, one of the young heirs to the Château de Cirlac—they were two brothers, co-inheritors—took Bernard into his service in order to accompany him in a voyage to the mountains that he wanted to undertake. The offer was good, and he was the master; in spite of his chagrin in quitting his wife for several months, Bernard accepted. The other brother, who was also to go on the voyage changed his mind at the last minute, and stayed at Cirlac until the return of the excursionists, which occurred in mid-August.

Now Sylvaine is almost running to the edge of the forest. That immense and black forest seems, before her, a formidable mouth ready to snap her up; but she knows all its coverts and detours well and now she disappears, a little shadow, into the great shadow.

That shadow is pierced and transpierced by reflections. The broken rays of the moonlight flow from the treetops and embroider their sheath of ice and their silvery jewels. But it is another fire than those white and tremulous gleams for which Sylvaine is searching. She is looking out for the red flame that ought to be lit for her on the threshold of a hut that she knows well, and suddenly, she sees it: an eye shining in the night. Then she hastens . . . a few branches crack around her and a whistle-blast resounds in the distance. She stops dead; she has recognized the signal agreed between her husband and his aides, whom he has summed to accompany him for the hunt. Then she sets off again, pushes a door made of dry wood and laths, and goes in after having seized in passing the torch placed at the door.

An old woman is sitting in from of a flat stone on which clods of earth and vine-stocks are smoking.

"Oh, there you are—I thought you weren't coming."

"Yes, it's me."

"How did you get away?"

"Bernard is in the woods tonight."

"Good! You're lucky!"

"Yes . . . I'm lucky."

Sylvaine is speaking as if she were asleep, but she suddenly utters a cry and sits up straight, with her beautiful hind's eyes full of fear.

"Aah!"

"Has it been working on you like that for long?"

"No, it's not yet strong enough . . . aah!" she exclaims again.

"Good, good—it will have done you good to run from your house to here . . . but tell me, my pretty beauty . . ." And the old woman draws closer. "With regard to running, is it far from here that the papa is running?"

Sylvaine remains mute.

"Good, good, one isn't asking you anything . . . inasmuch as one perhaps had eyes to see last summer . . ."

Sylvaine shivers. What does she know, exactly, the old bone-setter, to whom she has confided the shame of her present physical misery, and who might she tell?

"You know," murmurs Sylvaine, "I'll give you, as well as the promised money, my gold cross and my brooch . . . I'll say that I've lost them." She repeats the word lost . . . breathlessly, frightened . . . and the tortures are becoming more urgent, stronger. The hut is full of smoke and dolor. Outside, the night seems sculpted of silver and pearls, pure and delectable . . .

In the immense silence of the night, where all the respirations of nature are in lethargy, two faint sounds suddenly seem to respond to one another at the same moment: a whistle blast and a sigh. The sigh is that of a poor little human larva whom months of compression have half-crushed in the mother's womb; the whistle makes that mother sit up on her improvised couch.

"Hey la! Hey la! I asked you for a good hour, at least," says the old woman.

"But it's in, it's him!" cries Sylvaine. "He's going to come here, I'm sure of it! Oh, hide me!"

"Let's hide that, above all," mutters the other . . . My God, you've told him that you have a malady in your belly, haven't you? Well, you'll tell him a story if he finds you . . . that you felt ill, were afraid, and came to find me."

"That's impossible! Impossible!"

And they looked at one another fixedly without speaking, for, deep down, they both know that he would not believe—could not believe—that.

Then . . . then they distinctly heard a noise not far from the hut. In a second, the new-born, enveloped in a cloth, was hidden behind the bread-bin and Sylvaine, half-dead, slid silently outside through a sort of trap-door.

Scarcely had the trap closed on her than a door opened and the bone-setter saw Bernard appear, whom she knew well.

"I saw the light! I've come to warm myself for a moment if you don't mind! It's cold tonight, eh, witch! What are you doing at this hour?"

He laughed.

The old woman interrogates: "And the hunt? Are you content?"

"No, nothing—no one . . . !" But he interrupts himself and cocks an ear. "Noise there, outside! I heard a noise!"

"No, no!"

She had spoken too precipitately. Bernard, seized by suspicion, stared at her and murmured: "She's capable of hiding one, the old whore!"

He picked up his rifle and went out. Terrified, she was about to follow him, and stop him, but already, a rustle had risen from a nearby bush and simultaneously, the shot departed . . .

A groan . . .

"Ah, the rogue! All the same . . . !" cried Bernard. He whistled; his aides were already rallying.

"Light!" he said. "Nothing's budging."

With a torch, all four of them approach, and in the snow, brown, pale and covered in blood, they see Sylvaine lying on her back, her eyes open, gazing at the sky full of light.

POOR FIGURES
(*La Fronde*, 25 January 1900)

BETWEEN THE HOSPITAL AND THE SIDEWALK

"ROOM inside? Only one, at the back, the other on the platform."

And two women climb aboard. One prostitute, one child. The prostitute is bare-headed, with her black hair scented and curled, brought back in kiss-curls over the temples, her cheeks pink with make-up, her mouth well-designed in an eternal smile, her face still young, agreeable enough, with an air of insouciant good humor: the face of a strong country girl, all of whose health has not yet been eaten away by labor and misery; short, round, buckled in a thin black jacket ornamented with fake astrakhan open over a bright red bodice cut square, with laces, from which her white flesh seems to burst. Around the neck a pink ribbon, and shiny earrings.

Embarrassed by her skirt, lifted up over varnished cardboard shoes which are taking on water, with her streaming umbrella and the little girl she is leading, she sets forth confused and quick, on the perilous assault of the footstep, while the heavy vehicle, having scarcely stopped, launches forward in a zigzag descent

"Go on, child, go sit down over there . . . you see, at the back."

270

But the child does not budge. She looks over there, at the back, between two rows of parcels, which are seated persons, but it isn't certain that she can see . . . She has eyes of stupor and fear, immense dilated and empty eyes, between her waxy forehead and her hollow cheeks: a minuscule, poor, pitiful face, sculpted in full suffering, already covered by a patina of dolor and the horror of living, which resembles a heart-rending and terrible mask between the strip of cloth that surrounds her and the black woolen shawl knotted over her head: a mask devoid of age, placed by a ferocious and ironic hand on a little body that scarcely exists—a body ten years old, or six? Or a dwarf, perhaps sixty?

But no, really a child, those movements and those little white hands, almost pretty, the only delicate thing left intact by the malady—conserved, on the contrary, by the long days spent in the hospital bed . . . and after some malady, the emergence from the hospital, on this winter day when the mud of the street seems to invade the sky, where the purest snow becomes filthy in the gutter. But she still has a poor face of a little corpse whose eyes have been left open by neglect, and in those eyes, some vestige of a little soul, still wandering in that miserable flesh, astonished to find itself still having to gaze at life, fearful and seeming to say: "Oh, I'd just like to sleep, to sleep forever, to go away of my own accord from everything I know!"

But as long as that little soul animates that little flesh, that flesh is obliged to walk, to respond, to understand.

"Let's go and sit down . . ." And, still clinging to the skirts of her companion—her mother? Already? Her sister? Perhaps. Immobile and deaf to the injunctions of the conductor, the little livid mouth murmurs:

"Oh! No, not all alone!"

The other uses prayers, persuasion; her face is naturally mild even under the hoarse tone given to it by long nocturnal stations, feet in the gutter, heart God knows where! She does not seem to be putting much effort into it; she is maternal and desolate, with a timidity in the gaze that the métier—and a forceful streak of black pencil—makes hard, she implores the public in the interior. There are robust young men there; one of them might perhaps comprehend, yield a place to the poor creature who will otherwise remain outside, to her; she has seen others, of course, but who knows what might become of her little invalid, who does not want to, who is afraid . . . of what? Who can say? Are recent memories of the operating theater, of curious faces around her "case," of bandagings, gripping her again before all these unknown faces? She is afraid of humans, of everyone, not knowing who to blame for her obscure rancor, for her illness, for her tortures. One alone, her companion, doubtless represents to her the shadow of petty joys that repose, console, appease and bring to the lips the delightful smile that forgets, the divine sweetness of being loved . . .

And far away, in all the blackness of abandonment, redness, wounds, anguish and agony there is suddenly that gross, heavily made-up and vulgar face that shines again—eyelids painted and the mouth clearly designed—of such insouciant good humor, it is that face that appears: voice hoarse and tender, oranges, violets, sunlight and warmth in which her little frozen soul and her little frozen body relax, and it is obscurely to that, that gilded memory, that the child is still clinging, who is afraid and does not want to be alone with these strangers.

And those strangers are, moreover, hostile to her. No one responds to the mute appeal of "that creature," and there is between all of them a freemasonic and anonymous sentiment of instinctive common defense and almost ferocious relief in seeing "how things torment."

For in sum, that child has come out of the hospital, she is carrying on her, and within her, all the murderous germs. They are grateful, while fearing her, for the stubbornness of a hunted animal that is keeping her away, "in the wind."

And amid the grumbles, the grunts and the jostling, on the platform splashed with melted sleet and a layer of mortal ice, lashed by the wind, tossed about and huddled together, the prey of poverty, the two creatures no longer even dare to raise their eyes and look at one another, one with her eternal smile, the other with her stupor, which appears henceforth immortal. They sense that a hatred and a fear weigh upon them, enveloping them with a suggestion of all those wills and all those desires pushing them outside, horrified by being subjected to them, furious at their right of poor folk to be there . . .

And the prostitute, in the depths of her numb brain, sees some evening when one of her men might perhaps respond to her appeal from the corner of a street where only the red eye of a lantern gleams . . . perhaps he will have money in his pocket and jewelry on his person, and she will sense herself sustained by some brutal presence, invisible to the "bourgeois" but not far distant . . .

The little girl is not thinking about anything. But perhaps her mysterious scar will pale, her ageless mask will be refined, will take on a terrible grace of youth for one day, or one night; the stupor will slide away from her empty eyes, leaving there something like the reflection of a caress—and there will always be a place for her on the sidewalks of Paris . . .

Then, in those times, her bed of knife-flesh having become free, in the hospital that she has just quit, her companion will be able to go there to repose—because, in a well-organized society, it is necessary that everyone has their part.

THE BROKEN SCALDINO
(*La Fronde*, 1 February 1900)

A little town with the brilliant and bizarre name of Volterra, planted like a sword in the mountain, above the Maremme, in the heat of Etruscan terrain. Lorenzo, the so-called Magnificent, disemboweled it in order to posses it, and then, proud of his victory, embellished its already age-old beauty again, as a jewel of stone.

And it is in that little town, very similar to its name, kneaded from brutal history and delectable art, where the enraged mountain wind often blows, under a blue sky—one of those blues of which one dreams with despairs, whose like will never be painted—it is there that Syriane divined amour for the first time.

Syriane was a delicate and sad little girl who was traveling with her guardian and her governess. She was fourteen years old.

It had been necessary, for his interests, to summon her uncle and guardian to Volterra in order that, going from Pisa, where they lived, to Rome, in November, the travelers had made that detour into the mountains.

Already gorged with a great deal of blood, today weary Volterra is somnolent, in repose. It hardly stirs for the humble and quotidian movement of life, like a somnambulist with a fixed face, with eyes closed, but who retains in his demi-movement, floating between dream and wakefulness, such a harmony that one has a desire to kneel down in adoration.

Syriane, accustomed to splendors, was unmoved by the perfect grace in its precious dryness of a little Etruscan museum, nor by the palace of the Priors, nor by the chapels of the Dôme. She preferred infinitely to the shade of vaults and the light of canvases the gray neat streets where the north wind moaned under a sky in which the clouds rode like waves.

Syriane was an ardent and reflective little girl. Although she coughed frequently, as her defunct mother had for years, her blood was keen; her father, who had died after a fall from a horse, had been a signor prompt in anger, amour and arms.

Syriane had pale hair and somber eyes. She spoke little but often sang. She had many friends already, being rich, but did not love easily, being proud. However, something heavier than ennui sometimes swelled her heart, and she desired everything that she did not know.

Volterra pleased her.

One day, on one of her walks, a little weary, she sat down on the side of a road. Women passed by, each carrying one of the little brown clay vases known as scaldini, which, filled with red embers, warmed their hands on cold days; and their hands, around the slender handles and narrow flanks of the scaldino, had a delectable chilly and enveloping gesture of hereditary grace.

One of the women remained behind her companions, leaning on the rim of a well at the corner of the road. She was brown, tall and supple. A young man came to join her. He spoke to her. She gazed at him with a distracted and passionate air, as if, while only thinking about him, she did not hear what he was saying. Syriane could not hear what he was saying either, but suddenly, they took one another by the hand without saying any more, so abruptly that the scaldino fell to the ground and shattered into a thousand pieces, spreading the red embers at the feet of the lovers.

They scarcely seemed to notice it.

Then Syriane was seized by a frisson as violent as a pain; she stood up and went away rapidly, as if fleeing something terrible, and understood from that day on that only amour could devour her ennui and make her somber and veiled eyes clear and light.

Syriane continued to cough and to sing. Her fresh pallor and her passionate voice had such charm that many declared themselves ready to love her eternally. Syriane smiled and said that they were perhaps not promising anything much. Among them all she chose one. The wedding was very beautiful, and Syriane desired to return to Volterra for her honeymoon.

The town seemed shrunken and mediocre; nevertheless, she was loved there madly; but, always remembering the broken scaldino, she confessed that she had not felt at any moment the sacred folly that had extracted from the unknown woman she had once seen a gesture of such unconsciousness that she had dropped the vase of red embers on her feet without caring about it . . .

The north wind filled her head with lugubrious ideas and she returned to Pisa with her husband.

Again she was sad and her eyes became somber. She was so sad that it was thought that she would die.

However, she lived, as if by a miracle, and found herself prettier than ever. But she became very capricious. She expressed the desire to return to Volterra alone. The keen air of the mountain would cure her completely, she affirmed.

Her wish was granted and she departed alone. But someone followed her: a man who loved her. She had encountered him frequently at fêtes, knew about his amour and seemed to hate him. So he hid, but he was full of hope, because he was audacious and believed that the dread that is, it is said, the commencement of wisdom, might also be that of amour.

As before, Syriane fled the shadow of palaces and chapels; she only liked the road, the gray highway swept by the wind, with a horizon of gold or blood at dusk, and on certain evenings Syriane, alone on the road, felt so intoxicated and sad with desire that she would have liked to die right away. She no longer sang and almost no longer coughed, because she had no voice for that. She did not feel ill at all, however, and formed a thousand projects for the life, the beautiful life, that she would live *when she loved.* For she knew now that she had made a mistake, that she did not love the man she had chosen. And what did it matter? She waited, for she was resolved: she wanted to be burned by a fire stronger than the one that had been spread over that road one distant autumn evening.

One evening, she stopped in the same place, head bowed, and seemed to be searching on the ground for the dispersed ashes of that extinct furnace.

Then she heard a voice in the shadow, and quiet words carried, of a frightful gentleness, which stung her, tore her and devoured her.

She said: "Ah . . . ! I'm afraid . . . ! It's you . . ."

"I love you . . ."

He seized her in his arms and kissed her.

Then Syriane, seized by a frisson as violent as a pain, remembered how she had got up and departed rapidly before, as if to flee something terrible—but immediately, it seemed to her that her heart leapt out of her body and flew away, lightly, lightly, while that body became equally light—so light, truly, that she no longer felt it . . .

A strange smile was upon her lips, a marvelous and unique smile that enraptured the lover—but it was her soul that passed, and in his strong arms, with terror, he felt her collapse completely. She fell dead, ardent clay broken by the fire of amour . . .

YLLOS, THE KING'S FOOL
(*La Fronde*, 13 February 1900)

> "He was a fellow of infinite jest . . ."
> (Hamlet)

THE king had a mutinous son who found ceremonies repugnant, hating pomp and etiquette.

A great child, weak and pale, the king's son only liked Yllos,
the king's fool. Only Yllos succeeded in attracting him to fêtes
where the gold of fruits, the blood of wines and the sounding
of fanfares declared the abundance, the strength and the glory
of the hereditary realm. A singular heart, in those testimonies of
joy the king's son only saw misery. He saw the soil over which
men wearied by labor and hunger leaned from the rosy morning
to the ashen dusk; the fumes of wine gave him visions of frightful brutality, and brass instruments sang to him the carnage of
battlefields where a tide of cadavers fertilized for several generations the furrows in which a finer wheat would grow . . .

The king despaired then on seeing the sad face and the cold
eyes of his only son. He summoned Yllos.

"Go to the prince and make him smile and rejoice with us
all . . ."

Yllos obeyed.

Yllos was deformed and horrible to see; that is why the
people of the court were cheered up merely by the sight of

him. But when he spoke there was a folly of joy. Yllos had contortions and grimaces for each of his hilarious and contorting speeches.

Yllos, who was deformed by two beautiful Polichinelle humps, hopped on one leg, trailing the other like a sparrow caught in a trap. He had a mouth cleft all the way to the ears, under a desolate nose. His hands were claw-like and taloned, like the paws of a monkey. He imitated comedies of amour in such a fashion that handsome lords full of aplomb on their fine legs, in tight silk stockings, and ravishing ladies in fine clothes that their gallants had just crumpled, well made-up for youth, pleasure or art, writhed in convulsions of laughter and applauded him frenziedly.

And Yllos did not hate them. In counterfeiting the courtiers, Yllos obtained for them, from the master whom he amused to the point of tears, favors that the king would have refused to intrigue. Then Yllos kissed the ends of the floating ribbons that knotted in garters the handsome lords' lace and seemed to beg pardon for what they ought to have said "thank you" for . . . but they rarely said it. Even so, Yllos loved them.

Yllos had a vast heart in which all comprehensions and indulgences were lodged, but he hid them carefully in their abode with such a clownish architecture because there were companions in the court who looked at him with a malevolent eye.

To one alone Yllos showed his treasures, the precious gems of his soul, which, for the crowd, ought only to be decked with spangles, pearls of cut glass and bright colors—the eternal frippery of folly . . . to one alone, to the great pale child who found ceremonies repugnant, hating pomp and etiquette.

The king's son said to Yllos: "How I suffer in seeing you laugh!"

And Yllos said: "Milord, my heart, you are making me suffer by not smiling!"

To please Yllos, the prince smiled, and, seeing that from a distance, the king thought: *That Yllos is incomparable; he could make a dead man laugh.* But the dead have no need of a buffoon to laugh; their last expression is a definitive rictus, when they contemplate humanity on one side and eternity and the other.

But what his son and the fool knew well, the king did not want to know.

He organized a thousand fêtes for while he was alive, and when he thought about his "possible" death he only saw the sumptuous pomp of his funeral.

Now it happened precisely that he, the king, died a sudden death. The funeral celebrations were, in fact magnificent. Then there was the cry of: "The king is dead! Long live the king!"

Then the young prince, the royal child, elevated to his father's throne, was seized by despair and an infinite fear. Night and day he wept, taking refuge in an obscure room in the palace. Only Yllos had access to him, and Yllos alone, merely by talking to him, succeeded in appeasing that agony of anxiety.

Meanwhile, the people and the court demanded the presence of the king; a mannequin was necessary for their adorations, their baseness and their habitudes. The son of the defunct king was obliged to appear and was acclaimed by his subjects. His reign commenced immediately with, around him, the flood of the affairs of the kingdom, petitions, flatteries and insults—for he had a party of opposition.

In the evening, retired to his apartments with Yllos, the young king was manifestly terrified.

"All your follies, Yllos, will never equal the supreme folly: governing! I'm only a bauble, an instrument, a top that they spin, and if I want to reflect and make a firm decision of real importance, I sense, I see, I know that I'd unleash hatreds and murders . . . there would be, Yllos, there would be throats cut and blood spilled—and afterwards . . . afterwards, nothing would be better, nor more beautiful, nor more solid, nor nobler, for that which is built on soil steeped in blood is poisoned and corrupted in advance . . ."

Yllos shook his head with an expression that would have made the entire court swoon with laughter, so grotesque would his gravity have seemed—truly out of place in a body made for farce.

Meanwhile, the queen, the court and the kings of neighboring peoples were beginning to say: "It's necessary that the king marry. It's the sole remedy for his melancholy! Then the fêtes will recommence . . . it's necessary that the king marry . . ."

The young king said: "I'd very much like to marry; let someone bring me for a spouse a simple, mild and tender creature whose charming eyes will enable me to forget the world, and a heart pure enough for me to repose there and purify mine, already soiled and weary . . ."

"That's very easy!" they cried, and they presented the young king with a great number of royal heirs, young women of renowned beauty and ostentatious qualities. But the young king always sent them away, sighing, for he saw in all of them tastes that he did not have and in none of them the disgusts with which his soul was filled.

"The woman of whom I dream doesn't exist, then!" he cried.

Yllos said to him: "The woman you desire is neither a princess nor celebrated; she is obscure, hidden and ignorant of her grace; you won't find her by searching for her; you'll encounter her one day in the vast universe, one day when you despair of yourself and the entire world, and when you see her approach, compassionate and divine, to wipe away your tears . . ."

"Do you believe that I will make a good king, Yllos?" the young king asked the fool.

"No, Milord, I don't believe so," said Yllos. "You don't love your power; it embarrasses you, like an excessively heavy weapon; and it is indeed a weapon that has to be maneuvered for defense, protection or attack—but which always wounds someone. You, who don't want to wound anyone, will let it fall on one day of anguish, and others cruel and audacious, will take possession of it in order to dazzle and murder . . ."

What Yllos predicted was realized, in spite of the young king's heroic efforts. Then, with the same fever they had put into acclaiming him, he was solicited and summoned to abdicate—which he did.

"There are," Yllos said to him, "free countries" (this story is already ancient) "distant and beautiful; let us go, my master, my heart, to those countries, where, obscure, humble and energetic in labor, we will peacefully claim our share of liberty, the unknown and the sunlight. You will no longer be a king, but I will always be your fool, proud if, sometimes, in order for me no longer to suffer, you will be kind enough to smile at me a little—you, my heart, who, still a child, will suffer in order to see me laugh!"

And they set forth one bright morning of roseate gold, embarked on the vast sea, the son of the king and Yllos the king's fool, who was no longer a fool because he no longer had a king.

SLIGHT DELAY
(*La Fronde*, 20 February 1900)

A hotel room with two double windows, which held the entire ocean, as if seen through opera-glasses. It was yellow, smoky and drooling foam on that winter day. There was no longer either sea or sky, nothing but an infinite vertiginous gray and green expanse in which the waves and the clouds spat white flakes. But Loulie was scarcely occupied with what was happening outside! She was far too absorbed by her petty preparations for installation. She was unpacking feverishly and arranging things actively, which naturally produced a certain disorder in the room. Out of the vast leather trunk flowed a river of lace; and everywhere, on the well-to-do banality of varnished fir-wood furniture hung with old blue damask, Loulie disposed little doilies fringed with guipures.

That was already better; Loulie looked at her work and clapped her hands, laughing all alone. That was because Loulie was a cheerful person. Naturally, Loulie was not her real name; that was Juliette, but it was impossible to call by such a reasonable name a little woman so droll, so dainty and so pretty. Since childhood she had been called a thousand endearing names, and that one, Loulie, she owed to a friend she loved and whom she was expecting this very evening. Her friend was married, his wife was jealous. In Paris, Loulie and her friend saw one another often, but inconveniently. Loulie, who had become independent by virtue of a hasty widowhood, and who held to consideration just as much as was necessary to avoid deplorable scandal, had resolved to take advantage of a business trip that Jean had to undertake to Bordeaux to arrange a rendezvous with him in Biarritz, where they would not see much of one another, the time being limited by the jealous spouse—who was truly what is called in lists of dramatis personae "a nasty woman"—so they would not see one another for long, but well.

Thus was explained the prodigious urgency with which the lively Loulie was "making herself at home," as much as was possible. They would dine together lightly here, at that little table . . .

Loulie even took out of her unfathomable trunk minuscule Saxe plates for the delicacies, and a Murano cup enveloped with cotton wool like an excessively fragile baby; she trembled as she unwrapped it. No, not broken . . . what luck! Loulie looked at the clock frequently: it would soon be four o'clock! Time to change her clothes, go out for two or three little errands that she intended to run herself, come back and recommence doing her hair, making herself utterly beautiful in an adorable pink crepe and lace dress, which he had not seen yet, and then to wait for him, because he would not arrive until half past six. No, no, she didn't have too much time before her. She would hurry so rapidly that she would be quite out of breath . . . but so content, so content. She seemed to be on vacation, like a little girl, foolish and joyful, but the little woman, very young and very amorous and very coquettish, that she was, while recurling her blonde curls and reflecting her pink and bright face, like a lamp in which two large eyes were shining, that little woman observed with satisfaction that "I'm very pretty today . . ."

And that was true; she was more particularly pretty than in her ever-lovely prettiness of other days.

Quickly, she picked up her traveling dress made of coarse Scottish twill with immense blue and green squares, lined with scarlet silk, her sable mantle, her toque feathered like a fabulous bird, and went downstairs. Twenty minutes later she returned, carrying a bunch of flowers—roses, anemones, lilacs and carnations—and half a dozen small packets with the labels of confectioners, fruiterers, etc. It was thus laden that she appeared to the eyes of a tall brown monsieur with a lively stride and eyes that were bold but tender, who was descending the stairs at the moment when she was going up, pinker and more animated than ever. Immediately, the monsieur recognized Loulie.

Madame de Sèvres, here! And with such an enticed and enticing appearance!

He did not doubt for an instant what had brought her here.

Very perplexed, desirous that she should not see that she had been seen, he would have liked to fall through some unexpected trap-door when, raising her head and reaching the landing first, Loulie perceived him and also recognized him.

Monsieur Cimaise! Paul Cimaise!

One of her flirts—and one of the least indifferent of her flirts! What an inopportune encounter! However, with a genteel audacity, she smiled at him and saluted him, but without stopping or speaking to him, with an air of saying: "You see, I'm very polite, but that's all for the moment; I can't grant you any more. I'm awaited!"

And she passed by, returning to her room.

Awaited! It was entirely the contrary: she was waiting.

The lamps lit, and shaded with silk, the table laid, the delicacies unpacked, the flowers arranged here and there; dressed a little, and undressed a little, in her pink dress, in which she seemed a flower herself, Loulie waited . . .

And the hours went by inexorably, filtering the minutes—and Loulie had time to conjugate several times over the deplorable verb *to wait.*

But Loulie conjugated something much graver: her grievances against Jean—Jean, who was making her wait! For, in sum, what was he doing? What was he thinking? He had surely missed the train, for she had heard the hotel omnibus returning, bringing travelers from the express arriving at Bordeaux railway station, at six fifteen. So? She consulted her timetable feverishly: another train at twenty to nine. But she was already dying of hunger! How had he been able to do such a thing? It was inconceivable! Knowing that he was awaited thus!

Oh, but this proved to Loulie what she had suspected for some time. Jean did not love her as much . . . he was paying more attention to his wife, he was thinking more about his business affairs and not sacrificing them as much as in the early days of their liaison, etc., etc. . . .

Loulie felt herself penetrated by a mad and cold rage, with savage desires to break, to tear, all the small, delightful, fragile little things around her, prepared with so much care, so much love!

Love? Truly? As much as that? Loulie started to laugh, all alone, with an insolent and provocative laughter: did she truly love him so strongly! Habitude had a lot to do with it, and the natural appetite for amorous things heightened by tenderness and charm . . . but after all, why did Jean please her more than anther—more than Paul Cimaise, for example, with his manner of an elegant and supple swashbuckler, and very amusing, very intelligent . . . much more cheerful, she was sure of it, than Jean, who had a grave nature, a little tragic, and punctual . . . Punctual! Oh, yes, let's talk about that—not always, for rendezvous!

At that precise moment there was a knock on the door. Louise jumped. Her heart leapt. Come on, it was doubtless him; he had got off the train at Bayonne and taken the little train from Bayonne to Biarritz, known as the B-to-B; hence the delay; she loved him, she was about to forgive him . . .

But she found before her the hotel porter, who handed her a telegram, gravely. "Good," she said, closed the door again, opened it and read:

Slight delay. Will arrive tomorrow morning. Apologies. Tenderness. Jean.

"Slight delay!" she sniggered. Then she started to weep convulsively. Doubtless, it was not reasonable, such despair for such a slight motive, a *slight delay*. Her forehead a little creased she went to lean it on the window-pane. A livid moonlight illuminated the ocean, which was rising and commencing to growl angrily. That noise and that lugubrious sight exasperated Loulie. She showed her fist to the ocean: "Great imbecile! Great imbecile! Ha!" she murmured.

After that, she found herself suddenly calmer, and then thought that she had not dined.

That was abusive. After five seconds of reflection, with a half-smile that would have frightened Jean—with reason—had he been able to see it, Loulie rapidly took off her pink dress and put on with the same urgency, much more rapidly than a snake changing its skin, another very pretty dress in a pastel shade, very simple, but which "went well."

And she and her dress went, one wearing the other, to the restaurant, where there was a sensational entrance, for those feverish emotions and even more feverish resolutions gave Loulie a delectably provocative expression . . .

She did not hurry to select a place, which she ended up fixing next to a small table that was still unoccupied—the only one, apart from her own, which was prepared swiftly—where a single place-setting waited. But this time, the wait was not long; scarcely had she sat down than she saw Paul Cimaise appear, who, deliberately and joyfully, installed himself next to her, as a neighbor, and immediately, there were a thousand hypocritical exclamations:

"What! It's you!"

"I did in fact, think that I recognized you this afternoon."

"Yes, I've come to admire the sea a little."

"What an excellent idea."

"A charming—and unexpected—encounter!"

Etc., etc. And there were several people of good faith in the room who were sure that that encounter had been long meditated—of which they could not be too well-advised by fine perspicacity, aided by the most flagrant appearances, only exercised very prudently.

But the shortest stories are the best; the little supper so ingeniously prepared was not without consumers. With a tranquil and laudable frankness, Loulie declared, in fact, that she had expected anther partner.

"That delay is unpardonable!" exclaimed Cimaise—and he did not put any into declaring to Loulie the sentiments that had always animated him in her regard. She accepted the expression of them, both keen and fortunate.

The following morning, Loulie and Cimaise took the train to Saint-Jean-de-Luz, a matter of varying their horizon. Loulie left her luggage behind, not anticipating prolonging that detour in her itinerary. And toward five o'clock in the evening, from Guethary, she sent a telegram to the hotel she had quit that morning, addressed to Jean, who should have arrived there several hours before.

That telegram was as brief as any respectable telegram:

Slight delay. Will return at midnight. Pardon. Tenderness. L.

And when she returned, he pardoned her, believing it to be a stupid negligence and a slight rancor on the part of his "crazy little darling," and she apologized, and they were very happy.

Pail Cimaise took the train to Paris the same night with a pleasant memory, his valise and a certain philosophy.

THE LITTLE ORIENTAL QUESTION
(*La Fronde*, 26 February 1900)

"THROUGH the petty Bohemia of hotel life figures pass as varied as those in a good comedy-pantomime; some are grotesque, others are charming; such was a woman, almost a child, whom we had nicknamed 'the little Oriental Question.'"

Doremus had adopted the attitude of someone about to tell a story; and as, veritably, we had nothing better to do than listen on the warm and pale starry night that gave the impression of an Opéra stage-set to the terrace where, in a very banal fashion, after a good dinner, some were smoking and others respiring the perfume of roses; he was graciously invited him to continue, with the aid of a few interrogations simultaneously polite and curious.

The mistress of the house was surely enchanted to see her company distracted for a quarter of an hour without it being necessary to "launch a subject" or to have recourse to the inevitable gossip, sometimes skirting disquieting gaffes.

So Doremus spoke.

"She was sixteen years old; she arrived in a straight line from Constantinople with her parents. Her father, a businessman, had married a Levantine who had given him eleven children, all of whom had lived. He came to the thermal station for the health of one of his heirs—or, rather, his unique heir, for he only had one unfortunate son lost in the tumultuous flood of ten little sisters, all of them pretty, of which Seryem was the oldest. She was not pretty; she was the living and divine mystery of beauty itself. She wore that on her like a royalty, a harmony, to such a point that, on the first evening, when she went into the restaurant with her father and her brother, who was a year younger than her, there was a swell of admiration in gazes and murmurs, which seemed to rise from all the people gathered there to come and envelop her, to consecrate her as the priestess and the idol of a universal and superior worship . . ."

"He's both lyrical and unoriginal, our storyteller, don't you think?" murmured someone in the shadows to another someone, who acquiesced vaguely. And perhaps they were not wrong, but they had both racked their brains throughout dinner and had found nothing but exclamations without variety and English slang terms to make one shiver, concerning the different sports by means of which one awaits the regeneration of French youth.

Placidly, without hurrying, Doremus continued.

"Idol! She was certainly that: eyes that seemed to be carved in some undiscoverable black stone more brilliant and purer than crystal; eyes that could have dispensed her, for as long as she lived, from speaking, so many things did they say on their own! And yet they often seemed to sleep, motionless and indifferent, and one could have dedicated to her this phrase from *Salammbô*: 'and her large eyes, beneath her large eyebrows, were like suns beneath triumphal arches.'

"Her face was a narrow and neat oval, as if circled by the stroke of an ideal design. Within it, breaking the splendor of an amber and pearl complexion, was a sculpted mouth and the most admirable little nose that one could see: a rare nose, which did not offer in profile either the severe dryness of so-called Greek noses or the misplaced eccentricity of upturned noses, or noses crushed by excessive flatness. And that eighth wonder of the world held the universe so well between the heavy and obscure wave of her blue-black hair and her little neck of a straight and round statue that one could not weary of looking at her. That beauty, so admirable, but of a type that could so easily become tedious, was combined with an extraordinarily enigmatic grace. The slow movement of her eyelids only seemed to be one of multiple expressions of a secret magic and charm. Charm was exhaled from that individual like a perfume, and beauty seemed to float like the weight of an amour, an almost tragic pain or desire. That creature had attitudes immobilized in melancholy before the sea, the night and music. Her silences were an infinite comprehension. Of what was she dreaming thus, that child whose happy and luxurious life fulfilled, one could have believed, all her caprices?

"That was what we wondered about the Turk that we had come to call in our little group, I don't know how, 'the little Oriental question,' because she seemed to us to be complicated and obscure, to the point of being indecipherable.

"She spoke very little French, and, being conscious of speaking it very poorly, she scarcely indicated by a monosyllable, with an appearance of delectable alarm, that she had understood some topic of conversation or other.

"Her mother scarcely quit her apartment, where she remained collapsed among fans and cups of coffee; Seryem also lived somewhat apart from the rest of the smala. She was almost constantly with her father and her brother. The former scarcely seemed to occupy himself with anything but the latter, whom he seemed to surround with all dreads and desperate hopes, explained by the fact that the child in question was the only one of his species in that vast family. So it was generally thought that for some reason, Seryem was neglected and not much loved . . .

"Had she sketched a romance that had aroused wrath around her? More than one of us would have resumed the imaginable romance while Seryem passed like an ardent light through the bleak banality of the hotel sojourn.

"But, dazzling and irritating, 'the little Oriental question' passed by, in fact, and never stopped in response to any advance or attempt at flirtation. She followed the unreal path of her soul and her desire, as revealed by her eyes, her mouth and her entire being of mysterious and omniscient beauty . . ."

Doremus stopped. Thre was a short silence. We waited respectfully, for Doremus was not of the young phalanx, and we thought that he was taking his time to arrive at the culminating point of his story. However, as he did not go on, someone permitted himself to proffer: "And then?"

"Then? Well, the aftermath was last year—which is to say, twenty years later; you see, 'the little Oriental question' wasn't born yesterday . . . I was in the same town, at the same hotel, when a family disembarked identical to the one of which Seryem had once appeared to be the ideal and enigmatic jewel. The coincidence was amusing and I took an interest in that new smala: twelve children, this time . . . and what did I discover? The mother of that brood was the same Seryem! Reasons of health brought her back there. She spoke French well now, and I authorized myself on the basis of the distant encounter to permit me to introduce myself. She was prepared to believe me when I reminded her, but did not recognize me and admitted it to me frankly.

"Of her beauty there remained 'her large eyes under her large eyebrows,' but they had lost all mystery. Without telling her what they had lost, I recounted to her one day how much she had moved us and intrigued us before. She seemed excessively surprised, but a surprise without unexpectedness, without brilliance: an empty surprise, so to speak. She seemed to be thinking: 'What does that signify?'

"Seeing that simple astonishment, I persisted. 'Yes,' I said, 'we imagined I know not what drama and dream in your life.

You were like a heroine in fantastic and delightful tales, and your gaze, your thought, your entire heart seemed to be so far, far away, dreaming of we knew not what!'"

"'I only ever had one dream and one desire,' said Madame Seryem, gravely, 'and that for much longer than I can remember . . .'

"'And it was . . . ?' I interrogated, boldly.

"'To have twelve children . . . my mother had only had eleven; I wanted to surpass that figure.'

"She told me that placidly, simply, profoundly and sincerely, I sensed; and her eyes, her prodigious eyes of old, appeared to me then as those of an honest ruminant.

"And that was the solution of the 'little question of the Orient.'"

Immediately, some laughed and others started discussing the question of repopulation.

Meanwhile, Doremus sensed around him a certain surprise.

"You find my story absurd? Well, undoubtedly, because it's true, and I've disdained to ornament it with romantic peripeties. Such as it is, myself, I find it heart-rending, for there is nothing sadder than a beauty full of the attraction of a varied and passionate soul, in whom that appearance is a lie."

Many felt that Doremus was decidedly becoming what we call a bore.

THE THREE DOROTHÉES
(*La Fronde*, 6 March 1900)

THE three Dorothées were well-known in the village of Souize-la-Rivière. They lived in a single-story house surrounded by a narrow garden between the high road and the Benoit orchard.

There was old Dorothée, young Dorothée and little Dorothée.

The old one was a widow, and so was the young one.

The old one had a face like a little rennet apple crumpled by frost and the wind, a face puckered by a thousand wrinkles in which two black eyes shone like two black pearls, and which was always smiling. People even wondered where that smile came from, for old Dorothée's mouth hardly existed any longer, eaten away by age before being consumed by death; her lips, when she spoke, were merely a narrow gray line over her naked gums. Eternally clad in repeatedly-washed gray cotton cloth, always neat, her head swathed in a checkered kerchief, Old Dorothée was a pleasant sight.

Her daughter, who was habitually known as the Jewess, already appeared to have had no youth, although she was actually no older than forty. She was a strong woman with hair already gray, with a very red face, as shiny as if she had scrubbed it with the same care as the tiles of her kitchen, of which she was proud. That was because there had been money in the house a few years before. Dorothée had married Jean the miller, and commerce in flour was going well. But one afternoon in August Jean was brought back, crushed by his mill, and so horrible to behold that often, by night, she still awoke uttering screams because she had seen him again in a dream: a formless mass of bloody flesh, him, who had been so robust and so handsome. He left her a child, an only daughter, who had then attained her twelfth year.

Little Dorothée was so lively and cheerful that she made an endless sunshine and spring in the house all by herself. She grew up as straight and as beautiful as a strong little plant, with her brown curls always in a fringe over her golden eyes and her fresh and velvety cheeks; she seemed never to perceive that restriction reigned around her—more than restriction, almost poverty, for, forced to surrender the mill, the two Dorothées had seen themselves adroitly hoodwinked and robbed, and the sale of the vegetables cultivated in their narrow strip of land and the knitting and sewing work of the two women could barely nourish them.

Naturally, the grandmother and the mother had wanted to associate little Dorothée with those endeavors at an early age. They did not ask much of her, for she was adored and pampered, but the little that they asked of her she had the art of always avoiding. She was fatigued, or the weather was "too beautiful" or even that she "didn't know how." That was her best reason: "I don't know how . . ."

"Well, I'll teach you," said her mother, but then the little girl looked at her with her malign and desperate eyes, and if she consented to "try" it did not go very far.

She was intelligent, but of an eccentric, very particular, intelligence that made the people of Souize-la-Rivière say: "Little Dorothée is nice, but alas, she's loony."

When Dorothée learned to read, she unearthed illustrated pages left and right and God knows where, and was soon able to recount extraordinary stories that she read therein. That gave young Dorothée a high idea of her daughter's intelligence. She, so reasonable and so energetic, looked at that beloved child with the eyes of amour—which is to say, blindly. She saw her with pride become a very pretty creature, but she did not see that she was becoming greedy, coquettish and terribly slothful.

The Benoits having complained of numerous thefts committed in their orchard, and having kept watch, saw one moonlit night that the thief was none other than little Dorothée. Seeing that she had been discovered, the latter did not try to hide; she was full of bravado, and so seductive and repentant with regard to the rude Père Benoit, that he, who had sworn to administer a famous beating to the fellow when he caught him, contented himself with tugging the "little rascal's" ears and telling her that when she wanted apples she should come to ask him for them.

And little Dorothée went, audaciously, two days later.

When they learned that, old and young Dorothée felt a great shame, and strove to make the child understand and share that sentiment. But the child looked at them with her beautiful tender eyes and turned her little head like a kitten . . .

Meanwhile, the two women were killing themselves trying to maintain their house decently, which they feared having to sell one day, and to nourish and clothe their child. They sometimes said to her: "You won't find a boy to marry you if you don't know how to make soup, mend his clothes, weed a garden or milk a cow . . . or do anything, in sum!"

Furtive and light, little Dorothée escaped and ran to the river; she knew a calm and shady little creek where, leaning over the water, she saw a ravishing image.

That image was her own, and Dorothée, who, at fifteen years of age, knew nothing, knew very well that "in stories" little girls who have pretty faces do not remain all alone for long in their little corner. Now, Souize-la-Rivière was truly a "little corner" of the vast world. Life there was uniform between the mornings and the evenings, and between the evenings and the mornings. It was good there in shady or sunlit places, and little Dorothée, who did not have a wicked heart, liked the spoiling and tenderness that she found "at home." But more than all that—which she knew—Dorothée liked what she did not know . . . so she began to find it terribly black and sad, her little corner of the sunlit and placid village, but neither old Dorothée nor young Dorothée—her gray-haired mother—perceived it, because they could not conceive of any other world, any other life, or any other desires than those that attained, day after day, the possibility—quite simply—of living.

But one evening, like a bird, little Dorothée flew away.

How? Where? And with whom?

No one was able to say, exactly.

And the two Dorothées—almost immediately, they were called the two old ones—continued to toil, weeding and knitting, but their hearts had become so large and heavy that they seemed to be bent over the ground, as if it were only there that they would be able to repose from their toil. They had become almost mute, and walked bent double, humiliated, while Souize-la-Rivière repeated: "Ah, little Dorothée! She'll make her way, the rascal!"

If little Dorothée made her way, the two old ones were never able to do so. They ended up utterly miserable, had to sell their house and after dragging on a little further, died.

At about the same time, in the city, at the end of a supper flowery with women and roses, someone amused himself by asking those women for their stories. Some refused, others were sincere, the majority lied. One of them let it be understood that she had had an obscure childhood but a very flattering illegitimate birth.

She was able to narrate that admirably, with beautiful eyes charged with tender melancholy, while her mouth was sculpted for fascinating laughter. When someone said: "Show us your hands," she held them out, proud and sure of herself. Those hands, which had never worked, were slender and ravishing, and she agitated them gently, her frail, pink little hands, charged with gems, gazing unconsciously among the roses, into the mirror that covered the table, at her face, as she had gazed at it once in the calm and shady little creek, leaning over the water . . .

WINTER HEATHS
(*La Fronde*, 13 March 1900)

THE heath, as vast and changing as the sea, takes on all its beauty on winter mornings when it shivers, enveloped with the brilliant tulle of frost, melancholy and infinite, under the great pale sky in which the torn gauze of clouds fold up and deploy around the pale sun.

The russet ferns and the mauve heather give it a dappled adornment.

The clear atmosphere seems woven in crystal. The thickets, all thin branches and leafless twigs, are lacy and tremulous under a light wind that is scarcely perceptible as it passes. On the edge of the woods, on the hedges dotted with red berries, a population of birds takes flight with a rustle of silk and shrill cries.

A road cuts through the heath; that road is bordered by narrow ditches filled with stagnant water, and that water is half-frozen—not completely; all pink, all violet and all green, reflections of the earth and the branches, which give it their mirage like a kiss, that water resembles a mirror in broken fragments, a very ancient metallic mirror, tarnished by contact with too many faces—and those faces, annihilated a long time ago, it keeps forever: of their eyes, the extinct colors; of the fair or dark hair that veiled them, the veil of gold and shadow that trembles and still saddens its flat surface.

Who, then, has wanted to say that it is monotonous, the varied and magnificent heath?

It has no equal but the sea, and for having loved them as one loves animate and amorous creatures, one takes the rancor and horror of the monochrome landscapes of certain mountains that, like very beautiful women, seem to seize the pretext of that very beauty for the terrible insipidity of an invariable expression.

Here, there is an extreme grace in a detail of almost dry precision, apparently analogous to the delightful art of primitives in which all voluptuousness is dormant under the divinely calm harmony of lines.

A mysterious and magnetic beauty, which one pursues without wearying in order to adore and know all its roads, only marked by the double rut of heavy carts that hollow them out, roads that seem almost useless, dying who knows where, in the plain or the forest, where they are lost and rediscovered indefinitely in clumps of pines that cover them with an eternal shadow. Between the violet trunks of those trees, one can see the horizon scintillating like water.

Some of those roads, dulled by the gray of dried, ashy mud, intersect at crossroads where one would like to pause one's soul and one's life—in a dream, for those routes and that intersections seem to be chosen for the passage and the halt of a people of fays and witches. Oh, but very gentle witches of the woods, whose philters are devoid of poisons, and their incantations devoid of malefic spells. They must come on moonless nights, the queens of the trees and the plains, and dance silent rounds there, only illuminated by the whiteness of their interlaced hands. But those crossroads are deserted on winter mornings and solemn in silence.

The respiration of the world seems suspended here, and the heart is constricted as if before a beautiful dead woman one once loved.

That is because the land where one lived as child is alive with the individual and quivering life of an animate creature; it bears into the past the gilded hours of the joy of young mornings, and a little of the ingenuous and sacred alarm of evenings "when one was afraid!" Fear, a marvelous word, evocative of terrifying enchantments, the black sister of dusks dotted with stars when the lunar sky populates the earth with great dancing shadows!

Who has not traversed, in some evening of distant childhood, a large familiar garden, but which the night suddenly makes into a prodigious unknown, in order to search in the depth of pathways, behind the bushes, for some forgotten object? And who, that evening, at the blissful age when one sees further into the impossible than the real, has not sensed the irrational, mad and omnipotent fear that suddenly takes you by the throat and the legs, in order to prevent you from crying out or walking? And, with the eyes, peering into the obscurity, staring at horrible things that do not exist, and the ears filled with the sound of the ocean, whoever has known that fear has tasted a voluptuousness with a savor that the memory does not forget. They are the phantoms of evenings of old, of great, long summer evenings in which the light of the pink sky cannot die, but when that light remains suspended above the earth like a veil; it is them who populate the heath with their floating gait on this winter morning.

They emerge from beneath the clumps of russet furze and shake like feathers the frail little fir-trees what frost has made all rosy, fragile and implausible, like toys of spun glass. "It's us, it's us, don't you recognize us?" And they tell charming stories today to which one did not listen before when one sensed them palpitating in obscure thickets. They have the names of fays and beasts—how one would love, this evening, to see them again, with the same soul as of old, at the deserted crossroads . . .

But this will not be a summer evening—so soft that its blue pallor is less radiant than a pink dawn—this will be a winter evening when the wind will cry like a slaughtered beast in the branches, and skim the health with its mad gallop.

To see again this long-abandoned land where one was moved to puerile tenderness by details always identical—so that nothing seems to change here . . . In the old forest, trees have been felled and fires have eaten away entire kilometers of woodland with their ardent tongue—but on the corroded and rusted edges, an entire young forest is sprouting, thick and straight, and among the nascent plants are fir-trees so green that they seem artificially varnished; black and white herds in the far distance are like a game of dominoes symmetrically placed.

Yes, everything is immobile here—or seems so. The seasons, in passing, only change in eternal rhythm the color of the heath; autumn makes it pink with delicate heather with a thousand tightly-packed frail florets, and the golden gorse makes it all blonde in spring, with a river of flowers shaken in clusters, but it is less varied then than on a winter morning, when it is clad in the sumptuous grandeur of that which is placid and strong.

In traversing it, such as it is now, such as one loved it so much once, one senses how much the soul might be faithful to two various amours—for all the heart remains attached to the russet, melancholy and infinite heath; but because the enormous City that one has just quit holds you by all the senses, one cannot forget it even here—whereas within it, one forgets everything.

THE WHITE DONKEY
(*La Fronde*, 27 March 1900)

IT was a charming little Algerian donkey, white and lustrous, with beautiful innocent eyes, saddled and bridled with white reins trimmed with gold and a little saddle of white leather. As such, it was offered to a blonde child, who was enchanted with that plaything, larger and more amusing than all her others.

And she had a great many ingenious and magnificent playthings, Frilah, the spoiled and adored child, to charm her pretty young childhood, her delicate capricious childhood of a frail little girl who was stopped too often in the middle of her games in the midst of laughter, by obscure nasty pains, which prevented her from walking and running and fixed her big beautiful eyes in an expression of sad astonishment.

Frilah seemed to say: *Why? Why suffer when one is so small, when one has not much strength, and one has done nothing to deserve it?* And yet it was thus: Frilah suffered.

And because of that, because of the pains that often paralyzed her feeble little legs, she had been given this pretty little white Algerian donkey, which carried her along the pathways of the garden, very gently.

That little white donkey had been baptized with an Arabic name, but Frilah immediately suppressed that name, which did not say anything to her, and gave him another, which for her, summarized everything; she called him Treasure.

And Frilah and Treasure became great friends. However, Treasure had fits of melancholy. When the hand that was guiding him restrained his whims to gallop and hindered his impetus, Treasure thought about the plains of sand and short grass where he had trotted madly in his beautiful free youth, and as he was still young he suffered from the calm gait that was imposed on him. But for love of the little girl who had posed on his neck, simultaneously rude and soft, for the pity he had for the little tottering being who could scarcely take three steps without falling to her knees, Treasure allowed himself to be led obediently.

One day, Frilah perceived the sadness of that resigned mildness. She interrogated.

"What's the matter with my Treasure? He looks unhappy."

And stupidly, someone replied to her: "It's because he's accustomed to running, and he no longer runs."

"Ah!" said Frilah, pensively.

And she ordered that he be allowed to gallop freely every day before the hour of her excursion on her little white donkey. But Treasure did not rediscover in that tended park the intoxication of the plain with the vast horizon, the inciter of mad gallops and ridiculous and delightful bounds, and whatever effort was made to get a grip on him, on his nostalgia of an affectionate donkey. Treasure deteriorated visibly. And Frilah had such a chagrin in consequence that her excursions no longer did her any good.

Nervous and sensitive, she wept when she looked at Treasure's languid eyes, understanding that it was necessary either to see him dying slowly before her or to separate from him and send him to the wild liberty of the expanses of sand and short grass, where he would recover all his vigor by using his little hooves to run and run.

Was it just to make two prisoners where there was only one condemnation? Frilah knew full well the only one condemned was her, who would soon no longer be able to walk at all, not at all, and perhaps—who could tell?—would no longer even be able to have herself carried by Treasure for the slow excursions around the neat pathways of the park . . .

✳

Frilah can see her father and her mother hiding their tears when they look at her, and gradually, Frilah resigns herself; she almost forgets what the joy of free movement is, the allure of the noisy and rapid life of other children, but she does not forget that Treasure is ill . . .

Yes, Treasure, afflicted by a sudden illness, remains extended on the litter of blonde and fresh straw and only turns a languid eye when Frilah, carried in her father's arms, comes to flatter and caress her Treasure.

And Treasure hears someone say: "What a pity that that donkey is ill! He was the last pleasure of that little girl!"

And Treasure sees, in fact, with what desirous eyes Frilah gazes at the little saddle of white leather and the reins rimmed with gold, and that she is refusing everything that is offered to her in her great chagrin at seeing her favorite ill . . .

Then Treasure makes an effort—superhuman, one might say! He feigns strength, enthusiasm, raises himself up on his four thin feet and turns his intelligent muzzle toward the pretty harness . . .

And for day after day, Frilah, ever paler, on Treasure, ever weaker, make the little excursion at a slow pace, and it is Frilah who, definitively weary, lies down first, never to get up again, and one evening, closes her eyes, never to open them again.

By a thousand signs, Treasure has understood; his little mistress will no longer come to flatter his rude and soft neck. Then he too can also repose, and, dreaming of the plains of sand and short grass where he wore away his little hooves in mad gallops and ridiculous and delightful bounds, the little white donkey, the poor little exiled Algerian donkey, died one evening, exhausted by all the fine courage of his conscience of an affectionate donkey . . .

THE OLD WINDOW
(*La Fronde*, 3 April 1900)

AN old window carved like the calyx of a complicated flower in the old stone. In the hours of sunlight a scrap of red cloth closed the frame of the window, but at the calm moment of the gentle violet dusk that extended over things like a caress, that improvised blind was removed, and often, on the broad sill sculpted by some distant artist asleep under the soil of Italy and worn by the elbows of several generations, four thin young arms were often seen leaning on it and agitating like disorganized little stems, and two little faces that seemed the double heart of that old stone flower . . .

The curt and heavy little waves of the melancholy and yellow Arno licked the pillars of the old bridge that supported the ancient dwellings like the cells of a beehive in its thick flanks. The sky was golden-red in the west and a precious mauve like a rare amethyst in the pale and bright orient.

The great heat of the day vanished in light mists at the level of banks blue-tinted with shadow and frail breaths of exquisite freshness seemed to flow like a gentle atmospheric rain from the heights of unreal hills of ideal design and divine color.

Sellers of ice, lemons and licorice-water chanted their appeals in charming voices. The old stones and the heavy waters of the river prolonged those singsong voices in echoes. An infinite sweetness of living, which appeared eternal, trailed its soft web of beauty, harmony and indolence over beings and things. It was like a veil of precious lace cast in order to blur lines and attenuated collisions.

The two little girls with the naked brown arms that agitated like stems over the edge of the window, two little girls with fresh faces, were talking and laughing.

They were talking about amour, because it is good to talk about that at fifteen years of age—and at other ages—when one is amorous.

Barbarella and Isotta had many lovers, and they did not love any of their lovers, so they were laughing on that evening in June between the roses of the sky and the opal of the river.

There was Giuseppe, who always had such a funny expression as he gazed at Isotta when he came to visit her mother, and Barbarella, an orphan who lived with her aunt and her cousin Isotta, reminded the latter with forceful grimaces how Ludovico kissed her hands in the shadow of stairways when he encountered her going up or down—for Ludovico lived in the same house, but his windows did not overlook the Arno; he only had a little room on the corner over the street and the bridge.

"I believe he's very poor," said Barbarella. And Barbarella, who was poor herself, was smitten with splendors. Isotta's mother had a little shop of pewters, sequins and bronzes, all sculpted and gilded, brilliant trinkets that made the shop, opening under the arcade of the bridge, gleam like a huge yellow eye. That golden eye attracted enough buyers—and then, there were also those two living and fresh flowers in the boutique: Isotta and Barbarella. They were good and dainty little girls who worked hard in the narrow apartment open over the Arno and in the obscure and shiny boutique open on the bridge. They did the housework and the display; they were indefatigable and sage. But toward evening, when the boutique was closed and Isotta's mother went to chat with the neighbor, Isotta and Barbarella leaned out of the window that held the entire red horizon and

the golden river, to talk about amour, laughing like little luna-
tics because they did not love their lovers.

This evening, however, Isotta does not laugh at Barbarella's
pleasantries regarding Ludovico. She says: "Ah!" with a thoughtful expression.

Barbarella, who is shrewd and malicious, sees that and says
to her cousin: "If he pleases you, my lover, I give him to you!"

Isotta replies that she "can do better than that," and
Barbarella pricks up her ears, because Barbarella, whose father
married a daughter of a noble but ruined family has ideas of
grandeur. Barbarella often looks at her ankles and wrists, so
slender, thinking with pride that she has princely blood in her
veins. (She is doubtless exaggerating a little, but she is so young
and so sincere!)

Barbarella thinks that one day, a pale and handsome young
man will descend from an armoried caleche at the door of the
boutique of pewters and sequins, and while bargaining for the
brilliant trinkets will fall in love with her, Barbarella, who bears
such a pretty, proud and sweet name, because he will find in
her the manners of a queen and amorous eyes . . .

That is what Barbarella thinks.

And Isotta with the face as round as a fruit and the brilliant
eyes does not say what she is thinking while she watches the
fugitive reflection of tremulous stars opening, running and dying in the water . . .

Boats follow the thread of water with a silky sound. Red
lanterns light up along the banks and songs vibrate in the pure
nocturnal air; Florence is singing in the blue and delectable
night.

What is Isotta thinking? She shudders at Barbarella's voice . . .

Barbarella sighs and says: "I'd really like to eat a
watermelon"—for Barbarella has a taste for the realities of life.
Then she affirms: "I have some money. Come on, Isotta; Mama
hasn't come back; let's go to the square to eat watermelon . . ."

But Isotta withdraws her little bare brown arms with regret from the old window sill where she was leaning so limply. Barbarella is already looking for her headscarf in the gloom of the chamber—not to protect her from the cool of the evening but because it is red, silky and suits her very well.

Isotta calls her back, and hesitantly: "Tell me, Barba carissima—you don't love Ludovico?"

Barbarella laughs wholeheartedly. "Oh, cara, cara mia, no, no, I don't love him . . ."

"Then . . . then, me, I love him," declares Isotta.

Barbarella is delighted. Isotta was lying, then, jut now?

She loves Ludovico! Great God! As long as he loves her, and can forget me, Barbarella thinks, modestly. For then, the first young and handsome lord who stops his carriage at the door of the boutique will be for her—for her, Barbarella! And Barbarella's vivid imagination sees every scene of the marvelous romance, from the first—the disturbance of that lord before her, the humble Barbarella, who has already had the blood of a princess in her frail blue veins—until the glorious day when, trampling underfoot prejudices of birth and family opposition, the young lord will beg for the hand of Barbarella . . .

And confusedly, Barbarella, rendering confidence for confidence, initiates Isotta into the charming future that will be hers, while she drags her at a run down the stairs in order to go and eat watermelons in the square where Florence is singing in the blue and delectable night . . .

And the old window carved like the calyx of a complicated flower in the old stone seems to smile with its sculpted mascarons, and incline its broad sill, worn by the elbows of several generations, toward the river with the heavy and slow flow, for it is the accomplice, the old window, of all those follies and all those dreams . . .

THE RED PORTRAIT
(*La Fronde*, 10 April 1900)

IT was truly a very bizarre portrait. It seemed to be painted in a severe and formal manner, entirely covered in a patina of shadow by time, and in the dull light of gray days it seemed to be smeared with ocher, smoke-stained, devoid of relief and almost devoid of color—an utterly negligible painting, devoid of interest—and even its evident antiquity did not give it any value, because, not only did it not bear the signature of any of the innumerable masters of the abundant Italian epoch of the fourteenth century, but no invisible magical indication of some glorious name was revealed by the flamboyance of the brushwork, lines and colors.

No, it was a very ordinary portrait in its composition, and yet it was bizarre. To begin with, there was what it represented: a tall, seated figure, the face making a patch scarcely any brighter than the ensemble, a figure wholly enveloped in fabrics with heavy and obscure folds, which did not stand out clearly from a background of drapes that were equally somber and confused. That figure seemed so indistinct that one was not entirely sure whether it as a prelate, a queen or an image of symbolic fantasy.

To say all, and to be perfectly sincere, it was impossible to discern the identity and the meaning of the figure.

That portrait, placed above a mantelpiece in one of the rooms of the Sorona palace, did not differ sensibly from numerous paintings that encumbered the other rooms of the palace, pragmatically broken up into apartments that were hired out by the month or the year to strangers. Everywhere, there were frescoes and mediocre paintings, certainly going back one or two centuries, at least giving evidence of the furious but somewhat unreliable taste of ancestors for such decorations.

In the room where the painting in question was placed, situated at one of the corners of the palace—or, rather, the villa—three windows opened, two to the north and one to the west. Thus, poorly illuminated by the sunlight for most of the day, that room was invaded by light—and the most violent light, that of the setting sun, which darts its flames horizontally, burning and spreading rivers of gems—at about five o'clock in the evening in the summer months. Now, that was precisely the hour at which people deserted the palace in order to seek outside, in the gardens, on the terraces or on the strand, the exquisite freshness that fell in a long frisson from the paler sky after stifling days.

Thus, people rarely traversed that room at the moment when it was veritably illuminated. One evening, however, someone went through it, uttered a cry and called out; people came and were amazed: the portrait, the banal, black and wretched portrait, was shining with an extraordinary life.

The figure, of a dazzling pallor, was animated by the ardent reflection of the sumptuous crimson simarre that fell in magnificent unfurled pleats over the shoulders and flanks and around the feet. The hair, cut short over the forehead and flowing in straight and bushy tresses along the cheeks, was a fiery blonde, almost red, and one could hardly see anything of the face but the strong lips, very red: lips that gave the rare, intense, almost disagreeable sensation, so singular were they, of living lips stuck, moist and bleeding, to that icy canvas . . .

The almost-closed eyes were a scarcely-visible line of light under the lowered eyelids, the slender nose and the thin cheeks were strangely effaced between that russet mane and the ardent lips. A single hand appeared, the other being buried under the flood of crimson fabric; that long, pale hand, resting on the knee, was open and presented to the public a small casket in which jewels were shining, and from that same casket fell in delicately artful disorder a hand full of red flowers: carnations, dahlias, roses and ranunculi, slightly ragged and slightly withered.

Those details of composition had always escaped the gaze. Now, in the rays of the sun low over the horizon, facing the portrait and covering it with glory and gold, all of that seemed a work of exquisite genius, and the unique and infinite color of the portrait, the royal color crimson and blood, was so marvelously nuanced that the rutilance of the red hair, the violent or bright planes of the fabrics—velvets and damasks—the fires of the gems—pink and red rubies, almost bloody amethysts, chaplets of coral—and that entire ardent figure seemed to quiver with a magnificent life, ready to stand up, surge forth from its wooden frame and traverse that room with an imperial tread, strewing those gems and those flowers on the carpet . . .

But suddenly, the great golden light was extinguished, the window was pale and empty as the star slipped behind the hill, and people protested around the portrait; it had immediately become dark and insignificant again. From then on, however, it was known as "the red portrait," without anyone remembering exactly why, once that magic had vanished, or deciding whether it was a portrait of a very young prelate, a princess, or a simple symbolic image.

✳

In archives that I was reading through curiously one day for some study, I happened upon a series of notes, brief and terrible letters, visibly gathered together in a single file after the fact—too late!

The unsigned notes contained details that clearly designated their author: the illustrious Paolo Sorona, whose voluptuous and violent humor had once ravaged Florence. Paolo Sorona had married an adorable creature of a bizarre and perfect beauty and a soul so clear and pure that he was never able to recognize it as such, accustomed as he was to stirring up the worst disturbances of the heart and the senses under the most candid gazes. But Bianca, his wife, defied by her child-like innocence his most skillful experiments; and this is what can be reconstructed of such a dramatic romance by rereading those notes and letters: notes made by the husband, who, after having confided the care of executing a portrait of his wife to a young and celebrated painter, became absolutely convinced of the treason of that wife with the young man he was lodging, and between that certitude and the vengeance he decided, he did not even put the space of a single night . . .

One evening, at sunset, without wanting to listen to Bianca's tears, he killed her in the same room where the great portrait, finished the day before, had just been placed. Before the next day dawned, the young painter disappeared, and no one ever saw him again. It was a time of prompt justice . . .

Now, accompanying those tragic annals, a small wad was found of brief notes full of such touching emotion and such pure sincerity that one could not read them without suffering, and weeping a little.

They had, in fact, loved one another, Bianca and her young painter, who had slowly, amorously and strangely fixed her in such a curious portrait. All their amour was revealed there, entirely in his letters to her, and divinable in all her letters to him . . . and also all the severe prohibition of the woman: how she refused the adultery that, she said, would have "stained" her amour, that amour so sad: "All that I can give you will thus remain splendid and pure—always you will see me therein entire, and thus you will possess all my heart . . ."

For the rest, the lovely perishable beauty that he implored, she gave it for the last time, one beautiful evening, to the dagger that mingled her blood with the fire of the setting sun . . .

Had that correspondence been found too late by the spouse, or had it been added even later, by some mysterious care, to the written account of brutal appearances?

This, no one will ever know: whether, when alive, with a frisson, the husband ever saw at sunset, animated with a strange and magnificent life and, seeming to surge forth from its dull frame, the *red portrait* . . .

IN THE CHINESE STYLE
(*La Fronde*, 23 April 1900)

To Monsieur R.B.

"YOUR hair, drawn back over the temples, makes your eyes sharp, which are heightened and thinned further by a dab of kohl . . .

"Sitting on your rice mat with your legs crossed in a diamond-shape and your little feet shod in leather, wood and silk, placed one against the other like two absurd and delightful playthings, you seem to be painted on a complicated old fan, very 'porcelain lady . . .'

"Stay like that for a while, I beg you, and after having played in Chinese style for your own pleasure, for the taste of those multicolored, growing and brilliant satin adornments, where birds, chimeras, pagodas and mandarins fix immeasurable dreams with threads of silk, gold and silver, I beg you to prolong your game in order that I can lull my pain a little therein . . . You can't know, don't ask me anything . . ."

She fixed herself, obediently, in the clever and puerile attitude, very "porcelain lady," her eyes blinking slightly, fatigued by the tightening of her black hair over her amber temples.

He gazed at her with a tender attention. He loved her more in seeing her with a prettiness so different from her habitual fashion of being pretty. That attitude, entirely charming, presented to the crowds a thin little creature with a pale complexion enlivened by artificial touches of a delicate pink, with dark eyes painted very large but keen and brilliant as a bird's eyes, and dark hair perfectly undulated, which, by means of its arrangement, enlarged the oval of the face, a little too long and a little too thin, in which two sinuous lips smiled incessantly over the teeth of a puppy.

Now, those hermetically closed lips designed the mouth of a doll, very red and immobile. The hair, completely disengaged from the forehead and the temples, stacked in a complicated chignon, accentuated the length of the profile, all the fine details of which took on the value of a work of art curiously sculpted in beautiful luminous ivory.

With her usual make-up entirely removed and the face made up again with powders, pastes, unguents and pencils found amid the delightful unpacking of open caskets, Suzanne, known as Crampette to a few intimates, represented a perfect barbaric and comical figurine, and, because she was very conscious of her bizarre grace, she entered into her role so completely that it seemed that a fragment of the Chinese soul, as mysterious, infantile and attractive as a mask, had passed into her, with the slightly sickening odor of those fabrics saturated with perfume and the flash of the coral and jade heads of the long pins planted in her hair . . .

In the comfortable, luxurious and banal room, a kind of studio in which a billiard-table, books, a divan, a desk and drawings pinned to the walls contained all the habitual cycle of Pierre's life, there was suddenly that little idol covered in bright soft silks, living jade posed on a rice mat, like an image born of his reverie and his opium-smoking, disengaged from the slow blue puffs that he drew from his pipe while dreaming of things past.

Whence came that charming and bizarre little figure? Oh, from very far away, from a hot and heavy land, where the hous-

316

es, people and things, and even the dwarf trees in magnificent pots, forming such a marvelous museum decoration, have such an appearance of implausible trinkets uniquely created for the joy and amusement of the eyes that, in spite of the nostalgia, the maladies and the manias of exile, the European sometimes forgets everything in order to play with those absurd and delightful toys as children play with dolls and their tea-sets.

And he had played dolls, like so many others, with a nice little girl who had a name risible for us, but which could be translated into a poetic image.

But he had taken to the game madly, in order to forget, to forget a thousand things left behind . . . and he had arrived at wanting, at any price, to enable a soul to surge forth in the image of tender and supple souls of his own land, in the nice little girl who had fashions so neat, so mild and so fine that they would adapt so well to such a soul. But the little Chinese girl did not understand; and among the flowers of nacre that blossomed on the ebony furniture and under the indigo skies, she remained uniquely and terribly Chinese—adorably Chinese!

And when he left, Pierre had not taken anything of hers, nothing except all her habitual costumes, which he had replaced with others, even more beautiful, and all her apparatus of make-up and small complicated, mysterious and pretty trinkets, giving her identical new ones instead. But over the clear amber of the thin cheeks, not a tear had flowed, and the narrow and crimson lips over the teeth lacquered with gold had not even smiled in surprise. It really was a little idol that he had loved there . . .

And now this one, very modern, very supple, very much of his own race, Suzanne, was returning that already distant image to him, which had relaxed and charmed out there, in the warm and heavy land, his reveries and his opium dreams . . .

He gazed at her, therefore, with a tender attention—she was so similar to the other! And it even seemed that a little of the foreign, mysterious, infantile and attractive soul, like a mask, had passed to her with the slightly sickening odor of those fabrics saturated with perfume and the flash of the little balls of coral and jade that starred her hair . . .

The suggestion was so strong that Pierre wondered suddenly whether, in truth, there was such a vast difference between the souls of the two races. Perhaps Suzanne, like the nice little girl with the risible name revealing the name of a flower or a fruit, would not have wept or smiled, with an exact comprehension of the deflection of the emotions of her friend, if a subtle and innate art of simulation had been a great help to her on such occasions? Perhaps she would have remained just as motionless internally, with an identical soul of an idol, if only she knew her role better . . .

Now Pierre, who did not love Suzanne exclusively, suddenly began to tell her his Chinese story "to see what she would find to say."

And when he had finished, Suzanne exclaimed: "Well, old chap, that has cured you, I think, of your amours in the Chinese style. Pooh! Those women don't have sentiments like us, that's for sure!"

But Pierre remained perplexed. The only things that seemed certain to him was that, Suzanne having manifested a keen desire to possess the dresses and make-up of her distant twin, he gave them to her, judging that a refusal would have been impolite, albeit in accordance with his heart. For amid all that chinoiserie he still retained a predilection for the one *out there*, who, under the indigo skies, among the nacreous flowers blooming on ebony furniture, remained devoid of tears or smiles, in accordance with the mysterious verity of her little closed soul . . .

BIBLICAL MINUTES
(*Minutes Bibliques*, 1902)

RETURN TO GOMORRAH

Because the cry of Sodom and Gomorrah is great,
and because their sin is very grievous.
Genesis 18:20.

THE sky was violet and the valley, pink with mist, undulated like flesh or cloth lifted up toward the sky.

A wall of white mist closed the horizon, where the gold of the rising sun was fusing in triumphant dust.

Outside the city, before that light, she tottered and covered her eyes with her arm—a naked and pale arm. Her tunic was torn, her face bruised and her gait drunken.

At the opposite extremity of the city, twenty-four hours before, she had crossed the gates, leaving behind her, above the Jordan, the same beauty of the morning now displayed, immodest and superb, before her, lying between the flanks of scarcely-indicated mounds, as if in a bed easily accessible to violations.

She had entered directly, fresh in purity, and, going toward the plains of Mamre, where a man she loved was waiting for her, she hastened, thinking that she was choosing the shortest route.

The city was encumbered by women, and entirely burning, devastated like an amorous bed.

For Birsah, the king of Gomorrah, fighting in the valley of Siddim, had taken the men of his people with him, and the young women, alone and free, were living in the summer sunlight the life they loved.

Thus, a great disorder reigned; the gaping thresholds of dwellings were covered in crumpled flowers; between the ardent stones, on the shadowy margins of causeways, little girls were asleep, very weary; their feet, naked and pretty, were dangling in the gutter where water was running rapidly, heavy with oleander petals.

A tenacious, excessively sweet, odor charged the atmosphere.

The open doors and the obscure alleyways exhaled the plaints of doves incessantly: a long and tender murmur brushing the walls and filling the streets like the palpitation of an aviary in perpetual amour.

Over the city the wind from the South, with the sand of the plain, blew the madness of desire and thirst: the harsh thirst for kisses.

A profound breath of pleasure rippled the breasts of virgins spasmodically.

The stranger felt that breath upon her; her lips dried out and her legs were weary.

Unconsciously, she tightened her tunic around her loins.

Terrible old women, their eyes bloody with an unnamable fire and their cheeks livid, whistled monstrous appeals as she passed by.

Children not yet nubile, enlaced and already bearing an exquisite fatigue in their faces, were gazing with avid curiosity at a naked and mutilated boy lying on the ground between them—futile and scornful play for them . . .

The adolescent kept his face hidden, as motionless as a corpse.

But the young women were very beautiful, almost all naked, and under the sun, the splendor of flesh, on which the moisture of pleasure shone, was blinding.

Amid the melee of confounded bodies and limbs, the light of a face smiling with sensuality appeared even brighter; a few brief cries dominated the monotonous song of enjoyment.

The stranger lowered her eyes; a frisson of the knees and the arms left her inert, and she tottered, brushing couples and groups, seized by vertigo.

Two women stopped her.

"Where have you come from?"

With her hand she indicated the blue bright line, the blue line of the sky beyond the ramparts, to the west, and, her eyes encountering the drowned eyes of those women, she trembled.

"What is your name?"

"Ségor . . ." And, in a low voice: "Oh, don't do me any harm . . . I'm afraid."

They uttered a fine languid laugh, a fine cruel laugh.

"You're beautiful, come . . ."

And Ségor went with them.

Something as great as the sky, as troubled as the clouds and as implacable as the enormous sun rising behind her filled her heart and stifled her with an unknown malaise.

The roses of the dawn reminded her of those in which she had spent her night and its delights, in the glare of odorous torches, and, still moist with kisses, she shivered in the breeze—the good odorless breeze.

The fire that was burning her eyelids rendered the soft and light color of the dawn unsustainable to her gaze. Beyond the white fog the plains of Mamre extended, the goal of her journey. Her fiancé lived there.

Yesterday she had gone toward the rough and fecund wedding, and her virgin flanks desired it, of the man who already bore her heart. Today, she was afraid. However, she had fled the city . . . the sickening city of caresses . . .

So she was tottering and covering her eyes with her bare arm.

Beneath the shadow of that arm saturated with perfumes passed enflamed figures . . .

Oh, to fill her eyes with the morning splendor, to bathe them and drown them with light . . . that she might pass here like a strong tide, carrying away the recent and clear image of those frightful joys . . .

The water, the pure water of the dew, in order to wash her mouth, still thirsty, her moist hands, and all of her harassed body . . .

To spread her hair, and, in the fresh wind that passes, to sow the caresses that bind it, the flowers that charge it, the heavy charm that sticks it to the nape of her neck with sweat . . .

Finally, into the light, in the water and in the wind, to cast the dolor of her soul like a vain thing, a dead thing that will be forgotten . . .

Oh, not to drag it there all the way to death, perhaps further—and would it be remorse, or even regret?—but she sensed Gomorrah, attached to the mystery of her being, a terrified memory—a nostalgic memory . . .

THE QUEEN'S PERFUMES

There came no more such an abundance of spices as those
which the Queen of Sheba gave to King Solomon.
1 *Kings* 10:10.

IT was on the great parvis of the house of the park of Liban.
Kneeling on the precious carpet, where their feet sowed
the sand of the route, the yellow beasts enameled by bright
networks extended their heads toward the pure and bleak sky
visible between the columns of cedar.

Around, on the ground, out of bales of painted canvas, evis-
cerated, flowed a river of precious stones and fine gold.

At the back, under the shade of galleries, the queen stood,
upright and straight.

Dusted with a violet powder, she seemed coiffed with a
cloud descending from the edge of her forehead and weighing
upon her eyelids; from her gaze, almost entirely veiled, a little
light seemed to flow over her cheeks, uniform and pale with a
dazzling pallor.

Her arms and her feet were naked outside draperies woven
in silver and embroidered with sapphires; her fingernails, tinted
crimson, shone like fresh blood among the blue softness of her
adornment.

Beyond the porticoes a new caravan advanced, slow and
multicolored, like a giant serpent.

"Here," she said to the attentive king beside her, "are the gold of Ophir and the wood of Almugghim."

And Solomon, sensible to splendors, rejoiced and praised the Queen of Sheba for the abundance and rarity of her presents.

"There is nothing among what I have brought you," she replied, "with which you are not replete, and even this wood of Almugghim—greatly esteemed, it is true—Hiram, King of Tyr, would have sent you immediately, had you expressed the desire . . ."

"Do you not know that Hiram is discontented with your servant? I made him a gift of twenty towns in Galilee, but those towns do not please him."

"Truly?" said the queen, distractedly. She knew that very well, but at that moment, an intact cargo was brought to the foot of the onyx steps, carefully tied, and she could not remember hat it contained.

Leaning like a great flower over its stem, with the brilliant fracture of her garments marking the loins, she interrogated the Ethiopian who was leading the first beast, while the others were lined up—there were thirty, and some were in a second row.

"They're aromatics," he said.

The great flower of the land of the sun, the Queen of the South, stood up and gazed at him, her pupils like fiery flames, but said, modestly;

"It's very little; they're perfumes."

Then the camels were made to kneel down, immobile; they were stripped very rapidly, and, at a sign from the queen, the accumulated bales were all opened at the same time.

King Solomon went pale and shivered. A light smoke, an infinite vapor, filled the courtyard and rose, linking the cedar beams and the bronze columns until it hid the capitals of the columns completely—they measured eighteen cubits in height.

Whether the cloud came from outside through the porticoes of olive-wood or rose from the ground encumbered by riches, animals and strange men, Solomon could not imagine, but his voice changed when he asked: "What's this?"

The Queen of Sheba said: "O my master, they are only perfumes . . ."

The broken ewers exhaled their aroma, mingled with the violent odor of melted pastes; and sponges full of exquisite oils rolled amid the heavy trail of unguents and fards.

From split gourds rose an intoxicating mist of an unknown color, in which the blue of the sky and the royal robe, the mauve of precious woods and the gilded pink of the evening were confounded—an opaque veil that isolated Solomon from the universe.

He could no longer even see the queen, close by; only a glow in the mist indicated the form of that charming body heavy with silver and precious stones.

That glow brushed him, and it seemed to him that the odor, the ambient odor, penetrated him. Whether he drank the saturated air through his nostrils or aspired it through his mouth, whether it entered into his brain through the ears or into his heart by the taste of his tongue, he no longer knew.

But the offering of flesh was tangible, and, hidden from mortals, Solomon thus, as can be read in the Holy Book: "gave the Queen of Sheba all that she asked of him . . ."

A short time after the departure of the Queen of Sheba, King Solomon fell prey to a great anxiety.

His trouble was visible to everyone. It was then that he published a scandalous writing still known today under the name of the *Song of Songs*, but at that time people were blind to the meaning of the work, its author having a great reputation for wisdom.

Far from dissipating, however, his sadness increased. Then he gave himself to debauchery and idolatry—but nothing could make him forget the queen's perfumes.

DELILAH'S REGRET

And when Delilah saw that he had told her all his heart . . .
Judges 16:18.

. . . A ND afterwards, in the dark chamber, he went to sleep . . .

She, still naked, awake and pensive, was thrown back in an attitude of consent and charm . . . but, the heat being great, she got up and opened the door slightly.

The soft and violet evening blew a light air, and, as she turned round, she shivered: two things were shining in the darkness, one mobile and large, like a flame, the other neat and sharp . . .

The beautiful flame, beautiful and agitated, was her lover's hair, and she started to laugh happily—young women in sensual arousal are slightly mad—going toward him, ready for further caresses . . .

However, a thought stops her, and her gaze vacillates at that river of light spread over the neck of a young bull and the brown shoulders of Samson, at the cold and curt gleam of the instrument scintillating on the wall like a vindictive eye.

She remembers . . .

He had spoken before slumber in the dementia of desire; and there, not very far away, behind that door, scarcely open, through which the dying daylight and the perfumed night slid, men are waiting . . . to them she has promised . . .

Now, this evening, in the sad, exceeded accent of her lover—who has lied to her twice—she has sensed the truth pass; and her amorous face becomes attentive, altered by ennui, while she grips his hard throat with her two lovely little hands . . .

What murmur is emerging from his dry mouth?

It is his tender voice of the abandoned hours . . .

What words? Minuscule words, as light as wings, as futile as jewels, as soft as beauty.

"I loved . . . to feel your hair . . . on my face . . ."—and the frisson of a recent memory, the desire of a similar moment renewed chills her shoulders and burns her loins—"when you kissed my mouth . . ."

She approaches him and gazes . . .

Oh, she is going to wake him, wake him with the weight of her child's limbs wrapped around the rude limbs that wound her in the embrace.

"Samson . . . Samson . . ."

But her voice dies away, and Delilah bends her pink knees to the dust of the ground, and inclines her face, marked by pleasures, to the level of the veiled forehead that she wants to uncover . . .

Your fingers are trembling, Delilah—and yet you know that behind that door the governors are waiting, and that in their hands they are holding sacks heavy with silver.

Let's go! Exchange your gold—that fluid and warm gold—for their silver, their beautiful solid and icy silver . . .

But there is a mortal silence in the room, in which the night is eating the shiny things.

Samson, asleep, and Delilah, irresolute, do not move.

The torrent of Scorek, which runs past the house, caries away with the current of its waters the dream of the one and the thought of the latter . . . a blind dream . . . a mute thought . . .

Blind dream: Will Samson ever know what a shadow the insolent light of his forehead projects as far as that woman?

Mute thought: Will Delilah silence the voluptuous nostalgia that suspends her murderous gesture momentarily?

For it is not the anguish of knowing that the Invincible will soon be delivered and vanquished, and that he will be so by the work of feeble appearance and tragic reality, of your pale hands—too pale not to be cruel, and very skillful—it is not a dolor of your soul that holds you prostrate thus . . . no, it is because you are weeping, Delilah, it is the mild forest in which you put your fatigues to sleep after errands.

Listen, listen to the rapid torrent that licks the wall of your house; respire, respire the strong and fresh odor of the wind that has slackened in passing over the hills velveted with flowers—let your ears and your nostrils fill up with rumors and perfumes, be deafened and intoxicated, in order to forget the regret of the flesh before the sacrifice . . .

THE CRADLE

And the daughter of Pharaoh came down to wash herself
at the river.

Exodus 2:5

THE light song of the reeds soothed the young women who
were going—very slowly—toward the river. The slowest
and most languid of all was the one who walked in isolation,
a few paces in advance of the procession, trailing between the
gray and green of the trees of the bank the changing coloration
of fine veils tinted crimson and indigo.

The sunlight was full and rude over things; the plain dazzled
with gold and the waters carried gems of light as Pharaoh's
daughter, blinded and deafened, held her arm over her forehead in a gesture of defense.

Her face, with its eyelids thus closed, appeared to be asleep
and dreaming; the hidden magic of the gaze gave it a marvelous figure of death: a calm forehead beneath the heavy fold of
hair that negligence, fatigue or ennui had pushed back—and
the disengaged temples, bursting with youth, irradiated their
whiteness like an interior light.

The uniform and tender cheeks appealed for kisses still
pure, and the gaze had to descend the course of that ideal line
in order to be troubled and obscured by human desires, for the
mouth alone spoke of life: ardent, implacable, amorous life;

brilliant with color, sculpted in relief like a cup, ready to drink and offer sensualities.

The secret and rapid wave of blood and thought lifted her breast, and among the pleats of her veil as pale as the moon, the even paler flesh of her bosom appeared.

Emotions as frail as birds without down passed from that closed heart all the way to the eyes, and the royal child, who did not know suffering, suffered.

A nervous shock twisted her body when the supple reeds, the noisy reeds rustled, and she stopped, small amid the tall plants, with her respectful and reserved escort also stopping in the melodious green circle. Under the soft umbrella of foliage she raised her reposed eyelids. The water, very close, was not yet visible, and the virgin's eyes, having opened, were filled with an anguished mildness.

She was dreaming.

Her mouth trembled like an admirable flower in an excessively strong wind.

She was weeping.

Oh, had so many sobs around the palace for so many days saturated the atmosphere with an inevitable dolor?

Whence came that nostalgia for a boon that she did not know?

Sheathed in a mantle surcharged with ruby and turquoise scarabs, coiffed with a hawk with golden wings outspread around her head, she had witnessed the decree condemning to death the male children born to the Jewish people.

Her eyes, as starry and somber as a nocturnal sky, had then remained fixed and devoid of thought—indifferent.

Now, her body is no longer defended by jewels; it is naked and free under a light tunic; her soul is no longer torpid under the powerful words, the murderous words; it is vibrant and wounded in the pure air, the infinite air of life . . .

Palpitation in the branches . . . the breath of her heart . . . narrowly entangled . . . a diffuse life, a strong and supreme life, which she breathes in and out, weeping, as yet without thought—her gaze wandering around her—but no longer insouciant, and, sensing very close and very mysterious the hour that will open and deliver her soul from the weight of an unknown world.

Pharaoh's daughter goes toward the river, parting the reeds: they slip away and close up again before and behind her body, like a sumptuous and mobile fabric. She stops again . . . on the gleam of the river, at the limit of the shadow that is cast over the green bank, a frail object, white, with soft lines, is floating . . .

Amid that whiteness, that delicacy, a form even softer and more fragile: the pink nudity of a child . . .

And Pharaoh's daughter no longer feels the dolorous grip, but a peace and a rapturous joy penetrating her like a profound kiss, a secret kiss . . .

She knows why she was suffering, but her suffering is effaced and dies away before that cradle.

COLORED TALES:
CASTLE IN SPAIN
(A White Tale)

THEY were sisters, Princesse Lys and Princesse Fée.

Lys, sheathed in fine silver, had long hands and pale cheeks.

The pink nudity of Fée remained visible under the lace of her dress, her voice laughed with child-like laughter, and a light nacre beneath her eyes shaded her face with sensuality.

They lived in a castle in Spain, built on the summit of high dunes of blonde sand amid brilliant birches.

The men of their family were fighting far away to defend their beautiful castle, the ancestral castle, all of marble, in which statues of ivory—an immobile people—contemplated their eternal gestures in the clear and bright surfaces of innumerable mirrors.

On terraces florid with camellias, narcissi and jasmines, Princesse Lys and Princesse Fée were playing.

Their games were simple, with pearls, water and the feathers of doves.

Between their hands those frail things, those white things, lived a supple and strange life.

They played and they talked. They talked about life, which they did not know, and the future, which they would not live. Their hearts were tender and their bodies very weak.

Seeing, beyond the forests, the crowns of birch trees couched on the sides of the dunes; and seeing the bloody magic of the sunrise, they thought about the absent. The vision of brutal struggles made their foreheads heavy with a few thoughts of death; and over their eyes the color of cloud, the color of opal, the color of the moon, those thoughts descended like a veil: a little mist of presentiments.

Princesse Lys held out her bare arms with a sigh.

"I had a lover—and he has departed . . ."

Fée, such a very little girl, allowed her open hands to hang down like flowers, and gazes at the edge of her dress and the toenails of her bare feet—shining jewels.

Lys was astonished by her silence; and Fée, weeping very quietly, said: "I was engaged, and my knight will come back dead . . ."

But the ash of the night, like a dust of pearls, enveloped them and closed the horizon.

Thus, something very light and invincible tarnished their memories and they dreamed, wordlessly, of an amour from which fear and dolor would be banished.

Then, when the night rose from the forests and descended from the clouds, they dared to speak.

"I'm bored . . ."

"I'm weary . . ."

"He evoked the war, and kissed me . . ."

"He was thinking about distant victories while talking about our wedding . . ."

"Yes. Thus, the one remains while the other is already far away . . . and the one is intoxicated while the other retains all the pain . . .

✳

Then they hugged.

"My little Fée, don't be sad any more . . ."

"Why?"

"I love you."

"Why do you love me?"

"You're weak . . ."

"And you're beautiful . . ."

"That's sufficient . . ."

The fine silver sheath undulated in the shadow.

The crumpled lace, in the silence, made a furtive sigh . . .

Princesse Lys and Princesse Fée went to sleep together under the dew . . . then the beautiful castle in Spain—the dazzling castle, solid and pure—crumbled soundlessly while the men of the house were fighting far away for its eternal glory—but they had forgotten two amorous children.

THE PINK PARROT
(*La Fronde*, 19 May 1903)

For Mademoiselle Marie P***

YOU are named Rama, in a decorative spirit, but people call you Coco with an affectionate familiarity.

In a cage you have lost your manners of pompous hieratism and your imperious native decision. Old and weary you have weaknesses and manias.

You are accorded some liberty, aiding yourself with your beak, you crawl, with fatigue and without majesty, alas, all the way to the feet of friends posed on carpets, and you insist, with a certain turn of the neck and a guttural appeal, in order to be scratched on the top of your head, where the pink of your plumage is paling, because that is what you like.

That facile sensuality is given to you, with indulgence if not with ardor.

You are satisfied, with the nonchalance of a soul full of forbearance, rubbing your frontal bone between your two eyes as round as nails.

Your pink and gray costume is soft, and melts into Oriental wools. You are an old animate trinket between the pottery and the bronzes.

Golden gods with eyes in their navels and felt tucked up beneath the belly recognize you and appreciate you.

You have a place among the lacquer and the marquetry, even though no longer very beautiful and charged with infirmities.

A green garden behind the windows lined with red silk fills with sunlight to warm you up.

You certainly have ideas, but you do not always speak them, and you are right, for your accent is coarse.

You are wiser than men if you have unlearned their futile language.

A few gestures and a few keen desires would be sufficient to maintain exterior relations in society—at least, that is all that would be necessary to live, and to live well; all the rest is almost devoid of utility and almost always devoid of grace.

The more I think about you, Rama-Coco, the more I admire your chosen existence.

Doubtless, at the beginning of life, the limits assigned to your excursions must have appeared arbitrary to you. Your claws and your beak were judged to be full of danger with regard to varnishes and embroideries.

The spirit of investigation and curiosity offer inconvenience for furniture on the part of a parrot; but the energetic measures applied to liberty were, all things considered, excellent, and if you have the perspicacity that I like to believe, Rama, you ought to agree today the perfection of your life.

The limits of your horizon have taught you to concentrate your faculties of ecstasy; that is simply what the golden gods confronting their navels have striven for centuries to do, although it is claimed that that customary silence has become outdated and that sacred belies will soon seem insufficient panoramas to the sagest intelligences.

You, Coco, imitate such a noble exercise symbolically within the measure of your means.

Along with the usage of your wings and feet you have lost the flight of great dreams. O palm trees! Burning middays! Coppery skies! Lunar siestas! Hunts for nacreous little creatures! Those infinite pleasures are no longer yours; you would not recognize them and might even have a fearful disdain for them that is the final form of philosophy.

If your destiny had left you your natural life of a parrot, you would have suffered the inevitable detail of your adventurous joys and, decrepit and morose, you would no longer have any repose on earth.

Perceive therefore, on the contrary, what a lot full of charms is yours.

You have only retained one passion, but around you, people strive not to disappoint you, and you probably conserve intact the extreme sum of the enjoyments you expect, for it is improbable that a friendly foot will ever refuse your skull, where the pink plumage is paling, the light scratching in which you find your nirvana

So, it is good to learn in this world not to disperse one's desires and to submit over time to sometimes-incomprehensible slaveries; for only in a comprehensive renunciation and the cultivation of a unique goal has one any chance of encountering paradise on earth.

GIFTED
(*La Fronde*, 29 May 1903)

For Jeannot

"YES," he said, "there are debuts in amour as incomplete, uncertain and strange as the announcement of the first rehearsals of a play. Everything there is uneven, incoherent, formless and disquieting. One does not know yet, one knows nothing, one will never know; the gestures do not go with the words, nor the tone. Full of hesitations and breaks, the most beautiful role, the one that will enable frissons, ardor and enchantment, appears devoid of body and devoid of soul.

"Everything that will create beauty and emotion is there, however: the magnificent word on the armature of action, and the interpretation with the voice, the eyes and the movement that have already rendered it admirable. But nothing holds together . . .

"Thus, I remember that, one evening twenty years ago, in a province, at a desolating soirée held in honor of the young deputy that I was then in sojourn in X*** for the assizes of a still-celebrated drama—but I won't recall it, because it has nothing to do with my story—I encountered a creature who, amid so many mannequins, knew how to move and to gaze. Her eyes and her gestures were in accord. She did not speak rapidly or loudly, and she had throughout her being something nonchalant and concentrated, full of seduction. I was seduced, and that was immediately very agreeable, like an oasis in a desert.

"The young woman was free, as much as one can be in the provinces. An orphan and a widow with no children, she lived on a modest but sufficient income in a small house in the form of a charterhouse surrounded by a rather vast orchard of sorts, with an old maidservant and a few domestic animals.

"From an old bourgeois family of the locale, living calmly and without ostentation in solitude, although she frequented families linked by blood or amity with hers, and was spared by malicious gossip. No one talked about her in her petty and vain society agitated by minor intrigues and tedious occupations akin to hers; she passed almost unnoticed.

"'Madame A***?' people said. 'She's very nice, that little woman'—and that was all. I avoided asking questions about her. I divined that she was one of those almost dormant individuals, as if hypnotized in a waking state, unconscious of their true nature, submissive to atavistic habitudes, to hereditary privations and numbed by monotony—types that one scarcely encounters except in the provinces.

"If you are a reader you have already named a number of the people that it is necessary to invoke: Madame de Rénat rather than Madame de Mortsaut, for the former allows passion to devour her heart, while the latter succumbs to the desiccating invasion of duty. It is one of those maddening paradoxes that represent all the crime and all the glory of Valmont in the person of the Présidente.[1]

The most excessive and the most assured beauty can never struggle with certain graces of these seemingly-hypnotized creatures. They have all amour in their veins but they don't know

---

1 The author inserts footnotes to identify the sources of the named characters as Stendhal's *Le Rouge et le noir* (1830; tr. as *Scarlet and Black*), Balzac's *Le lys dans la vallée* (1835; tr. as *The Lily in the Valley*) and Laclos' *Les Liaisons dangereuses* (1782; tr. as *Dangerous Liaisons*).

it—or don't want to know it—but if you succeed in teaching them the price of the fire that makes their movements similar to regrets and their eyelids so heavy . . ."

"Well?"

"Well, yes . . . ! I'll continue. So, Madame A*** pleased me. But could I please Madame A***? I've never been very conceited. I encountered Madame A*** almost daily, while out walking, at soirées or dinners, and sometimes chance made us neighbors. We chatted. I considered the young woman with a great desire several times, while passing through a poorly-illuminated vestibule or on the threshold of her garden, to which I accompanied her, for on those spring evenings in the country, we went out in groups from our hosts, and separated to escort our female companions to their doors. Several times I nearly seized her in my arms and covered her face with kisses—that would at least have been a commencement.

"She was so pale and flavorsome to see, but I always dreaded having mistaken her attitude and risking losing by such moderate movements what I hoped of her in the future: an avowed trouble. It was assuredly stupid, for the future did not exist for her and me, or did not appear to exist. In a fortnight the session would be over, and I would rejoin my position.

"In any case, she did not inspire any sentimentality in me; I would have been incapable of expressing it to her with a polite elegance the impression that she produced in me, and on the other hand, that impression was sufficiently delicate and profound for me to have a horror of making it understood by excessively vulgar gallant evidence.

"In default of all that I could not say—for all those reasons—I talked a great deal, at random. She was not alarmed, testifying neither perverse curiosity nor stupid reserve. She was good-natured, and did not take the trouble to hide it, thank God.

"At every moment I thought with more decision that she would be a delightful mistress, but, at the same time, I judged that she certainly did not consider me as a possible lover. Was she even thinking, in any case, of taking a lover? She had neither coquetry, nor caprices, nor enervations. She was merely pale, with her slow eyes, her becoming voice and her fashion of sitting down, getting up or walking, full of natural nonchalance. What was particular between us was that I did not pay court to her.

"Our long conversations were animated by indifferent words, at least with regard to the sentiment that occupied me. One day, at table, I don't know why, I said to her: 'You, who are a passionate woman . . .' Then I stopped, surprised myself, and looked at her. She had lowered her head a little and was playing with her knife . . . I did not see either the very ordinary circle of faces surrounding us, or the tablecloth and the banal décor of a formal dinner, but only her, with her pale face charged with the weight of her brown hair, her bare arm, her charming hand, with the shiny blade between the fingers, and all of that, very isolated and distinct, was so full of strength and sensuality that it was all futile . . . I would no longer wait, I would no longer hope, but that very night I would go into her house with her and I would know how she loved . . . if she were able to love me . . .

"It was more than a month since that amour, which I had not recognized immediately, had entered into the marrow of my bones, slyly and inevitably, like a mortal malady. And so, that same night, when she opened the little wooden gate of her garden and turned round, as usual, to half-extend her hand to me: '*Au revoir*, thank you very much, *bonsoir!*' and while the silhouettes of three common friends were still visible at the corner of the street, going home talking and laughing, I didn't take her hand, but I pushed the gate, went in with her and I kissed her on the mouth. She did not utter a cry, and, after that kiss, not a word. Attached by desire, we traversed the garden between the low and wide fruit trees, and were in the house. A small lamp was burning in the drawing room.

"She opened a door, that of her bedroom. The open window and the bed were all white in the darkness.

"The garden and the linen had a fresh odor . . .

"Some time afterwards she said to me: 'I love you.' Her voice and her skin were incomparable. It was not until much later that she explained to me that she had not thought that she had made any impression on me during the beginnings of our acquaintance.

"A sort of touching stupidity, which is sometimes one of the forms that malign amour takes, had rendered us both an exaggerated modesty.

"The following week, when I left, she went with me, with an admirably passionate tranquility.

"She was gifted and had understood the necessity of happiness in amour. It requires a certain genius that is rare in our fatigued races."

"That's all?"

"Yes, that's all."

LILY
(*La Fronde*, 29 June 1903)

SHE looked at herself in the mirror and shook her head.

"You see," she said, "how ugly I am . . ." and as they had not known one another for very long, she added: "What a pity," and then she looked her lover in the eyes, took his head abruptly in her two hands and covered that head with kisses with a sort of desperate fury.

When she stopped in order to take a deep breath she said to him in a low voice: "Don't look at me, close your eyes . . . it's true, you see, I no longer have a body, no longer anything . . . but if you can't see me, you can sense my flesh and my blood and all of the me that 'doesn't want to die,' but to love you so forcefully that you'll also love me, madly, and you'll no longer able to forget me."

A little later, she coughed. He closed the window and then he had to leave, to go back to his house, his family and his business affairs.

She remained alone.

She was a little Montmartre prostitute. She might have been thirty years old, or twenty. She gave the impression of a child and a creature. She was very thin, 'bodiless,' as she said, and as she thought when she was twenty-eight and her face was pink, and her beautiful little breasts.

All that was finished.

"I don't want to die," she said, ardently, but she knew very well that it wasn't true, and that the death that had arrived insidiously with her fevers, her oppressions and all the graces and terror of tuberculosis, she loved and desired.

For, after all, she could have dragged out her life—couldn't she?—like Marcelle, who had a big bosom, good health and lovers who left her all the time, or . . . but it fatigued Lily even to think about all that.

She was loved, thank God! One doesn't need to be intelligent to perceive these things.

What man for whom her friends suddenly had, in the caress, those emotions almost ready for tears, and as he came back soon, after having departed late, and after her, had said: "Let's stay in this evening without talking, without moving, hugging one another," as all of a sudden he couldn't remain thus, only tender next to her; or again, sometimes after a wait full of folly, fainting at the first kiss, they remained motionless, breathless, looking one another in the eyes in an enchanted agony, as if they had just escaped death . . . ?

All that was certainly not ordinary. At eighteen, rosy, gay and beautiful, Lily had not known those things, and now she found them good.

The trouble of her beloved friend gave her a kind of terrible joy: her, little Lily, nothing at all—wasn't she?—with her little thin face, well, she would be regretted!

Sometimes by night—and sometimes by day—he would still believe that he felt her, burning and tenacious, bound to his limbs and to his heart, with reckless kisses, inconsequential words and all that force of life that she stole from life, since life no longer wanted her.

Little Lily gazes into the mirror and sees herself all ardent and all pale, something very hot fills her chest, her veins are swollen with amour and joy, and furtively, she turns her eyes toward the door as if he were still there, the man who, a little while ago, on the threshold, took her against him for the adieu, until this evening, as if they had not seen one another for . . .

a week! Lily thinks, for her a week is the infinity of time, a number of eternity!

In her mirror, when Lily, alone in her dressing room, looks at her arm, so thin, she feels a wicked hand grab her abruptly by the throat and squeeze hard, it is chagrin, great chagrin, that is strangling her. She's afraid . . . Can one love such a poor little creature? For dolor and malady exalt terrible pity, and not amour . . .

But in the street, sometimes, Lily encounters pretty women, visibly full of muscles and blood under harmonious flesh, and sometimes those women have sad eyes and an air of not being happy, and then, everywhere, people tell Lily frightful stories of abandonment and cowardice, and she sees beautiful and healthy friends weeping every day. Then an implacable happiness grips Lily and carries her away, she sees, in flames, hours passing when amour holds her and breaks her, ready to crush her without caring about her air of weakness, because amour, which knows the price of life and death, has no pity. How happy Lily is! She would not have the time to be more loved, and, after brief and solitary despairs, Lily feels an admirable pride.

She is the mistress of omniscient death. The latter might come with the air of an assassin toward the little whore, so thin that she "no longer has a body" as she says; tenacious and hasty, it can prepare that prey by means of sly and rude maneuvers, but Lily will not cease smiling, and remains the stronger.

"See how ugly I've become," she will say to her lover, and they will only see one another for a furious minute, which he will not forget.

She will not have the time to forget it.

Lily says: "I don't want to die," but she knows that she is lying. Lily curls her hair, gets dressed carefully, passes some light make-up over her pale cheeks, and marches toward life and amour, among beings and things, savoring the implacable brutality of the world. Lily, with much pride and joy, thinks: "I shall die standing up."

It is unnecessary to feel sorry for Lily.